House Of Legions

The Angel Descendants, Volume 1

Shan R.K

Published by Shan R.K, 2018.

This is a work of fiction. Similarities to real people, places, or events are entirely coincidental.

HOUSE OF LEGIONS

First edition. June 1, 2018.

ISBN: 978-1393540526

Written by Shan R.K.

To All People Who Dream of More

Also by Author
Beggar
Kylie Bray
Prince of souls 2018
Possess my body
River's Keeper
School me part 1
School me part 2

Note from Author:
This book is a work of fiction. All characters are fictional.
Any religious references made was done solely for the purpose of
Bringing the story to reality and making it believable to the readers.
No dis-respect to religious beliefs was intended.

A Descendant dictionary

A

ADAULA – (VERB) ELVAN word for Run

Alurya – (noun) Mark of the knower- possessed only by Irin

Aquadore mountain- (noun) mountain of deceased Lightwatchers

Asguardians – (noun) off spring of Angels, pure bloods who have not earned a place in the Infinity

aveu – greetings

C

C aster – (noun) child of a Tempter
Cadre – (noun) Leaders of hell (Paros)
Cherub – (noun) Name for Angels in the Infinity

D

Deceptor – (noun) human beings

Demon – (noun) creatures created by Tempters

Descendants – (noun) created by the seven children of Adonai and Archangels, or born to the Angels and Tempters. (Shifters, Casters, Naturahs, Lightwatchers, Asgaurdians, Fuized, Elvan.)

Dresta - (noun) Angelic laced whip named and made by Azazy-el (The master of weapons)

F

Fuized – (noun) only partial Lightwatcher eg, mother is a lightwatcher but the father is a shifter

G

Garde – (noun) Lightwatchers or Fuized who bring justice to those who have broken the law, and hold up the descendants treaty. They are the policeman of the descendant world.

Gazool – (noun) energy

Guiders – (noun) birds of the Angels

H

Harpien blade – (noun) angel blades, can not be wielded by any other besides a full angel or someone even more powerful

HOL – (abv) house of legions

I

I chor – (noun) demon blood

Igori – (noun) the original watchers

Infinity – (noun) heaven

Irin - (noun) Angel of a high rank in the Infinity, but not as powerful as an Archangel

K

K^{hiron} – (noun) land of the Lightwatchers

L

Legions- (noun) Lightwatchers who ascend and gain legacies. The Lightwatchers assassins

Legacies – (noun) Angelic abilities only possessed by Legions

Lightwatchers – (noun) part Venusian, part angel, (descendants of four archangels Mikael , Gabriel , Raziel , Casteal)

P

P aros - hell

R

R ealm – country

S

Seals- verses mixed with souls of the Lightwatchers dead or blood from the living... Sometimes found on the body of Lightwatchers and angelic descendants or in rare angelic stones

Seeker – (noun) half caster and half shapeshifter's (rarest of matings)

Seraph – (noun) Guardians of Infinity, minor angels still earning a higher rank

Sytna- (noun) the mark of a new birth

T

Tempters - The 200 hundred fallen angels who were kicked out of the Infinity

V

Verses – (noun) spells that are angelic in nature, Used by Lightwatchers. Found in the book of Watchers.

House of Legions

The Angel descendants
Book 1

By
Shan R.K

Prologue

William Blackwyll stood motionless on the roof of an old rundown building. A lone figure shrouded in the darkness of night waiting with infinite patience for his guest to arrive.

Months passed since he'd last spoken to Franchesca. It was the day she showed up in his New York building demanding his presence. He was pissed that she thought she could demand anything from him, obviously at first he refused. But Franchesca never deterred in the slightest. No, Draiken women were known for their persistence, and Franchesca proved her bloodline true when she stormed into his office in a state. And not the good kind, more the 'I'm in dire need of help' kind. So reluctantly he agreed to listen.

"Just look at her William, one look, a minute of your time, maximum five," she'd said, those months ago.

Staring at the night sky moonlight he thought back to his decision. There was no agreement reached as he walked her out of his office toward the elevator. Unlike his siblings he wasn't ruled by emotions, but he recalled the hair on his nape rise to attention when he considered her request.

The sensation passed, she left and all was forgotten.

Two weeks later an unexpected trip to London was the changing tide of his decision. He was in West Central London with hours to spare before his next meeting. He should've never tracked the girl, he should have walked away, but cowardice wasn't a suit William wore and that was what stayed on his mind right until he stopped across the park from where the girl stood.

There was no doubt in his mind of who she was or how she looked. The instant he set his sight on the young Lightwatcher, behold his virgin sister. She was jumping up, trying to reach a branch in the tree. William Blackwyll knew then, that this green eyed beauty across from him was the greatest treasure on earth.

And so it began, the path which led him to now, standing on a rooftop, waiting.

Gazing upon the stars, home crossed his mind. In the past an overwhelming sense of loss sired him because he missed his family, he yearned for his mother. Now, the pain he festered in leaving his birth place those many years ago no longer mattered, only his decision to stay did.

Frustrated with a sensory overload of emotions that were just too dangerous to accept he clenched his jaw, something he had done much too often over recent months.

His father will call his name and soon. So will the time come to pick a side.

The drum of footsteps snapped William out of his reverie. Turning, he faced the rapid click of heels on concrete approaching at a brisk pace,

"Franchesca, aveu," his voice echoed through the space of the thirty story roof top.

Franchesca walked closer to him, her black hair windblown, attire somewhat out of ordinary for a private meeting amongst their own kind, "Dressing as a deceptor, nice."

The woman smiled and bowed her head in respect. The 'old fashioned' formality held a touch of reverence. Because while he appeared to be in his mid twenties he was much older.

His long wool coat moved with the easterly wind as he took two steps toward her.

"William." Franchesca paused, her eyes twitching, "Sorry, Clare's difficult to avoid, I'm running out of reasons for leaving at odd hours, she believes..."

"Clare believes as she wants. Deception fuels inquisitors, Franchesca. Please, call me Liam."

The shortened name was something new he'd gained from his brother, Kole. The same night Kole started drinking himself into foolishness for which new woman, William never wanted to know. He'd grown accustomed to the nickname as Kole continued using it to goad him and it stuck.

"Liam," She corrected, "You needed to speak. Sending a Seeker, isn't that risky?"

"No, I trust Quintin, longer than I, you."

She flinched at the unvarnished truth which he ignored and continued, "There's more important matter's at hand."

A long time ago Liam faced facts regarding his involvement in people's affairs, he was terrible at meddling. It took three wars which he caused to figure that out. The plausible solution was simple, emotions of any kind needed to stay inviolate to those besides his siblings.

Doing this kindness and priceless favour went far beyond his level of niceties - his sisters words not his. He was immortal with a considerable longevity and three thousand years on earth.

There was only one reason for him warning Franchesca –

Her name was Clare.

Which brought him to his decision of what he said next, "Clare has been spotted at a club by Asguardians. They recognized the Da Vinci boy and alerted the Garde."

Franchesca's heart thumped in imminent danger of collapsing. Her eyes frantic. She stumbled back,

"I, ah, I've got to get her. My son, please warn him."

The abject terror on Franchesca's face made him pause and

ponder of what he undoubtedly missed. William narrowed his eyes as he witnessed Franchesca stumble and shake. Until this point he'd been unconcerned about them finding her. Truth was, he wanted Clare to find out who she was, then perhaps his interest in her would dim and he'd finally bed a woman without feeling guilty. Francesca however didn't share his enthusiasm, in fact she looked scared.

What was so bad about Clare finding out who she was? He thought.

And Why oh why was Franchesca protecting the girl, she wasn't the one they wanted. The Garde would never harm Clare, of that he was most certain.

Liam hated when he missed important details, but New York wasn't built over night. Franchesca's reaction was a puzzle that just didn't fit, one he was starting to dislike very quickly. From what he knew about Franchesca, she had accepted her death after the war of descendants years ago. Liam had been there and seen the life shed her eyes as it had many before her. The ultimate curse of the assassin. However, the same attitude didn't apply when the threat related to Clare, which pleased him more than he cared to admit.

He knew the addiction to the girl. After one glimpse of Clare those months ago he couldn't stay away. One misguided look at the girl was a shot of adrenaline spiked through his entire system and 'short circuited' his brain. For months he had shadowed Clare from a distance and for months he fought the temptation of facing her, talking to her.

There were moments when he'd tortured himself watching her shower. The sight brought him to his knees.

He thought back to that first day he watched her from across the road trying to reach the branch of that ridiculous tree. He'd used his will to bend the branch ever so slightly so she could reach. It was the day he was irrevocably changed, more like screwed as his brother would put it. People had stopped and stared at Clare as she spun around cheering her victory, and for some reason his anger had risen in seconds as a swell of possession over powered him.

Take her... A voice had whispered, *take her.*

What started off as a few days of watching her, quickly became his new pass time..

His excuse- fascination rendering to obsession. Everything drew him in- her existence as a deceptor, her uncanny belief of humans being the superior species on the earth, her easy relationship with people, and competitive streak which had delighted his sister. He could listen to Clare for hours arguing about something she knew was wrong, but insisted it to be correct.

She was so full life and living.

One other reason came to mind, which frequented more often in the past week. He refused to allow the thought to seep into his knowledge, or be spoken of. Instead he reverted his attention to the matter at hand.

Franchesca...

Who stood frozen as he crowded her space. Knowing the implications of what he had to do would change things, didn't make it easier.

Liam took an oath not to intervene in Clare's life, to only help from afar if he needed to. But now she was a key in something bigger which meant danger, and if Clare's life was in danger he wanted facts. Oaths were to be bent, his, more often than not.

With his right hand he grabbed Franchesca's head. She screamed and tried to push back as he applied pressure, but to no avail. She wasn't strong enough to take him on. Linking his mind to hers he watched it all unfold- the visions, the memories, the accident, rushing through him as he relived the years in the minutes passed. What he found was unspeakable, even to his own mind.

Little Clare was about to become the most hunted being on this planet.

The wind blew in his eyes, but he didn't blink, not even when Franchesca stumbled away from him to flee from the roof.

Liam's fury seeped through his body at the thought of any harm coming to her, his beautiful Clare, his princess, who had yet to still blossom and grow into the woman she would become, his.

Wisps of ice involuntarily flickered like frozen torches on his fingers as he commanded, "Franchesca, stop!" His words rumbling through the wind as her dress crept up her thighs.

Facing him she took out her heels as the evident tears cascaded down her cheeks, as darkness invaded their space.

Liam didn't need light to see, his vision never dimmed, only enhanced. Franchesca's lips narrowed and he knew the stubbornness in her gaze. After what he'd seen, he should rip her limbs apart, shred her to pieces. Clare however would never forgive him for taking the life of her mother. Jullie and Nathan wouldn't understand, not like it bothered him

Much. However Franchesca had been loyal all these years. And then there was Caleb, though a boy, Liam considered him a good friend and maybe something more in the future.

The fear in her breathing was foreign to his ears. Franchesca, always the warrior and protector he had never seen scared. But fear of the unknown was a weakness bound to happen to any mortal who found out their daughter was about to be hunted down like a rabid dog.

Watching her closely, she dropped her shoes on the ground and swung her body around. Her knees lowered, and she begged, "I have to save her, please William, let me go, you've seen enough, please, if you wish to kill me do it once she's safe."

Her crest fallen face was a torment to his will but not enough to succumb him to its desire. Liam would protect Clare himself while he put a stop to all those who wanted her dead. For now he was going to need help and information from a closer source. Starting with what happened eight years ago. Which meant he'd have to leave, without knowing when he'd see Clare again.

The mere thought of not seeing her caused foreign emotions to gather inside him. If he'd possessed a beating heart the organ would've ached as his stomach did now. He heard about it from his sister, maybe he'd ask her what it felt like. But the solution to this was simple, he had to see Clare before he left. And that knowledge relieved him of the ache, which he chose not to decipher just yet.

With the authority instilled in him from before his birth, he finally spoke "I'll help you."

Franchesca gasped as the words left his mouth in the ancient tongue. It was difficult to digest and he didn't blame her. Help was not something he offered to others without a price, no matter how bad he was at it, and he wasn't starting now. After all, he was his father's son.

His reasons for helping Clare were among the most selfish. But he kept his features neutral as he waited for Franchesca to get her grips, "You're one Caster," she said, "I doubt your siblings would jump to protect a Lightwatcher's young. What could you do?"

Her lack of confidence in his abilities tempted him to unleash his anger, what an insult, "The terms Warlock now!" he said dryly, schooling his features, a task he'd mastered thousands of years ago, "And to answer your question, more than you."

He paused and waited for her to calm down, "neither of us are strangers to false identities and lying about who we are, Franchesca. I being superior at it of course, but you heed my point Lightwatcher."

He listened to the rise in her heartbeat, the gulps she swallowed and watched as the sheen of sweat on her forehead glistened. Denial was pointless, she was as guilty as Lucifer. He should rip her throat out, but he was no lousy Warlock to everyone's disappointment, so no throat ripping for him today.

Lucky for her, she didn't know who fathered him, well at least not yet.

The words tumbled out of her mouth, a wasted attempt to negotiate, considering he was warning her and not killing her, "I'll take her to the realms, you've seen what follows, they all coming for her." When he just stared at her she huffed in frustration, "Whether you agree or not she's my blood, it's my right."

Ignoring her disrespect he sighed , "You wound me Franchesca to trust the word of a stranger, and brand me as your enemy." She narrowed her eyes, and he shook his head in disappointment, "You think you've got me figured out Lightwatcher. You'll be enlightened soon enough to discover you're sorely mistaken."

The look she gave him did little to alter his mood. Because for the first time in years, finally a glimmer of hope shrouded Franchesca,

redemption,

even if she was yet to realize it, she would. Self sacrifice wasn't something to take lightly, it showed courage, if done to protect the one you love.

"I'll get your son to safety is he still at the HOL?"

Her eyes widened in surprise before recovering quickly with a shake of her head, "No, he said he was going to the Irish country, but your brother..."

Understanding what she'd meant when she referred to his drunken mess of a brother, he nodded. Trust Kole to put a tracker on the kid's cellphone. He just hoped it was only the cellphone.

He turned to walk away when he heard it, the soft discernible sounds they made as they crept up the stairs. Weight shifting to the balls of his feet, white knuckle fists clenched at his sides, he took a fighting pose,

"Franchesca."

The woman who moments ago walked up to him with every appearance of a vulnerable deceptor, shifted into something far more dangerous right before his eyes. The fear in her gaze swirled, gathering into a storm of towering rage and fearless determination. She now stood as a killer, and a protector.

The door to the stairwell crashed open. Liam turned to her with a sadistic quip of his eyebrow, "ladies first," he said as he held out his hand to her in a gentlemanly gesture.

The moment she placed her hand in his, he tightened his grip, pivoted and let go, sending her hurtling toward the doorway where her own kind waited to end her.

One

*C**lare Miller*** sipped her black coffee watching the sea water darken as day became night. A gentle breeze caressed her face, and blew her long brown and newly ironed hair as it flowed like a river of gleaming satin over the back of a comfortable rattan sofa. Curling back into the sofa she shut her eyes to watch the kaleidoscope of colours dance behind her eyelids.

South Africa was so much warmer than London. No gloomy skies with incessant rainfall, no falling on your ass in Boulevard , or walking for miles in soaked boots because you lost your stupid pass. South Africa was about waking to the echo of the ocean, sipping coffee in the sun while wearing shorts and vest as you waited for the heat to drift away in the grip of winter. Well, it was that to Clare and more, but it wasn't home, it wasn't West London, and she missed home.

The non-stop activity since their hurried departure from London was enough a reason to spend a weekend in bed. Adding on the jet lag was the last straw as her body succumbed to the exhaustion that'd been weighing on her in recent weeks.

For the first time in weeks her mind and body began to relax, well attempted to. Instead, she got lost in her thoughts as they flashed over the recent course of events, specifically to that one night. The night which tossed her life into chaos, and precipitated their sudden arrival in Durban, South Africa.

It was after three a.m when her mother returned that night from the 'medical association meeting' in a totally dishevelled state. Clare was engrossed in a rerun of cribs when her mother stormed through the front door. A torn skirt, broken heel, hair in a total mess, dried blood, her mother was the prime image of a woman who'd been raped or mugged, except her bag was still over her shoulder. Her mother just stared at her with those big eyes, before she beat her feet to the bedroom. Clare ran up the stairs and banged with the heel of her palms on her mother's door and shouted, "mom, mom? MOM, open up! Mom, should I call the police?" Her mother didn't reply, even as she rattled the locked door.

"Mom, come on, open up, talk to me." She banged on the door, kicked it, but it was no use. She knew that, even as she screamed, "MOM, please, don't do this, tell me what to do."

The hours after passed in silence as the sun bled in through the bathroom window, but she wouldn't move from the bedroom door.

Stubbornness eventually cost her a numb butt on the cold tiled floor as she waited for any sign from her mother. The ache in her back from the cold wall and cramps in her legs from staying in the same position for so long meant nothing in the end. Because she never got a response, not then, or the next afternoon when her mother, Michelle, finally left her room, acting as if nothing happened.

The pretence lasted until Clare mentioned she was leaving for school, then things had gotten strange and confusing. Her mother flat out refused, "NO!" She'd all but screamed, "I need you home."

After that, it pretty much said it all. Her normally calm and collected overbearing mother became a nervous wreck overnight. Moody and short-tempered replaced the calm and collected. Her mother was continuously agitated, nerves constantly on edge, snapping at people for the silliest of reasons.

She recalled the evening her mother had shrieked, startled by something out of the window. Clare was sure she saw her slice her hand chopping potatoes. Instinct had Clare grab her mother's hand to place it under the cold tap but there wasn't any injury. Her mother brushed it off as her over reacting and insisted Clare imagined the incident because the blood was from the meat. Which didn't make sense, her mother never touched the meat, or anything red. But Clare left it alone.

With all those episodes, she still couldn't fathom what'd been behind her mother's decision to bring her half way across the world, to a place so foreign to her. They could've went anywhere, America was the most logical option. Clare had lived in Washington for two years after the car accident which changed her life in more ways than one. It was the reason behind them fleeing to London in the first place.

Six years in The UK and she never lost her accent. Her birth certificate confirmed her birthplace, Washington DC. The small piece of paper was the difference between her sanity and going crazy from not knowing. Without it she'd be lost, because her mother never spoke of the past. Her mothers adamant refusal to talk about life before the accident was contradicted by the look in her eyes when Clare brought it up, like a longing for something.

Of what? Clare didn't even have the basics to begin. She despised her mother's decision of remaining tight lipped about her past. What was so bad, she'd never know, because the choice was never given to her.

Ten years, TEN! She hated the number, it marked her life, it marked the years. Those many years that she'll never get back because eight years ago, a car accident had stolen it all.

"A head concussion," one doctor had said, "haemorrhage on the brain"

A few months later a surgeon from New York said, "She'll never remember", and finally the last blow, "Sorry Ms Miller but there's nothing we can do." Those were only some of the stuff she heard those years ago.

Her mother never went further, she simply chose acceptance. But Clare couldn't, she was the one living with the emptiness not her mother. Over the course of years she'd bring up questions of the past, but always came up short. Her mother would just leave the room, or give her one of the famous 'you don't understand' lectures, which were the worst, because, duh... how could she understand something, when she didn't even know where it began?.

The impression she got was that something horrible happened eight years ago, something her mother wanted to forget. It must have had something to do with the father she couldn't remember.

And after eight years the hollowness of her life, with all the unasked questions and unspoken truths was now a black hole. For years Clare yearned to know what her mother hid, hoping it would fill the void burning deep within her soul. But recently there was that whisper that held her back from figuring it out, a warning bell going off inside her head. Telling her, screaming at her- once she knew whatever it was, there was no going back, it would change her life. And of that she was certain.

So years later Clare finally caved, accepted faith and everyday since, a part of her soul died taking a piece of her life with it.

'*This is life now,*' She would say to herself whenever the thought of finding out more became a nagging insistent thought. Her amnesia was the least of her problems, she had other seeds to roast. Starting with why she'd uprooted from the only home she could remember. And where was her best friend, Phillip, who just upped and vanished, without even a phone call, *nothing*.

– '*gosh, my life sucks.*'

It wasn't as bad as not remembering the first ten years of her life, so she always said, "If I can handle not knowing, I can handle anything."

She thought back to when her mother started rambling about how some time away from 'London's cold' would be great. Just the thought of it stirred up her anger at how foolish she was for the lack of concern. Clare presumed her mother was blowing off steam, or some psychological bullshit after whatever happened to her. Fearing it was rape Flare could only hope not, because she'd seen the after effect, especially on people like her mother, who liked control. A shudder went through her at the vision of her mother ending up like her friend Stacy's.

What Clare couldn't understand about the whole ordeal was what was so damn important that she had to drop school and leave straight away, two weeks before her interview with Oxford University. That was what stayed on her mind, unsolved as she finally drifted off.

CLARE OPEN HER SLEEP filled eyes. Her stiff neck begging to be stretched as her lower back felt like it was run over by a train, leaving her groaning in discomfort. Lifting her head, a wave of lead greeted her before the constant pound of drumming made her want to drill a nail in her skull and dig her brain out. Talk about an alcohol free hangover.

Side effects of awkward sleeping, '*shit*,' she swore inwardly. She scrunched her face and slowly straightened her long legs.

Five minutes into stretching her body on the sofa she felt great. Well not that great but totally what she needed.

"Honey,"

Clare squealed before falling side first to the tiled floor, "Jesus, mom, just scare the sleep right outta me, don't ya."

Michelle's only response was the quirk of her brow and the tilt of her lip. Comfortably leaning against the door jamb, she waited until Clare finally got up off the floor, no doubt frowning. Flagging a menu in her hand, Michelle shook her head on an exhale, "Just thought you were hungry."

Clare looked at the woman who had supposedly given birth to her. And it wasn't the first time that she had really looked at her mother. The light powder blue eyes so different to Clare's green emeralds, yet almost identical to Phillip's, Clare's friend, looked back at her.

Now, the slacks were normal, but the straight black hair tied by Chinese forks on the top of her mother's head could mean either two things- they were getting a visitor, or the visitor was her mother. Judging from the flushed freckles on Michelle's cheeks and the slight frown to her brow, Clare figured neither. Her mother had already been the visitor. Which meant that she must've slept for hours, no wonder her body felt like hell all over.

Her mother straightened her stance; of course doing it in a timeless grace and elegance that was an innate part of her, something that Clare herself couldn't even feign. It was somehow ingrained in her to wear boots and always choose practicality over fashion. Unfortunately there was no way of confirming how true that assessment of hers was, memory loss and all.

Michelle normally dressed for comfort herself, with loose slacks or chinos. She never showed too much skin even though she was five foot eleven and fit comfortably in a European eight. That night which changed everything, was the exception. The one and only time Clare could remember seeing her mother in a slim black fitted figure hugging dress, was that dreadful night.

Sometimes Clare wondered if she was adopted. They had nothing in common when it came to looks, style, or temperament. The things that kept Clare from believing her presumptions true was firstly, Michelle's height, she was almost as tall as Clare's six foot figure. Which was relatively rare for American women, so it had to count for something, right...

The other obvious, was the blood type O-, which they both shared, surprise, surprise. Those weren't the deciding factors. No, that was left to the obligation that Michelle always saw her as. Clare wasn't a child wanted in Michelle's mind, but one to protect. She doubted her mother would've kept her if it wasn't for the blood ties, and that hurt. But Clare always told herself, *"If I can handle not knowing, I can handle anything,"* and that was exactly what she was doing, handling anything.

"Clare, why are you looking at me like that?" She didn't answer her mother. Not that she didn't want to, she didn't know the answer, so she just kept on staring.

If she didn't look like her mother, she thought, almost in a wistful daze then she must look like him. The mystery sperm donor. She had no recollection of her father, or even his name. Her relationship with him unknown. Why had he never looked for her.

Was he even alive? Not knowing, never stopped her conjuring him up. A rugged brown hair man, with paler skin and a sharp jaw line to match unnaturally dark green eyes. She could almost see him, the male version of her. After all her looks had to have come from somewhere.

Considering her extensive sporty nature which she must've inherited also from her dad, Clare moved well. She was solid on her feet. So what if she couldn't pull off the grace that Michelle possessed. She could tackle a ball from between opponents' legs without losing a step.

Clare also had a swing to be reckoned with. If it wasn't for her need to be academically stimulated, she would've taken the offer from her tennis coach to play professional tennis. Which was why, she applied to Oxford law. Getting the interview was one thing, and getting through it, was a whole lot of ball game and respect. Both of which she flunked. She was rude, filter-less and self absorbed.

Apart from her mother, Clare was incapable of biting her tongue. And well, her ball game started and ended with Phillip. Being the only Oxford student she knew, he was supposed to help her out, but he'd just upped and vanished. All in all she wasn't left with much. She wasn't so sure that her outgoing nature and looks would contribute to the deciding factor. In fact she considered the negative impact it'd have on acceptance.

One couldn't hide their out-there come and get me features. Her sharp jaw line was way too strong to ignore. And lips utterly out of character. They always scrunched up in a pout which only amplified when she was upset. Let's not forget the deep emerald-green eyes. The one feature she loved and never complained about especially since it came with excellent vision. Lastly the out of control chocolate-brown locks cascading down her back that she just couldn't cut. She always imagined running to her dad with her hair swishing from side to side. That long hair of hers kept the image alive. It was depressing holding on to childish fantasies but she had her way of dealing, it was what it was.

Stretching her hands toward the dark sky, dragging her feet toward her mother, who unsurprisingly had taken up leaning on the door frame again. Watching Clare as intently as she watched one of her patients. Clare wanted nothing more than to shake her head in disgust at the lack of affection in her mother's silent scrutiny. It was hard to refrain, but refrain she did.

When it concerned her mother, Clare always held her tongue, which was a complete contrast to her persona. She didn't need a psychologist to tell her that their relationship was bullshit, naturally Clare had figured it out years ago. Regardless of the distance that lurked between them, she loved her mother, but liking her was pushing it. A step into the apartment she stopped short at the sound of Michelle's soft commanding voice, "There's a lot you don't know about the world, Clare, you wouldn't last a day alone, not yet."

Clare didn't turn her head, she wouldn't give her mother any satisfaction, nor did she raise her voice, "of course mother." Michelle stiffened and the silence which followed was enough confirmation to Clare, that she hit her mark.

Frustrated with her thoughts, and knowing full well that the one-sided conversation wasn't going to get any better she huffed and stormed down the white-walled passage. Turning to the first room on the right she slammed the door, taking a small pleasure in the loud noise.

She threw herself on her bed frowning at the ceiling and ignoring the black jeans and red t-shirt sticking to her clammy skin from the afternoon heat. Any other focal point in the small space was pointless. Already knowing the colour scheme of the whole apartment - white or similar to, but still white. Which wasn't a surprise considering her mother's obsession with the bland colour.

Two

Clare
Her attempts at envisioning a life without an obsessive mother always trying to control her, turned out impossible and a complete waste of hours because she'd never known another mother, and was never going to.

Being eighteen and never having a boyfriend because her mother forbid it, made her mind scream for retribution. Her love life started and ended with a hand full of kisses from a couple of guys. And a minor crush on Phillip, who had zilch interest in dating her. The guy couldn't be any clearer than to have it tattooed on his forehead. Oh, but how she missed his nagging British voice and thin smiles. If only he'd been around, but he wasn't. Thousands of miles separated them. And even if she was there, it wouldn't guarantee his presence because he was MIA and had been for two weeks. She had to face reality, she wasn't as important to him as she once presumed and it hurt more than she admitted to herself.

He was supposed to be her best friend but where was he.

Using her index finger and thumb she pulled her cell out from the front of her jeans pocket. A quick check of the time told her everything she needed to know. Which included that her cells network was still SFS (searching for service).

She cracked open the door with the least noise she could muster, to find the apartment drenched in darkness. After a quick spy on her mother who was fast asleep two doors away on the left, she snuck back to her room on soundless flat feet. Changing into a blue t-shirt that said 'MUSIC IS FOR ROCKERS' and a black tights that went well with her laced black boots, she was done in under ten minutes. Wasting no more time than necessary Clare grabbed her boots and headed for the front door.

Sliding the bolt open she turned the key until it clicked and pulled the door ajar. Stopping shortly only to grab the set of spare keys from the hook by the door, she walked out. Her biggest test was locking the door from the outside without waking up her mother.

Boots on the ground, she gripped the handle and twisted the knob. She placed her left foot as a door stopper. And finally with a skill that could only be mastered by practice, closed the door inch by inch. Once the door shut, gently she let go of the handle..

As she bent and tucked the keys into her left boot before slipping it on and zipping it up, Phillips words chose the moment to ring in her head, "*If you don't get out now, you always going to be stuck.*"

Clare refused to be ridden by guilt for this. She never had in the past four years and wasn't starting now. She was an adult and her mother damn well better remember that. Hopping down the stairs to where the small piece of freedom awaited her, she thought of the night before she left London. Her girlfriend's had slept over at her place, telling violent stories about South Africa, and its increasing crime rate. Scared or not, there was nothing that could sway her to turn around, she needed this.

She never participated in her mother's meaningful 'you don't get it' conversations. Instead she shut the woman out and waited until it was safe to escape, and that was what she was doing now. Without further hesitation she looked up at the eight story mustard painted building and walked out the gates.

The night rejoiced as a scenic breeze teased her cheeks, calling her name. The temptation of what awaited proved too good to resist a second longer. Clare strolled past the gates to experience the foreign land.

On the left, the road descended into a slope and the right was a hill. Left or right, she considered them both but didn't take long, because logic won out since there was more light higher up, the hill was the route to take.

Dragging feet and a thoughtless mind ten minutes later, proved to be just what she needed. Alone time. Out in the open night with no destination in mind, *perfect*, she sighed.

Pausing near an oak tree, she absorbed in the peace and serenity her surroundings delivered to her. The stillness of sound, the smell of the ocean, the empty roads, even the lights had this relaxing aura to it, and in these minutes her mind cleared. This was the first time since that night her mother came home covered in blood that she felt eased.

Inhaling the night sea breeze a chill brushed up her spine. Clare smiled to herself not regretting her decision in the least, but- "I should've worn the jacket." she mumbled, as the jitters escaped her lips. Continuing up the hill, she turned a few unfamiliar corners until she arrived in front of a huge white domed church half an hour later,

"St MARY's CATHOLIC CHURCH," She muttered to the empty air.

Clare didn't mind church and religion, it gave people a meaning to life. Although she herself attended Sunday service with her mother she often fell asleep or took prolonged bathroom sessions until church ended. She couldn't sit and listen to a priest when she had memorized the bible in two days. The curse of a photographic memory.

The church in front of her was painted white with hints of dark varnished wood serving as the edging. A St. Mary statue stood as a bodyguard on the outside.

How symbolic, she thought on a gleeful note. Opening the green gate she hurried through the pathway toward the door. The fresh scent of newly blossomed roses carried with the breeze brought her attention to a rose-tree on her left as she continued on her way through the path. Stopping for a second she picked a rose and stuck it under her t-shirt between her cleavage.

The wind blew her hair forward blocking her view. Not wanting to take the chance of falling on her butt because it was so dark, she paused long enough to gather the long mass in a tight grip. Moving into a slight jog she barged into the church. A loud bang echoed as the door parted ways.

Clare gasped and snared at the sound, knowing without a doubt she had awoken someone.

The rose chose that moment to poke her, she cursed, and slapped a hand over her mouth. Slipping the rose from her breast she dropped it carelessly on the bench nearest to the door.

The holy place was much bigger on the inside that it looked, with stained glass windows of at least a meter and a half on the right. Various shades of neutrals coloured the Altar floors. And a deep brown wooden finish made up the rest of the church's flooring. High stretched ceilings that crossed with wooden beams left no place for ceiling lights. A soft glow from the candles on the side walls showed the pole styled lampshades at the end of every second row of wooden benches.

Hearing faint voices coming from outside, she moved toward the Altar. *Just people walking past*, was her first thought. She dismissed the voices until they became clearer. For reasons she knew came solely from hearing bad stories about South Africa, she felt the urge to hide. Not wasting a second to think, Clare ran to the middle aisle of wooden seats bumping her knee in the process. It didn't slow her rush to the row of seats. Or the speed her heart was racing.

Ducking under one of the plank benches she sent a silent thanks to herself for being thin. The throb in her knee protested the cramped space. It was a stark reminder not to jinx her luck. The louder the voices grew, the faster her heart beat. She drew in a long breath. Without releasing the air which now filled her lungs, she froze at the loud screeching sound of the church doors opening.

The people were moving with a speed that said they were in a rush. Their boots clattered the ground like a pack of soldiers competing to the beat that drummed in her chest.

Where they would've been rushing too, Clare couldn't figure out. *It's a church for crying out loud, and after midnight,* she harrumphed inwardly.

At the sound of a male voice, someone in their twenties, she tried to sneak a peep. Not wanting to get caught, her attempt was futile. She wouldn't take the chance. After all she was no fool to late nights, these people could be killers.

Though this particular guy spiked her curiosity because he sounded more like her, American. With an eagerness to his tone his voice drew louder, "We need the extra weapons Alonso, demons are pouring in by the day, Azazel's loose doing hell knows what."

Pause, more walking, shuffling, "We have no help from the other realms since the attacks. Four found dead in the last forty-eight hours and descendants are still blaming each other, even the Asguardians are now hiding."

He was no doubt American, someone educated, if his proper tone was something to go by. The words however, though spoken in English sounded more gibberish to Clare's ears. Was it her imagination or did she walk in on a movie set. But that voice, she had this vision or was it a sense of recognition, and as fast as it came, it vanished.

The clearer the voice became, the faster her heart raced. *What were they talking about,* she prayed they weren't drunk.

After minutes that felt like hours, she heard another guy, "Taking weapons from the dead isn't the smartest of your plans, Nathan, the Garde won't be as forgiving as the last time."

The silence which followed was intense before the second talker said, "Listen man, you just nervous 'bout tomorrow, you not thinking."

Nathan's growl warning sounded so inhuman, she almost stumbled in the small space, "Stop telling me what I am, and what to do," his voice got nearer, harder, "I'm older than you, which means you do as I say." Pause, "You'll make a good Garde one day but you will still take orders from me."

Feeling like a hammer was knocking nails in her chest from holding her breath, she released her lungful of air. The cramps in her legs from being in a constant crouch fought to be subsided. Clare couldn't take the pins and needles prodding beneath the skin in her limbs much longer. The sensation of her calf being crushed made her grit her teeth.

She listened attentively to the sound of heels thumping fast, down towards the aisle near where she hid. It was an attempt to block out her bodies feelings. Clare scrunched up her face because it wasn't working as well as she'd hoped.

Not able to see anything she instead paid attention to the woman's sultry voice,

"Men, why must you gauge each other? It's not like we have a mission together every day. Nathan doesn't plan on using the weapons. Kalbreal asked him to retrieve it but we need to be quick. The Caster won't stand by the gates forever."

The woman paused and lowered her voice, "We are who we are, don't let everything become a battle. One blood, one cause, one path together makes one soul, forever united, don't you remember?"

Nathan she presumed was the one who sighed in frustration, "Now's not the time or place for ceremonial quotes Nadia, let's get what we came for and get outa here."

In normal circumstances Clare would've laughed at these people and told them how ridiculous they sounded. But if she didn't change her position and soon, her legs were going to fall off from the feelings attacking them. Trying to do just that she moved her arms first, doing her best to go for that subtle way her mother was able to do things, bit by bit without making a sound.

All was going well until her foot slipped as she moved her leg, hitting her head in the process. A loud yelp escaped her. If her loud 'ow' didn't alert them to her presence, the smack across the mouth she gave herself did. She cringed right before she inhaled another breath of air.

It took only seconds before she felt the fingers of a masculine hand curling around her waist lifting her up and spinning her around with an effortless yet aggressive force. Desperate to get away from him she kicked and screamed trying to dislodge his hands from its powerful grip around her waist. But he was huge, like almost 7 feet, and too strong for her to take on.

The church lights went on.

She squeaked, "hey."

Clare's heart wanted to collapse with terror when she looked at him. His caramel skin under the dim light was darker than hers. Someone born that way, definitely. And very muscular with broad shoulders resembling a well groomed German warrior, or maybe a Therian warrior she read about in one of her books. She could see hints of Asian blood by the upper tilts of his eyes, but his American side won out with the strong nose and unusual tall height. Black shoulder length hair covered his thick eyebrows. Harsh hazel eyes, which now focused furiously on her, wouldn't define him as handsome. More like scary, crazy dude scary in her book.

This is the end, she cringed, *I'm going to die and my mother wouldn't even know where to find the body.*

His mouth was moving, but she caught only the last part of what he said, "...it's a sin to break into a church at the Tempters hour."

Clare gave the guy a scattering look who she presumed was Alonso by the sound of his voice, "I have no idea of what you said, put me down."

She skimmed her eyes down his body. The long sleeved Henley was a shade lighter than the brown leather pants straining his muscular thighs. Spotting the heavy army boots, that looked as if they had been through a bloody carnival of dead bodies was very intimidating. Now focused back on his face, she gulped at the serious angry gaze that marred his features. Whoever said looks can be deceiving had certainly got the wrong memo. Alonso's spoke volumes of a guy with lots of darkness around him and it scared her, shitless.

Kicking her legs out, she realized how tall he was. Clare always thought she was tall herself but nothing compared to Alonso the giant. He made her height seem like an adolescents. As if that wasn't bad enough, he shouted, "How in the realms name did you even get in. It's after midnight." He looked at his watch to stress his point, and the movement made her flinch because he still kept a tight grip on her waist with one hand, "I stand corrected, it's one in the morning. You know, now I'll have to call the cops. They'll probably arrest you for trespassing on holy grounds or, if you lucky, which is highly unlikely, call your mother."

Clare didn't want to seem scared but her face gave her away when she grimaced at the mention of her mother. She struggled in his hold but only made it worse, the man didn't let her go. Instead he put both hands on either side of her waist and held her mid-air with his arms stretched out; similar to how one would hold a wailing baby. Which in her case wasn't far off as she yelled, "Get your hands off me, you freak, I came through the door just like YOU."

Whatever he saw in her face as she frowned worked, because the giant bastard let her go like she was made of fire. Which in his mind she probably was after listening to the crap they spewed. Finally her feet touched the ground, but she knew this wasn't over.

It didn't take long before she was manhandled, yet again, when another guy grabbed her left arm and tugged with a firm grip that was close to painful. She was pulled up towards the end of the aisle.

"Do your parents know where you are?" His voice strained, "What if you got raped or mugged, and eavesdropping on others conversations is rude, what were you thinking?" He asked, more like demanded through clenched teeth, barely holding in his anger.

His name was Nathan, the guy with the strong voice that now sounded extremely angry, great, just great.

This guy had a light olive tan from standing in the sun for long periods. His hand that pulled her was darker from driving than his neck proving her theory further.

His muscular built was more pronounced than Alonso by the splay of broad shoulders, and the veins visible on his forearms. Judging by his height which put him at least four inches shorter than Alonso, hopefully, he was the more saner one. Clare was going with her assessment knowing full well it was bullshit. But if she could convince her teacher lime green is yellow, she could make herself believe her theory that a shorter guy equalled a saner one. After all she was technically a genius. One in hiding, as she always remembered to write a few incorrect answers in her papers. She was already considered a freak and a 'nasty insensitive bitch' she didn't need another reason for the female population to despise her.

When Clare looked into Nathan's eyes to say something, the gravity left her as her knees buckled at his reflection. Luckily he held her steady, she was too transfixed on his eyes to worry about falling. They were Green, dark green, the same as hers, 'devilish' she thought. That was what they called it at school, Devils eyes.

Never had she seen another person with eyes like hers, that was dark yet so visible. Her friend once said it was freakishly unreal. Her mind raced with possibilities at him being her relative, he looked familiar, yet not so much. The hairstyle of shaven off sides and long black hair kept in the middle, was too modern to ring any bells.

But those eyes, though harsher than hers, colder, they were still hers.

Capturing the knowledge from her brain of anything familiar was like trying to solve a puzzle without the border pieces, pointless. Without the foundation you couldn't do anything, you were just simply stuck. And as memory went, it was harder to know what you sought if you couldn't remember, and even more to capture it, when you didn't even know what it is you were searching for.

His jaw clenched as she openly stared, rude as it might be Clare couldn't look away even if she wanted to. And maybe she was acting a little crazy, but he must see it, he couldn't be blind. Surly a relative of hers would have some brains.

"It's rude to stare just take a picture, it's more permanent, post it," he suggested with a careless shrug, "Instagram is quite popular these days."

She hesitated and then blurted out, "Dude, you seriously can't be that dumb." When he quirked his brow, something her mother did, she huffed in annoyance, "We have the exact same eyes, come on."

When she saw the blank stare he gave her, she could tell he wasn't going to say a thing, so she shrieked, "I don't want your picture. It is obvious that you are no relative of mine. When I first heard you, I got excited for a second thinking you sounded so educated, and then again when I saw your eyes, but then just as quickly I realized you lack an awful lot. Mostly that which includes intellect and vision, so just in case you lack hearing read my lips slowly, LET. ME. GO."

A woman's voice shouted from the altar, "This girl is wasting our time, we have a job to do, we can deal with her la...ter..." The female voice trailed off, her words lost in her view of Clare.

These people were really starting to freak the be-Jesus out of her, in the sense that they somehow knew her. She was no fool, she knew when people had recognition in their eyes, and Nathan had it written all over his almost familiar face.

With a gentle push he let go of her arm. Squeezing his eyes shut he grunted at her, "Leave now and go straight back." A daring warning in his voice, he snarled, "No more wandering places, if I see you around at night, alone, I will beat your ass, understood." She narrowed her eyes, trying to get a read on his mood. There was no smirk on his face or sign of joking, he was serious and definitely the one to be wary of among the three.

Nobody had ever spoken to her like that before, and if they did, she never remembered it.

Fear aside, she squared her shoulders and stared at him smack in the face, "I was leaving anyway."

Clare then gave the other two pointed looks, snapping her fingers in the air, "Clearly you all need to get your heads examined. And news flash, giant guy," She arched her brow at Alonso, "The church is a place of peace not weapons dumb ass."

"Ooh someone's getting grumpy," he mocked, "You shouldn't name call guys with daggers."

She watched as Alonso put his hand on the butt of the dagger which fitted into the side of his pants.

Turning, her boots skidded as she stormed down the aisle of the church. She refused a backward glance as the sound of their laughter echoed through the church walls.

Welcoming the icy breeze creeping through her cotton t-shirt as she opened the door and barged out not slowing down until she was out the main gate.

A sudden relief washed over her, as she cut the corner from the church. She was glad to be alive. But she couldn't rattle the sense that something wasn't quite right with those people she'd met. They all wore similar clothes, brown leather material and light Henley t-shirts, which looked extremely soft, except the girl wore high heels, which in Clare's opinion, totally unnecessary. If they weren't so clearly crazy and she didn't know better, the trio could've easily passed as some special force team. She highly doubted that, clearly they lack the brains and were all Braun.

As the minutes went by, the only thing on her mind as she walked was the bone deep anger and the sound of their voices laughing at her. Her body was riled up, she couldn't wait to get back to the apartment and get some sleep. Clare picked up her pace as the sudden urgency to get home filled her with a shot of adrenaline. Clare always thought better on a clear head.

Three

C**lare**

Clare took the corner when she saw trouble shaped in the form of a car. The light captured her figure and the music grew louder as the car lowered speed. The front window wound down and she turned her head to the white Chevrolet, that was full of men. The one in the front seat mocked her in a drunken deep Indian accent "Hey, what's your name, where you going? come on, I'll give you a ride."

She frowned with saliva thick in her mouth. For a second she contemplated bolting it, but looking up at the sky she screamed, "God how about some help, or miracle will do."

When she heard them laughing in the car, she caught the whiff of alcohol, they were plastered, and most likely on something more. Her fear rose to panic and she kicked her legs into a sprint. Building her speed, she ran the corner she needed to take to get to the hill she came from. She wished she'd stayed with the other guys, they seemed safer, scarier and stronger, but safer,

"Aarck" she screamed as she sprinted down the road toward what she hoped was safety. The men continued to follow her in the car, laughing and mocking her attempts. They drove down the road and for a moment her body slowed in instant relief, thinking they lost interest. But no, the car paused a few blocks below and parked off , waiting.

She ran down the hill thinking she could pass them before any ONE of them jumped out of the car, and possibly duck in one of the hotels. To her disgruntled surprise and horrible luck, a bald guy from the back seat jumped out. He was fat with a thick silver chain locked around his neck and slightly shorter than Clare.

Clare ran, going deeper on the pavement to avoid him.

The man grabbed her as she passed the car. She screamed as loud as she could, "HELP!, HELP ME." She kicked his shin and elbowed him in his big belly. He cursed in pain swearing her profanities but let her go even if it was with a hard shove. She stumbled but didn't lose balance.

The men in the car threatened her with bodily harm, but didn't jump out. Checking the road for any cars or signs of life, she looked profusely from side to side, but there wasn't any.

She turned at the sound of the fat guy now a few feet away, screaming like a woman. Spying the wetness on his jeans, and twisted position of his leg she was shocked, it looked broken. Clare didn't think she could've kicked him that hard, could she?

Bending over, hands to her knees, ignoring the men in the car while trying to catch her breath. The banging on the window frightened her at the thought of them jumping out, causing her to lose her balance. A sharp pain tore through Clare's left shoulder as she fell, landing hard on an idle brick in the center of the pavement. Her face contorted with discomfort. Squeezing her eyes shut, she opened them slowly looking up into the darkness.

"What the hell.."

With her right hand she rubbed at her eyes, not certain or believing what she was seeing was real. Pulse racing, breathing escalating she was definitely seeing something, and it was falling from the sky, at a missile speed,

"Can shit get any deeper!?"

Ignoring the men in the car, her focus detained on the

descending object that now looked an awful lot like a meteor.

Why did it seem like her time to die. Maybe it was all a dream and she was asleep in her room.

Unfortunately the pain in her shoulder quickly assured her of how real it was, and if that wasn't enough, the car load of angry men who still scorned her would have done the job.

Lost in the fire blaze that just kept falling way too fast, she was mute besides for the two words that split her lips, "holy shit."

Pushing herself up, moving in a backward crawl, using her heels and her hands and ignoring the pain that tore with every flex of her shoulder. The men in the car oblivious to what was now so close still screamed saying only hell knew what. They were the least of her problems. She was too busy gawking at the fiery light dying down as it drew closer, and closer.

Clare screamed and screamed, her lungs hurt, her shoulder desperate for restraint, until finally in front of her, stood

a man,

She had no idea where he'd come from, well she did, it was the light, or meteor thing. *Shit, this wasn't happening*, she was supposed to go for a walk and get back. Crazy guys in leather and drunken ass wipes weren't part of the plan. And a guy that glowed like he'd been sent straight down from heaven, had no business being anywhere, holy shit, was he an Angel.

The mysterious man landed on his right knee and one really large hand firmly splayed on the stone ground. And at that moment her mouth blurted loudly, "oh thank you god."

He stood up like some sort of saviour with feet plastered to the ground and legs slightly parted. Blocking Clare from the other men which she thought was the bravest thing to do.

His attention focused solely on her as his voice drifted through her like molten lava, "I am not god." He then gifted her with the most cockiest and leg melting smile she had ever seen. Which sent shock waves coursing through her body, as her cheeks turned crimson.

She caught the streaks of ginger or was it orange, and black that made up the colour of his hair, as the wind blew the volcanic mass in his undefined gorgeous face.

The hue of his eyes remained a mystery but for the shimmering ray of light the glowed behind it. What the hell was this guy. Corded muscles displayed his long length as his ripped v waist peaked out of his loosely fitted shirt as the wind blew from the west.

His muscular arms hidden in the loose long-sleeved shirt he wore was enough to leave a lot to the imagination. The silky fabric teased a woman, but what made him sinful was his juicy dark pink lips that looked ripe, if only she ...., eyes widening she gaped at the direction of her thoughts.

What the hell is wrong with me, she groaned inwardly. Why was she feeling like this all of a sudden. Why couldn't she stop staring? It was like his body gave off instant heat waves flooding her senses with intimate emotions that she knew was not the time or place for.

There was something in his features and the piercings in his ears that gave a dark impression. He was no average boyfriend material, well not any material, unless it came with lots and lots of heat.

He stood there watching her like he had no deterrence of looking away. Her heartbeat knocked hard in her chest.

THUMP, THUMP. Raging with insanity to get out of its confines, her heart beat was fierce, while his spellbinding gaze sucked the left over adrenaline she had in her. Drained and suddenly light-headed, she hunched herself further toward the floor still gazing at him through a curtain of long lashes with unmasked amazement.

His attention altered, sending the men in the car staggering with one look. Purposely he left the guy on the floor for last as his calm façade diminished. Only to be replaced by a hunting predator with precision and swift movement, because he now stood right in front of the guy Clare had kicked. Her mind told her that he was standing right by her, how was that possible.

The saviours hand grabbed the bald man in a choke hold and lifted the screaming guy effortlessly into mid-air, throwing him away like a piece of trash in the middle of the road. The guys body twisting in the air before it landed on the road made Clare grimace. A loud screeching sound left the man, anguish and regret clear as he screamed, "Sorry lady, I didn't mean it..I..I m sorry."

The words from his lips playing in her head over and over were strained, and she knew it was because of the blood pooling from his mouth.

The amazing stranger then kicked the headlight of the car the men still sat in. Their shock and horror confirmed by their silence was not enough for the extraordinary man. Proving it, he flipped the car over effortlessly, landing it, upside down.

He bent over and asked the guys struggling to get out of the car in an almost bored voice, "Anyone dead, or about to die in let's say 10 seconds from now?" In shock they just nodded.

He stood up and clapped his hands together, "Perfect, guess I'm all good to go."

She was kneeling on the pavement. Her heart feeling like going into cardiac arrest. How could a guy be so strong, move so fast. What was happening to her? This shit was not real, it only happened in movies or books.

Frozen in place, she didn't lift her hands to her face. Clare didn't blink. She wasn't even certain she was breathing. This was too much for her, she couldn't keep up with this. The trio in the church was enough to raise her shackles. This, it was just too messed up, but why wasn't she screaming for help.

Why was she kneeling on the hard rough stone? And why the hell was she staring at him in awe instead of terror?, he did just flip a car like he was turning a bucket over.

The tall stranger looked at her again. Not sure of what she expected to find on his face. She wouldn't have guessed it'd be the annoyed frown marring his brows,

okay then she huffed inwardly.

His voice was gruff, extremely deep, "Try to use a little of your brains next time you have an epiphany." So much power emanating from just a voice, making her ears ache, "South Africa is no place for loafing in the dark, ALONE."

The details of what she saw still played in her head. A scene she'd only seen in a movie, but this was waaay more better, it was so real. In a little tone barely audible and foreign to her own ears, she stammered, "thank y..y..you for your help, I'll just be leaving now."

She looked at him waiting for him to laugh at her stunned expression. When he didn't, she saw his jaw tick. And something told her that was bad, very bad. Strangely enough, however there was no fear in her emotions. Awe, yes, amazement, undoubtedly. But fear, nope, there was none.

Logic told her to be frightened, she should've pissed her pants in fear of this super strong man, but she wasn't scared. As reality soaked in, at how cool it was that she had seen all that, she sighed, giving him a lopsided grin. When he didn't return it, she shook her head, "Too soon I suppose. Are these guys going to be okay?"

He just stared at her like she asked the stupidest question. Which she probably did, because these men that seemed silent to the world wouldn't have shown her the same curtesy. She exhaled with a huff, "Can you please quit staring at me, it's freaky."

The guy arched his brow, as he shook his head. She caught the quick smile, before he muttered "London's left its mark."

"Still American, mostly." She replied.

"You sound like both, get up, I'll walk you back." He didn't help as she struggled, even with the pain noises leaving her lips as she held her bruised shoulder. Limping and not hiding her annoyance of his lack of remorse to her pain, Clare was determined to keep pace behind him.

A thought struck her as she watched him walking up front. This male was somehow connected to those guys at the church, so maybe they weren't as crazy as she first accused. Which meant they were like him, but no, she didn't know what they were, but she was certain no one was like her saviour.

His voice was otherworldly. His lithe predatory walk unseen. And that hair that resembled fire couldn't possibly come from a box, the perfect blend of fire was too distinguishable. But the connection was there. Perhaps they were all different species, or some lab experiment of special ops team. She recalled the word for word article she read a year earlier on genetic mutation. One had to wonder all possibilities when faced with cold hard evidence. In her case really hot evidence.

This particular guy was supernatural somehow, she couldn't quite put a finger on what he might be, not yet anyway. But knowing herself she'd figure it out.

He was almost as tall as Alonso, a little too Gothic to be human. Though, now that she observed him, there was this light that came from him, too weird to wrap her mind around. Her first thought was Angel, but Angels had wings, so that was out. She huffed and swung her arms cringing as her left shoulder protested the movement.

Legs tired and body aching with whiplash, Clare slowed her pace even more, still expecting help from the guy. Cursing when he continued ahead she gave up on his help.

The man didn't turn to see if she was following him, not once. They reached the apartment where she stayed thirty minutes later.

Leaning on the green fencing gate of the entrance to the building he crossed his legs. Hip to the gate, and hands shoved into the pocket of his grey leather pants, which she could see clearly under the spot light, as he waited for her limping form.

She stopped three feet short from him before lifting her leg to get the keys from her boot. Keys in hand Clare looked up at him. Instantly losing her balance, she stumbled barely managing to catch herself as the air escaped her. Gosh, his eyes, she was sure she stopped breathing because it certainly felt like it.

She moved closer, uncaring that he grew completely still with the two steps she took to close the gap. Too entranced by what held her captive.

Blazing hot lava, molten fire, dancing in his gaze, it was a live rhythm of red, orange, yellow and black flames threatening to be unleashed. What the hell is this man? His eyes snapped shut and she realized with dread that she said that out loud, shoot, "Sorry."

When he didn't look at her, knowing it was trite but she had to say something she added, "They are exquisite, like the sun at the height of its brightness." *You are exquisite,* she completed to herself, *with thick brows that are perfectly shaped.*

Geared in a grey leather pants and a light shirt that hanged loosely on his body. Whilst a hilt of a dagger stuck out on the right of his pants wrapped in a chain sheath made out of gold and heavy metal. He looked as if he'd been born to wear this attire. It matched him perfectly.

She couldn't say he looked ancient because he wasn't. In fact the world seemed under developed and small for this warrior man.

The tall stranger stood there waiting for her to say something else, *was that hope on his face.* After what felt like hours getting lost in his lava gaze, she managed to get more control of herself and a thought struck her, "Hey, how do you know where I'm staying, do you know me?"

Clare felt flushed when he tightened his jaw line, his features sharp and pointy. He had the sexiest nose ever, a perfect slope, defining the crease on his lip.

However, the said lips didn't answer her question but warned her instead, "Whatever you saw tonight keep it to yourself, we wouldn't want any awkward occurrences happening."

She frowned staring in to his molten eyes, "What are you anyway?"

He flinched so quickly, she almost missed it, but she didn't, nor did she miss the tension in his shoulders, "lets' just say I'm special."

Unconsciously she touched her shoulder with her right hand rubbing it, "Are the guys I saw at the church like you?"

He smiled as if holding a laugh, "No actually, they a lot like you." He opened his mouth then closed it before a full tooth smile broke out, and holy was he beautiful, "Let's slow down with the questions!"

She blurted, "You not thinking about erasing my memory are you ? I hope not, I've watched some series with that shit and it ain't cool, but on second thought, if I have to choose between that and death, I think I'll go with the first option. Oh gosh I'm rambling. I tend to do that, amongst other things but I'm sure you don't care, I'm not gonna see you again am I."

He looked confused, and going by his slight gapped mouth, well, she wasn't going to look deep into that, "Okay, well."

He shook his mane, naturally to clear his head, "If hypothetically you did supposedly tell anybody, they'd just think your crazy, now that, I've heard of."

Examining her from head to toe he didn't change his pose, "You should eat more," he muttered. She stared at him thinking maybe he was teasing her, but no, the guy was deadly serious.

His gaze paused on her chest, his breathing laboured, "Saving your life was a favour. I'm not interested in bedding you.."

What an arrogant prick, and to think she called him her saviour. *Jack ass,* she all but screamed in her head, "I asked a simple question. Sex wasn't in my question Angel-boy, and quit staring at my boobs." When he didn't look away, she snarled, "All Braun and no brains, you are more like those crazies from the church than you think."

He was amused by Clare's sudden outburst which just pissed her off more. She ignored him and opened the gate. She walked four steps when he appeared in front of her. Startled, she jumped back, hand on her chest, gawking at him.

His fiery vision burned her with intensity, regret, there was no smiling or amusement now, "I'm sorry, please, I wasn't trying to be rude. Just don't, aah." He turned his back to her, then spun back around, his eyes narrowed, "Don't expect much from me. You'd just be disappointed."

Learning along time ago to hide her emotions she rolled her eyes, belying the lump stuck in her throat, that he actually apologized. He was the first one to ever utter those words to her, "Story of my life Angel-boy. Whatever, it's late. I really just wanna forget this night and I'll keep your secret for saving me and all."

His eyes widened and a worry frown marred his skin. Talking just loud enough that she could hear him, "Put some ice on that."

He looked at her shoulder, "It'll be fine in the morning, You'll see me sooner than you think."

His eyes sparkled with the light reflected from the moon, "Unfortunately for today our meeting is over, the others are waiting for me," he turned his head, hair blocking his face and laughed aloud as though he couldn't believe his words.

Clare laughed a little too, she couldn't explain it, but for some unknown reason she couldn't be upset with the guy. He did save her life even though he was a bit of an arrogant ass.

When she finally paid him more attention it was to notice he'd been staring at her, eyes wide in wonder, lips tight, nostril flared, "Goodbye Clarebella." He bowed his head, turned his back and walked out the gate. Which automatically opened for him.

She wasn't surprised by this, maybe she was too tired or just really good at supernatural shit, she didn't know. The only thing she was certain of as she walked the flight of stairs to the apartment was that he called her, "Clarebella." It didn't sound bad, as she said it out loud. A tad bit too old school for her taste but she could deal.

After sneaking into the apartment she went straight to her room. Another teenager would have run to their parent, but not Clare, this was something she'd deal with herself. Her mother wouldn't know comfort, she wouldn't have the words Clare wanted to hear, she never did.

As Clare stripped and winced at every ache and pain in her body, she was well aware that her mother could fix the physical problems. Michelle Miller was the best general surgeon you could find, but Clare needed something deeper, she yearned for a mother's touch. She wrapped her arms around her naked skin, swallowing the lodge in her throat. "If I can handle not knowing, I can handle anything." She repeated the mantra until her breathing steadied. She wasn't a crier, no matter how bad she wanted to howl at times.

Thirty minutes later she lowered her naked form into the bath tub and relaxed. Closing her eyes, she tried not to think of her strange encounters. But the picture of the guy at the church kept popping in her head. He did look surprisingly similar to her, except for the hair.

There was more to it than that, Clare knew she had seen him somewhere. It was in the past year or so, but where. Then it hit her, it was on the Harvard website. So he was educated after all. She mentally added that to her checkout list, Nathan.

Feeling remotely better once she had on her pink and blue silk pyjamas. She didn't dawdle around the room picking up her clothes, nope, she was wiped and barely managed to put the light off before she threw her body on the bed. Careful not to land on her injured side.

Her shoulder still throbbed from the fall, so she put a cushion underneath it, giving it some support. Clare rested silently in pain, thinking the worst about what would've happened if those guys in the car had taken her. They would've raped and killed her, that was certain. She felt the wetness on her cheek, chastising herself for not paying attention, and now crying about it like a baby. She was blaming it solely on fear of the unknown.

Angel-boys faced popped in her head, he had saved her and for that she'll always be grateful. She was safe in her bed, because god had answered her prayers. Her eyes grew heavy, but not before she realized that god was the answer to all her prayers.

Four

L^{iam}

LIAM ARRIVED IN THE ally an hour ago. He was in the middle of a meeting with a scientist from Hong Kong when his sister had called. The news about Clare's encounters was beyond unsettling, and had him storming out of the building.

He barely made it to a confined space before his fury reached his skin. Kalbreal was supposed to watch over her. Liam never trusted the guy, always thought he was too young and tacky, but his sister seemed to think different at the time. Now, not so much. Liam had no idea why he'd expected Kalbreal to be able to keep Clare safe, but then he always had a soft spot for his sister and forgot how trusting she was.

A lapse of judgement he had no intention of repeating.

Barely a week gone since he'd seen his princess. And two days since his sister had shadowed her and already she was in danger. That of a mortal kind, not the immortals who were actually hunting her down. To say he was having a bad day was understating it.

The one good thing that came from his day was the reason he was still dressed in a silver Armani suit and black Italian coat standing in an alley where he was certain deceptors used as a toilet going by the stench of urine and other smells he was not going to acknowledge, or decipher. It was one of the few places he couldn't be tracked to, the stench would put off almost anyone.

His black layered hair blew in all angles as the wind swept through the narrow space. The two buildings he stood between, housed street kids and a shelter for woman. He didn't like the way the earth turned out. He always helped, but being immortal, he wasn't allowed to intervene enough to make a difference. It was an unspoken law. To help the deceptors were to curse them. They needed to learn from their mistakes. As long as they ruled with power and greed they would continue to fall. He just hoped the deceptors learned differently before it was too late.

Sliding his hands in his coat pockets, waiting the minutes before his visitor arrived. An early arrival was his small price at making sure he wouldn't be tracked. Knowing the shady character he was dealing with Liam wouldn't put it pass the man.

It had taken days to track down anybody with some answers involving anything concerning Clare. And extra days in making a decision when he barely scratched the surface about the young Lightwatcher. But he was immortal with no regrets and until he knew for sure, he wasn't taking chances with Clare's life.

A shadow figure emerged from the smog on the ground. Just a little out of the dead-hour, when the figure closed in toward the entrance of the dark narrow parting of the two run down flats in Brooklyn.

Liam hated downtown in every state, but be it as it may, New York was the best place for what had to be done. He stopped a few steps in front of the male, "Do you have it?"

The man who confronted him was covered in a dark hooded coat, his identity hidden, with comfort. Which was the way Liam preferred it.

The man pulled out a necklace from his coat pocket and wrapped it in a cloth before he handed it to Liam, "When it's done a blood vow will commence to have my involvement erased from your mind and all else that you know." It wasn't a request and the male knew it.

The mysterious figure lifted his head that remained covered from sight, "Can I ask why?" His tone sounded of one who spoke of authority and power but luckily for him he knew to ask a question, not demand an answer.

Liam's face brushed with a malicious smile of mystery, "I prefer to keep my involvement.. distant."

The man argued, confusion creeping up, "Your sacrifice is anything but small, if you wish to bed her..."

Liam raised his voice, his eyes sparkling with specks, as his true blue irises showed itself through his brown contact lenses, "BED her, I need no heroic acts to do such."

His voice deadpan as he admitted, "I've bedded enough woman. Emotion is a weakness I have never encountered. She's different from her kind, I want her alive and breathing, for now."

"You keep my boy protected. You have my full discretions as you will it."

Liam knew there was no guarantee that the male's son would live but he had to promise. There was too much going on that he needed to know, and unfortunately this male was his primary source of getting him the information he needed, like-

Who was killing the Lightwatchers and what was so special about his Clare that three millenniums of tradition was broken. He didn't want to bring his men in just yet, so he was left dealing with shady characters. Playing his hands too early would be a fools move and William Blackwyll had never been foolish.

Once his princess was safe in his clutches, he would protect her at all cost, regardless on whether she agreed or not.

Focusing on the hooded figure he dismissed him, "I shall send word, until such, you have a task, you would see it done." The shadowy figure bowed before it transformed into smoke. His remains winding its way like a moving cloud through the fog.

Liam turned and clasped his hands behind his back. His mind already galaxies away. When he heard the hoot of a taxi, he knew exactly who it was.

Staring at the necklace, he took the pendant out of his grey coat pocket. It was a flat stone made with yellow liquid that glittered in the inside, forming patterns of a cross. On its surface was gold crested writing forming Angelic runes, which he recognised instantly,

"Let's hope I'm right mother, let's hope I am."

He walked to the end of the pavement, and looked toward the sky. A spark of lightening sparked the clouds, and he smiled.

The door of the yellow cab opened just before he got there. Inside at the back of the cab sat a girl with a red wig. Gazing one last time at the deadbeat sky, he slid into the cab. The lady smiled at him, her glee infectious as she removed the hideous wig she insisted on wearing. Once she shook out her dark wavy blonde hair, she looked at him with her light green eyes, "Where to now?"

His mind made up and he sighed with dread, "South Africa."

She looked confused, and surprised but she couldn't hide the smirk tipping her lips, "Why there? Why now?" He touched her cheek, "Because sister. It's time I summoned the Angel."

Five

C^{lare}

Clare groaned at the bright light filtering through the curtain. A quick flex of her shoulder blade confirmed her pain was almost non-existent. Guess Angel-boy had been spot on about it feeling better. Just to make sure she wasn't imagining it, she moved her bone around in circular motions. Her brain didn't register much on the thought, Clare was just glad that she didn't have to tell her mother, because that would be awkward.

After her teeth was brushed and bed made, she changed into her green knee-length skirt that sat snuggly on her waist, and a black blouse which she tucked in before slipping on her 'home shoes' which was a thick strapped slip on..

Clare looked at her phone, it was almost eleven. She practically ran to the dining area. Her mother couldn't be anywhere near her room, not with the bloody clothes still decorating the floor.

Surprise had her stop in her tracks, it was a table set with breakfast. Toasted bread, fresh fruit and honey with muesli, all Clare's favourites and a glass pot filled with black coffee, which her mother equally enjoyed. She hoped this didn't mean they were moving to Timbuktu.

Noticing her mothers absence she checked around the apartment, finally spotting her standing outside on the phone. Clare stayed inside not wanting to seem inquisitive, especially now, with her guilt still intact. It was one thing to get away unscathed but this time things had gone sour. But with her fading bruises and almost fully healed shoulder her mother shouldn't notice Clare was gone, which brought her instant relief.

Michelle Miller took overprotective mother to another level, so her morning encounters and occurrence she was keeping to herself, regardless of what almost happened.

Clare tried to eavesdrop on her mother's conversation but all she managed to hear was, "... understand, I need more time. No, Wesley needs to keep his distance."

Her mother looked concerned, and angry. Whoever she spoke to on the phone really got to her, but with her job Clare figured it was work.

Dismissing her mother's conversation as unimportant, Clare sat at the breakfast table and poured herself a cup of coffee.

The crazy morning she had came rushing back to her, and the people she met at the church. Having some shut eye Clare now thought with a clearer head. She figured the guy at the church who had her eyes, probably would've mentioned something if he knew her. Coffee paused to her lips, now that she thought about it, maybe he did know her, it was not her imagination, she had seen the recognition in his eyes. The question was not if but how did Nathan know her?.

She sipped her coffee, picturing the guy with the streak ginger and black hair, and his flaming eyes, she wondered how he had managed to jump from so high. He was an interesting character, though arrogant, he was better mannered than the church people, after all he did apologise. A secret smile played on her lips. The way he looked at her, while leaning casually against the gate, he was the epitome of goth God.

If she HADN'T known better, or if he hadn't told her otherwise, she would have considered the possibility that he might've been interested in her. He was possibly genetically engineered, a guy so gorgeous and strong clearly couldn't exist, and it did explain his ability to lift a car up and jump down from very high anonymous places. And then there was the looks, in honesty if it wasn't for his broad built and ginger streaks in his black mane, he would have been annoyingly too perfect.

She didn't get butterflies in her stomach or tumble when she saw him, she wasn't scared of him either. Intimidated and maybe a little awed by his presence, yes, but she knew she hadn't fallen head over heels for him, like it happened in the movies when a hot supernatural guy saves the female. There was nothing drawing her in, no pull, no sudden attraction, maybe something was wrong with her, because any woman in their right mind would fall flat at his feet.

Clare brushed the thoughts of Angel-boy away and focused on Nathan as she dunked the end of her toast in some honey, unable to shake that feeling she was overlooking an important piece in the puzzle.

Think Clare, just think, and that's exactly what she did, ending up so lost in thought she didn't hear Michelle come in. Nor did she hear what her mother said.

"CLARE," Michelle screamed in a wavering voice. She raised her eyebrows, no doubt at Clare's complete lack of concern for her presence. When Clare arched her own brow, coffee cup tipping her bottom lip, her mother narrowed her eyes with a knowing smirk, "How was your midnight stroll?"

Clare flushed, she hadn't expected her mother to have noticed that she went out, let alone confront her so early about it. Normally her mother worked up to what she wanted to know, never was she blunt and straightforward. That was Clare's route.

"Mom, I'm sorry I left, okay, but if I'd asked you.."

"I would've said NO, of course." Her voice louder, "Clare the worlds a cruel place, what if something happened to you." Clare gritted her teeth, resisting the urge to throw the coffee cup on the wall. Instead she sighed and sipped her drink.

Knowing Clare would say nothing further on the topic Michelle sat down next to her, "I'd never be able to get through life without you Clare. You are older now, yes. It's understandable for you to need space and feel that I'm smothering you, but I care for you, you know that honey." She paused as if giving extra thought to her next words, "I don't know what goes on in that crazy head of yours."

Clare felt like saying something but just thought better of it. She knew her mother 'cared' for her. But that wasn't what your daughter wanted to hear. Her mother never neglected her, far from it. Her motherly duties went far and beyond when it came to earthly needs. She was supportive as a parent should be. Clare couldn't complain that she lacked for anything, it'd make her look ungrateful. But how she did lack for that warmth and touch of a caring mother, or anyone for that matter. She was like a starved pup seeking comfort, willing to take any scraps people were willing to give.

Clare never really minded her mother's insecurities, and domineering ways after the accident. She was a familiar face, and as a ten year old, you tend to attach yourself to that which you know. At first she mistook her mother's hovering for love and nurturing, thinking that was her mother's way. She wasn't observant enough to notice the obvious. That unfortunately changed the day she'd seen Philip with his mother, and the unmistakable love in her eyes as she dropped him off. It didn't take Clare long after to figure out her mother saw her as a task, a job, hence the overbearing obsessive mother.

As she got older, she thrived in the freedom and fun that came with friends. It made her life bearable, she went out with her friends on weekends. Parties were a rarity with her mother knowing, though nothing stopped her from having her fun, not even her mother. Phillip would wait for her by the gate outside her house. After, she would change in his car to something more appealing, she lived for her nights out. But they were always better when her mother at least thought she knew where Clare was.

Ignoring her mother's worried frown, Clare shrugged and grabbed a piece of fruit stuffing it into her mouth. "So mother dearest, what're we doing today?"

Her mother smiled, though she could tell it was forced. Mother dearest looked awfully troubled by something, AND what her mother said next confirmed her suspicion, "A trip to the mall. Shopping; distress, the usual." Clare laughed though hollow, she made it loud. Her mother loved to shop, especially on bad days. Michelle liked crowded places. Clare on the other hand only enjoyed it when it came with hot guys, loud music and kegs.

Clare grunted, "fine." She got up taking her plate with her, striding slowly to the kitchen, "You know how to get around this place, or are we gonna get lost like we did in Bali, cause I heard the traffics shit here." Her mother never gave her grief on bad language, which was one upside. "GPS Clare, GPS, oh and I was thinking we should stop by the church nearby."

Clare's eyes went big, not wanting her mother to notice her expression, she yelled from the kitchen "Oh come on, It's Friday. Relax. If you need to confess I'm all ears."

"I'm sure there's a law somewhere against confessing ones sins to their children."

And that was how the next two hours of conversation went between mother and daughter. Both unaware of how a few hours of an average day could change your whole life.

After replacing her shoes for black lace up boots, Clare applied some mascara and a little pink lipstick, which matched her lips and brushed her long hair, they finally headed out.

Finding a mall and a parking, her mother brought it up, "So ,what happened last night on your charade, you seem different, lost in thought." Clare's face turned white, and she gulped. She needed to remain cool, and go with partial truth, she knew the drill. Her mother could sniff her lie out before she even said it, "Actually, ahm, uh..."

"Spit it out Clare." She hated it, when her mother used her name whenever she addressed her, "I met this guy, Okay, he seemed really sweet, walked me home. I think he's American or something, didn't quite catch his name." Not wanting to get into too many details Clare quickly added not giving her mother a chance to speak, "Don't stress I probably wouldn't see him again." She shrugged, "He's not my type anyway."

Hastening her steps, she let her mother know the conversation was mute. She paused in front of the malls sliding door. Looking up she caught the name, muttering it, "GATEWAY." From the outside it was a three or four story building, not much to look at. Painted in a mustard colour with a bit of blue which she presumed was supposed to resemble a wave.

A loud yawn escaped her knowing the hours ahead was going to be no picnic in the park, seeing as Clare hated shopping of any kind. But when she spotted her mother sidling up to her, the dead look in Michelle's eyes and lack of interest, Clare felt a new surge of energy kick in. The woman could be difficult, but she was still her mother, and right now that said mother was hanging on by a thread. Plastering a smile so wide her face might crack Clare rubbed her hands together, "Come on mother dearest lets go shopping."

Unexpectedly she pinched Clare's butt, as she brushed passed her, muttering "Smart ass." Talking louder than usual Clare chastised her, "Woman, we in public, behave."

They were parading the second floor when they came across a jewellery shop, when the gem caught Clare's eye, "Mom," she gestured with her head that they should go inside, "I wanna see that chain." By the time her mother followed her inside, Clare had already shown the man in the shop the platinum chain, with a heart shaped locket embedded with blue sapphires. She might not like shopping, but it didn't mean she didn't know how.

Michelle looked at it, "It's stunning, put it on."

"What's the verdict?"

"An early birthday present, what do you say?" Clare pretended to think about it before she beamed and nodded. Having come from old money her mother never worried about cost and being a general surgeon was an added benefit. But Michelle never spoilt Clare. So she was stunned when her mother agreed to buy her a pricey gift, even if it was an early birthday present.

Fingers on the clasp of the chain, she was seconds away from taking it off when a hand brushed her fingers away. Goosebumps rose on her neck, she sucked in air and froze. Attached to a masculine scent the heat of breath startling, as the man whispered in her ear, "Let me help you with that dear." The voice was so sharp and cunning it could cut you like a razor.

Clare turned quickly to face him. He was dressed in a black tailored suit, and a grey shirt loosened at his collarbone. Long brown hair neatly combed back, slightly taller than Clare with a trim waist and broad shoulders, this man looked sleek for someone in his thirties. When Clare opened her mouth, to say just that, her mother grabbed her arm a bit too harshly, but the look on her mothers face made her shut up, "Take my card, go pay, let me talk to this man very quickly,"

FRANCHESCA

"She would've made a remarkable warrior. Such a pity she can't remember, if it was up to me, I would return her memory now, at a small fee."

Franchesca clenched her hands in a fist, "Leave her alone, she's no threat to you,"

The man smiled cunningly as he spoke, "Well. I don't know about that, soon she'll become a full descendant, who knows what she might do in the future. What is that saying that deceptors use? Ah, yes, prevention is better than cure."

Franchesca glowered, "The place is crowded with people there's not much you can do here Tempter."

"I didn't come for a fight Franchesca." He dropped the act, and sighed, "I came to warn you, a heads up, think of it as a kindness to the girl. I always did have a softness for little Clare, isn't that what you call her these days?. I had my Seekers on her since she became a 'mortal.'" He made a gesture with his hand.

"Even if she ascends into one of them, she's harmless, please Azazel leave her be,"

"I am a prince, don't test my patience. You have been warned. Consider this my only act of kindness Draiken, for when I bring hell, I bring it unaltered"

Azazel left, walking out of the store humming. When he was out of sight only then did Franchesca turn around to look for Clare, who was standing by the counter. Franchesca didn't like the situation she was forced in, nor did she like the wall she had put up between Clare and herself over the years. But love and affection was not going to keep Clare alive. Franchesca prayed when the time came, Clare was strong enough to survive.

Clare smiled and Franchesca flushed with the guilt she wore as a second skin, before she steeled herself. Clare wasn't going to be smiling for long when she found out the truth. She was going to have to delay the inevitable because until she had back up, the best place for Clare right now was the mall.

CLARE

It was nearing sundown when Clare had enough. She was tired, groggy, hungry and not a happy shopper. She put her foot down when her mother wanted to watch a movie. Since that guy at the jewellery shop, her mother had taken her through the whole mall. Twice. That pretty much summed it up. The cars boot now choked with clothes.

They were sitting at a restaurant, waiting for their order. The place was very old fashioned reminding her of the little diner in the British capital. Dark wooden chairs and lightly varnished tables reflecting the warm roof lights created a relaxed feel.

When Michelle's phone rang, Clare groaned. She wasn't going to sit and listen to her mother talk about MRI's and X-rays a minute longer. After a quick signal to her mother that she was going to the bathroom, she left.

She was nearing the toilet sign when she heard familiar voices laughing. An instant knot formed in her stomach. At first thought Clare figured she was just imagining it, because she was beyond exhaustion. Her mother wore her out. The woman was relentless. Who knew there was eleven different styles of plain white t-shirts.

The voices carried louder as she focused on them. She always had better senses than most people, but kept it to herself after reading an article about heightened senses being a sign of extra brain activity. Her intellect was her secret weapon against the world. Too bad it didn't cure amnesia.

Blocking out the other people in the mall her steps didn't falter as she followed the voices, in a trance. She stopped in her tracks and turned to see inside a small ice-cream shop. Her instincts took over and before she even registered her actions, she was walking in.

Cursing under her breath for her unyieldingly inquisitive nature.

There they were. The first familiar guy she noticed was the Fire eyed hottie, who was wearing contacts, *wow*, she didn't figure anything could hide that blaze. Next to him sat the Asian guy, Alonso, who wasn't too hard on the eyes either, dressed in a light blue golfer, if you liked the giant cave man type who grew up in royalty. To her, he was the asshole who grabbed and threatened her in a church. It was no shocker to see them together.

Making her way to the table confidently, straightening her posture and narrowing her eyes. Today was a new day, and though she was tired, nothing was going to send her running without some answers.

Sitting at a corner table and eating ice-cream, the duo was completely oblivious or ignoring the fact that she was practically in their vision as she made her way to the table. Feeling a little nervous she cleared her throat and sucked in the stuffy air as she stood in front of them. Angel-boy smiled slowly as he addressed her, melodically with his wavering fingers. "The girl who couldn't stay away."

Alonso was not bothered by her presence, he didn't even acknowledge her, which ticked her off. But she shrugged, "I'm on holiday, it's a coincidence and unfortunate one in your case that we meet twice on the same day." She made sure the scepticism was laced heavily in her snarky tone.

Both of the men laughed, but just as sudden Angel-boy stopped and gazed at her with those unnatural black contacts. His features hardened as curiosity masked his face, "Did you come to spoil our fun, or are you going to tell me why you blocking my view? I was admiring the beautiful women that walked by but then you stood in front of me."

He rubbed his chin, eyes narrowing as it held her captive with a broody stare. Something tugged in her stomach, it seemed forced or unnatural. Tilting her head to the side, maybe her first assessment of her attraction to him was wrong. She frowned at the direction of her thoughts. He smirked as if he read her mind, or maybe he could have messed with it. No, She shook her head, that was crazy.

"Let me guess," Angel-boy gestured with his hands, "You have a habit of stalking hot guys like myself, not particularly saying that there are any guys like myself, so to speak."

Her temper blazed, "Oh just fu.." a small growl emanated from behind her, interrupting before she could finish, "ah ah ah, no cursing allowed, there are kids here."

Clare turned to stare at Nathan from the church, "Nathan, right?" she sighed at him. Waiting for him to be rude as well. Instead he smiled, a huge toothy grin, transforming his face to a sports star, with killing GQ looks. Since when did she become so obsessed with how hot guys looked. *Always*, because she was only eighteen.

"Someone was paying attention, if it isn't the church burglar, sorry about last night or early morning."

Nathan winked, and she flushed from embarrassment, "Would you like to join us, sit down? I can get you an ice-cream to make up for my friends manners."

He shrugged, "It's not every day that we are graced with London's finest."

Clare was surprised, that he was acting really nice. These guys voices. So masculine but full of silk. Intoxicating, like your finest brandy gliding down your throat. She cleared her own throat at that thought, before she pointed to the duo sitting, "I think your friends here, especially the guy with the gingered weirdo streaks in his hair, who thinks he is heavens gift to earth, would prefer it, if I left, so I'm just going to head out."

Alonso looked at her, "I don't, I'd personally be happy if you stayed, and Kalbreal's hair's naturally like that, it's weird, but freak of nature is what I'd go for."

So Angel-boys name was Kalbreal, she thought. She looked from Alonso to Kalbreal, who now had his hands covering his face. Turning her attention back to Nathan who now stood beside her, she sniffed the Dunhill desire blue, mixed with a potent leather and metal smell.

He must wear leather a lot considering today him and his pals were donning jeans and t-shirts, smiling like he never threatened her bodily harm a few hours ago. But logic said he had answers, and those eyes of his was proof that there was more behind Nathan. As if a decision crossed her face, he said, "Well I guess it's settled then."

Gesturing for her to sit down, he pulled out a chair. She nodded, too tempted by the offer to pass it.

All these gorgeous guys, who could resist, she was about to say something as such when her mother walked in. Silence descended amongst them, Clare included. Nathan stood like he'd seen a dead body, as his focus switched solely to her mother.

Clare felt the hairs on her nape tingle with tension, her mother walking up to her slowly. Her eyes moving back and forth between Clare and Nathan.

Michelle smiled as if she wanted to cry but chose another route, confusion set into Clare's mind knowing she was missing something very important.

Michelle hugged Nathan, kissing his lips as though she had done it a thousand times.

Clare stunned but not as surprised as she masked her face to be, "Mom do you...ah.. know these people?"

A weariness shadowed her mother's face before she nodded, "Yes I do, I wanted to do this after lunch, I didn't expect you to see them here. But you're all here now, so we might as well get on with it."

Clare's puzzled face turned to Nathan, then back to her mother, "Get on with what?"

Michelle looked at Clare touching her cheek, "Oh, honey,

Nathan is your brother."

Five

Clare stood there in the ice-cream shop. The noise around her, a background sound as everything else just slowed down, everything besides those four words, "Nathan is your brother," that was deafening, the words echoing so loud she wanted to rip her ears off.

The urge to scream strong but she couldn't find her voice. How could she have a brother and not know about him. It was so obvious now that she had heard the words. Nathan was her brother.

All of her eight years of what she remembered she'd wanted another sibling, yearned for it like a second limb. Yet, here he stood, so close but she felt like they were mountains apart.

She was played for a fool, her own mother rolled the dice. How much other lies followed, how much more was there to tell. Clare didn't hear the others talk. She didn't hear Nathan calling her name. Her mind too caught up in how her own mother had betrayed her, she knew the woman didn't want her, but this. Clare shook her head.

A wave of anger coursed through her veins as her mothers long fingers brushed her cheek. Clare snarled at the woman who she had refrained from meeting the end of her tongue all the years. Her lip curled in disgust, but her voice came out steady, dead, belying her anger, "You think this is so funny, don't you mother, mine, huh? Playing god with my life, lying to me."

She ran her fingers in her hair, hoping to feel a knot to tug, to ground her, make her feel strong, "I want to leave now." She stammered, "I wanna go back to London, I.. I can't do this."

When Clare met the sorrowful gaze of Nathan she flinched, dropping her head. She didn't want his pity, she didn't need it. Unconsciously, Clare sat down next to Alonso, dismissing her mother completely. But Michelle wasn't having that, she stopped right in front of Clare, her commanding voice in full force, "We are leaving now, we can talk on the way."

Clare shook her head, "So you just thought you could play me? Clare the unwanted daughter, let me punish the bitch, lemme not tell her, THAT SHE HAS A BROTHER!" People in the ice-cream shop turned around to look at Clare who was without a doubt making a scene. She was aware that she in fact was making a scene but just didn't care.

Clare ignored the onlookers and glowered at Kalbreal, "And you, correct me if I'm wrong." She laughed at the obscenity of how it happened, but dropped her voice, "This morning when you saw me, you knew who I was, you could have said something, but you chose not to, instead you brushed it off, acting as if you'd never seen me in your life. My question for you is, did you get your kick out of it? Was that apology worth anything?" She asked in a hostile manner,

The arrogant ass grinned at her, grinned! Seriously? "Really? you wanna have this conversation NOW, in front of her?" He answered in a hush voice with a question of his own, not wanting the others to hear him. She frowned and shrugged, "Well you did make it known that I am by far not your type, so yes, I want to know now!"

Alonso snorted a laugh under his breath, "LIAR"

Before Kalbreal could reply Michelle screeched, "Kalbreal is the guy? Oh come on Clare, a guy with piercings and gingered hair, really?"

Clare snapped, "Now you wanna lecture me, you LIED to me woman. On top of that I was played for a fool by these idiots, and you want to give me grief about my choice in men?"

Kalbreal smiled at Clare, in awe, "Well I did save her life twice, just saying."

Her mother shot a blatant look at Kalbreal, "I'm thankful for that, but it doesn't mean you have full rights to her, Kalbreal. We all know about your kind and their history with our women, and Clare is certainly not going to be one of your playmates or weekend pastime."

Clare looked at Kalbreal, focusing on one thing, "When was the second time?"

"Not here, let's go" he said. Kalbreal looked almost, tainted.

His narrowed gaze aimed at her mother, "I shall remember that hostility the next time you are praying for a miracle Franchesca Draiken."

He turned to Clare, his voice held the same power she'd felt when he took her home, "Stop this. You don't really have much to be upset about, it is Nathan who had to grow up without a mother after all, not you, and I am sure if you allowed your mother to explain you would realize that there is always more to the story, isn't that right Franchesca."

He turned to look at Michelle.

Clare was speechless as he finished his ice-cream, got up and gave his hand out to her. She was about to touch it with her fingers when he pulled his away, "Sorry, I have this thing about touching the unmarked."

Michelle insisted Kalbreal and Alonso follow them in a separate car. Nathan must've known his mother had a bad temper, because he didn't even bother saying anything when she handed him the keys to the car.

Her mother only spoke to Nathan once in the car to give him directions which somehow grated on Clare's nerves. Clare was relieved to see him smiling while he drove, and clamped her mouth shut. She wasn't angry at her brother. Kalbreal wasn't lying when he said she was the lucky one, but just as she realized that, curiosity won out, "Does your mother know what a crazy son she has, looking for weapons in a church?"

He shrugged, smiling in the rear-view mirror, "I never said I'm sane, but I'm sure she figured it out."

Clare addressed her mother for the first time since they had left the mall, "Why did Kalbreal call you Franchesca?"

"Clare, it's complicated, Nathan lives with." She paused, "your father. We separated after the accident, well actually..." her mother sighed, "It wasn't an accident Clare, somebody was trying to kill you. I'll explain, you'll understand and I'll answer all your questions honey, I promise, just, let's get back to the apartment."

Clare screeched, "Trying to KILL me and what, you just stumbled on telling me, what eight years later?"

Nathan's voice drafted through the car, "We've all made sacrifices, you should be grateful you had a normal life,"

She snapped, "Grateful. I spent eight years living a lie. Being controlled. I don't consider my life the least bit normal. I have amnesia, I can't even remember my own father. I had an accident with no damn scar to even remind me of the loss, is that normal? How could I ever be normal."

Not wanting Nathan to see her this way, the moment they reached the apartment and the car switched off she jumped out and slammed the door, denting the side of it. Clare didn't notice, but her brother did, as she turned her face towards the sun's rays.

"I see you got your temper from your mother," smiling as he pointed out.

Clare snorted, the mother she knew was a lie. She thought her mother was a person who would never just leave her children. But not only did her mother leave one child, she separated them. She took Clare's brother away from her, and Clare wouldn't forgive her for that. Because there she was, with a brother she didn't know, and a memory forgotten like a bag of old clothes shoved in the darkest corner of a wardrobe. *Why was this happening now.*

Clare wouldn't allow herself to be overwhelmed. Deep down she knew that there were frightening truths which dwelled in the air waiting to be unleashed on to her, and above all that, now stood a boy, a person who didn't grow up with a mother, but knew that they existed.

What could have been the reason for her mother's biggest betrayal, WHAT could be the reason for abandoning her son?.

Heading upstairs. The sound of their feet thumping as they hit the ground, her brother and mother walking in uttered silence from one step to another.

Finally at the top floor feeling as though she was approaching a trap set especially for her, something which she would never come out of Clare lowered her pace. Taking deep breaths of air whilst trying to control the hammering of her heart inside her chest.

Nathan noticed her panick and fell into step beside her, leaving her mother to look for her keys, as they walked towards the apartment door,

"You don't choose your family, sister, but forgiveness is strengthened in numbers, remember that will you."

Liam

The necklace had been safely handed to Franchesca before she left for the mall. But Liam wasn't feeling relief. He was still furious that Kalbreal waited so long before he helped Clare. Not only was she injured, but Liam knew that the incident would be haunting, and Clare didn't need more haunting experiences. She'd have enough of that to deal with once she found out the truth. Her mood swings and temper tantrums were only going to get worse before it got better as well.

Not catching a glimpse of Clare's sleeping form didn't help his mood, especially since the reason was Kalbreal. Liam was just about to go into her room, when he sensed the Angel.

Liam cloaked himself and was about to leave, but stopped at the eye full he got of Kalbreal leaving Clare's room. The urge to wreck havoc was so potent, he barely maintained his cloaked form. His impulse to claim Clare and mark her as his, after he ripped Kalbreal's eyes out for looking at what was his, almost had him going blind. But he had refrained, barely, by a breath and only because the Angel had left, and Liam's rationality knew Clare was his and Kalbreal wouldn't be able to touch her, because she was still fully mortal. It was enough to appease his instinct for the time being.

Now he was sitting at a table of a crappy restaurant on Umhlanga Rocks drive waiting for said Angel. He hadn't heard back from Kalbreal since he'd arrived, but he was certain Kalbreal got his message. Liam needed to see Kalbreal face to face. Kalbreal lied way too much for Liam to take his word for anything. The guy was his definition of an arrogant prick. He wondered what Clare thought of Kalbreal, but at the first sign of unease he blanked it out of his mind. It seemed his body didn't like any association of Clare thinking about another man, which surprisingly perked his mood up instantly, ha.

His coffee arrived. When the lady didn't move he lifted his head up to the ladies crooked toothy grin and then to the others in the restaurant, as they exerted minutes of their existence pondering his handsomeness. Which he felt a nuisance, but not too much to keep having to hide, especially from today's deceptors. So keen on outer appearance, no wonder it was such an ease when Satan tricked Eve.

Liam's phone vibrated for the umpteenth time, he'd been ignoring the call from Kole, another brooding problem. Liam rejected the call, which he knew he would have to pick up eventually. But not now. If Kole was going to help, it'd be on his own revenue, especially since the alcoholic bastard had ditched him for a full year.

Ignoring the people in the restaurant he focused on the red

lantern light on the pine wood table. It wasn't long before the cool breeze blew from the open door when the one who he waited for approached him with that smug grin on. Rethinking his decision to be at mercy to one like Angel-boy, Liam had to remind himself that if he were to get answers, and fast, he was gonna have to act nice.

His lip twitched in an attempt to play nice and stood up, "Kalbreal, who's the guy in the car?"

"Alonso, but I wouldn't trust him, just met him recently."

"So." Liam asked, "did Franchesca do what she agreed to?"

"No, I sensed her feelings changed, something different. I presume she holds more secrets but it's not why I asked you here."

Liam's face remained cold and hard, he had known Franchesca, and nothing was ever so simple when her name was involved, "I wonder what could be the reason to her sudden change of heart?"

"There's mention about her being a target, possibly Clare too, I need you to find out why William. If I ask it'll raise too many suspicions. And could you PLEASE answer your phone when Kole calls. He's making it really difficult to be understanding. He wants no part in this, and I need all of you to help protect her."

Answering his brother was not going to happen, he listened to Kalbreal give him DAMN orders. But Kalbreal knew the chance of Liam doing anything was slim to none.

Liam ignored most of it, "The Legions, why don't they help?"

"Wesley is on board, he'll see the message spread. I saw Jullie this morning, playing, 'lets follow Clare.' You know for a Caster you seem to underestimate my capabilities of keeping a young girl safe."

Liam would have felt offended if he were human. But he wasn't, he discouraged human emotions and found it amusing that Kalbreal seemed to be battling them. Not bothering to comment on that, Liam tapped his finger on the table, "Jokes aside, I don't wish Franchesca to give herself up like a weak deceptor nor do I think she would. I mean she has spent ALL those years with me by her side, I must have taught her something."

Kalbreal slammed his hands on the table. The people in the room looked at them, and the waiter moved toward Liam, "Is everything ok sir?"

Liam smiled, causing the ladies knees to buckle by his beauty and Kalbreal's heating presence not helping, "My friend here is not one for humour."

Kalbreal dropped his head near to Liam's, "Watch your place William, might I remind you of who you speak with."

Liam stood up, completely immune to Kalbreal's threats. He walked outside after he dropped money on the table for the coffee he hadn't even touched. Kalbreal followed him after noticing Alonso was gone.

The sun was setting. Cars drove by. People walking around. But nothing could stop Liam from what he was about to do. They walked together down an ally, neither of them in a hurry. Once they were safe from prying eyes Liam grabbed Kalbreal's arm in a firm lock, making sure not to touch the Angel's skin, "Firstly, you don't order me around, secondly my patience has run out. You don't question me boy, and you don't disrespect me. For that, you would answer my questions regarding Clare and then you would be my eyes and ears."

Kalbreal laughed, "I am not your boy, maybe our time together has weakened your mind Blackwyll. I only serve myself, my involvement with Clare is as beyond as I want it to be."

Liam put his hands behind his back, and took a step back, his cool persona back in place, "Do you want to know what's going on? Or better yet, the identity of the one you truly crave? Yes, I know why you truly here. Known it for years actually."

Kalbreal's face creased, and paled, "How do you..."

"I seek answers, news travels fast, blah blah blah."

"That information isn't worth the risk. You need to be careful, if you are dabbling in dangerous grounds."

Liam's temper decreased mildly, "If I weren't so smothered in emotionless conflict I would consider a possibility of you caring."

"You know I consider you family."

"Family?" he stared at Kalbreal, dumbfounded, surely he wasn't serious, "Family, ha, no need to lie, we both know that's not true. You might've fooled Kole but not me and neither Jullie." Liam's lip tipped up, "You can never be family to those you consider dirt Kalbreal and I would never accept one who I consider weak."

Kalbreal stepped back from Liam as if he had been hit in the chest. Liam walked closer to him, his arctic eyes a complete contrast to Kalbreal's lava ones, "I know your orders but if you hurt Clare.."

"I won't. I'll meet you at home." As if he was suddenly out of pretence, Kalbreal looked sad. The Angel amazed Liam at how pitiful he became when his feelings got hurt. Bloody hell, Liam had forgotten how young Kalbreal actually was. But the boy needed to learn, he knew Kole kept him close feeling obligated to look after him, well actually Kole pushed that burden on Liam.

He felt the pinch, but didn't show it, at Kalbreal words,- "Sometimes it's hard to remember you're a Caster who's much older than me, I really thought you considered me family."

Liam stopped short, hearing it like a siren ringing in his ear, the pain in his chest, "DEMONS."

Kalbreal's face graved, "Where?"

Liam closed his eyes, tracking them, "They there, GO NOW." At the command Kalbreal dissipated in a speck of bright light, like a flash.

Wanting to go help but knowing he shouldn't intervene, not as long as he was him, and not with Kalbreal there, had him clenching his jaw. So far he had managed to keep the Angel at a distance but still close enough not to get suspicious, but Angel-boy would figure it out. And when that day came Kalbreal would meet the end of his blade. Liam wouldn't risk his siblings safety for the life of an Angel that didn't mean much to him. Ignoring the voice in his head which questioned that thought, he turned and saw a woman standing on the street.

Tall and tanned in complexion, her French accent no doubt a turn on for most but Liam just found it a bore and thorn in his shoulder when it came to this one, "I normally mutilate my stalkers." His annoyance unmasked in his comment.

But she didn't take the hint, "I'm looking for Franchesca, she's wanted by the Garde."

He looked down at the navy Italian cottoned shirt paired with black Armani pants and shoes his sister had just gotten him. He wasn't dressed for this. Black hair as straight and unkempt as the day he was born, tickled his jaw as he walked up to her,

"What's your name again?"

She flared her nostrils, "Nadia."

"I would be of help but I'm just a lost beastly creature who knows nothing of the name."

"Boo hoo, William Blackwyll, If your reputation weren't so renowned for treating women like sex slaves then maybe I might have considered you a real charmer."

Faster than the eye could catch, he closed the distance, hand gripped on her waist.

Racing heart and arousal, sickening, her eyes dazed in desire, her lips parted with lust, he let her go. It took her a few steps to get her footing. Hands behind his back, he shook his head, "You want me like all the women out there."

She smiled, and shrugged, "Maybe, but after, I might just kill you."

She put her hand on his chest but he stepped back, "Touch me again and be you a female or not, I'll tear the skin off your hands."

Death glare, eyes narrowed at him, he smiled as if she had blown him a kiss, "Desperation is not a good quality on a woman, nor is revenge."

Walking away, back turned he spun around so quickly, catching the tip of the knife she had thrown at him. Flinging it back, seconds later the knife went right through the same hand that had dared injure him.

Hissing, her face scrunched up in pain as she tried to take the knife out, but the thing twisted deeper and deeper. Realization hit her and she dropped her hand and paled. Ah cleaver girl, but not bright enough, because she had made an enemy, "tut, tut tut, no wonder you are just a Garde Nadia, I know a girl who would've done some serious damage with that knife, now be gone before I kill you out of boredom."

Smiling to himself as she ran away, he continued toward the main road to his parked Jaguar. His phone rang, flipping it open as he slipped in, "Any good news."

The voice on the other end fainted, after the words had slipped through his speaker. He dropped his phone and all that around him had changed.

Six

Clare

Franchesca placed her hand on the knob of the front door just as a black hand with sharp clawed fingers gripped her wrist and hauled her into the apartment, slamming the door, latching it from the inside. The whole scene took merely seconds.

An extra second too long to register what Clare just saw before her. Clare screamed as loud as she could. She screamed until her voice cracked. Nathan didn't waist time in knocking her out of the way and throwing himself against the wooden door that burst open. A shiny gold knife was pulled out from his buckle under his jacket before he charged into the apartment.

Crawling toward the door, her eyes bulging. On the verge of wetting her pants, Clare watched in stunned silence as Nathan sprung himself up in mid-air and jumped on top of the monstrous creature with the gold dagger in his hand like he was diving in the middle of a war zone, and had done it a thousand times over.

Eyes fixed on her brother's movement, he was that amazing. Shocked to the spot as he continuously plunged the dagger into the creature, Clare didn't notice at first the black and slimy monstrous creature with bloodied horns protruding from its back or the red eyes that stuck out of its head. She only paid it attention when the pupil-less eyes of the creature focused on her before it bellowed in pain.

The creature whined, but Nathan relentless with his blade didn't pause with his continuous assault. The acidic stench of rotten flesh filled the air. Knife in. Knife out. He didn't stop, but the creature wouldn't let up, and Clare could see why. Her mother was embedded under its body, not moving. The image enough to shake her out of the shock that threatened to hold her captive. Clare got up and ran into the house. Grabbing a vase by the front door she cracked it on the wall. Keeping the sharp point in her left hand she struck the creature, the piece didn't come out. Screaming, she kicked the wailing beast.

"LET. HER. GO," kick, "You disgusting," kick, kick, "Ah, piece of shit." "LET," kick, "HER," hard kick, "GO.".

Dislodging Nathan off like he was a bug, sending him through the balcony window, the evil gosling finally got off her mother.

Now facing her, the beast began to transform. Too stunned, she didn't see her mother grabbing Nathan's dagger from the floor until her mother plunged it into the creatures neck.

"Clare RUN."

But Clare couldn't move, a slash and a strange pain prickling in her stomach had her looking down. Claw marks parted her shirt and flesh, blood gushing out of her abdomen, hands to the gaping wounds as the warm liquid dripped over and through her fingers, she felt herself falling down, her body shuddering with pain as her head made contact with the hard tiled floor.

Was this what death felt like, Was it so easy. Even in death, her mind remained curious, refusing to accept scraps. She tried focusing, but a sharp needle stabbed her brain. Voices, what were those voices. Why did she keep hearing voices. Loud screaming hurt her ears, then nothing, silence. A sudden burn torching her stomach took over all of her senses, melting it into one- excruciating pain..

What felt like hours, she knew must've been minutes before she was invaded by blackness. Not understanding it, Clare welcomed the bright light coming from the far end of her psyche. Her heavy eyelids slowly opening.

Laying helpless on the floor Clare focused on the first thing she could see, her mother kneeling and gasping for air. Next to her mother sat a frowning Alonso and an out of breath sweaty Nathan who crouched next to Clare's head. Swallowing the tears that threatened to flow from upon seeing the worry in her brother's face she placed her hands flat on the floor, "Mom, are you okay, Jesus what the hell was that thing?"

Clare lifted herself up expecting to feel pain from the ab curl being done, she frowned, pausing. She was more than certain the blood on her stomach was hers, she lifted the ripped t-shirt up slowly. Sucking in air, she contemplated what she'd find under it.

Not feeling pain anymore is a good thing, she told herself even as she hesitated.

Tightening her spine in preparation, there wasn't much that could shock her after what she had just witnessed. Having already pieced together that there was something more to her. In a place kept inside her head, locked away, she'd always known she was different.

Steeling herself, Clare lifted the rest of her top up. Unsurprised that the wound was healed, but still a soft gasped escaped her parting lips, "It's gone."

Tracing the red cursive marks that now marred her stomach she didn't say anything after that.

Clare was scared, yes, her entire world was spinning on a different axis, and it was only the beginning.

Her body functioning on its own accord, her fingers traced the imprint on her flesh. Not ever having had a scar, it fascinated her enough to ground her, remembering the most basic thing to living-inhale and exhale.

A demon, she somehow knew what it was. *How?* she had no clue. Raking information from her mind, knowing that if she could just remember something factual written about it, her nerves would relax. Disappointed, she got nothing but the feeling of a head concussion.

The pressure of warmth on her cheek brought her out of her mind to focus on the green eyes very much like her own and the mouth that was trying to tell her something important.

"Seals." Nathan said looking confused and relieved at the same time, "When creatures of the fallen harms us in any way we heal leaving signatures of sorts, we call it seals, it'll go away." He looked down to where her fingers still brushed her stomach.

Speechless, she nodded her head slowly, repeating, "Seals, fallen, healing, wait what?!"

Alonso sighed, "Fallen are the Tempters, demons are the makings of the Tempters, completely different, uhm Angels of hell, ring a bell?"

Her mother grabbed her arm, "I know you want to process this," her words hurried, anxious, "but I need you to go with your brother, I'll be right behind you I promise." Not waiting for an answer Franchesca turned to Nathan, "Take her, alert the Garde, get word to Ray, tell her Calub has been kidnapped, you have to protect her, Alonso you stay with me, there'll be more."

Nathan nodded, his eyes bleak, like he held a secret, a deadly secret. Of what Clare didn't even want to guess. There was obviously something more happening here.

Giving Nathan some privacy as he spoke with Alonso in hushed tones, she spared neither of them a backward glance. Stepping over the broken door splinters she scanned the passage way.

A sudden thought occurred, why with all that noise the security guards didn't check on them or police or anyone else. The place was dead silent apart from the three in the house.

It is a good thing she thought, and shrugged her curiosity off, heading toward the staircase. She needed time to think, and figure out why the hell wasn't she freaking the crap out.

A man appeared from the staircase, halting her mid-step. Dressed in a navy blue pin striped suit, one would mistake him for a harmless businessman man at first glance. The coldness and lethal intent in his eyes as he smiled brightly at Clare confirmed he was anything but. Raising her brow she returned his gesture, trying to act casual, like nothing had just happened and her heart wasn't threatening to burst open from terror..

She couldn't say how it happened, or when, but one tick of a second he was five feet away and in a tock, he had a long sharp metal string wrapped around her neck and unyielding grip locking her hands together between their bodies.

"Nathan, Mom," Clare screamed in horror, the man holding her didn't stop her as she wailed for help.

By the strength of his hold on her hands and neck, Clare doubted he cared and that thought brought unbidden tears to her already glossy eyes. Quietening in case she was bait, he couldn't possibly want her, she was a nobody, right?

It was Obvious Clare was no match for him, didn't mean she'd just wait for her death, didn't mean she'd just let this stranger use her to lure whoever it was he wanted. Struggling in the hopes of getting lucky, she squirmed. The more she tried the tighter his fingers squeezed her wrist, feeling like her bones were being crushed, she stopped and whimpered as the pain became numbingly excruciating.

A spark of hope rose in her chest upon the sight of her brother.

Knife in hand, Nathan didn't flinch as he ran, aiming the sharp object, hitting her captor in the shoulder attached to the hand that held the metal string to her neck. The man barely jerked, grip still tight on her, she froze, certain this was no man.

Shaking her head as her brother approached, she mouthed "no". Relief didn't meet her when Nathan listened and stopped walking , but he was safe, well safer than her.

"Your immortality will bring Infinity to your knees." Her captor whispered in her ear, the tip of his tongue wetting her earlobe, making her stomach wrench, at the sickly sweet scent assaulting her nose, "Too bad I have been ordered to kill you. If it was up to me, I'd make you my consort."

She snarled, "Bastard," through clenched teeth, not wanting Nathan to lose it. The crushing sound of her wrist bone breaking weakened her. Clare ignored her body's need to release the pain by screaming, and snorted, her whimper just a whisper, "With your putrid breath I won't even let you kiss my ass."

She felt it rather than saw it first, like an invisible shield going up, before her mother appeared from nothing but smoke, her eyes blazing with blue flames, that sparked like a live wire. The same licks of fire light caught on her mother's hands in the colour of a blue flamed torch. A scenario that should've caused her captor to loosen his hold, or let her go. But not him, this one was determined to finish the job.

This woman no stranger to her eyes, but Clare knew she was really seeing her mother for the first time. There was so much rage and anger, so much strength in those flame filled eyes that resembled a warrior. And all of it focused on the man who held Clare captive.

Franchesca grabbed the metal rope from the man's hand but he tightens it just in time, slicing all of Franchesca fingers open in the process. Red liquid sprayed out, Franchesca clenched her bleeding hand in a tight fist, showing no sign of pain, only a sight of pure anger and determination.

Clare kicked the man who was holding as the metal string loosened around her neck, sprinting behind her mother. Seconds after, he crossed the floor grabbing her mother by the neck. Franchesca screamed in pain, her agony echoing in the passageway as he scraped his claws across Franchesca neck, her voice cracked and hoarse from the blood gushing out, "RUN Clare! Run, NOW."

Franchesca pushed back, and spun around in seconds, kicking the guy with enough momentum that it lifted him in the air, and back down, only to land on his feet. Franchesca somersaulted in the air, with blazing eyes, screaming , "She's not like the others, we'll protect her, he can't fight us all!"

The man's face turned red, his body burning into a fever so high his eyes protruded as they stared daggers on Franchesca who still stood in mid-air standing guard, like an avenging angel, her fingers sliced almost completely off, neck oozing blood but she didn't show weakness.

Nathan flung the dagger in the man's carotid and grabbed Clare's arms, shaking her, so she'd look at him, but all she saw was her mother.

Nathan yelling, "Let's get out of here," went like liquid through Clare's ears, as she stood there, mouth open, watching. The man's head spinning, his neck breaking, a huge sharp thing protruding from his back. Inching closer toward him, involuntary, wanting to see what it was crawling out of the man shoulders, Clare was stopped short by Nathan.

But she still watched in terror and amazement as whatever it was coming out of the man's back got bigger and more visible, until she saw it properly from where she stood, shuddering she scrunched her face.

Black and the darkest shade of green wings were now visible, with jagged edges and unsightly oozing blood dripping from the bottom, bedded in millions of thorns. The right wing disfigured and for some unknown, unexplainable reason she felt sorry for the guy, why ? It looked painful.

Seeing her mother still in all her glory, Clare ducked her head in Nathan's chest.

Alonso screamed something, in a language Clare didn't understand but sounded familiar, "EL ELOAH YAHWEH-JIREH who brings you forth Tempter?"

The Tempter laughed, "Only that which is greater has power over me, Boy. I am Barbatos, Duke of hell." His voice powerful, confident.

Barbatos's confession shocked them all besides Clare. Not understanding why Nathan started pulling her with renewed vigour, hastening her to move, "Now we really have to go, there's no way out of this alive, we aren't armed for this."

Clare tried to pull her arm out of his grip. She was petrified, horrified too, but she was stubborn and that only worsened in horrific cases, "We have to wait for mom, we can't just leave her."

Her mother was so quiet, body blazing. Not able to see her mother face as Franchesca was mid-air between Clare, separating the three of them from Barbatos. Clare yelled at her mother to get her attention but she didn't acknowledge Clare.

About to yell again, she caught the movement from the corner of her eye as a man from the back of Barbatos flew straight up in the air screaming something. Lifting her head toward the man attacking the Tempter. Everything moved so fast, her eyes barely able to keep steady to see what was happening. With the same flaming eyes as her mother, the unknown man plunged a thin sword from the top of the Tempters head down his middle section, swift and elegant.

Mouth opened wide, a huff left Clare at feeling instant relief of this unsightly occurrence and uttered disbelief of her own eyes. Ignoring the persistent urgings from her brother to leave, she looked closer and saw the demons body knit together, healing fast.

A brisk and steadied movement later Barbatos bolted straight for Franchesca, plunging his hand into her body.

Everything slowed as Clare and the others watched Franchesca's body fall lifelessly to the cold hard cemented floor, leaving her dripping heart in Barbatos's hands. Clare bared witness to the entire thing, she broke free of her brother's grasp and ran to Franchesca's side screaming,

"Mom, talk to me, mom, MOM, mom," she lifted her mother's head onto her hand, holding it screaming,

"You can't be dead mom, please, don't leave , MOM ,mom." She slapped her mother, once, twice.

She looked up at the Tempter, holding her mother's heart like a trophy to be discarded, Barbatos, duke of hell. And in that time Clare's body burned with a heat of rage.

No tears shed her eyes, no thought deluded her mind as Clare gently put her mother's head on the ground. Her challenging gaze never left Barbatos as she got up. A taunt, he tightened his fingers around her mother's heart. Clare charged him and for once she wasn't thinking, she was doing.

Her brother screamed behind her, "Clare. NO." Nathan went to grab her, missing her body by millimetres. Barbatos taking his position gleefully to defend himself, making his answer to battle obvious.

Thick fingers dug into Clare's nape torching her skin like a skillet burn stopping her in her tracks. Turning to punch the person, she came face to face with a pissed off Kalbreal. Teeth grinding as the burn worsened but he didn't let go, she growled, "Lemme go." He pushed her slightly but it was enough that she fell down, hard.

Kalbreal pulled out a sword, his voice a loud commandment as he ordered, "Gastav." No second wasted, he plunged it into the Tempters brain. Feet slightly parted, sword dripping of blood, Kalbreal watched Barbatos, as the Tempter said his last words,

"Angel of fire, how yield thee grace when thy sire naught Infinity nay Paros." Kalbreal smiled, and with a quick brisk of his feet, he moved whilst using the sword to slice off Barbatos head. The Tempters body burst into blue and green flames melting into lava that burnt through the floor as Kalbreal's blade shattered into thousands of tiny pieces.

Kalbreal dropped to the ground on one knee, his gaze a new as he took in all that was Clare like he had just seen her for the first time. Feeling uncomfortable with the way he stared, she focused on his chest, surprised to see it not moving at all, like he didn't just kill a Tempter, like it took no strength at all.

His face softened, eyes dropped, "I was too late, MY APOLOGIES Clarebella."

"You can't save every soul Kalbreal, Adonai be with you," That came from the older man, before his back turned to the four of them. Clare didn't take a minute longer to register what had just happened before she rushed to her mothers' side. Hair falling down her back she dropped her body on the floor beside her mother's now lifeless form, "mom, mom, talk to me mom please I'm sorry, please, I didn't mean it, I love you, just wake up, please, please."

Her eyes burnt with unshed tears as the misfortune of ungodly minutes consumed her, taking in her mother's body laying there, motionless. The pool of blood which covered her mother's blue shirt soaked in a puddle of what Clare's mind refused to register, her missing heart. Another child would have lost it, howled, screamed but Clare couldn't do it. Even as the tears ran silently down her cheeks, passing her lips, landing onto her mothers face, she couldn't break down. It wouldn't change faith, it wouldn't bring her mother back. No amount of weakness would bring her back. But Clare knew that in her strength, as she looked at her lifeless mother in her arms, she would seek justice until her own death.

Nathan sat next to Clare, chest to her back and held her tightly, "It'll be ok, it has to be."

He cooed, "I've got you, now you must let her go. You have to be strong sister, it'll be ok," as if to convince himself.

Clare knew it wouldn't be for a long time, but she wasn't going to tell him that.

This day would haunt her, but not because of the reasons Nathan thought. She'll miss her mother and mourn her death, but she'll move on. It was part of life, but what would haunt her was the burning truth behind her tears, even now as they came down faster. The real reason her heartache burnt into her veins, the confession behind the sorrow that took over every emotion in her body, as she closed her mother's eyes and sang, "I was looking out the window, when I saw the stars were bright, but then I saw the reflection of your eyes and I said to myself, it's a beautiful day, but I don't know where I'm going but I know I'll be with you till the end of time.." Beckoning her mother's body, on top of her lap. Clare sang for all the words that were never said, the feelings that were never shown.

"So close your eyes, and lay your head down on my pillow, and when you wake, I will be there with you, I will be there with you." And lastly, she sang for the love her mother never shared, truth was, her mother never loved her. Clare wondered why, but as her mother's vessel rested on her lap, Clare finally knew the reason, because she didn't know how. So Clare sang for the person her mother couldn't be, but sacrificed her own life, so Clare could.

Nathan unable to handle it got up, and walked a few steps away. He grabbed Kalbreal by his arm, "Help her, you're an Angel, save her, please." Kalbreal dropped his gaze in response.

Alonso, Nathan, Kalbreal and Clare were standing downstairs in silence, neither of them wanting to talk about what had just happened. It was though none of them really registered the reality of the situation.

Kalbreal moved slowly toward her, stopping a foot away he stared at her without an uttered word. He didn't need to say a thing, when his expression said it all. At that moment Clare looked at him and knew the look of regret and remorse. Joining Kalbreal and Clare before either one of them looked away was the older man with her mother's body cradled in his arms. The corpse looked so alive, but gone at the same time, like her soul still remained trapped in its skin.

Seeing her mother's body like that hurt Clare, she spun on her heel and walked away. Once a safe distance was reached, Clare kept her vision pinned on the older man who was at least in his late thirties. If she had to sum him up in two words, she'd say unpolished and rugged.

Thick eyebrows, a forty eight hour shadow, with short curly unkempt hair, he didn't give a damn about how he looked. She herself always obsessed with what people looked like. Maybe too outsiders Clare was shallow, but people didn't understand.

The only thing staring back at her was what she saw when she looked in the mirror, looks. She didn't have all the memories that came with it. She didn't even know who was her father.

The brown leather pants and t-shirt the older man wore was an exact replica of what the others had worn that morning. Only his was strapped and loaded with a vast amount of weaponry, from knives and swords to two gun holsters packed with silver guns.

He gave her mother's lifeless body to Nathan, "Take her." he said to Nathan in a deep baritone voice, "We can still perform the moon ceremony without Calub. If Barbatos has come, that means there's a much greater Tempter. I'm sure your mother gave you a message." At Nathan's grim nod, the continued with his orders, "Alert the Garde, put a flame in the Aquadore mountain, we going to need all the help we can get."

Nathan obeyed the order without a word, then rushed toward the black BMW. Alonso acknowledged her, as he spoke to the older man, who seemed to be in charge, "Caidrian, What about Clare? She's a mess." Even though she had no tears evident she didn't bother arguing with that statement as she sat at bottom of the steps.

"I'll bring her myself, and next time it's best to carry proper weapons."

Kalbreal ordered, "I'll alert the Orderian, I'm quicker."

Caidrian nodded, "Thank you," not having anything else to say to the boys Nathan and Alonso left a while after, taking the jeep, leaving just Clare, Caidrian and Kalbreal standing in the parking lot.

Caidrian watched her, his emotions closed off, "I'll get the car, a lift Kalbreal?"

Kalbreal pointed to a black Porsche parked a few cars away from them, "I'm good."

Caidrian left, and she turned to face Kalbreal, "What are you still doing here?" Smiling at her question he tilted his head, eyes on hers, "Gonna clean the mess upstairs, I don't think the other's thought about it."

She wiped the dust from her eyes with the back of her hand, as a heavy wind blew.

"CLARE, I'm sorry I couldn't save her, I don't know your hurt and pain, but what you did back there was reckless."

"Please Kalbreal don't, I..." he went closer to her, his breath kissed her neck as he whispered in her ear, making her forget all that she was going to say, but not in a sexual way, but a temporary lull, "I have waited eight years to meet you again, I always imagined it with smiles, I'm sorry it has come to this."

She looked at him, curious, as to, what did he mean 'again' when Caidrian drove up right next to where they stood, interrupting her on getting any answers. Kalbreal stepped back and lowered his eyes, but never bowed his head, she noted that he never did drop his head. It was a sign of pride, and he was always proud, she wished she could have had some of his.

Caidrian revved the engine, "Clare let's go, See you in the realm, Kalbreal."

Clare looked at Kalbreal before he turned, but he didn't look back, just continued up the stairs.

"Who dented the car?" Caidrian asked her as she jumped in the car. It was the first time he had addressed her head on,. Having no interest in his questions, or even a slight inclination to answer it, her eyes stayed glued to the window.

The urge to kill should have lessened by the death of the Tempter, but all she could feel was a slow burning fire waiting to be released from her chest, a need for justice. She thought of her history teacher's last lesson, he said that there was power in vengeance, but the true power was how you chose to apply it. Watching the trees pass by, Clare knew that the only application she'll make was the one with Tempters' blood, and just that very thought eased something inside her, it wasn't much but she would find a way to keep it.

They parked outside a forest entrance. The whole drive Caidrian had stayed quiet, now however, he was holding her gaze with a pained expression, making her want to flinch at his pitiful face, "How much did Franchesca tell you. Do you know who I am?" Her no answer was answer enough, "It was Franchesca's idea to separate you from all this and the rest of us for so long."

"Franchesca meaning Michelle, my mother, I know Nathan's my brother, and my mother's dead, so I guess there isn't much left to know, is there." "I'm your father, there's that, and a whole lot more, which I'll explain to you soon, if you give me a chance."

Clare looked at him as if he was insane as she considered the possibility, he was too young to be her father, and looked nothing like her, she already had an image of her father in her head, even if it was made up, and he wasn't it, "I don't know what world you're from dude, but in this world, you don't just save someone and inherit a kid!" Shrugging she added, "You gotta do things the old fashion way, OR ADOPT, Carl or wait! - what's your name again?."

He gave her a small smile, jumping out of the car. She didn't expect him to answer, people tended to mistake her bluntness for rudeness, her mother always did, she flinched at the thought, and buried it deep down where no one would know the truth.

Pulling open her door, she was relieved and surprised when he held out his hand, "Caidrian, though I would prefer father at best.

You used to call me dad." He paused, as she shook his offered hand, then added, "Supporting you for the first ten years of your life, and paying for that expensive fancy school you go to should count for something, besides there's a resemblance, see." he pointed to the small mirror on the outside of the car.

Pouting her lips, which was a force of habit, she frowned at the cars mirror, and her reflection, "Liar, we look nothing alike."

He laughed, as she stared again at her reflection, swollen lips and puffy eyes, with smudged mascara. Bad was understating how she really looked and felt with all the dirt on her skin, and torn blouse now painted in dried blood stuck to her body.

Touching her tongue to her pellet the taste of iron from her blood still lingered in her mouth.

Thinking of how she could fix this, a small grin tugged on her lips when she looked at the car they'd arrived in. Not wasting a minute Clare went to the boot, which was filled with clothes her mom and her bought today. Unperturbed by Caidrians presence, whose name, she had remembered perfectly well the first time, but would never admit it, she stripped down to her bra and panties, taking some bottle water, and washed herself up.

Replacing her tattered bra with a black lacy one, she rummaged through the packet until she found a skinny jeans and black shirt.

Noticing Caidrians stiff back, she suppressed the urge to poke at him as she pulled up her jeans, asking instead, "What's the difference between a demon and a Tempter, Alonso explained it to me but.."

Back seeming to relax a slight bit, he replied, "Tempters are the fallen Angels, Barbatos, Lucifer, Azazel, Amon, Abbaddon and a whole lot more, there are 200 or more fallen, but the demons, are the beast that the Tempters create, like an Aggrammon demon, or Ravenor, Drugbard, Dragonfiely they're normally horrible looking things, sometimes the stronger demons could take the shape of fog, or even deceptors."

She tossed the destroyed clothes in the 4x4, threw her hair forward, finger combing it, "So is the Tempter completely dead?, I'm Done."

"Well, not quite." He walked toward the forest as she tied her hair in a knot, "He's as dead as he can be, Kalbreal just cut his soul into pieces, scattering them all over the planet, so give or take maybe a hundred or so years, Barbatos will be himself." He shrugged, "Can't really kill that which was never alive you know."

She walked closer toward him, meeting him there, "What are we doing here in the middle of nowhere, it's creepy, and where's Nathan?" Arms folded across her chest, expectant mask on her face, she waited for an answer, he sighed, "We have to go to the realms, inform the Garde and bury your mother, we don't have much time, if they're killing and hunting us we need to be at our stations." He paused, "Tempters have managed to get passed the seals before, you should prepare yourself girl, you need training as soon as possible."

She flinched, "Why? I don't need training!" When he ignored her and started toward the car with what looked like gasoline, Clare got the bags from the back of the car. There was no reason to leave it, and she'd need the clothes wherever it was they were headed. Putting the bags on the ground a good distance away from the car, Clare watched him pour the liquid on the vehicle.

When he turn toward her she sighed, "It's like we speak two different languages, how about tryna explain in English."

Caidrian took her arm in a firm grip, gently shoving her in front of him, "We got to move I'd portal us but it's too risky since you've never done it before, let's go, I'll explain it all to you, just not right now." Clare shot him a wicked look, before they started the journey into the forest, both of them carrying the stuff from the trunk.

Silence thick as the tension in the air, they walked deeper into the forest. When the vehicle exploded, she jumped by the shock and vibration of the ground, and with it came the brutal and horrifying reality, of her situation. She was stuck! Now blindly, having to trust strangers, and this man who laid a serious claim of being the one person she'd hoped to find for eight long years, her father.

There was something not right with it, something she knew she was missing. The feeling so potent and strong that she could physically feel it kicking and screaming in her mind with a powerful rage. Her mind wanted her to remember what it lost, it had always been greedy, but now it starved with need.

Clare tried to push the thoughts of her mother's sudden death out of her head as it threatened to flood her memory. After every attempt, trying to figure out why her mind and body were at war, she had to give up because all it caused was nausea.

Caidrian looked at her, shaking his head. They moved in silence, until he huffed in annoyance breaking the silence, "Your name is Gabriella Moonstone of the sixth realm, I've spent the first years of your life with you but after the accident your memory was gone and so was everything that made you a descendant, if the rest of the Garde or the Advisors found out, they would have branded you as a curse and left you to die on the Elvan mountains." He spoke too calmly, matter of factly, like it was the most natural thing in the world.

"What, seriously? Why would they do that?" Clare was anything but calm at the mention of her and death in the same sentence. Why would these people want to kill her.

He nodded, "Descendants are very strong on tradition, something to remember when we get to the realm."

When he didn't explain further, her anger rose, "No one has spoken about my amnesia for years, my mother never mentioned anything to me. I asked her, I wondered why would my father just abandon me. I always wanted a brother, a father, family." She paused, swallowing the lump lodged in her throat, "do you know what it's like spending your holidays alone. I like things to make sense, I need it to make sense, I need facts." When he remained quiet she added softly, "If there's one thing I know about life Caidrian it's that death is easier than betrayal. I've been surrounded by a cocoon of lies for years. So if you are my father, I need you to explain it to me, I need you to give me the facts."

Even a stranger could see the pain in Caidrians eyes as he listened to Clare, she didn't mean to poke a nerve, she needed answers. But he didn't budge, "We'll talk later."

His finality of the statement left no room for argument. Noticing his clenching hand as it balled in a tight fist around the packet handles, unwanted images of Barbatos holding her mother's heart while it dripped of blood, invaded her frontal lobe. It was like the world spun at an unusual fast pace, but as much as she tried to join in she was standing still, an invisible force holding her to the ground.

Caidrian spoke but she couldn't register what he was saying, her mind refused to process it. Clare stared at him but it was like she was actually staring through him really. Her mother was dead, and all she felt was shock and anger, the need for blood, but there was no sorrow, no heart ache.

What did it say about her? Was she herself a monster? Was she one of the demons that Caidrian had explained looked like human?! Questions that she couldn't answer filled her mind in a maddening repetition.

Caidrian's eyes darted around the trees, until he finally caught her frozen status, as if he understood what was happening to her, he pushed her, causing her to fall unceremoniously on the ground, "OW, What the hell." Clare yelled as her eyes glared at him from the ground.

Caidrian stopped walking, and looked down at her form resting on the floor. He reached his hand out to assist her. But she didn't accept it, instead she put her hands on the sandy pathway, and as the small stones poked into the palms of her hands, she got up and dusted herself off.

"You were going into shock, do it again I'll slap you."

Deeper into the forest, silence distanced them yet again, Clare, too wrapped up in questions to let the man's cold demeanour affect her.

Why was her mother hiding her? Was she hiding her? Why were these people helping her? What were these people doing in her life now after all these years? What changed? Did something transpire that she didn't know about?

Her mind bombarded with these thoughts, but the biggest question lingered in the air like a silent blade of thorns waiting to be unleashed- If she weren't human then what was she. Words flowed from her lips before her mind even processed it happening, "If I'm not human then what am I?" She was not certain she would like the answer, but knowing was better than not knowing.

Caidrian looked at her, deciding what to say or how to start, or if this was a good time kept him quiet. His indecision however was written clearly on his face, "let's get you to a safe place, I'll explain it to you later."

She screamed, "NOW," her voice echoed through the forest. The birds in the trees leaving their resting place.

His hand cupped her mouth silencing her. "Quiet, we're being followed." He hissed.

Her eyes widened as her gaze skittered around the forest, the tall trees intimidating her with their height as she sized them with envy. The birds chirped in a melody which Clare interpreted as a hymn of sorrow taunting her with the knowledge of her lack of affection, was she being judged? Shaking her head at how ridiculous an insinuation she conjured up, she dropped her head not sure what to believe anymore.

Caidrian grabbed hold of her shoulders beckoning her towards him. He yielded her in as she pushed away, still resisting him, but as he pulled her closer toward him, he gripped her into a strong embrace.

She released her rage and anger, hitting him on his chest, shouting, "I hate you, you left me you bastard, you COWARD, you fucking left me, I hate you."

"I know, I'm sorry, ssshhh, I'm so sorry Clare."

Wetness on her cheek spilled as the softness of his voice lulled her. He cooed her like one would a new born baby, reassuring her with gentle words. But what should've eased her, hardened her instead as it poured over her like acid withering away the little happiness she had in her, of meeting her father.

In its place now an impenetrable thick cloud of obsidian darkness. She wouldn't allow another parent to leave her tattered, not when she had already so little to offer those who deserved it, who deserved her love, no matter how little of it she had to offer. It was the one thing she'd do for her mother, she would love those deserving of her love unconditionally. She refused to waste a fraction of it for this man who held her now when she was an adult and her heart already hardened by the ages. It was far too late.

He held her tight, swaying her body like a ragged doll in the middle of the forest. Realizing the wetness on her cheek was his and his intent was not to comfort her, but to reassure himself, her legs caved. Nobody had ever cried for her, cried for the person she was, but this man did. She expected to hit the ground but he didn't let her fall, no, he held her up, and gave her the support she needed. They stood holding each other, like a long awaited reunion, like two people who had experienced great loss, but where one was strong, the other one was just learning to walk.

There was no comfort in his arms, and as if he sensed so, he stiffened. Without a sound, she dropped her hands, and took a few steps back, picked up the packets she had discarded on the sandy ground beside her, and stood there, with a determined look, "You got your hug, my daughter duty is done, now it's your turn, I need some solid information, what am I?, or who am I?, at least tell my why the hell were those Tempters after me?"

She glared at him, stubbornness penetrated through her eyes letting him see the brick he was dealing with, "Dude you gotta give me something."

In his attempt to try and keep his calm, which Clare was making disturbingly hard, Caidrian said softly, "You are going to get yourself killed, there's a time and place to tell you all that you need to know, and now is neither."

She pouted her lips which was a habit, and arched her brow, before she dropped herself to the floor sitting on her butt. If he wanted to play tough ball then so be it.

"Suit yourself, I'm just going to sit here and wait for the demons and Tempters to arrive, maybe they'll be more co-operative. I really have nothing to lose."

She stared at Caidrian, waiting for him to reply her, but a sudden pain pocked inside her stomach, it was something she'd never felt before, her stomach contracted and with it a deep agonizing pain. Fisting both hands to apply pressure she howled in agony, "Aaah, shit, aaahhh, it hurts," the pain similar to a severe case of food poisoning.

Caidrian knelt down beside Clare as she held her hands around her stomach rocking back and forth with her knees to her chest. Just a few hours ago she was with her mother, the woman who had not one nurturing bone in her body, the only parent she ever knew. The same person who carried her down Hyde-park when she hurt her knee and stitched it up. Her mother would've known what to do, she was a healer, a cold one, but a good healer. Clare wanted to scream for her, but there was no use, she wasn't coming back.

Now in a matter of hours Clare was motherless, orphaned, by the ultimate sacrifice a parent can make. It was then she recalled the last words her mother said to Barbatos before he ripped the life out of her, "better my life than hers."

At first she didn't remember but now she did, what did it mean. Even with the pain and her constant rocking motions it didn't stop the questions.

Caidrian lifted her up by her shoulders and looked deeply into her eyes, "You're my daughter, no death or loss is going to change that, and I know you have questions, but the pain you're feeling is only going to get worse, it's a reminder that times passing, you need to walk, if you're not safe, your mother would've died in vain. We have to bury her and draw out her power, her wishes fulfilled." He let her go and with a firm voice "Now get up, the Caster is waiting at the entrance."

Clare got up staggering quietly without a sound besides her footsteps pounding on the ground as she walked. Listening to the forest birds, the only sort of comfort she had, as the pain in her stomach lurked through her abdomen, like a curse, reminding her of the loss.

Caidrian broke the silence, "You really want to know who you are, I'm not sure you'll be able to handle it, you lived as a deceptor for a long time." She didn't miss the curiosity in his voice, as they walked.

The path deepened further into the forest, leading to a higher spiralled walkway with sanded spots, it looked as though the entry had been blocked, deserted, and retained to its natural habitat with sky high trees, and colourful birds.

Clare looked up at the trees, noticing the fading sun, darkness would soon follow. She thought about checking the time on her phone, but remembered she lost it at the apartment. They started to close in toward the trees and branches which blocked their way, but the closer they moved, something extraordinary happened- the trees moved out of the way, bending. Clare gulped as she jerked back in a wonder of horror. "CAIDRIAN."

He laughed, "Relax, they're giving us way, how else are we suppose to keep the deceptors out of the way." She relaxed a little, but still weary with each passing step she took and each bend the trees made, it was way too much for her eyes to handle, especially after all that had already happened, but it was an incredible site for her sight

Caidrian muttered, "Never ceases to amaze,"

She said softly, "I wanna know everything."

Seven

Caidrian breathed soundly, "Fine. Quick history lesson, about 3000 bc, there was a planet with life on it, famously known as Venusta, now it's just a ball of rock, which deceptors call Venus."

Clare interrupted, as she screeched, "So I'm an alien"

Chuckling at her expression, he shook his head, "Not quite, before humans, Adonai, created Venusians. They once lived on earth before the first reckoning, but only a few of them who were worthy got sent to another planet to continue their legacy." When he saw her mouth open, he cut her off, "Na ah, just listen."

She half smiled and nodded, "Venusian people were superior to humans, they were perfected versions, masters of all arts, guardians of the realms, their technology and infrastructure was advanced. But they were the most god fearing of all creation, so much so that an Angel became jealous at Adonai's affection for them, and in a fit of rage he opened a portal, allowing demons to enter. It wasn't long before Venus became riddled with demons, so the Venusians decided to seek shelter on another planet, but the demons saw through their plan and destroyed Venus by flooding it with water, killing all but 100 soldiers, who were locked underground. Most of whom survived were royalty." He paused,

"Now you must understand that in Venus the strongest of soldiers were always woman, they were the leaders, so with only enough metal and blue energy for one ship they sent 50 of the strongest woman to seek their ancestral planet called earth. When they landed on earth 3000 years before Christ, they found human beings, instead of killing them, they decided to try and teach the humans to be civilized so they may grow as a species. The Venusian women noticed the humans were very similar to them, so they taught them language, farming and sewing, but after just a few years of peace, came the Tempters and their demons.

The Venusians knew they couldn't defeat them without the help of the Angels, so they summoned two Angels, they begged the Angels for help but they refused and left. The Angels said the humans needed to be destroyed, they were the first to call them deceptors. The Angels said it was not their fight, but as time went the women fought the demons, dying by their cursed blades, dooming them for eternity."

Caidrian stopped, but Clare was still trying to absorb what Caidrian had already told her, she looked at him with raised eyebrows, her expression that of shock,

"Well are you going to tell me what happened?"

Satisfied with her response he smiled, "Four of the Venusian women were at the bayou, when they noticed a deceptor or human as you would call them, giving birth to a baby with a cone shaped head, as the women went closer they noticed the child had razored teeth and beaded black eyes.

Devastated by this, one of the Venusian women made a last attempt to summon an Archangel, she summoned the Angel Mikael, and intrigued by her beauty and bravery, the Angel agreed to help her, Mikael returned in mortal form bringing with him Gabriel, Raziel, and Casteal, they each married a Venusian woman and all the women bore kids. The Angels raised their first born by teaching them skills and how to use their abilities, making them elite servants of god, for all eternity. The demons didn't dare enter the earth where the Angels lived. One of the woman, the wife of Casteal, Samara, noticed that unlike on Venusta they aged quicker on earth.

Mikael, wanting to help, ascended to the heavens, and on the third year returned to earth. On his arrival back to earth he bestowed a gift on the children so when they reached the age of 34 they all aged three times slower than the deceptors, and lived three times longer, making them superior but still mortal, calling them Lightwatchers. After the first of the Lightwatchers were grown up to twenty years, the angels left and said never to return. Though we are visited often by other angels never those four.

Clare stood still for a few seconds, her brain perished with thoughts of what she just heard, "Whoa, so what you're saying is that I'm a Lightwatcher, correct."

Caidrian wasn't looking at her, instead his eyes searched the forest, lower ground and up toward the trees, "Not just any Lightwatcher, you are the descendant of the Archangels Gabriel and Mikael, and the last born female of the Draiken bloodline."

She smiled, "So what I'm special somehow?" He nudged his head so she could walk, "Somebody is following us."

He hadn't met her eyes, but placed his finger on his lips, signalling her silence, on her nod he took out a long sword from his weapon belt, her instincts telling her to move closer toward him, and follow his gaze. Both of them startled by a squirrel running down the tree near them. In an attempt to break the embarrassing moment Clare mused, "WOW, imagine that."

"A creepy little creature," was Caidrians reply before they moved on, making higher ground, further up.

"There must be a reason the Tempter was after me, he said he HAD to kill me, it wasn't his choice.."

The words were not complete in her mouth when he touched her lips with dirty fingers, as if he ignored the last words or didn't hear them, he said, "Reason isn't important now, there could be many reasons why." He added, before he walked on in front of her, his voice still clear to her ears, "You ARE a female and your mother's daughter, which makes you naturally one of the strongest Lightwatchers, and also makes YOU a big target, Franchesca made a lot of enemies along the years."

His mind lost itself in his memories, she could hear the distance in his voice, and moved closer to him, "You know child, we all lived together once, you training with your brothers, and Nadia at the Washington faculty. Raphael, an Asguardian, an angels spawn was always around keeping you busy, in verses and offense training, I didn't know why he stayed. But the day you killed your first Ravenor demon, I was with you, both of us thrilled we wanted to celebrate. You wanted to go ice-skating and have strawberry and berry ice-cream at the square. Nathan was sick that day so he stayed at home, Calub, well in his moods AGAIN."

"Calub,"

"Yes, Calubeal is your brother, not much younger than you. Your mother was driving that night, we just turned the corner when we saw this bright blue light, at first we thought it was harmless, but there he stood, an Angel, your mother swerved the car, but the Angel was determined. He lifted the car while we were still in it, and threw it against a block of flats, he still tried to grab you but another Angel came, he had these red wings, they were magnificent and I remember him saying, 'don't worry I will finish her off,' but instead of killing you, he showed you mercy, and let us go, Franchesca and I were ok, we healed quickly, but you just weren't healing, we rushed you to the hospital, after hours of waiting, doctors said you were fine physically but had suffered a major blow to the head, and you couldn't remember. You didn't recognize me, you only knew your mother, your seal of strength was gone, all that made you part Angel had vanished, you were DECEPTOR, human."

Clare looked at him dazed, but chose not to speak only listen. He wasn't really paying much attention as he spoke, and she was too scared to break this moment of truth,

"We did what we had to Clare, someone had to look after Nathan and Calub and run the faculty, after that I didn't know much, if there was another reason, I'm the last person Franchesca would've told, always so private and protective, Franchesca always had her secrets."

Clare hastened as his steps got bigger, it seemed that he was making a conscious effort to walk slow earlier, because now that he wasn't paying attention he walked so fast that Clare had to speed up in a slight jog.

Caidrian spun around, suddenly, and she stopped, putting her hands on her knees to catch her breath, packets in hands.

Caidrian's breathing was normal when he said, "This war we have fought for years." He continued, "There is no winning it, lives are lost constantly, I consider you lucky having that time to live like a deceptor."

This guy had seriously lost his mind, she thought, "It weren't the first time, an angel and a Tempter hunted down Draiken blood and it won't be the last, I'm sure of it." It was the matter-of fact tone he used again that raised her shackles.

Clare's throat scratched from dryness, "Draiken?"

"It's your mother's bloodline, Franchesca Draiken, her family is the first descendants of Mikael. There was a time many years before, the Draikens' were a big family, hundreds of leaders, until the battle of descendants, the Tempters and Angels hunted your mother's family based on a myth. After, there remained a handful of them. When your great grandmother, Alinore Draiken and the others got of age to marry, it was forced that descendants of Raziel and Gabriel marry the women, to strengthen the bloodline, to keep the Draikens' blood alive, and strong, many agreed because their offspring was guaranteed good fighters."

"Is that why you and mom married?"

"Franchesca was truly something special, she hated the thought of getting married. Do you know that she was the last of the girls her age to get tied down. I asked her countless of times before, and I loved her, but she could never really be mine, she always belonged to him. I believed she could be persuaded, but now I see she gave her heart to him. It was always him, though in the end she married me, she was never truly mine."

The words were sad, Clare felt remorse for Caidrian, her mother was something. She wanted to know who the 'he' was, but she couldn't bring herself to ask, "She's been mostly single so maybe you're wrong."

He smiled at her thoughtfulness, his sharp jaw working, the only sign that he was partially aware, "The Draiken bloodline is the only ones who can absorb energy from the dead of the Lightwatchers, do that, and your strengths are far beyond understanding."

"What if I don't absorb her energy from her body?" "You don't have a choice, it's a gift that you can't reject, her soul won't rest until it's done."

She muttered, "It just keeps getting better." "Clare this isn't a game or a joke, this is real, as real as you're going to get, and there are worse fates out there."

"So, basically I'm a Lightwatcher, descendant of an Angel and because I'm the last female of a special family I'm now fair prey for demons." She paused, "Okay, call me crazy." Making hand gestures in the air, with the packets, dangling in her hands, "but that doesn't make sense."

His gaze hardened, he spun on her, "Firstly you are the last born female, not the last female, secondly, I don't know why you being attacked purposely by Tempters, that's why we need to get you to Khiron where you safe, so I can find out." He said walking on, "Your mother did what she could to protect you, but there's so much we could do without breaking laws girl, even the deceptors have them."

He shook his head, "Franchesca knew the outcome of her actions, your brothers and I stayed in America, we had no choice. The Legions would have come for all of us if we left. Your brothers are too much of a weapon to let them leave unscathed, and then there was the demons to consider. You can slay demons after demons but there is never an end to it. We have all this strength and some honored to fight for Adonai but at a price, because to be born a Lightwatcher is to die a Warrior."

He raked his hands through his hair in frustration "It's not an easy life, many are orphaned young, but we move forward, because we are born to kill and protect."

The rawness of his voice, the unmasked terror and insanity in his gaze shocked her. Acting on pure impulse she grabbed him by his arm turning him towards her, clearly he lost his mind, but the only thing that she wanted to know was, "Where is he? Where's Calub?" The guarded frame surrounding him at her question raised her shackles, her brain focused. Caidrian had no clue who he was dealing with.

When she thought he wouldn't answer he replied, "Taken hostage by a greater Tempter, one of hells cadre, Asmodeus, king of the succubus demons, he's as good as dead now."

"What? As in, the Asmodeus! I've always had a fascination in demonology, this certainly explains it." She sighed, exasperated, "He's your son, there has to be something, you said you going to see the Garde maybe I could talk with them."

Caidrian shouted, in a loud whisper, "There's a lot you don't understand, traditions for one, and if you did that the Garde would be the least of your problems. If you asked for help, we would need an Asguardian or Caster to open the portals, and you want to stay far away from them right now."

"No" she frowned, "I'm going to find my brother, there has to be a way."

"I'm sorry there's no way, the angel blood in us, will weaken going into the demons realms and our abilities along with it, this is reality, it's never a happy ending in the real world girl, you better get used to it."

She stomped her feet as they continued on their trek towards the gate of Khiron, she was beyond pissed as her mind tried to think of solutions. "Why would my mother want me to meet Nathan after eight years?"

She waited for him to answer but when he didn't, raised her brow in challenge, regardless, he just kept walking forward. Fuming, with the obvious signs of exhaustion, her sharp breath intakes, her sweat drenched skin, she was running out of reserves keeping pace with this fuel injected man. Clare's mind tracked, and replayed everything she had learned today, ignoring the pain and loss, focusing on finding her smaller brother. She was not giving up. As they walked, and darkness neared she finally was on something. Clare had a point and she was going to see it planted,

"The only reason I can think about my mother introducing me to Nathan is it must have something to do with Calub, and I have known her for a long time, my mother wouldn't want me to give up on my brother."

"You don't understand what you're saying, you're naïve, you don't even remember who you are. You wouldn't last five minutes in the ring with our weakest ten year old forget a hundred demons." He laughed at the thought, but kept his focus on their surroundings.

His gaze kept wandering toward the upper parts of the trees, "Your body is healing quicker, your temper getting worse. It would've been too risky not to tell you, imagine if you just wandered around without knowing your strength? you could easily harm a deceptor unintentionally."

Various emotions sketched his face from confusion, sorrow, frustration to maybe even anger before his body visibly relaxed, sighing, "Your brothers have a special connection to you. You and Nathan might be able to track Calub down. I'm not sure if that was the reason you were meeting your brother but it was what I heard Nathan saying to Kalbreal and like your mother he doesn't tell me anything, he knows way more than I."

"So what Nathan doesn't trust good old papa?"

Caidrian shook his head, as if the thought was as frustrating as it was necessary, "I know as much as I'm trusted, my position as a Garde means there are something's I can't know. If I did I'd be forced to inform the Advisors, where as your brother mostly answers to himself."

She nodded, getting the message that Nathan was obviously higher up than him, "FINE, I'll speak to Nathan."

He stared at her from the corner of his eye, "Your mother's side of the family has many fatal secrets. Draikens have always had loyalties with Casters and Elvan that I still don't even know about. But I do know that when the Draiken women have babies there's a ritual performed by Elvan and the Draiken family. It is said to bound siblings of their bloodline together. A brother which is always the first born, may choose when he is older to transfer some of his energy into his siblings making the bond stronger. Linking oneself to the other, they would be able to find one another and feel emotions of the other, like an invisible link between them."

"What?" A whisper escaped her, "How is that even possible?" She didn't mean for him to hear her.

He shrugged, as he walked further and tilted his head, "Beats me, when you find out I would love to know."

Slapping away the mosquito bitting her leg, she caught the worry crease on Caidrians forehead. Following the direction of his gaze, she peeped down. It took everything in her not to scream, she hadn't noticed that they were walking up a spiral, heading toward a mountains peak. So lost in conversation, not paying much attention to her surroundings. Or lack of...

It wasn't long after, she caught the blur movement of white hair, unfortunately that was no rabbits, but hair attached to skin, which meant one thing, "Caidrian, what's going on?",

Not sparing her a glance, he answered, "I'm not sure, they're Asguardians."

Ok, "Are they good or bad?"

"THEY are the Angels offspring." She relaxed at that, and muttered "Good then."

"I can't chance it, let's move." She didn't argue as they hurried back on the path making tracks.

Frozen mid-step when a pack of wolves appeared in the front of her, four, to be exact, she stuttered, "Ah, Caidrian, w..what are we gonna do."

By his confused furrow it was obvious Caidrian was at a lost for words but those thoughts were quickly dispelled into rage, when the wolves jumped forward circling him.

Lips peeled back, snapping teeth, there was no mistaking the wolves hunger for flesh. Clare shuddered knocking her head on the tall thin tree, she skittered across the pathway. The plastic and contents of clothes scattering on the ground. A quick glance over her shoulder, she watched Caidrian fighting the wolves. Some of them howled as he flung them across the pathway, like they were nothing more than stray dogs, he wasn't fighting with all his strength as he maintained his human form.

She yelled, "Caidrian," when she saw the Asguardians approaching faster.

His back bent, slightly over the edge of the high drop as he beheaded the wolf with one quick glide of his sword.

She was almost convinced that she was having a concussion when she saw the body turn into a headless woman, naked. Across from her the head rolled, resembling a ball wrapped in blue hair, and red liquid.

Mouth open, and eyes wide Clare swivelled to the howl of another wolf. Spine ramrod her body turned instinctively toward a third howl. Caidrian pierced the sword through its heart at the same time the wolf transformed into a man with dark blue hair, and darkish skin.

Further down the Asguardians were almost in her line of sight. Raking her brain for some contingent plan or delay tactic she drew herself away from the fight, careful not to gain unwanted attention to herself. Once a few meters away she turned her back on the fight and lifted her hands to flag the Asguardians attention.

When a hooded figure jumped down from the nearest tree blocking her from the Angels spawn Clare squeaked before losing balance. Expecting to hit the hard ground, she gasped as a huge male arm surrounded her waist, holding her in place.

The hooded males eyes glowing like the gleam of a predator, giving only the faintest semblance of his features. Instinctive, and compelled like an invisible magnet, her hand shot out to caress his face. He let her go so quickly, positive she would have fallen this time for real if some invisible force didn't keep her in place. Disappointment stark when she looked up only to be greeted by the hooded males back. Which meticulously blocked her from the Asguardians he now held in assembly. Brushing away the thought as another howl filled the air. Clare could only hope for the stranger dressed in an old robe like those you use in a monarchy, was friend and not foe.

There was something so potent about his demeanour, that Kalbreal who she would have described as a strong powerful male didn't even niche the raw strength from this hooded man. From his broad shouldered back, to his stance as he shielded her, he screamed leader. She thought of Kalbreal, the way he always looked down on people, his head always held high, but this man wasn't like that, he didn't need to command anything.

Frowning at the pull she had to him. This stranger to her eyes was intoxication, compulsion and intimidation. It made her want to drop to her knees and make vows of her loyalty, before she stroked his back. The message was obvious,

He bowed to no man. And Clare feared him.

She watched as the Asguardians conversed softly with this man who made the monarchy robe, look like a warrior's suit. Eventually with curt nods they turned around and walked back down. As though just awakened from an induced haze, Clare turned to see Caidrian still fighting the last wolf. Giving him silent due that he was holding his own, unsurprised, she returned her attention back to the man in the robe.

He was gone, vanished, or was never even there. She spun around as a grey wolf bit into Caidrians arm, blood oozed out, "Go Clare, NOW," before fear or dread even touched her mind the strange man appeared like a wind blew his presence.

Those strong hands that had held her up with such intimacy now gripped the wolf in a pair of very manly hands, 'the big knuckles and thick fingers kind of hands', long, alluring.

She watched as those fingers dug into the fur of the wolf and heard rather than saw the shattered ribs. Flinching at the cry of the wolf, she meant to turn her head, but didn't do it fast enough as she bared witness to the brutal force of this powerful being as he twisted the wolfs spine, the snapping sound unmistakable.

Watching in part horror and the other part bewilderment as to who he might be, as the dead wolf transformed into a blue haired man, she couldn't move. The tingle in her veins, the shiver that ran down her spine, familiar to her, only now it was more intense.

The pinpricks she felt behind her neck, and the invisible magnet attracting her to this man was something she felt at times in the last four months. There were times when these feelings became more palpable, but nothing like this.

Having had only a glimpse of his face she couldn't be sure of who he was or whether she'd seen him before this. Though a man in monks clothing, he was a stone cold killer who she knew with the surest certainty would see again, it was inevitable and that thought sparked something in her. Clare brushed the feeling away, not ready for its intensity.

He's a killer, your mother just died, you should not be thinking about a man, she chastised herself. Walking toward her, she watched his lithe form, his confidence stark in the field of dead bodies, it should have scared her.

"Because where there is strength there's darkness." His voice- so intense, deep, hypnotic, it left her spellbound. Clare had never heard a stronger, yet sensual voice that appealed to her as much.

It took her almost a minute to comprehend what he'd said, and why. Her eyes widened when she finally did. He had answered what her mind was still going to conclude. He had invaded her thoughts. Heat flushed her cheeks Crimson when she recalled the way she eyed him a few moments ago.

Standing tall, face hooded, he was intoxication at its most matured as she walked up to him. He made no attempt to move, until she was in touching distance. Tilting his head, he took her right hand in his own, engulfing it as he tugged her close until she was encased in his hold. Face tucked in his broad chest, She inhaled the musky scent of him, and closed her eyes, revelling in the perfection of his hold.

The heat of his lips on her hair was her undoing, gripping the robe tighter in response. The comfort too great to warrant any explanation. No words to understand it, it was what it was, like she'd spent her whole life in this mans embrace. His voice quiet in her presence, embrace strong and possessive. Clare raised her head to look at him, though she could see blackness in the hood, his cold eyes froze her in place.

She looked closer, air caught in her chest, when she saw the pair of mesmerizing sapphire blue eyes. They had the luminescent of a cheetah at night, but his, defined the word exquisite. A true perfection, without seeing his face, she knew he was perfect, he would be to her. Looks weren't important to her now, just him.

The heat of his breath on her forehead as he brushed his lips across her skin, his voice melodious to her ears, "Caidrians waiting. I have to let you go now." After her reluctant nod, she heard his soft chuckle as he moved toward the edge of the cliff pathway. Apparently he was going to jump down to the bottom. Clare screamed in panic, "WAIT."

The man's hood turned with his body, his face a shadow, but she could see his eyes that glow resembled an aqua gem, "Who are you?"

His voice was deep, his accent- none, his tone that of an ageless perfection, "That Princess is for you to decide."

The words stood between them, just when she thought he would speak again he jumped, and instinctively she ran to the end of the pathway to see him drop but instead watched him vanish mid-air , gone.

Her heart pulsed at the glimpse of this man, his touch alone held her spellbound. All her worries vanished, all the blood spilt around them, mindless in that space of time, it was just her and him.

His voice, inhumanly masculine as the words left with the tune of addiction , it lured her, entranced her, compelled her and now she starved for more.

She pushed the thoughts away and for some reason her mother flashed in her mind, punishingly brushing the image of Barbatos as he stood with her mother's heart in his hand. Choosing to ignore the worried frown on Caidrian's face she asked, "Are you okay?"

"Yeah, shifter bites heal fast." He showed her his arm, the bleeding had stopped, and the tissue was only red and scarred where the wolf had bitten into his flesh.

She cleared her throat, "So does he have a name?"

Instead of answering her Caidrian pointed to the dead on the floor, "Those are Shapeshifter's, stray ones." Wiping his sword on his pants he added, "The Asguardians were hunting them, we're to side with Asguard in most situations, so they saw us as a threat the minute we arrived, and the guy in the robe is someone you should stay away from, far away from."

"I didn't even see his face."

"He can see you, that's all that matters, unfortunately I've given my word to keep his identity hidden from you for now, why I agreed to something so stupid is beyond me but I did."

"So what! We never really keep to our word! it's just a lame way of getting people to tell you stuff."

He inhaled a breath, "You are a deceptor full in, aren't you, let's go."

"A statement isn't an answer to my question."

Caidrian speeded his pace, holding the packets with what looked like a lot less clothes "You can't understand, until you know your place. Lightwatchers are restorers of balance, our existence is to protect the earth, and all kinds in it, how are we to be taken seriously if we can't even keep to our word."

She had nothing to say to that, he was right, she didn't understand. Clare couldn't deny that there was honour in keeping your word, no matter how ancient it sounded. Dropping her head in shame, his pace slowed as he put a hand over her shoulder, "This world has a lot of darkness but there's also good in it. Deceptors are a good example, their compassion is that which we can never understand, you should know, you have lived as one for eight years. Your emotions are more human than a descendants', but you are still a Lightwatcher, and in our line of work human emotions will just get you killed. Holding on to him." He gestured behind Clare with his indicating by 'him' he meant the mysterious man, "He will just make it sooner for you Clare."

She glared at the harsh undertone, "So you don't love, or feel, soulless hah? You said you loved my mother?"

Caidrian didn't look at her, as he walked with the packets hitting his legs, making swooshing sounds, "I do love and feel, but I learnt to control my emotions, you have to if you want to stay alive. Tempters manipulate the weak, they feed on pain, fear, heartache, I wouldn't give them that satisfaction."

Clare ignored the man claiming to be her father and picked up her feet. A few meters away she shouted half heartedly, "Where exactly is this realm, this walking is just making me sick, we've been doing it for hours, might I remind you it's almost completely dark, and my stomach isn't getting any better." When she received no answer, she huffed, "How's Nathan getting to the realms?"

He shook his head, "He used a portal, stop being so lazy, it's actually not that far."

She hunched her shoulders as they walked up a steep hill, "I feel like I've been walking for hours, and all this, it's a lot to take in, and In my defence I'm tired, exhausted actually, INCASE, you didn't know, let me inform you of my day,

I was out till early this morning, getting massacred by the gigantic Alonso, that guy is huge, have you seen him?"

Caidrian hissed, "Yes, and you should stay away from him, I don't trust him."

Clare rolled her eyes, "Sure you don't."

Clare watched Caidrian walk leisurely beside her, at first glance he was the epitome of an underdog warrior, long torso, solid statue, not too broad shoulders. One would think he looked very young to be her father, but not to her, she could see the wisdom hidden in his eyes. The pain and loss which hardened his features and emotions could only have come from years of horror.

"Stop staring at me Clare, you do that to the wrong descendant they'll see it as a challenge of dominance."

She was tired and her feet ached, applying unwanted pressure on the blisters forming underneath her feet wasn't helping. Nor was Caidrian who carried on talking, expecting her to keep up, "The mark on your stomach is a seal, most Lightwatchers have many of those, if the demon dies the mark goes away eventually, but a Tempters mark, never fully heals, so it's not wise to stare, some are marked on their faces.

Also I must warn you, over the years our kind have mixed with other species, they called Fuized, but our ANGELIC blood remains strong, no matter how different some may seem. Unfortunately some Lightwatchers don't feel that way, so keep your mouth shut if you hear anything, or see one of them."

She half smiled, "Am I going to freak out, just tell me now, this place is sounding more and more like a refugee camp." Her throat was parched, which was totally understandable considering that she had been walking for hours with nothing to drink. She looked at her packets, her eyes widening a fraction in hope remembering the muffins she'd gotten, but she'd forgotten it in the car. And even if she didn't they wouldn't have survived the treatment the clothes had gotten when they were discarded on the floor earlier.

Thoughts back on water, she welcomed the set of blue eyes that clouded her mind, as the strangers words played in her head, "That princess is for you to decide." What did it mean, was it really all up to her, did he feel the connection as she did when he held her in his arms and kissed her head with such tenderness. A contrast to the lethally cold killer that lived within him.

"Clare walk on, you're wasting time."

Ten minutes later they stopped, the view was magnificent. Virgin territory that went on forever, with born landscapes of tall mountains clothed in green grass and shoed with sandy floors and generous slopes, as they stretched over the hill tops covering the bottom. Parts of the mountain covered in forests of greenery whilst others were embedded with solid rocks and caves. The sun touching on tips of the mountain beds as it set.

It wasn't long before a man appeared from behind the tree, attired in a white leather coat and a green grass stick mixed with gold bindings attached to his left hand. Older in age, an easy fifty years or so, his eyes, black, no eyebrows, instead in its place were tattoos of small S's locked in one another. A bit dramatic in appearance to the common eye but beautiful to an artistic mind.

Clare greeted him but he ignored her. She brushed it off, not taking it as an insult more of an urgency to avoid chit chat.

"Do you both confirm your status of Angelic descendants?" The man asked in a roughened voice, evil with malice, causing her chills of gravely displeasure. Clare followed Caidrian and nodded her head in a vigilant manner. The Caster hit his stick twice on the ground and a high stretched golden door became visible before her very eyes. It was like watching a photo drawn from thousands of small dots joining together to form an architecture that was exquisite and unexplainably, magical in its true form.

Sizing the door from the bottom to top, an easy thirty feet high and two meters wide, it was discomforting. Regardless, the brilliant golden metal shined like it had been newly made, only just minutes ago. It was what hid behind the big door that had her twitching.

Caidrian stared at her with a mysterious sigh, which challenged her to find out, join him, which she did. Together they stepped inside a light flow fountain with blue crystallized liquid. Glittering specks of liquid, full of multiple shades of colour covered her, but didn't wet her. The liquid, warm on her body as she walked her final step into the unearthed area. Her first discovery was that her clothes were dry.

Clare's mouth wide open with the amount of variables she collected in her mind explaining to her what had just happened.

Advanced species, *way advanced* she thought. Mouth agape, she moved closer to Caidrian, who waited on the other side of the fountain, which had now taken its real shape of a waterfall with steps moving right down to the bottom of this grand expanse.

Clare's mouth shut, her eyes ravened, as Caidrian said, "WELCOME to KHIRON, Realm of the Lightwatchers."

Eight

L^{iam}

Liam rumbled through the draws for the hundredth time, "It can't just disappear, try tracking it again."

His sister clomped her black ankle boots towards him from the passage, trampling on glass, cracking it with her heels, the noise not bothering either of them.

Her legs encased in a vintage pair of dark maroon leather pants, she lifted up the sleeve of her black and silver jersey which sat loosely on her bodice, and pushed her open blonde wavy hair back. Her Australian accent rushed through the room, "I have done it over and over again, if it was here I'd know."

"Nobody knows about the necklace besides the three of us, I delivered it myself, who would take it."

He looked at the girl, her eyes greener than the summers grass, shinier than a gemstone in the sun, the eyes of his mother. "Liam I don't even know much about the necklace myself, you still haven't told me what's it for? the scent tells me it's strong, and that brother always equals trouble."

"I told you I will in time, try again, I'm going to talk to the police, and try 'n keep it to yourself will you."

She threw her hands in the air, "I don't have to help you, a little trust brother will go a long way."

Fiddling with her hair he smiled before he bent down to kiss her forehead, "Why can't you wear a dress once in a while Jullie." A fleeting wave of her hand, she then pushed him lightly, "Because dressing fittingly for a mission, ready to fight or flight is more logical."

He fought the urge to laugh, although the necklace was missing he had held Clare in his arms, inhaling her essence. She never shunned from him, if anything she was reluctant to leave his embrace. Liam had wanted to be there with her, have more time with her. The possessiveness he felt of her went beyond reason, but his need to protect her first was without thought. After a call to Nathan, he knew Clare was in good hands. That thought appeased his need to claim her just yet.

A man dressed in a brown chino's and green golfer walked toward him. "you must be the detective," Liam's voice echoed loudly before the man approached.

Liam had put his brown contacts on, and wore a black suit pants and white shirt, leaving it open slightly down the chest, in an attempt to apply himself as a deceptor. Unfortunately his ego was still much intact when the light skinned man offered his hand in good faith. Liam did not touch humans.

So instead he gave a nod, It made him look like a pretentious bastard, but what was he to do? No, he wasn't wearing gloves for anyone. They would know instantly that he was different, either way.

The demon scent masked by his own in the room, caused the air around him to rise, making him a minimum of a hundred times more intimidating than any deceptor in the world.

He heard the deceptors heart race, because his profound presence was hard enough for one not to feel undermined with his stature, the man stuttered,

"Ccccall me Ian."

The deceptor dropped his hand, and Liam didn't have time to talk much. Casually he looked at his watch, it was a few after six, then he looked behind him, but the men in the police outfits were talking outside, oblivious to the detective and himself.

He focused his hearing toward Jullie who had made herself scarce moving toward the bedroom. She hated deceptors and tried to refrain heavily from any contact with them unless necessary. Which suited him just perfect because he liked his sister safe. His eyes darted back at the man facing him.

Liam played close attention to the detectives features, rounded face, redness from eating forbidden fruits and meats, then he went deeper. The man stood there but had absolutely no recollection of what Liam was doing, no clue that he was reading the man's mind. His thoughts flashed in Liam's eyes, watching if the man had suspected anything out of the ordinary, he was just about done when he heard the drop of wind coming from the balcony.

Stopping only once he was completely satisfied of what all the detectives now concluded in their minds about the crime scene- it was a fight, and the people had left, either than that it was a closed case, nothing worth reporting. Because that is what Liam had put in the mortals mind.

Staring at the mortal man he commanded in a gentle voice , "You and your men leave now, and forget you ever saw me." He appreciated how easy it was to control the thoughts of the deceptors, so easily intercepted.

Liam stood in the lounge watching the deceptor Ian leave with his guys. The place was in a chaotic mess, glass and table parts scattered across the floor. His body felt the anger drafting up to the surface, but his mind reminded him that his princess was safe.

Attempting to control his anger, on what stood outside the balcony, or who, he opened the door, his persona cold and lethal as his voice dropped, "You lied to me, you said you knew nothing."

Kalbreal stood there, bare chested as his eyes boldly scanned the traffic of car's beneath them, "I didn't intentionally lie, William, I just didn't see the need of you knowing everything."

Turning his body he acknowledged Liam. Eyes a blaze with the Infinity fires distantly burning continuously, pleading to come out, begging to torch this earth in its flames. Liam was no fool, he knew how it felt to have a constant power seething in your body. He knew the burning desire to unleash it even more.

"But then again," Kalbreal added, locking his hands behind his back. Deceptors would think the pose was casual, relaxed, but Liam knew better, and it was confirmed by what Kalbreal said next, "I find myself having to remind you, I do not hold the answers to your asked question, where as you taunt me with information regarding mine."

"The way I see it Boy, with-holding information is the same as lying, you want my help I suggest you start talking. I want to know everything, including why she has been stripped of her identity, yes might I repeat STRIPPED."

The Angel tilted his head, a smile as hot with anger as the magma of his heated stare, "Meet me in Khiron, first light tomorrow, I will tell you everything that I can."

Jullie ran from behind Liam and hugged Kalbreal, who again had no shirt on. His body covered in circular pieces of drawings, in the middle of the circles were letters written in beautiful Angelic designs of burnt orange and black specks around it.

Kalbreal lifted Jullie up with a genuine laugh in his vocal cords, "What, Australia isn't doing it for you already." Broad shoulders flexed, as he swung Jullie around. He was almost as tall as Liam, but more bulky in his built, and an arrogant ass, who got under Liam's skin, and they say Angels aren't conceited. He just hoped the Angel kept his tools away from Clare, because Liam's generosity to Kalbreal only stretched so far, and Clare was beyond a hard limit-untouchable.

Which got him thinking of Calub, it had been days since they'd spoken. A thought of what his friend would say about Kalbreal shirtless and holding Jullie was enough to make anybody smile, especially since Calub had made claim to Jullie. His sister thought Calub was another notch in her bed, she was going to be pissed when she found out just how wrong she was.

She got down, and touched Kalbreal's chest, where one of the sketched drawings had been slashed across. It was the only full black marking with an orange diagonal cut down the middle.

Jullie whispered, "Not the same without my three boys." She couldn't hide the sadness in her eyes, which always got to Liam. But the reason behind it got to him more, his Jullie wanted a family of her own, she wanted kids. Unfortunately it just wasn't happening.

Moving to Australia to stay with Calub while he trained was Liam's suggestion. She was only back because Liam had asked her too. She had been running in circles with him and for him since she arrived, but he knew she wanted to be with Calub, as much as she fought it' his sister always held her heart on her sleeves. He'd treat her with a new car when this was done, and maybe another boat, if she behaves, just the thought of spoiling his sister made him feel better. Jullie loved her presents from her eldest brother.

Liam looked at Kalbreal's chest and the scar Jullie's fingers brushed, knowing exactly what it meant to have your abilities weakened. Luckily he wasn't an Angel, but a part of him dare crossed the thought to his mind, instead he brushed it off with a question to his sister, "Jullie did you find it?"

"No, but I was picking up something of Tempter origin in this place, what happened?"

"Franchesca Draiken is now deceased," Kalbreal answered, slipping on a t-shirt, *how convenient*, "killed by Barbatos, the others should be in the realm by now, preparing for the moon ceremony. I came back to see if there was anything I should take Clarebella."

Liam touched at his pocket, the phone, her phone, he almost slipped it out, but decided to hang on to it instead, keeping his hand in his pocket, "Such a sweet boy," Liam said dryly.

Jullie gave him one of her famous death glares, before she smiled so sweetly and touched Kalbreal's face, "Give me a minute to get some stuff, and I better see you at home soon Kal."

Liam was in no mood to argue about home and houses but he loathed the idea of Kalbreal living with them. For the past seven years it had been a constant confinement with Kalbreal around, especially this last one when Kole up and left without a trace for a year.

Kalbreal was always in his face, his space, challenging him, and just being there. To sum it up, it was the worst and torturous year of his immortality and he had some bad years. Liam secretly didn't dislike the Angel as much as he wanted to, the boy was young, barely a millennium. In Angel growth, he was a teenager becoming a man, he hadn't even ascended yet. Many times Liam had wondered how his parents felt about him staying on the earth, Angels were very protective of their young at that age. Ones born as powerful as Kalbreal never lived in Asguard, they stayed in the Infinity. Where they were honed to be lethal.

He shook those thoughts out, he needed to check on Clare.

Kalbreal took out his hand, "Not going to shake it?" he said, "Afraid I'll melt you away with my hotness."

Liam bemused at Kalbreal wanting skin privileges again, asked, "I've known you for decades and I have not touched you yet, what makes now any different?"

"Perhaps you've changed your mind." Kalbreal shrugged, "I have patience," dropping his hand. Liam laughed at Kalbreal's remark as Jullie returned with a suitcase of Clare's stuff, "You should take it to Andraya." She said, "I got a feeling Clare might be there sooner than intended."

Kalbreal nodded in agreement, "Do you sense something."

Jullie's eyes went distant , leaving her irises full white, before purple slits splashed diagonally across, turning back to green, "She's fine, better than expected for a girl who lost her mother. We should go, the moon ceremony will start shortly."

Kalbreal took the black suitcase bag and was gone, leaving a sweet aura behind of musk and grapefruit.

Jullie snuffled in the air, "I love that smell."

Liam pulled at her hair, as a brother would do in annoyance. She responded with a kick to his butt, following him into the apartment, "Are you EVER going to stop doing that, you should cut him some slack, he's helping us, even if he doesn't know how much, and come on his young, just admit you like him."

Liam welcomed the thought with a loud cough, "I'll clear this place up, should be as good as new, you clean her scent off everything."

Jullie smiled that knowing gleam in her eyes, "Is everything set? Kole keeps calling, are we going to tell him?"

"Not just yet, there's a few things I need to find out first."

"You could just lure her with your charm if you want to sleep with her, instead of all this." She gestured with her hands.

His eyes widened, his chest tightened, "Where do you come up with all your conclusions little one."

"It seems obvious that this isn't purely platonic, and I've spent two thousand years in hell remember, meaning I'm technically almost your age." She shrugged, "By the way."

"In your dreams, enough now with all this insane thinking, you need to go to L.A and keep Andraya busy, she can't attend the funeral. If she doesn't budge tell her that there'd be eyes everywhere, those waiting for gaps. And pick a new car, when you done, something safe and not too fast."

She jumped and clapped her hands, her face transformed instantly into a huge smile, "I booked my ticket yesterday, Andraya would want more answer's. We can't keep them running in circles for long. We need another plan, maybe we should find out who's killing the Lightwatchers, it could be linked."

He nodded, it was a good plan, "Contact Tash she'll know what to do, I'll get the answers we need in Asguard."

"Ha, I'm sure we're still banned for another three decades, risky."

"It keeps things exciting, quick question, if you're going to L.A why not take the suitcase yourself?"

"I gathered earlier by your choice in attire our involvement is still under wrap, besides do you really want him spending all that time with her." She moved her eyes across him to the robe laid across the Persian sofa, an amused smile crossed his lips, "Impressive, Little sister,

what would I do without you."

"Live, of course, though it would be miserable and pathetic, possibly a little boring."

Clare

Clare stood on the fountain steps, frozen in amazement, her mind refused to acknowledge what her eyes were clearly seeing. She was high enough to see only a minority of Khiron in its beauty, because the houses were actually rows of castles, some taller than the mountain she stood on.

Shinning castles made of gold material stretched beyond normal heights, as peaks of light shimmered from the tall building walls. There wasn't much of a sun left, but the light surrounding Khiron seemed to seep through from something beyond the air, high above her, but not so distant as the stars. But not particularly close to the moon either, which still held in its shadowed phase. It was further than reaching distance, but not high enough to dismiss, however, it didn't captivate her as the realm did. There were hundreds OR thousands of castles, some bigger than the others, rounded roofs made of milky glass fabrics of some kind, maybe marble.

On distant parts, she could spot smaller houses, tinier versions of the castles. *Maybe they were double stories*, she guessed as her eyes shuffled around the top parts of what she could watch.

The nearest castle had no windows, it was like a fully covered shell of gold. The smell of musk and roses seeped in her lungs as she deeply inhaled the crisp air. Caidrian nudged her, "Come on, we've been standing here for twenty minutes let's get down."

"Are the castles made of gold?"

"Not entirely. Marble exterior, but you can't see it clearly, it is being shielded by a liquid gold because of the Orderian. It's a protection Verse to protect our homes from intruders or our visitors if they happened to double cross us."

Clare coughed the word out, "Orderian?"

"Your brother can explain it all to you, let us get you inside, I got to check in at the Garde's fortress."

She turned her head but kept her eyes fixated on this visionary place, as they made their way down the steps. The fountain flowed down the stairs, but wherever she walked the water parted for her feet, a silent invitation, so she wouldn't slip.

Clare felt like Alice walking into Wonderland, only this one wasn't filled with big cats and rabbits, but rolled in death, inhabited by descendants of Angels and demons, and whatever else awaited her. Only her bravery would be earned in the form of death.

Her legs didn't throb as they had earlier, so she took her steps with more urgency to make her way down. When she heard a cry of a bird from the sky, she stopped and looked up, knowing she was way below Caidrian, who had been carrying the packets from earlier. Her eyes instinctively encountered the bird, that was larger than a eagle, almost the size of what she would have presumed a dragon would've been as it skirted, breezing through the air.

Circling her, as it flaunted its brilliant bright colour wings, of green and purples feathers. The bird gazed at her from a distance, and she could swear that she felt the wind a knot stronger as it flapped its wings. It drifted further down, as if her notice was a silent invitation. Catching the wind in her hair as the bird flapped its wings in rapid beats, she squinted her eyes. Seeing the size of this creature so close made her palms sweat.

She never liked anything that could fly. When she was little, her mother took her to a bird park, and Clare touched one of the birds, it attacked her, pecking her hands and her head. She remembered her screams, and the way she grabbed the bird by its beak and flung it across a tree, by the end of it she was riddled with small bites. She should've known that she was different when the scars healed without a trace but she didn't, she was naïve and foolish, things she'd never be again.

Her focus intensely on the bird whose wings kept getting closer and closer to her, her hair moving slightly by the breeze.

Caidrian touched her back, startled she jumped with a squeak, *way to go Clare*, she sighed.

"Guider's." he pointed at the bird, seemingly unaffected by her edginess, "Don't stare at it, he'll take your eyes out."

"Are there other awful beasts around I should know about?"

"They aren't beasts, but our eyes, the angels birds are rarest of creatures you will ever set eyes on, Ruzak, is his name, he's circling the area, making sure no unwanted guest have attended for the moon ceremony."

Something brushed her cheek at her nod, it made a ruffling sound like paper getting squashed. Noticing Caidrian was almost to the bottom she followed.

It happened again, and that's when she saw what it was -a tree. Trees lived yes, but not like this, its movement resembled a dance as she lifted her hand as if it were a wounded pup before she touched the leaf. The roughness brushed her fingers, taking a bold step she pinched the leaf, it was spring soft to the touch, but ROUGH like a tongue on the outside. *BREATHTAKING and freaky*, she thought.

Following the leaves movements as it left her, eyes wide, she ignored Caidrian as he repeatedly called to her to hurry down. Finding its origin on the opposite side of the waterfall with a whole forest of the trees and fruits filling it with colours. The trees moved, making noises of cracking branches. They looked alive, and the mysterious sky light reflected on the forest, made its aliveness shine.

This place was not just a different place, but a new found world, one of exceptional beauty. A final look across, she went downstairs.

Standing on the ground that resembled a road but very smooth with a high gloss finish, she waited at the top of a long pathway, which led to different road ways and paths. Next to it, was grass, gold grass, that also seemed to be moving on its own. Spotting Caidrian walk on it, she almost shouted, but the grass flattened before his foot touched the spot. Further down was a man riding a white horse near the second castle from where they stood.

She couldn't see any cars, or anything normal, it was dark, but Khiron had a glowing dimmed white light in the sky. There was no reason in trying to understand why, she didn't bother asking. The city spoke for itself, it was extraordinary and Angelic. The air around her, light, clean and untouched, made her skin tickle. Maybe she had been here before.

She thought about the possibility of living here, maybe it would jog her memory. These people might be family by blood but she didn't remember them, she needed to remember them. With that said, there was something about Calub, where ever he was. On hearing he was missing she felt the love for him, it was like she had loved him forever. Her instincts told her to find him, protect him and that was what she was going to do.

Staring across the land of Lightwatchers, the little bit of heaven. She felt a sort of peace and familiarity about this majestic land, the sweet smell of honey suckle and rose trees now scented in her nose, she was sure she smelt musk earlier.

A while later she asked, "So that vacant land is it all part of Khiron"

"Yes, but I assure you the realm is much larger than that, there's a lot of science involved, alternate spaces, it has height as well, made by the Angels themselves."

Intrigued by Caidrians response, she queried, "So why couldn't I see it earlier?"

Caidrian impatiently pulled her to walk in front of him, "Invisible seals surround the place. This is the land where the Angels lived, everything is more alive in the Angelic realm, the trees, including the water, it's how some Lightwatchers are able to stay here and survive for long periods without any help from the deceptors." he continued , "We don't need the deceptors crops or food, it makes us self sufficient without the aid of deceptors."

"Figured, so, do you stay here?"

He laughed ,"Don't be silly, I'm one of the Garde, those who live here are mostly the older ones and the makers, sometimes new orphans who want to train here before they are put in others care. Generally Lightwatchers stay all over the world, there isn't much of us, so if we do come home it's for a break or a problem, like in your case."

She walked next to him, keeping her feet on the narrow black path, the grass seemed creepy to her, the way it moved, like swollen seaweed in the ocean but without the water.

They turned toward the first castle when she spotted a guy leaning on the castle wall, "Nathan."

He gave Clare a sideward smile, "SO sister, how was my fathers company."

Smirking with a wide-eyed glance as he touched her shoulder, affectionately, he added, "I hope not too depressing." She didn't reply him, not because she didn't want to, she didn't know how to. These people, her supposedly rediscovered family was different from her.

The truth was that her walk with Caidrian was life changing, she had her entire life explained to her by a stranger she barely knew.

Nathan made to put his arm on her shoulder but she shook him off, "Still got that stick up your ass hah." Nathan stormed off without allowing her to respond, she didn't know whether to run after him. How was she to know what to do in these situations.

Caidrian moved to take a place on her right, "Give him time, he'll come around, you know how big brothers are," he gestured with a pat on her back. She flinched, because she didn't and whose fault was it, if she didn't know how big brother's were. Following Caidrian inside the second castle, she made her mind up to talk to Nathan.

The marble under the liquid gold was noticeable close-up, there was no sign of brick work. Stepping inside the automated door, it moved in an up and downward circular motion before it finally opened showing an empty space. Visioning high rise ceilings and gold brackets cushioning it in place, she paralleled her head to her feet and furthered her eyes to the marbled floor. Her jaw went slack, she was standing on no ordinary marble floor. This one was white with beige patterns moving constantly in the inside of it, making no permanent attached markings, but millions of intricate patterns.

She had seen Buckingham palace but that was merely an old faction of a castle compared to this.

Screening the place out, from the paintings to the fine craft, which positioned itself perfectly on a centre piece table that she had completely missed when she'd walked in. It was made of the same marble material as the floor. A sculpture of an Angel with wings that was too big for the small body, as little as the size of a kitten attached to it.

The sculpture was a work of art, the intricate details she saw from afar drew her nearer, admiration in her eyes, she could see the crafting of every eyelash and every line. Curiosity getting the better of her, she touched the Angel sculpture.

A flap of its wings, Clare stumbled and screamed, but not before its eyes opened, revealing big black irises. The sculpture was alive, there was no doubt by what she was clearly seeing, as its face twisted into a frown. It's mouth moved before it ascended toward the opposite side of the room.

Clare fell back, and looked up in terror as it flew around the room. Its body now grey, still sculptured like stone, but alive. Flapping across to the top of the hall, where a part of the rounded room was shown. Her eyes followed its out stretched wings, which appeared to be similar to an Angel, at least a sculptured one.

"ISADES."

Clare turned to the commanding voice, "It got a name?"

Nathan walked into the room, as the sculptured Angel settled on his arm, looking at Clare, "Yes, one you should respect, he's small but a real Angel."

"Angel? OKAY."

"You do know Kalbreal is an Angel right?"

Clare's ears itched, she couldn't say she didn't believe it, because she did know, and Kalbreal as an Angel made sense. "So what Angel is ISADES?"

"He's a protector, he's given the Moonstones protection for a thousand years, a debt which was paid months ago, but he still chooses to stay, he won't say why."

Isades pierced her with his eyes, pitch black beady things, it got to her, like it knew something she did not.

The staring was broken at the sound of Caidrian, "This is our home, made by the Angel Gabriel, the marble alone is a protective seal so if our invisible seals got destroyed we can still seek shelters in our homes."

"Seals? Verses? This all seems confusing."

Caidrian explained, "Verses are like spells, it's Angelic in nature, those from the Book of watchers, the Igori, and seals are Verses mixed with the souls of our dead, or blood of the living, it's an offering for protection, only those of Angelic presence has them, you find them in stones as well, or appearing on our body."

Nathan's confidence screamed heart robber, he was gorgeous, well built, which she noticed was a common factor among the men she'd met in the past twenty four hours, "It's much more than that, a whole lot more, Calub is good at explaining that kind of stuff."

She spun herself around slowly, absorbing in her surroundings, inhaling the lingering smell of musk mixed with cinnamon.

"Come, you need to get ready for the crescent ceremony, you have tomorrow to admire the place."

She looked at her brother who was leaning against the wall cutting a mango, as he spoke, "When one of our own dies in battle." Nathan's voice echoed in the open space, like a wave of sounds, "We preserve their soul until we absorb the Gazool or energy in english, of the deceased, unfortunately Calub won't be able to join in."

She looked at the floating lights just beneath the ceiling. They were small and bright, drifting in the air, with no destination, three across the entrance hall where she stood, "What's up with the floating lights?"

"We're Lightwatchers." Nathan's eyes weary, "Everything about us is light, we just verse a stone and it comes to life, simple." Her brother held a piece of cut mango to her as he spoke melodically, but she could feel the hurt and pain that strained his heart, she could see it behind his eyes, the longer she looked at him the more sorrow her own heart could feel. Unfortunate that it was sorrow for him and not her mother.

How might he have felt seeing his mother, after so long and losing her on the same day. Smiling, she walked toward him, she didn't want him to feel like she hated him, because she didn't, she had a feeling that if she knew him, she'd love him.

He looked just like his mother, the big oval eye shape, his straight dark hair, even his sharp chin. She leaned in, attentively thinking how similar he was to Michelle- Franchesca, EXCEPT the eyes, "You look a lot like our mother, does Calub look like her too?"

"No, he looks like you actually, you would think you look like our aunt, but you're more like our grandmother than anything else." She didn't know how to talk to Nathan or what to say, now that she knew he was her brother.

Put blood into it and everything becomes complicated, she huffed inwardly.

What would she have said to Phillip? Could she talk to him and tell him about all of this? What would she say? If she could tell him, would he even believe her?

Did they tell humans about this stuff? obviously not, or else they wouldn't have all the secrecy.

Would she even see him again. Her stomach toiled at the idea of never seeing him again, she didn't get to say goodbye the day her flight left for South Africa.

Phillip, her best-friend for six years strong and she always knew what to say to him. They were both rude and impulsive, but not much else in similarities, nonetheless, comforting him would have been as easy as walking. But here he stood patiently, her own flesh and blood, her heart softened with how his resemblance brought up her mother, but the words got stuck. The tightness in her jaw and flex of her chin, she looked away from him, as if his face had burnt her, which wasn't too far off the mark, as she Silently cursed herself. Her thoughts sobered as she heard the tap of a boot, and realized she was staring, awkward, "Nathan, nice name! Why couldn't I get a name so cool, Gabriella, urgh."

He laughed, "Yeah, that's a bit hectic, but unfortunately choosing random names doesn't work around here, tomorrow's a birth at our family house, I'll take you with me." His voice seemed different now, more relaxed after Caidrian had left with Isades.

"What do I have to do to get ready for the moon ceremony, is there a bathroom I can use? And a glass of water."

He pointed, "Turn right down the passage, second door on the left, I'll make you a sandwich and bring the water." he paused, "Use the room on the right across the bathroom, I put a robe on the bed."

He turned to leave through another open area instead of the passage, and paused, "Oh and you might want to shower, you stink."

She walked down the passageway directed to her, smelling under her arms, he was right she hadn't smelt so bad since she went to the farm and slipped in horses dunk. The scent of musk carried through the air never lessening or increasing. Floating lights lit her way, through the expanse as her mind wondered.

What should she make out of all this. The things Caidrian had told her, to this place, wasn't something she could just digest and move on from, her entire life had changed. She was going to need days to process, and it wasn't starting now. At least not with the pain poking in on her stomach, reminding her of her mother's death, a mother who lied about her name to her child. And not only child, apparently, because she now had not one, but two brothers. What was next, since she'd seen these people, it was like she was pushed into a maze of dreams, curved out of a gruesomely ancient and horrific Grimm's brother's tale.

She should hate her mother, but she couldn't. Franchesca never loved Clare but she cared for her enough to sacrifice her life. Getting her heart ripped out of her like she was nothing, such a quick death, yet so violent, and honourable.

Clare shuddered at the thought, and willed herself to an excruciate level not to break down, not to lose her strength, to remain pensive. *There would be a time to break, just not NOW.*

She opened the bathroom and took in the smell of lemon, and orange. Inhaling the welcoming scent she shut the door.

A stone toilet, and grey moon shaped built in sink took the left side corner. Above the sink was a round mirror with no edging, and behind her was a shower fit for three, with black tiles on the floor and white tiles on the one wall, the rest was open, *interesting* she thought, and *tsked* at the shower beams which peeped from every direction, *this is going to be interesting*.

Next to the shower was a dozen of neatly stacked grey turkey cottoned towels, picking one from the pile, she opened the shower, and looked down at the scar that marked her skin, but it was already gone, almost no sign of it left. Caidrian was right, she thought, shaking her head, of course he was, she was standing in the proof.

As the water hit her skin, massaging her muscles with its powerful jet, she thought of how she was going to save her brother, she couldn't even remember him, not one single memory or emotion attached to him. She knew she loved him, but Nathan, she considered him, he stood a stranger to her eyes, but he resembled her mother, right to her heart, she should trust him. There was that spark when they spoke, ten minutes ago, but she wouldn't fall for it, not yet.

It was a task knowing what was real when she just saw her mother become a celestial being in front of her very eyes, and then death. Unimaginable death. Those memories would haunt her until her own death became her, it was something she feared, she just hoped her subconscious had prepared.

Nine

Liam

The night in Khiron was a bustle of chaos, Liam had done almost everything he could to stay unnoticed, keeping his distance by staying across the bayou, but Ruzak had other plans.

Sitting on the bench, Liam watched from across the water, the fire crackle and listened to the descendants gossip, and next to him laid Ruzak. His wings stretched across the ground, head nudging Liam's thigh, but he never complained.

The bird had awaited his presence long enough. Liam, being the only one who was allowed to stroke the wings of Ruzak even if it was done in secret, because Casters were forbidden to make such close relationships with the Guiders. Like a stupid rule would stop him from doing what he wanted.

Shaking his head in silent disbelief he stroked Ruzak's wing, pausing when he heard the sound of grass moving, "Ah, I was wondering when you'll be joining me."

A tall woman showed herself, Ruzak snapped his beak, and flew up into the air.

"Not all is pleased, obviously." A strong, deep feminine voice answered before her face was seen. Some found her voice enchanting. Her body planted next to him, attired in a long light powder blue dress. Platinum hair shined as bright as the shimmers of stars, and eyes black as midnight. She was strikingly beautiful but not shockingly so to Liam's eyes.

She was different compared to the other Elvan, and he knew her struggles that came with it, "Alexandra."

When he saw her grim face his voice dropped, "What's with the hair?"

"The moon ceremony, my mother suggested I blend in with the Elvan and not with the Lightwatcher's."

"So she made you dye your hair? Is there no end to her madness, you should consider living with me."

"Then I would be just one of your mistresses." She teased.

He couldn't argue, he had considered it many times in the early years. She was the Elvan Princess and half Lightwatcher, he knew she would've made an exceptional distraction, but he also knew he hated their diet, just the thought of it made him pale, but he decided why not amuse her, "The thought did cross my mind."

"So did it mine."

Her black eyes daring him the way it did, would have made any man squirm with the invitation it had given him, but he didn't even look amused, instead his eyes dropped on the glittering water, which sparkled with the reflection of the full moon. There was no mistaking his message, he was not in the mood for mind games.

"In a few days." he paused, "I'll be brought to the Elvan mountain by Asguardians." His eyes not reaching the princess, "I would need your help to escape."

"Whenever you ask for my help it means betraying my own." She snarled, "I have settled my alliance with you years ago."

The long silence between them said more than the words had, "I have not seen you in months William and you send messages summoning ME, do you forget who I am."

She stood up, his eyes changed, as he stared at her, he knew he could be intimidating, but so could she, which is why he kept his voice gentle, "Yes you don't owe anything to me, but in believing we are allies, I thought you'd be willing to assist."

She stamped the ground, for the fifth time with the grass shoes she was wearing, like a school girl who didn't get her way, "Really, you are going to go there now? The ally thing oh, okay let us use that."

Her face was flushed, and her breathing heightened, she was ticked, "Tell me the plan, If I like it I'll join, if I don't, forget me, ask Calub, he can enter Safiereal at will."

Liam had known Alexandra for years, he knew how easily perceptive to words she was, he got up as she walked toward the back path she came from, "haven't you heard Alexa?"

"Heard what?"

"Calub has been kidnapped."

Alexandra- Alexa stood still, her mouth opened, her face whitened even in the shadows, PALED, like a ghostly creature of the night, "Impossible, I saw him a few days ago, I would've known."

"It's very recent, I heard it myself like an hour ago."

She didn't move, "Are you going to save him?"

"I have to save his sister first, I'm sure you heard of her, Clare."

He had liked talking her name, it was short and simple, like his nickname Liam, just the thought of the beauty made his mood lighter. She had been breathless when he spoke to her, and he felt the pull toward her, his body's urge to hold her. It took a lot of restraint not to touch her, or grab her, or reveal his identity. In the end he succumbed to his desire, and held his princess.

He wondered how she was, did she settle in, what was she doing, he began to rid himself of the thoughts, but it was so intense, that he had to create a shield. He didn't understand this reaction to her, he really needed to stop thinking of Clare, for his own good and many others.

Alexa walked closer to him, lost in her own phantom, "I did, my mother's calling her a weakling, apparently her memory's wiped out."

Her voice dropped with every word said, it was softer than he had ever heard, an extra effort made on her part to sound more trusting or convincing perhaps. He wouldn't put it past Alexa, and with his own shields held in place, he didn't want to invade her mind, and risk losing control and hunting down Clare and laying a public claim to her.

"I have deep feelings for Calub." Her confession was final, Liam held her midnight vision, with his blank one, he had just seen something at that moment which was not his to witness- Love, it was personal, but she wanted him to see it.

Alexa kept her sights on the sky, oblivious to what he might have thought but he didn't blame her. Alexa had succumbed to decades of worrying what other's thought and said, mostly by her mother's own doing. Unfortunately unlike her sister Wuzana, Alexa had taken majority of her father's genes, she had looked and thought mostly like a Lightwatcher, and being the youngest meant she would be queen, made it all harder to fill the shoes of her mother.

"I want to see him safe, William, so whatever plan you have on saving him, you have my alliance, there, only."

Her dress showed her slender figure and curve between her hip bone and ribcage, one side more curvaceous than the other. Liam had remembered that day, when it happened- the war of descendants.

They all had their scars of that day, but Alexa's was more permanent, because on that day twenty years ago, had marked her as one who had lost another. She had kept the deformity in her spine as a constant reminder of that which had been savagely taken from her- a sister, a friend and a warrior and though, her limp was a disability, she was still one of the best Fuized fighters he had ever seen in two thousand years, on this earth.

Liam tightened his jaw, there was no remorse in his eyes, no hatred, nothing. He was emotionless when it came to most, there were only a few who he ever cared for, and only two who he placed above others, they were his siblings, and part of him knew that innocent little Clare was too fast becoming a vital part of his existence in more ways than one.

He had known the loss of family, the absence of that which was a part of you slipped away. He had once lost, more than most, which was why he never got too deep, too emotionally involved. He urged himself not to drop his guard, to hold his own, BUT it was time Alexa's trust be tested.

Eyes on her, recalling what she said, he couldn't say he was not entirely stunned by the Princess's confession. In his absence from Khiron, he had still heard stuff from Jullie.

The on-going complaints of Calub's play days with Alexa, but he knew Calub well enough to know how this was going to turn out. Liam wanted to highlight the obvious, but another part knew not to meddle, especially when it got him what he wanted, he never claimed sainthood, "Isn't he a little young for you?"

"Not as old as you are for Natarsha."

His blue eyes seeped into the sky, as the stars sparkled in its miles, "She's just a friend."

"Okay, then, enlighten me, what are you doing across the lake?" she grinned, "When there's a ceremony happening, and might I point out, of a dead woman which happens to be your student?"

She spun around slowly, showing her knee length hair, clinging to her satin dress.

"We both know you aren't big on love William, but you are one of honour, seeing Franchesca's burial is honourable, even I am here, but it doesn't explain why you're sitting out here."

She didn't face him, he didn't move, "The last time you hid was when you met Roselletta Rulaen."

He had forgotten how blunt and straightforward Alexa could be. Elvan always the bitter bastards he thought, "I'm here to protect

Clare, I don't want the distraction, so I'm keeping my distance."

As if he said it all, she gasped, "You have feelings for HER, the weakling? But you barely know her, I'm intrigued."

He clenched his fists, his guard defensive, Alexa knew how to get under his skin, he told himself to be careful, keep the shield up, "She can't even ward off a Shapeshifter, Her body is too weak to handle my presence and she cries A LOT."

Alexa raised her voice, sarcasm unfiltered, "She would, she just lost her mother."

He almost smiled at that, "Now you defend her."

Alexa turned quickly, and pushed out her hands, before she pointed at him "I'm not, but it sounds like you are making excuses and finding logical reasons to your actions." She arched her eyebrow waiting for him to deny it, but he didn't, she continued, "When the most logical one of all is that which you refuse to acknowledge, but fair enough, your personal life isn't one with many red ticks is it, how is Roselletta doing, are you still her run to guy."

He grimaced at the thought, "You certainly know how to get me thinking don't you?"

"I know you for almost three hundred years, William Blackwyll, our friendship is one based on mutual ground and a barely there honesty, you didn't just call me here for a mere escape plan, you wanted my council on whether she might break you. You are always too secretive."

She continued, "She had been living as a deceptor for so long, William, I want to meet her myself, but you are in the wrong company if you seek answers."

Alexa assured him, "You speak to my cousin, he's in L.A, I'll send his number, but I could tell you that the death of her mother is a certain dampener to things, so give her space."

Liam didn't say anything, he had wanted her to tell him that Clare was bad news, and he should stay away, but she didn't, though he wasn't surprised that she didn't.

He knew that the only true way of knowing would be through experience and that was not something he could afford to do. Distractions were only going to keep him off course, and he knew that failure was not an option. When the time came, Clare's life could end up in his hands, just the thought of it, left his body in an instant rage. Somebody was to blame for all of this, he had to find out who before they attacked Clare, and his own secrets came crashing down.

He focused his eyes across the water toward the ceremony, he used his extensive vision to see further, everything appearing before him, zooming in as if he were standing right there, "The ceremony is about to start, head back, before your mother sends her bats out for you."

Alexa touched his shoulder, "Your looks are one of a rarity, if she fails to recognize your inner greatness she wouldn't be able to resist the outer."

He wore a black tracksuit with a hood covering his hair, he was not dressed to impress anyone, "She was able to resist Kalbreal."

Alexa smiled, "She just lost her mother, she needs time, or it could mean that she's getting her angelic side back, good luck with those hormones of hers, the girl is going to be a walking Aphrodite."

Clare

CLARE ENTERED THE ROOM, her vision taking time to adjust to the darkness. Narrowing her gaze to the only thing she could make out, a king size bed, which she could barely see as it was, besides its shape.

Everything else was camouflaged in darkness, the curtains that draped the windows sealed, she couldn't see anything else.

Annoyed,

She tried looking for the light switch by the door. Searching the walls with her fingers. The walls felt SMOOTH under her finger tips, unlike the cold marble they had in the bathroom.

No switch.

She was so tired, her eyes burned from exhaustion. The shower helped but not much in freshening her up, as she hoped it would. Instead it reminded her of how she just wanted the day to end.

She drank the bathroom water from the taps in desperation of some long needed rehydration. It was delicious. It wasn't magical like she'd hoped, it didn't cure the hunger pangs or the heartburn from the emptiness in her belly. And it definitely didn't ease the constant cramps she had to endure until the moon ceremony was completed.

Nathan said that he'd prepare her something to eat. All she wanted to do now, looking at the bed, was get into it, relax her aching feet from all that walking in the forest and maybe have a nap. While she laid on her stomach and forgot this day ever happened.

Clare was still yet to recover from her flight, and the morning at the church. She had almost forgotten about that. Everything which happened from the time she'd seen Nathan, seemed so long ago, but not her mother, not her death. That would always be something too sudden, too fresh, something that altered Clare's life in so many ways. The moment it happened, it marked her heart with an obsidian marker that would continue to leave its scar every day, in the future.

The towel cinched snuggly around her body, she rubbed at her burning eyes, succumbing in to her desire. Clare threw herself on the bed without wasting a single thought. Expecting a soft drop, she squealed in pain and surprise as her body hit a hard surface. The pain shot right up her back as she let out a string of curses, and yelled, "GOD dammit."

At first, her mind boggled with the idea of how tired she really was AND the bed she imagined was not really there. OR maybe she missed it.

Her fingers wandered around, to confirm her accuracy. She felt a hard lumpy thing. Fingers spread out she touched on something soft and cushy. But nonetheless there was something hard on the bed, directly beneath her. She touched it with her hands, FLESH, "Shit." It was another person under the sheets, and the victims touch was blistering hot, which meant only one thing,

She jumped off quickly. Her towel falling off, she grabbed the soft cloth and straightened it as fast as her life depended on it. Tightening the towel as tight as she could whilst her hand stung and burned from the heat of his skin.

A deep growling voice yelled from under the sheet, "This better be good."

The guy clapped his hands and the curtains opened and lights went on, brightening the room, "What are you doing in my room?"

She stood up straighter, her face flushed with embarrassment at the sight of him. His sun blazed eyes and furrowed eyebrows taking her in, with lustful heat, but there was something in the way he stared her down, something that made her take a step back. He did not look happy, scratch that, he looked pissed.

She muttered, "Kalbreal,"

She hadn't seen him since the afternoon. Her mind puzzled on what to say, how to say it. He was an Angel, she didn't know what powers Angels had, but looking into his orange and red sunrise eyes she couldn't see anything Angelic about him. He was more like a bad boy, satanic worshipper with all his piercings on his ears, gothic eyes, and hard firm lips.

She stumbled into her words, "I..I'm ss..sorry, Nathan said I should change here, blame him."

She stood frozen to her spot watching him stand up. He wore only silk cotton black boxer shorts that hanged dangerously low on his abdomen, revealing a bit too much of his stomach, and what belonged underneath.

He had no happy trail like most men, his body was hair less, even his arms, and legs. Wow, his legs were toned, and muscular, inviting, she felt an urge to touch it, taste it, her neck tilted at the forbidden thought.

She jumped when he spoke,

"I'm sure changing doesn't entail jumping on my bed with a wet towel." His lips tilted, as though he was amused, "I could've burned you, how's your hands."

She put them behind her back, ignoring his impute words, "Angel-boy likes black, who would've thought." Not sure whether she referred to the room which was draped and decorated in full black, or his boxers.

Clare couldn't help herself, there was something in his eyes, telling her to remain cautious. They spoke of fire, heat - burning things, there was a lot of kindness in them, a hard sort. Thinking about it, there was something Angelic in him, but she remembered what Caidrian said about an Angel wanting her dead.

"ANGEL-BOY," he said in disbelief, "You couldn't think of anything better, hero, knight, prince, just ANGEL-BOY."

Was he actually attempting to have a normal conversation with her, while she wore a towel, with NOTHING underneath. Sizing his body with an appreciative gaze, she halted on his neck.

There was energy in the room coming off Kalbreal that wasn't there a moment ago. It was highly alluring as it drew her in, yet resisted at the same time. An aphrodisiac- teasing you, compelling you, but never giving you a taste of its drug, never giving you the full pleasure of its addiction.

His muscular torso flexed, as he walked toward her. Kalbreal was lined, ripped, bulkier than she'd ever thought she would like. Yet- Neither had she considered a possibility of standing with only a towel, in a room with a man, or Angel built like a man, with his ribcage hidden away behind corsets of muscle.

His stature was lean, with an extensive eight pack, broadened shoulders to match a tall powerful frame. She stood and stared longer than she knew could be legal. Her eyes sketching on his imprinted tattoos. The few on his chest resembling a signature of something, surrounded by circles. There was one which caught her eye, it was the only one which was black, with an orange slash crossing through it. He was an Angel.

an Angel,

She repeated the words in her mind, in hopes it might absorb into her emotions. She walked a step closer, her face fixated on the mark marring his flesh above his heart.

Was it all orange or was it red? She couldn't make out, but for the small bits of black.

He turned toward the left, grabbing a t-shirt from the floor, only a few feet away from her, which gave her a side view.

She admired the black tattoo on his arm, it was symbolic, like fire wrapped in a pair of wings, but the wings bled by a red vine of roses, as the thorns pierced through causing the blood to drip.

He noticed her examining his body and interrupted her, "So are you just going to stand there and stare at me? Or are you going to take out your towel."

Flushed by the gesture and the sudden exhilarating heat in the room, her cheeks turned red as thoughts penetrated her brain, *was he inviting me to bed*. His eyes twinkled in clear amusement, by her reaction to his words, "Relax, I meant to change into your robe."

He touched his chest, "This, it takes some getting used to, us Angels can be very appealing to one without a mark."

She exhaled loudly not sure whether to be relieved or not, she asked him, "Mark?"

"Nathan's been assigned to explain it all to you tomorrow."

"If that's the case, can you wait outside, please."

He looked at her with tiresome eyes, "No, Go change in the closet."

She looked around from side to side, remaining in one place, too nervous to take a step. She didn't hear him, sneak up behind her, not touching her, but still just a breath away, he whispered in her ear, every breath he took as he spoke tickled her earlobe

"Turn around"

Her heart thumped, as she obeyed, she was instantly drawn in confusion to see him a few feet away from her, sitting comfortably on a black suede chair.

He pointed to the closet, and she understood it, he was playing with her, making her weak, in places she didn't want to feel weak, she knew it by the glimmer in his eyes, the arch of his eyebrow, and the lick of his lip.

Clare grabbed the white robe off the bed and marched angrily toward the closet, too scared to approach him in case he hurt her or worse, she killed an Angel, and became a fugitive on the run, because if he didn't watch himself she was going to lose it, very fast.

She slammed the door shut, it was really stupid she thought, but since she met Kalbreal it always seemed like she was a game, a tease, YET he said it himself, he would take some getting use too..

She recalled the guy in the robe, as she changed into her own, panty less, luckily for her perky breast, she didn't really procure a bra. There was some connection she felt when he spoke to her, a loosening in her threshold. It wasn't like the tension in the room with Kalbreal, the lust, she felt for a forbidden fruit. She had rethought his words, over and over again, a silent mantra, "That princess is for you to decide."

The words lingered in her head, a passing memory. A small spark of something sizzled in her veins too microscopic to name.

DRESSED IN A FULL RED robe, Kalbreal waited for her. He deliberately raked up her body ever so slowly, pausing when he reached her lips, "A true Lightwatcher, no doubt."

Clare brushed the unwanted feelings that hummed in her body, "Thanks," was all she could say, before he opened the door. Turning around but facing his head to the side as if trying not to look at her while he spoke, he gestured, "Tie your hair, you look too distracting for the others."

Baffled by his gravel voice she asked, "Is that your idea of a compliment?"

He didn't answer, instead he turned and walked away leaving the door open behind him. That was a dismissal, she guessed Angel-boy didn't like to be questioned.

Well if he was going to ignore her, so would she. Door slammed shut, she went down the narrow hallway. Caidrian caught her arm, the grip firm but not sore, "You look good, but tie your hair up it's a crescent ceremony not a wedding Clare."

She resisted the urge to roll her eyes, and begrudgingly knotted her locks up in a bun. From the corner of her eye she caught Alonso staring at her, secretly smiling from the end of the passage way.

Alonso, Nadia and Caidrian wore red robe, whilst Nathan the only other one dressed in white. All left the castle together making their way slowly further into Khiron. It was easily past seven by now, but the realm still looked bright, the skies darkness overhead, from where a beam of light shadowed the city, like sparkling diamonds of pearlescent light glittering in the air.

She spoke to Alonso who walked next to her, "What is that light up there, it's beautiful,"

He smiled, not looking at her, "Well, I like to think of this realm as the city of lights, those are protective seals." He said pointing to the dazzling glimmer, "Souls of Lightwatchers, it's like fragments of their souls falling around us, they do that all the time, but at night, you just see it better."

"The souls never lose its lights, so that's like dust from it?"

He nodded his head, "You catch on quickly for a newbie. I never had a chance to tell you."

She looked up at Alonso, his long hair falling on his nape, he was a few inches taller than Kalbreal, and almost twice Angel-boys size, Clare was happy he was one of the 'good guys', "Tell me what Alonso?"

He looked at her as they walked behind the others, his Asian blood seemed to be more prominent in the dark, causing the olive undertone of his skin to give him an almost dream look.

"I'm sorry for the loss of your mother, her name shall echo as a hero in Aquadore mountain, and her soul shall be the brightness in the darkest of hours."

She didn't really understand what he said, but it sounded pleasant and remorseful, "Thank you Alonso,"

They approached the ceremonial grounds, with small fires marking the corners. Groups of unfamiliar people scattered across, all dressed in different attire, but still respectable.

She noticed a few of the people, the ones who walked together muttering in a foreign tongue, all wearing red robes with golden links of rope tired around the waist holding the garment closed.

Their skin shimmered in their unnatural fairness, and as she got closer to them she focused on their hair, which was a bright shining white, or platinum.

Her first thought was Angels, before she said anything, she caught a glimpse of their eyes. They were black, but not like Isades was, these ones had SO much hatred in them, her bones jittered.

Nathan startled her, by clicking his fingers in front of her eyes, she snapped out of her mind, "Hey, I didn't see you there."

"Don't stare, they're Elvan, from the 4th realm, Safiereal, the shimmering on their skin is just a hoax, to piss the Caster's off. They would look just like us if it weren't for the white hair and fake diamond teeth." She gave him an incredulous look, which earned her one of his rare smiles, "On second thought, scratch that, they are just freaky, but Calub stands them so." He shrugged

She looked at him, curiosity marked her gaze, but she was only caught by part of his sentence- "There are other realms?"

He put his arm on her shoulder, and part of his wrist bands dug into her skin. She dropped her eyes to the floor and back at him, he was dressed just like her, and his dark green eyes a stark reflection of her own, but jealousy seeped in by the obvious features of her mother, she pushed it away.

He was taller and more muscular than she remembered from the day before, especially since he put his arm around her, she could feel the weight drag her down, but she liked it, she needed to hug someone, especially someone who reminded her of her mother.

"Sister, sister, there are many realms, eleven to be exact, but we only have alliance with five others, Elvan, as you've seen, the Shapeshifter's," he said pointing to a group of men. One of them stood out, with a tattoo on his face, but all of them possessed dark blue hair, shocking or metallic, it showed brightly even in the fire light.

The Shapeshifter's wore dark green robes with beads of white around their necks, some of them were fair skin, others dark like Asian, she recognized the appearance from earlier when they'd attacked her and Caidrian. Those ones were dead, most of them beheaded to be more precise, except the one.

Clare swallowed her saliva as if water dripped in her mouth, as the memory of the Shapeshifter in the hands of the faceless man, surfaced. The man who held her mind captive, by seven simple words, who was he.

Her body waited to be recalled by the hooded stranger, as if her senses were intertwined to seek him out, her eyes darted involuntarily across the lake, she saw... him, a figure, staring across the lake. She knew it was him, every sense of her body awakened, as the very reason she was there in the first place left her.

He stood directly opposite her but in this case he was unreachable, a little too far. She withdrew herself away from the foreign stranger knowing that it was pointless to strain her eyes so far, when she could hardly see him, even if her body yearned for it. A small voice whispered in her ear, "*He would come to you.*"

Though Khiron never had a dark night, not really, that was according to Alonso, who had informed her that the souls lighted Khiron, but even so, Clare could hardly make out much but a shape and size of the figure across the lake, but she knew, it was strange how, but she knew it was him, the robe guy.

She felt the pressure of Nathan's hand as he squeezed her left shoulder, she stared at him, "What realm are the Shapeshifter's from?"

"The fifth, It's called Rughonia, but the ones you need to know about is the Asguardians."

"Asguardians? You mean Thor and stuff?" his eyes widened, as he moved her forward, further from the crowd. They stood so close to the water, any closer and they would've been in it, "Ssshhh, don't mention those names around here, its forbidden."

"Jee wiz dude, I was just saying, no need to get weird." She whispered back, with a poor attempt of a scowl, "Who are they anyway, the Asguardians."

Nathan stared directly into her irises, grave distress envisioned in the pain of his eyes. His turmoil, opened up for that moment, but she didn't look away, because she knew if she was sure about anything - he was her brother, and all she wanted to do was hold him, and tell him it'll be okay, but she couldn't, because them being okay wasn't certain. He dropped his eyes and gazed behind Clare, past her shoulder.

His guard up and tightened in his features, "Asguardian's are the off-spring of Angels, they don't have Angelic abilities but they can use seraph verses nonetheless, you should watch yourself around them, our own have a habit of disappearing when it's convenient for them."

Clare gasped out a breath after she had held it a minute too long, she caught a sweet incensed smell of citronella from the near fire which burnt a few feet away from them, "What? Where are they?"

Clare could smell brandy on her brother's breath as they walked close together, moving in toward the crowd. He was practically bringing her down, leaning on her, inconspicuously. She didn't confront him, or moan about it, she wouldn't care if he was drunk, she didn't blame him either, he just lost his mother, "We tend to purposely lose the invites addressed to Asguardians, unless we really have to."

"Offspring of Angels, I didn't know they did stuff like that, amongst themselves."

Her brother's smile broadened at her, "You have much to learn sister. It'll be easier if we could get that memory back, and I got someone who might be able to help with that, but first."

He pointed to a coffin, as he did she looked around them, small bonfires burned in small holes dug up around the bayou.

Clare saw something, and a thought projected from her mind, "Who's those people, one of them got their hood up, how weird is that, I saw a guy dressed just like that."

Nathan thought before he answered, he looked as though he wished she had never asked, "They're the Casters, descendants of Tempters."

The thought of her mother's heart in the Tempters hand, flooded into her like hot liquid being poured on her flesh, "Why are you allies with these monsters,"

He gripped her arm and pulled her to one side, "Not so loud, they're not monsters, they choose to be good and for thousands of years they've proved greater allies than the Angels themselves, especially to us Draikens." Nathan paused, and outstretched his fingers around her arm, but his voice was low, his eyes peeled on the crowd, as he gritted out, "Just give them a chance."

He gently brushed Clare's shoulder. Upon her frown, he whispered in her ear, "You should brace yourself, the Casters and Elvan are not always welcoming, especially the elders, my guess is that they heard you."

She didn't reply, there was nothing she could have said, it was not like she knew anything about them, or the realms. Nathan stalked away, like his body was on fire, and she was the lighter.

There were people everywhere, some had hoods on, whilst others had them dropped down but one stood out, the only person who had not wore a robe but a dress, it was odd at first, but the lady turned around, as if she sensed Clare's eyes on her.

She likened the lady to an enchanting beauty from a fairytale story, the snow queen.

The woman's skin was like milk in flesh, the fire lights were not enough to wash out her fairness, her beauty, RADIANT.

Clare had always wanted skin colorless as the lady's, who stood at least ten feet away from her, dressed in a light silky blue dress which dropped to the floor.

She stared harder at the woman, noticing how her lips thinned, and her eyes sunk, from a lack of sleep and possibly poor diet. The woman's black eyes never altered from Clare's face, as she made her way closer to this unknown woman.

A hand held Clare's arm, she turned to see who it was, but it was nobody. She scanned further down but the bayou was stacked with people, it could've been anyone or her imagination. Some dwelled on the high squared gold coffin, which got her attention soon enough.

She had subconsciously tried not to think of whose body laid in the gold coffin, which was positioned flat on a twelve inch squared brick stand, that looked decades old, with parts of the bricks missing. She would have to face the obvious sooner.

"Your innocence is quite fascinating."

Clare heard a woman's voice from behind her. She turned as her hair slipped out of its bun, it was the woman from earlier.

"I am Alexandra, call me Alexa," She smiled at Clare, her teeth surprisingly not diamonds but ordinary white.

"Did you know my mother."

Alexa had a black charcoal eye-shadow surround her eyelids and a grey smudge underneath her black eyes. The Elvan woman looked well made up, but false. She had a feeling that those weren't her real eyes, as much as the platinum hair color was not her own, but Clare wasn't about to point that out.

"Yes, we fought together, but Franchesca has undoubtedly made more enemies than she had friends or allies."

Clare didn't know how that was possible, there were lots of people at the ceremony, how could her mother have made more enemies.

She couldn't get used of the name Franchesca. Not Michelle, but Franchesca, was it normal that she was angry at her mother but at the same time frustrated and hurt that she had to die so soon. Clare's stomach tightened into knots. Bile rose up and she flinched with the sick feeling. She had forgotten the pain cramping in her stomach, but now it worsened tenfold.

She looked at Alexa's expressionless face. This woman, who looked in her early twenties, didn't even blink, but just stood up straight directly opposite Clare, refusing to lower her eyes, which just seemed to tick Clare off, "My mother is dead, if you have nothing good to say I suggest you leave."

Alexa dropped her eyes and looked ahead toward the shore of the lake, "It's not that simple, we're all descendants after all, and I'm the Elvan Princess and half Lightwatcher, a friend of your brother's."

"Nathan?"

"No, Calub, I heard he's missing. I'm here to honor your mother's death for his sake, but I'm also here to seek answers from others."

"You mean Caster's."

"It isn't wise to assume that which you do not know."

"You don't like me very much do you?"

"Elvan do not express emotion mildly."

"Ah, but you are half Lightwatcher."

Alexa turned her gazes back to Clare, who was certain that the Elvan woman's face was pulled into a frown, "I really don't know what he sees in you." She took in Clare's appearance as though she was taking in an unappealing view, "You're not even blonde, you are barely mature."

Clare's stomach felt assaulted as the pain grew to new heights, she felt a bead of sweat trickle her temple, as she bit down the urge to weep, "I don't know who the hell you are talking about." She gritted out, through clenched teeth, "and frankly I don't care."

Clare marched away from Alexa, her hand stuck on her stomach and limped her way toward the crowd. The pain began to numb in the core of her stomach.

She felt her body now being drawn to the coffin. Inhaling, she smelt a stronger scent of musk, mixed with the citronella. She walked, crossing paths with a group of Elvan who wore red robes, that resembled blood, and worked her way closer to the gold coffin, which glistened in the light of the fire and the Lightwatcher's souls.

The coffin was decorated with engravings written in ancient script embedded on the golden casket and in it laid her mother, lifeless, blue eyes now closed by flesh and freckles and deadened by the blueness in her skin. Breathless, Clare swallowed, her throat squeezing in.

The lifeless body was covered in a shiny dust of red, but Clare got closer, her body tensed, the hairs on her skin stood up, she took a step closer, it wasn't dust, or dry powder, but a slimy liquid that smelt like musk. It had red shiny beads inside the jelly substance.

She let out a harsh exhale and inhaled a strong smell of musk, which had come from the coffin, before she put her hand on her mouth, attempting not to scream, but it was too much.

The noise from the crowd had dissipated around her, suddenly it was just her and what was left of her mother whose skin was so pale, she could've sworn it was almost surreal.

Clare's heart pulsed at higher beats with every second passed, the yearning for her mother's eyes to open and stare at her. The smell of her mother's hands when she would touch her skin, always smelling of rubber from wearing gloves. Just yesterday that face had smiled at her, those lips had spoken to her, just yesterday her mother's arms had held her. She hated the way it happened, she wished she hadn't said those things to her. She should've tried to understand when her mother told her that Nathan was her brother, now she would live with this feeling, this hatred of herself, and all the unasked questions.

She wanted to scream, she wanted to yell, parts of her felt like it was exploding, but all Clare could do, all she could effort to do, was stand there with her hand on her mouth, gasping for air.

Her body wanted to tear itself up from the inside out, rip her heart out, like her mothers had been. She remembered her mother's words a year ago, it was a day after she won the swim offs, "You can never truly love until you have lost, Clare."

Now she stood there, and she understood, what her mother meant, she understood, loss, and it undid her. The last threshold she had, the last of her strength, her willpower, gone.

Her mother's face was the only thing not covered in the coffin, and Clare wanted to touch it, wanted to feel her mother's skin for the last time.

She tasted the salt in her mouth, the wretched feeling in her stomach and the lump in her throat. The hot tears rolling down her eyes, was this really happening. She prayed that it was all just a dream, that her mother had not been killed so quickly, defeated so easily, but most of all she wished that her mother hadn't sacrificed herself to save her.

'better me than her'

The words killed the rest of the restraint Clare had left in herself and she screamed louder than she ever had, and dropped to her knees hitting the ground with unsheltered force. Her knees and body crumbled with pain but nothing was enough to keep her heart from crushing, nothing was enough to exceed this pain, this unbearable, wretched pain, as it tore from her heart, from her chest, burnt into her veins.

She didn't see the descendants staring at her, she didn't care if they did, she cried, and her stomach ached, her long curly hair falling around her face and body. Her head throbbed, her body perspired from the heat of her despair but she couldn't stop crying, she couldn't stop the anguish she felt, the fear that had come with this loss, stolen from her in a matter of seconds, her mother was all she had, all she knew to be real in her life, it was the one true thing that kept her from destroying herself.

Clare gripped on the coffin, outstretched her fingers to pull herself up, putting her hand to touch her mother's head, she was so close, strangely enough her mother's body was not cold as it looked, she was almost certain, she could feel some heat surrounding the body, only an inch away.

A hand gripped tightly at her wrist, it was hard and hurt, she wiggled her wrist free, "What the hell is your problem." She yelled, sniffing.

She stood up, her face wet from the tears, hair stuck to her forehead, and no wind to dry it for her but she didn't make eye contact with the person, she attempted to put her hand on the body again but was stopped by a voice,

"NO, you do not touch the dead, her body will be cursed."

It was a deep voice, she noticed him from earlier, he was the Elvan she saw on the way to the bayou.

He was slightly taller than her, his diamond looking teeth barely showing, which somehow made him look younger in appearance, black eyes poked her like stab wounds.

She didn't respond to him, she couldn't, she wanted to cry more, but urged herself not too. She moved swiftly towards Caidrian who was standing near a fire and talking to a man in brown leather attire, he met her eyes when she neared him, she was grateful when he didn't mention her outburst, or try to console her, she wouldn't take it,

"What do I do now?"

Caidrian pointed to a chair that was placed a few feet from her mother's body, "You sit there, Nathan will sit on the other side."

She couldn't put a finger on it, but Caidrian sounded like her mother's death was a minor implication, he seemed distressed and worried in his eyes, but no sorrow. She hesitated before she turned and made her way solemnly to the chair keeping her head to the ground.

She graced the night sky, tranquility in its stillness, clarity in the stars that decorated it. A thought occurred to her, she tilted her head to the crowd, catching her brother's eyes glared at clear spaces, he was sitting directly opposite her.

The place started to quiet down, there were not many Lightwatcher's around, majority were the other descendants, as Alexa had explained to her, they were all descendants. She wondered what that meant, the girl had seemed so young but old at the same time.

Clare stared at a fire, a few feet away from her, its blue and orange flames rose and dropped, she recalled what Alexa said, her mother had more enemies than friends. She looked at the golden coffin and met her brother's green eyes glistening in the shadows of the fires, she could see the tear in his eye as it fell on his right cheek, almost like a forbidden gem.

"The invisible shield is down, a must when these things happen."

She turned her body, to the deep voice, "Alonso, you startled me."

"Take this," He handed her a glass of white thick liquid.

"What is it?"

"Litchi juice, you haven't eaten, it'll take the edge off, Nathan said I should give it to you."

She directed her eyes to her brother for reassurance which she got in a form of a simple nod of his head, "Thanks."

She gobbled the juice, it was thick and fresh, too fresh, but it had done the job.

She sat there for what seemed like forever, with eyes on her from all corners. Most of them from other realms, either dressed in white, or red, accept for Alexa who wore blue, and the occasional Caster's in there dark robes.

She sat beside her mother, her brother on the other side.

A man with a grey dark robe made his way to the centre, where her mother's body laid. Gold cloths draped around his wrist, a stick in his hand which looked like a broken off branch, but Clare suspected it probably wasn't.

She kept her eyes on the stick, at the same time concentrating on what was going on, she wanted to cry but parts of her inner self willed the outer to be strong. The Caster hit his stick on the ground as he moved slowly to the casket. He approached the body with caution. Clare's eyes transfixed on his cane, his hood up, face covered. The way he walked, hunched in the shoulders, but tall framed, thin, he must've been old.

The man looked down at Franchesca's body, and lifted his stick up in the air.

Clare looked passed him, over his shoulder. The branches creaked, and the trees moved their roots, and trunks out of the way, they moved backwards, allowing more space. Something about the act made her nervous, but at the same time it was incredible, something she would never get use too.

Her eyes darted back to the Caster standing close to her mother's body as he hit his stick again on the ground, and a siren noise echoed, coming from the staff.

Clare blocked her ears, the sound rattling in the ground, she saw where the stick knocked the ground. A fire light, now burned just inches close to her mother, leaving her mother's coffin surrounded by its flames.

Clare's heart sank, with the sound of the stick, realization overcrowding her mind that this was happening, so soon. They did not mourn their dead, they burnt them as soon as the last light had set, she hated it, she had not even got a proper goodbye. How was she going to move on from this, live without her mother, her eyes burned as the anger filled up inside her chest.

The fury in her captivated, when she caught her sights on the Caster, he was a foot away from the fire, she couldn't see his face, but when he spoke his voice echoed through the bayou, "Lightwatchers, Caster's, Elvan, Shapeshifter's and descendants of Draiken blood, set your mind."

Ten

Liam

Liam frowned as a figure announced itself next to him, "I wasn't expecting you here so soon."

Kalbreal appeared from the air itself, sitting directly next to Liam, who had remained on the other side of the Bayou where Alexa had left him. The night sky still, windless, regardless of the invisible and protective shields lifted. He was watching the activities that were taking place across the Saltril lake, just to keep tabs on Clare. He wanted to make certain she was safe before he left, and get his fill of her presence.

He sipped from the bottle of cognac he had brought with him, to quench his thirst as he watched the ceremony. First he eavesdropped on Alexa and Clare's conversation, which really rallied him in the wrong way, for reasons he didn't want to admit. And then Clare's loss of control. When she screamed, he hated that nobody even held her, or consoled her, that made him glow. He decided to loosen his mind, as his brother Kole, solemnly would put it.

He should've insisted Jullie be there, she would've known what to do, he was on his third bottle, when he was now interrupted.

Kalbreal's face was faint, he wore a dark stone denim and a cream loose linen shirt which was opened to the chest, revealing his chest.

Liam knew that look, there was something wrong, but Liam was not one to really care much, so he took a swig of his cognac, and

Kalbreal scowled. He was not amused by Liam's lack of compassion, clearly daunted by something, and that almost brought a smile to Liam's face.

He knew Kalbreal better than he would openly admit, even to himself. The Angel was not easily swayed, his suspicion was confirmed by Kalbreal's voice, it, was too soft, not crowded by his conceitedness, "Ceremonies are not my thing."

"The rare few things we have in common, cognac." He held it up, a bottle of Camus.

Kalbreal took it without a thought and gulped quarter from the bottles half in one go, "Deceptors, they do make a good drink."

Liam slanted his mouth into a weak smile, "And food too, what's up with you."

He tried to keep his voice neutral, he was pretty versatile with all his years of speaking. When there was things to do he knew how to get it done, but now Kalbreal needed him, no matter how much he hated the annoyance of the Angels' constant uninvited arrivals.

Liam felt sorry for him, there was distress in his eyes, and Liam knew it weren't good for anyone especially now.

Kalbreal drank swig after swig of the Camus. Liam considered reminding the Angel whose stash he was drinking, but then again, what better way to seek some satisfaction for his brother's recent incompetence.

Kalbreal's quietness gave him a chance to check what was happening with the ceremony. He stood up from the old wooden bench and walked a few steps to the lake.

Liam's eyes darted across x-raying his vision to see what was happening parallel from him, "The ceremony has started."

"Armatos is here, his son is ascending tomorrow." Another Angel Liam thought, like he hadn't had enough on his plate already. He kept his back faced to Kalbreal, he'd known him long enough to know that Kalbreal was not one who you fooled easily but then neither was he - "Oh, when did he arrive?"

"First light, apparently, why cause so much attention, he could've been more discreet."

"That's going to be all over CNN."

Kalbreal got up off the bench and walked toward Liam, "UFO'S," he muttered, taking another sip of Camus.

Liam figured he weren't getting it back by the looks of it, "Aliens and flying saucers, I wonder what's next, you never could put anything pass them."

Kalbreal shook his head, "you would think by now they would have figured it out, it could never be more obvious."

Liam turned his attention to Kalbreal when he came shoulder to shoulder with him. Liam was two inches taller than Kalbreal, but much less bulkier, but older by at least a few thousand years, "There's a reason why we have named them deceptors."

Kalbreal looked up into the night sky and laughed, "I would drink to that, except, do you have another?"

Liam could see the worry in Kalbreal's eyes. There was a lot on the young winged warriors mind, a small part of him wanted to grab the Angel and see his thoughts, sooth his horrors, but he knew there was no good going to come from it, especially if Clare was still in danger. He hadn't found out exactly why yet, but he didn't blame Kalbreal, regardless of his part in this whole mess.

Armatos was an older Angel, you never knew with him, and he was one who did not hold favor on the deceptors either, so from what Liam gathered, the Angel's arrival seemed to stem from more than just the ascending of his son, "No, but I'm sure there's more at the manor, why don't you get it."

"Not so fast, what's going on with Clarebella, have you met with her yet."

He faced the lake, and looked from far, but he didn't extend his eyesight to see what lay in the distance, instead he just admired the fire which mirrored on the lakes waters and the reflecting stars which dusted with glitter on the calm surface,

"No, you know my track record when it comes to the opposite sex," Liam said, as he willed himself to stay calm, from hearing her full name spoken from Kalbreal's lips, "I was hoping you'll be more informative." Liam flexed his jaw muscle, hating the sarcasm in his own words, and continued, "When I agreed to help Franchesca, I didn't consider you to have an interest in Clare, my interest is in her protection." For now, he thought.

Kalbreal nodded, "Tomorrow, as we agreed, I'll be here but I need time to think. Clare is safe for now, there's much more happening here, like the deaths of the Lightwatcher's, it has scarred even Asguardians. Now that Armatos is here I have to keep him away from Clare."

This peaked at Liam's curiosity, but he didn't show any of it, not even a brief flicker, "Why, are you afraid he might try to harm her?"

"My fears are much worse, than her death."

Liam wanted to push further, but he had to have patience, he knew Kalbreal was not one who liked to be pushed around, "Did you hear about Calub?"

Kalbreal's tone was dry, "Yeah, she knows too, I suspect she'd want to get right to saving him."

Liam laughed mildly, "She can barely swat a fly, I wonder how she would be if she was raised as a Lightwatcher all her life, she is already a fascination."

Kalbreal didn't respond straight away, but Liam caught his jaw tighten, from the corner of his eyes and his throat glitch, but Kalbreal refrained any eye contact, instead he looked straight ahead, "Yes, she would have been dead, if it was left, Kadreal was the one who tried to kill her all those years ago."

"Kadreal!"

Liam was about to say more, when he remembered something,

and instead he kept quiet, his eyes darted for a second to catch a glimpse of Clare, but was filled up with what was happening on the other side, something wasn't right.

Kalbreal shouted, in agreement to his own instincts, "You need to go, now, GO."

Liam closed his eyes he knew the risk of what he was about to do but this was the most sensible option.

Clare

The Caster standing by Franchesca's body requested all the descendants excluding Clare and Nathan who wished to participate, to say specific words.

It was when she lifted her head finding her brother that a sharp pain jolted through her spine, rocketing straight to her brain. She screamed, as thousands of needles poked through her whole body falling to the ground. Not one of them came to her aid. Endless time passed. What felt like forever, before it stopped, just stopped, and left her out of breath, covered in sweat. Her torso ached, like she'd ran a marathon. Getting up off the floor she sat back on the old wooden chair.

The descendants were all in a trance, their feet lifted off the ground, as they slowly moved in a circular ring, creating a closed circumference around Nathan, her mother and herself.

They all held hands, some of them had blue and green neon lights coming from their eyes, chanting, "araeh mareal barah masah jibraeel amara," the words chanted over and over again.

Clare looked at Nathan, his eyes closed. His body a sight of peace whereas hers ached all over, something had to be wrong, her hands getting hotter, feeling sweaty, she stared at it. Veins protruding out through Clare's flesh, as a beam of light emanated from Franchesca's corpse, like a spirited blue electric wave. Splitting like a slower form of lightening, she watched as the beam struck her brother, before it forcefully penetrated the tips of her own fingers.

The pain was death defying, she screamed her lungs dry, the depth of which left her body shaken.

The pain rose from her hands to her arms, to her neck slowly draining itself through her veins up to her brain, and finally her heart.

The pain kicked at her, she fell onto the floor still screaming, as she scratched her chest, attempting to remove the robe, she couldn't breathe, still nobody aided her.

Her brother's scream lowered, he was saying something, but her body fitted on the floor. Her thorax choked down, her stomach burned, like it was getting eaten, she pulled at her hair, as she kept hearing chanting.

Her body lifted up off the ground, she wanted to panic and throw a tantrum, but instead she shook in the air. Epileptic agonizing shivers passed through her nerves, her body electrified by the current as it penetrated flesh and bones. What was happening to her, she couldn't stop moving, spine twisting, neck pulling. The bright light bursting out her chest shocking her with electric volts.

Eyes dazed, tracking a shadow of something, somebody in front of her, a figure. A chill set of hands landed on her chest. Forcing her heavy lids open, a tall figure loomed over her. Just the knowledge of his presence made her pulse quicken. His hand cold to the touch placed flat underneath the crest of her breast, directly on her flesh.

The chill of his skin, so comforting, beautiful, peaceful, she wanted to cry with the relief it brought her, as his hand removed the light that had come into her so violently, and rapidly from her mother's body, raping her senses. His hand sucking it up like a vacuum as it stole out the wrong inside her.

The physical pain subsided with every second passed, but the emotional brainstorm which consumed her regarding this man, was sending her dangerously close to the end of her rationality. How could she feel so strongly about a stranger that she had met just one time, yet let him embrace her, kiss her. The more he absorbed, the steadier her heart soared.

Not seeing his face, she knew who he was, he was the same one, who saved them that afternoon, the same one who she had asked, "Who are you."

And he had replied, the same mantra that had played in her mind, "That princess is for you to decide."

She looked down to where his hand settled. The light was gone, the pain a dull ache, but still his hand lingered just underneath the curve of her breast. He made to move it, but she put her hand on top of his, to halt it.

She was certain she heard the hiss of his breath, as her sex clenched with the pleasure it brought her. He was here, when nobody else helped her, he was here. She couldn't see his face, but she didn't need to, she just needed to touch him, so she lifted her hand to his hood, and moved it in slowly to touch his face.

When she did, a bolt of electricity drizzled on her fingers, how was that possible. The hair on his face poked at her finger tips, as they wandered shamelessly. It caressed his stubble, so inviting was he, when he tilted his head, slightly into the palm of her hand. She rubbed her thumb on his cheekbone, brushing it down until it skimmed on the indent of his lips. Hesitantly, she dropped her hand.

She didn't want to push, but as the thought brushed her mind, he brushed the side of her breast, luckily the robe managed to conceal it. She had completely forgotten about the people, she was utterly lost to this faceless man, who she had began to trust without knowing anything about him, even his name.

She didn't need her brother's knowledge, to know that this man was incredible, there was a deep yearning when she touched him, "You think I'm incredible."

She could hear the amusement in his voice, he sounded English, but it wasn't distinctive, his voice was soothing, a fluent tone, something deep and masculine, deeper than Kalbreal's. Confidence poured through his words, her mind whirled with the realization, had he just read her thoughts, she should have been nervous, or scared, but instead she was aroused.

Her mind had come to its senses moments later, when he removed his hand. She was levitated in the air. Just as the thought registered, the gravity pulled her down to the ground. She braced for the impact of the fall. The awaited pain never came, because her mysterious stranger, who enchanted her with his touch, had caught her in his arms.

He held her like she was a weightless bride, hand brushing her nape, sending chills down her spine, she lost herself by the intensity of his actions.

His other arm gripped under her knees. This man made her nervous, and highly aware of all his caresses and touches. She tried to see his face, now that she was cradled against his firm, hard chest, but the hood was pulled down and it was so dark she couldn't make out anything besides his eyes. Its color was not shadowed by the darkness of the hood, it was illuminate, the color of the night sky with the billions of stars lighting its hue, mesmerizing.

"You can read my mind?"

Putting her down, he brushed his fingers on her lips, she closed her eyes, waiting, expecting him to kiss her, neck slanted, her invitation obvious, lost to his touch, slave to his want. When his hand dropped, instead, she opened her eyes. A stab of disappointment assailed her, was it something she said. Before she could speak and ask, she saw the descendants as they stood in utter shock. Reality clicked, where they were. The others must've seen everything, she held back her groan, at what an awful daughter she was, allowing herself to be consumed by this man, who just saw it quite okay to hide his face from her, and manipulate her body to bend to his will.

He walked a few steps away from her, and she noticed the guider, sitting in a predatory position. The same one she had seen earlier upon entering Khiron.

She walked closer to the strange man, as he jumped on the guider's back. His robe opened at the bottom, noticing his jeans underneath the robe, didn't give her much besides show her that he had a well defined muscle tone on his thighs, he yelled, "See you soon princess."

The bird carried him in the air, higher into the dark sky. She watched with amazement as the birds wings stretched out in lengths as a dragon, gliding through the midnight air with the mysterious stranger riding freely on its back.

She wished he would've offered to take her with him, whisk her away like a fairy tale, 'a true Angelic warrior' she thought, how enticing. She watched him until she could no longer see the man who enticed her body with just a brush of his fingers as it danced on her lips.

Turning, around her the descendants stood stunned but no one walked up to her, or spoke to her at first. They just stood like obedient soldiers, she found it strange, but remembered that guiders are feared, they had a connection to Angels, so how was a Caster riding one, she'd decided to ask Kalbreal when she saw him.

The small fires that were made around the bayou had been replaced by dust and smoke. She heard people around her, whispers and laughs, but it was like her world had slowed down, making seconds minutes, because it had never crossed her mind that she lusted for a man who was bred from the very own breed that descended from the same beasts she had pledged to kill.

It was much later that Nathan stood a few feet away from her, she broke from his glaring eyes, when somebody shook her from the back. She spun around, about to put a fake smile on her face, when she saw the perpetrator,

Alexa.

She didn't seem impressed, or amused as the others were but rather impatient, "Your body rejected Franchesca's gift, luckily it didn't kill you."

Clare forced a sarcastic smile, "I kinda figured, who's that.."

She was caught off guard when Nathan pulled her to one side, away from Alexa, before she could finish her sentence. When he was sure they were away from the other's he whispered, "Something wasn't right, I felt it, it's the first time I've seen that, I don't want you talking to anybody about this just yet, not even our father, nobody saw much, they were put in a trance, Kalbreal no doubt."

She moved a step back keeping her voice low, "Wait, just a minute dude, firstly why didn't you help me, and secondly that guy that just saved me, he just flew on a freaking bird, I mean who the hell is he."

"I'm your older brother, and right now, I'm ALL you got." He paused, "I couldn't save you because I couldn't move, something, blocked me."

His eyes grew wider, anger filled them, tinting the green darker, "And that guy is a Caster, the same monster's you dislike so much, except I dislike him too, so stay away from him, he's way too old for you, and that goes for Kalbreal as well, you wanna date, find a nice Lightwatcher you own age, or younger."

Clare pushed her lips together, Nathan had a point, and he was older, and her brother, and when it came to dating, she never considered getting sloshed by a brother, but the look Nathan gave her, told her, he wasn't going to hear about it, so she shut her mouth, because what she had to say wouldn't make a difference.

She dropped her head angry and pissed off that she had to listen, but Nathan looked like he was not going to hear to any of it, he was so much like Franchesca. He ordered, "Stand still, I'm going to calm your nerves, I think you might go into shock."

He didn't wait for her to respond, just touched her wrist before she could say anything else. A warm sensation passed through her body, quickly like a dose of valium passing through her veins except this method did not sting. Her body relaxed as the warmth spread, her mind felt feathery, the world around her seemed to move, or her feet did, she felt like she was drunk, in a way, but sane.

"What did you do to me." Her words came out soft and dead, like she made no effort to speak, when she actually had to try pretty darn hard.

"I weakened your emotions and heightened your senses." His smile was wicked, "You lucky I'm not Calub, he would've given a mean shot, with catastrophic side effects, it lasts for days sometimes."

The green in his eyes protruded, his jaw tightened, it was more prominent when he smiled so gleefully. His hair was not gelled, so the middle hair which was far longer fell flat to the side of his right cheekbone, and the front swept to the right eye. He was a beautiful site and looked just like her mother except for the eyes, the resemblance was astounding.

"I have to go greet the Elvan before they leave, the effects should last till morning." He winked at her, and walked away.

She looked around the people staring openly at her. She wanted to talk to them, but the looks they were giving her told her to do otherwise, turn and run.

The place was darker without the fire, as people moved around, most wearing brown leather pants and t-shirts, discarding their robes at some time. They walked with sheaths on the waist, swords protruding proudly out. She scattered her eyes across the bayou, able to see the glint on the water bed, reflecting the protective shield.

She looked up at the sky and saw that the seals had been put up and the place was lighting up slowly, but that was not what caught her breath, it was when she dropped her sight and saw a pair of eyes. The rich golden hues belonged to the Caster, who she saw stare at her, when Nathan and her passed him to walk to the lake. There was something familiar about him, but she brushed it off, now she wished she hadn't.

The eyes stared back at her, it gave her a shiver. She thought of Kalbreal, but he was an Angel, this was a Caster. Instincts had her look more closely. Her eyes blinked twice, just to be sure she wasn't imagining things because the person was gone. she looked around, but nothing, poof, gone. These people were strange, it was hard to believe she had been one of them, especially harder to believe she had been raised a Lightwatcher for ten years.

The Caster who did the ceremony, held his hand out and shook hers. It had been a half an hour, wondering aimlessly in the bayou, before she turned, when some strange person called to her, she turned and saw everybody lined up to hug her. She thought it was weird at first, but realized that they didn't know her body rejected the Gazool, if they had, she gathered these fake welcoming's wouldn't be so false or welcome.

She considered what Nathan told her and played along, hugging the people. Finding the whole thing so much easier because of what Nathan had done to her. She felt different, more like a buzzed out high different, and for the first time since her mother passed away today she didn't feel sad, or entranced by a faceless man. Only peace, as if she said it aloud, a voice whispered, a mere breath from her neck, "how do you feel?"

It was Kalbreal, she smiled at him, she could've replied with dizzy, high, good, peaceful, a little overwhelmed, but instead, she crooned, "Don't tell, Angel-boy wants a hug too."

He paused at the thought, taken off guard by her boldness, "No, I'll pass."

She teased, "You not going to change your mind? the offer is closing. What's it gonna be Angel-boy?" She waited, then shook her head in mock horror, "Your loss, offer's sealed."

"Maybe if you offer me something more lucrative than just a hug, like a touch of those gorgeous breasts."

Clare stared at him, in shock, her mouth making a big oh. Her cheeks turned crimson, when she saw the knowing look he gave her.

His ginger and black hair was so straight down his neck, and shone in the glistening night, especially now that the seals were back up in the sky. She thought about his question, and a smart come back, but she kept coming up blank, opening and shutting her mouth.

She wondered if he saw what the mystery Caster did, but she knew that he couldn't, nobody could, his hand was in the robe, surely Kalbreal was just bluffing, not even her brother could've seen it. The eyes that stared at her, told her different.

"Where were you?"

"Around." His demeanor straightened, so quickly as the playfulness left him, "Your presence is requested at the chambers of descendants."

"The what? Where's that?"

Nathan was behind her in an instant, she was certain she saw him leave, but she didn't see him return. He walked a little in front of her, almost to shield her, "We just lost our mother, the Garde can wait until sunrise."

Kalbreal flinched, and then he laughed. In that, was beauty, it was loud, as it transformed his face into what one may consider a god. Angel-boy was gorgeous, even though his sudden happy mood was in complete contrast to the seriousness that was so obviously sketched in his eyes a minute ago. Kalbreal had to state the obvious, "I was just messing with her, What's with you."

He pushed comically at Nathan, who grabbed at Kalbreal's hand and gave him a brotherly hug, that surprised Clare, since his touch had only burnt her. She had the blister marks on her finger to prove it, yup, it hadn't healed. Apparently Caidrian forgot to mention that they didn't heal from Angel burns, "How are Casters able to fly guiders, I thought they're Angel birds."

Kalbreal stood next to Nathan, the Angel was taller than she led herself to believe. Clare was sure she remembered him not having so much height, considering she was supermodel tall herself, he was at least a foot taller than her brother, a bare few inches shorter than her mystery man.

Nathan laughed, starkly, "He's a special type of Caster, and you're my sister, his name is..."

Kalbreal blurted, "His name isn't your concern, leave it be Nathan."

Nathan was as confused as she was, as to why Kalbreal didn't want her to know, "It's just a name man, it's William."

She smiled and squeezed him tightly, *'William' how heroic* she thought.

Kalbreal looked upset, but Clare didn't care. Prying information out was like removing a thorn from your foot, you had to keep digging.

Kalbreal was good to look at, his stares very seductive, but parts of her chose to see pass that, she knew he was an Angel and he probably had some power of temptation but she was not going to allow herself to be played with, she needed to tread carefully, and William, her faceless William, if Nathan knew she was crushing on him, she doubted he'd be so giving.

Nathan kissed her head, "He's not as bad, once you get to know him, I promise, Kalbreal is known for his charm, but remember what I said." She laughed, and looked at her brother then Kalbreal, his orange pupils softened after meeting hers',

"I don't doubt that." She turned her attention to her brother, "What did you do to me, I feel so different, I almost forgot my mother's dead, what will happen to her body?"

Nathan replied, but not before his eyes darted at Kalbreal, and

Clare could tell that both men were hiding something, "They'll burn it tomorrow and drop her ashes in the Saltril lake."

He pointed at the water, eyes on it, she wondered how many thousands of Lightwatcher's ashes had been dropped in the lake along the years. It made her heart sour, but she felt it ease as soon as it began, "how long does this feeling last? What's got you so happy? Wanna share?"

"Temporary I'm afraid, I'll do it again if you like, I asked one, well more like my fist did the talking," He smirked as if in thought, "one of the Garde to do the same thing to me."

She smiled and shook her head, Nathan was turning out to be trouble with a bold T. She saw it, by a hairs breath, when Nathan and Kalbreal exchanged furious glares, it was almost annoying, that they try to get along for her sake, she despised the falseness, "When do you plan of telling me what's going on, I might not remember much but I'm certain you both know more than you claim."

Nathan turned his head, she could see people still hanging around, talking, Shapeshifter's laughed a few feet away, "Not here, Orderian are everywhere."

"Orderian? I heard Caidrian say something about them, and Advisors right?"

Kalbreal said, "Orderian are, all those who are part of the Angelic order, besides the Lightwatchers. Advisors are the prime leaders of the Lightwatcher's."

Caidrian cleared his throat, "Both my children together after all these years, embracing, Adonai has been good to us."

Nathan looked at his father, with unhidden disgust, before he stormed off. Kalbreal sped off into the mist, no sooner, like a camera trick. One minute he's there, then poof, gone. Except, this was very real, so much real, that his scent was left behind, musky and citrus, almost like grapefruit, not the cologne she smelt on William, like black rich aromatic coffee wrapped up in a decadent brand of honey, and drizzled with dried lilies, the recipe of seduction, her seduction, she thought.

The clearing of a throat brought her back from the forbidden thoughts that stirred her mind. Clare stared at Caidrian, trying very hard to keep her eyes from wandering. The way Nathan fled, and his admission of physically forcing a guy to his whim, was all she needed to know that playing juju with one another's senses was not allowed, but curiosity was a power on it's own, when she asked, with as much casualness that she could muster up, "What was that about?"

"Don't worry about it, I'm off, Nadia will walk you back."

Clare scanned the area, looking around the Bayou, to see where Nadia was. She hadn't seen her when the people had hugged her. She never really had an opportunity to speak with the girl, she barely caught a glimpse of her. Finally Clare spotted her sitting on a chair under the tree, near the lake. She waved when she saw Clare stare at her. She was just the person that Clare needed to speak to.

Clare kept her eyes strained on Nadia whilst she spoke to Caidrian, "Ya fine, see you later."

She left Caidrian and made her way to Nadia, without so much as a backward glance. A lady stopped her, by standing in her way.

The female wore a white robe, "Hello, Clarebella, I am Valeri Draiken, your mothers sister." She had a soft but daunting voice.

Clare stared at the lady, unashamedly sizing her up, and instantly hugged the woman, she didn't know why she did it, but she did, and she was going to kill Nathan, but her fuzzy brain couldn't explain the impulse of that either, urgh, she wanted to groan.

She took a few steps back. The woman did look like her mother, it was slight, but there, and she did have brown hair like Clare's, she didn't trust her feelings now that she was only conquering one emotion, so she said, "I can see the resemblance, I'm really glad to meet you, maybe we could have a talk sometime?"

Valeri smiled, sadly, "I'm a maker, we don't see our family often, mostly in death, once we are initiated, relationships are forbidden, but Franchesca's my sister, she never did anything without cause, so I presume her death served one as well." She said it looking passed Clare. Clare turned to see Kalbreal standing further down.

She didn't know what to tell Valeri, or how to? Her sister died protecting Her, so she settled with, "Thank you Valeri,"

Valeri whispered into Clare's ear, "You are a Draiken, you'll be loved by many but feared by most, with fear comes death and a high price, trust your heart, I have to go child, take care."

Clare stood there, dazed in thought, how weird was that conversation, the lady really needed to get out more, but maybe it meant something.

Nadia interrupted her, ongoing thoughts, "Hello? I don't have all day, let's go, you can daze at Adams,"

"Whose Adam?"

Nadia sighed, "You just have to find out," she pulled Clare to walk.

They stalked their way into the path going toward the trees, as people moved around them, some greeting as they walked by.

Clare's mind, too riddled in questions to notice much, "I never had a chance to speak to you, since well..."

Nadia replied, "You don't remember me, it's really not important, I'm three years older than you, we hardly trained together, though we lived together, that's it."

They continued down a road, in silence, when they reached the other side of the pathway, passing the bayou. The place was busy for a late night. Clare kept staring at Nadia, who kept pace ahead. An obvious tell, that she wanted to avoid conversation.

Clare assessed her, she was tall, not as tall as Clare was even though she wore flat boots, but like five seven.

Nadia had a small frame, with curvy hips and bigger breasts. Whereas Clare's was straight, with a solid B cup, which for a eighteen year old, with a small waist, was above average in her grade books. Nadia was definitely in the C's, at least and a great ass.

The thought made Clare a tad bit self conscious about her small figure, considering her height. Nadia's posture made her body more pronounced. She wasn't the prettiest thing in the world but she was attractive, with her shoulder length light brown hair, and hazel eyes, not forgetting the highly tanned olive skin tone. Nadia was sweet, attractive but very well guarded.

Clare asked, "What are people still doing out so late, it must be about ten?"

Nadia huffed, "It's almost eleven, they're leaving, we don't stay here." A few minutes passed, and she was ready to give up, there was no point if Nadia was going to be so evasive.

The lightwatcher surprised her, "There was an emergency meeting last night, someone's killing our kind, so they've ordered a global search for the killer, besides who's going to kill demons if we are here."

Clare stepped on her robe, "Shit, Nadia by any chance, do you have something else for me to wear."

"Yes it's all at Adams don't sweat."

They walked further up a hill, away from the busy roads, "Why is everybody so tall, and I haven't seen a fat person, not to mention, is there any guy who isn't strikingly handsome."

Nadia looked at Clare as though she was crazy, "Looks are important to you. Well for the Casters and Lightwatchers, We are descendants of Angels, we're suppose to be tall and good looking, we're part Angel. And we train constantly, which you'll start from scratch soon, five hours a day. It's almost impossible to get fat, and as for the other descendants whom aren't Angelic, they also train like us, they have a purpose, it might be a mild one and less deadly but they do have a purpose, and for the record they're not all good to look at, you haven't seen all of them, Naturahs are the most hideous of the lot, with scaly green skin."

Clare shuddered at the thought of that, "So Casters, are Nefilim, children of fallen Angels right, I thought it's just a myth, but I guess not?"

"Yes, except the children of Tempters get to choose their path, we don't." They turned right onto a road that read 'Zoid Creek',

On the right hand side was street lights that looked like floating metal lanterns, lighting the way up the steep hill.

She spotted Nathan on the top of the road. His arms opened as he screamed, in an over exerted show of relief, "FINALLY, I thought you were resurrected."

Nadia replied wryly, but just as loud, "How would you function without me kicking your ass."

They approached her brother while he yelled, on the top of the incline, "history paper, due next week, don't forget, I'm not saving your ass this time."

Clare's ear peeked at this, curiosity etched on her face, "You're studying, with all this?"

She opened her hands in the air, to gesture her point, her eyes wide, as she waited for answers. Nathan was too relaxed, and eased, so was she but she wouldn't be able to be so calm as Nathan was, no matter how deluded her senses became.

He laughed as he put his arm around her shoulder, "Sister, sister, of course I study, the brown I'm wearing symbolizes that I'm a member of the Garde, true, but I'm also a science major at the University of Washington, Final year."

Clare was amazed, "Wow how do you manage all of this, and still try to be normal?"

He said, "I accept that I'm not normal but extraordinary, plus I have a photographic memory, didn't you apply for college?"

Clare had forgotten all about school and her normal life since yesterday, "Yes Harvard, Yale and Oxford. Actually, I have or had an interview with Oxford in two weeks, don't think it really matters now."

Nathan squeezed her tight, his voice almost comical, "Of course it matters, we have to maintain normal lives, demon slaying is only our night jobs."

"But don't your'll get paid to kill demons and whatever else you guys do?"

Nathan shook his head, "We do get allowances, according to our status, and we have inheritance, money isn't really a problem for descendants from any race, but some of us choose to work in the world. Obviously, there're some who don't, like Caidrian, he's second in command, and head leader of the Washington faculty, he chooses not to have any contact with the deceptors, but for me I see it important we blend in with them. We can learn from them. Most of our kind tend to stay away from them. I feel there's a lot to learn, if we just listened, but nonetheless, all younger Lightwatchers are forced by the Advisors to study in the deceptors schools, further education is your choice."

"That's the most words I've heard you speak, what's the point if you don't need education?"

"How else do we keep our kind a secret, besides what better way of spying on our enemies, especially if they think we're deceptors."

Nadia stood there with her legs slightly apart, in her robe, and her boobs sticking out. Clare couldn't help just looking at them, there was seriously something messed up about this, she was so going to kill Nathan tomorrow,

"Come on guys, party's inside."

Clare repeated, "Party? I'm so not dressed for a party."

Eleven

Adams turned out to be a double storey building, covered in grey rocks, which made up the walls of the outside, like the Scottish stone houses.

When they entered it, Clare saw a huge flat screen television, showing a football match in full swing, as lots of people scattered around, talking, dancing to the loud rock song playing. Some just lounged on maroon couches, whilst others stood, eating, drinking and screaming strings of sailors words, it was no doubt a party scene.

The place looked human, and ordinary, young people lurked around, ranging from ages between eighteen to thirties, maybe. Waiters took orders. The people who stood out, on the left corner reminded her of where she was, the Elvan, who still wore their robes.

Majority of the people blended in with her brother, wearing brown, some wore normal jeans and t-shirts. The Shapeshifter's hogged the pool tables at the back, she loved the blue hair, she wondered what they did with it in the real world.

She sighed, "This place is awesome."

Alonso touched her back as she walked further into the place, toward the wooden tables and chairs on the left, she turned, "Hey, dude,"

He handed her a bag and smiled. When he did this, his eyes seemed to stand out more, she wanted to laugh, at her wayward thought, but held it in, "Compliments from Nadia."

She took the pack, "Thanks dude, what is this place?"

"It's a joint, like a hangout place for students mostly, they serve a mean steak, if you're hungry, come on it's too crowded here lets go upstairs."

She followed him up two flights of green neon tiled stairs. Giving the bottom floor one last and quick scan because she hadn't seen where Nathan disappeared too.

The upstairs of Adams place had soft music playing, and dimmed purple lights coming from behind a large circular shape fish tank. On the right side, a small flat screen TV hung on the wall, which served no purpose, at the moment.

Nearer to her, was what looked like white couches designed to represent a huge almost full on circle made to surround a rounded low rise table.

She spotted Nathan, Kalbreal, and Nadia, seated on opposite ends.

Alonso bumped her, "It's great right?"

She agreed, but didn't face him. "Definitely, I'm going to change," noticing the bathroom straight away, because of the sign.

The bathroom was simple with a lime green toilet and sink. She changed into her clothes, a blue shirt which was on the big side and denim jeans, which was a little too short and fit like three quarters.

Clare opened her hair, and walked out of the bathroom, barely managing to back up a step, before she hit into his chest, "Kalbreal, do you want to use the bathroom? Or do you just get the thrill of burning my skin."

He looked ridiculed "I was waiting for you,"

"Oh, really, why?"

He searched her face, she could see the redness in his eyes, the flicker of gold on his irises. They were so beautiful, she almost didn't see them stopping at her lips.

Her pulse seemed to race, as his mouth opened slightly. His eyes narrowed when she dropped hers, instantly, to look away from him, "We need to discuss something. Privately."

He opened the bathroom door, just expecting her to cower to his demand, and waited for her to go back inside. When they did, he opened the sink taps wide, "Franchesca was no patriarch or warrior, but when she died she became much more than that, I would see to it that she gets a good place in my home, but I'm afraid her death would be for nothing." He ran his fingers through his hair, she could tell he was agitated, "you see there's other Angels on the earth, a few actually." He moved a step closer to her, and then hesitated, "I don't know where the others are, but I do know of one's whereabouts."

She could smell alcohol on him, it wasn't strong, but clouded by his strong distinctive seductive scent. Something she wasn't familiar with, but he didn't look the least bit drunk, he just seemed haunted with worries.

His mouth didn't twist into a smile either, as it had a few times, and he blinked way too often for a normal guy, "Okay." She said, "If you want to talk that's fine, but what does the angels presence have to do with me or my mother, is it something to do with my brother, Calub."

"No. One of them might be after you, which is why I need you to be safe, I know you're looking for people to trust, but right now I suggest the only person you can trust is your brother, he'll protect you."

"What about William?"

Kalbreal put his hand on his face, and peeped at her through his index and middle finger, "He doesn't count, he isn't the most reliable when it comes to women."

"What is that suppose to mean?" Kalbreal looked up at the bathroom ceiling, "He's helping because of loyalties to your mother, and myself, you can't trust one who refuses to meet you."

"How do you know that."

His tone was defensive, Clare could tell she hit a nerve, if he had any, "I'm an Angel I know things, now why are we talking about someone who you don't even know."

She could see something flicker in his eyes, the annoyance in his voice, "If you're going to be jealous at least make an effort first."

His cheeks flushed, even for an Angel he couldn't hide it, "Nobody has ever said that to me before."

"Well maybe they just haven't had reason to," she replied with as much sarcasm she could muster, watching his body movement.

The bathroom was small for a big man like Kalbreal, but there was place to move around, instead he stayed near her, without actually touching her.

She could see the lines on his chest, his shirt unbuttoned on the top, and the long bridge of his neck. The sharpness of his chin that curved at just the right angle, was enough to make a woman bend to her knees. The plush of his lips that promised for the best seduction, was his wickedest feature, and finally she reached his flaming eyes. So unreal, the guy was gorgeous, regardless of his piercings there was no denying the obvious, though he didn't make her feel the way William did, but she would play along.

"Do you have wings Kalbreal?"

"Yes."

"Can I see them?"

He laughed, "They need space, they are really hot, BUT without your name you won't be able to see it, it'll blind you."

"You mean the name on my skin right? If you want to say no, just say it."

He moved closer to her, she took a step back, until her back was flat against the bathroom door. He placed his hand on the wall beside her head, making the hairs on her neck stand up at the close contact. His heat seeping from his skin, imprisoning her.

"I don't want to say no, let me pick you up tomorrow, show you around." Kalbreal's eyes were so appealing, unyielding in its request, but she wasn't going to give into his temptations so easily, this feeling wasn't like what she felt for William, this was strange.

"First, I'm not your type and now you want to take me on a date, the day after I just lost my mother."

He dropped his hand, but kept his eyes focused on hers, showing no attempt to rekindle its course. The hollows in his face and the piercings in his ears were stark at the close distance. Taking a closer look at his ear, they weren't piercings, but small shining tattoos on his skin, it was part of his flesh, a shiny silver metal.

He was no doubt an un-captured beauty, "No, not a date, just a tour, I find you fascinating Clarebella." He paused, it was the second time he had called her that, "I was married before, not so long ago, and she was taken from me, you remind me of her. I wished to touch your skin the other day, it had been years..."

Kalbreal's eyes dropped to the floor, he didn't continue with what he was going to say, she exhaled a burst of warm carbon dioxide. Clare turned her head to the left, her hair falling in her eyes. She wanted to push it back, but his gaze was so captivating, so unrealistically burning. Was it arousal, or need, or hunger, she couldn't tell, but all of a sudden she felt like the room just got fifty degrees hotter. "But without your name on your skin it'll never be possible, the heavenly fire in my veins will burn through you with one touch."

She didn't know what to say by the little peak into his life, he had given her, "I'm sorry to hear about your wife, she would've had to be perfect to marry you, but you shouldn't compare me to her." She didn't know what she had expected from Kalbreal, but this was certainly not it, "I'm not sure if sightseeing alone with you is a good idea, as you said, trust issues."

"I am ageless, I have patience."

She muttered, "I don't doubt that."

She fanned her face, and took a painful swallow of saliva, "Is there anything else Angel-boy, I'm kinda hungry."

"Yes, tomorrow one of those Angels are going to attend the meeting with the Orderian, I'll try to summon another Harpien blade tonight, in the event I tell you to run, you need to listen, do you understand."

"Am I that transparent or is it you super mind-reading skills?"

Kalbreal closed the water by the sink after he washed his hands, his eyes finally moved off her, "I can't read minds, I'm made from fire, it has its perks but also limits, but I hear you are quite the stubborn one."

She thought it was interesting, because she was certain, William had read her mind, and he was a Caster, she thought of saying something, but shrugged it off, "That's me, what's a Harpien blade?"

"Angel blades, made from the Infinity. As Angels, we can summon them at will, there was once a time you knew them better than any Lightwatcher around."

"Seriously, I feel like all my memories are lost forever." She meant to be sarcastic but it came out tired.

He closed the window behind the toilet, "It's for the best, trust me."

"As stupid as it sounds, I kinda do, to an extent." She said, lying coolly, "I'm meeting with the Orderian, my brother's out there, somewhere being tortured and god knows what else is being done to him, I feel it's my duty to save him or die trying, just thought you should know."

There was a knock on the door and Kalbreal vanished into thin air, before she got to asking about Calub. Her body tensed and she paused with her hand on the door knob, gathering herself up.

Nathan stood with his legs apart in the front of the doors frame, he peeped at her threw his hair, which was full over his eyes brushing his cheeks. Clare could see that he himself had a dangerous deadly spark to him. He had that bad streak, which woman craved, just like Kalbreal, accept both of them were made from light, and yet-

"Come on, little sister, let's eat."

She walked a few steps when he gripped her arm, her breath caught from surprise. He bridged the gap between them, whispering into her ear, "Kalbreal is an Angel but I wouldn't trust him with your life and neither should you."

She nodded, speechless, because yet again, she found herself thinking that her brother was a smart ass, who never missed anything. She wanted to tell him that Kalbreal told her to trust only him, but that would've been awkward considering what he just said, but she didn't deny facts, and it surely felt good to have an older brother looking out for her, even a possessive one like Nathan.

Nathan let her go as they approached the couches, "Come on, I want you to meet Adam, he's a partial shifter, one of the Fuized, awesome guy."

Clare followed her brother to a door which led to a kitchen. She stuck her head inside the door frame.

A few guys cooked, as flames sizzled. They all looked ordinary at first, but the longer she stared, the more she noticed. The guy who stood washing dishes, and whistling, his eyes were enlarged like an ants might be if it were his size. His head shaped in an elongated cone.

Her brother bumped her, getting her attention instantly. Guilt written all over her face from staring, and he shook his head. She knew he was telling her to cut it out.

He spoke loudly, to no one in particular, "Where's Adam?"

A soft sweet man's voice replied from the back, "You late what happened, bro."

Clare followed the voice, it was the guy who was walking towards her. Pulling her into a bear hug, her response was automatic.

Adam smelt like Chinese food, his blue hair shorter than the other shifters, and his blue eyebrow hair thicker than average. He had brown eyes, and a tattoo on his neck. She couldn't make out what it was, beside the v shape peeking out.

Adam queried, "Clare right? Your brother hasn't shut up about meeting you for the past week."

Nathan laughed and walked to stand next to the guy, he was several inches shorter than Nathan, "Don't scare my sister away."

Adam looked around Clare, curious to what he was looking for, she turned around to see what he was so interested in, but she was lost,

Adam looked at Nathan, "Where's Calub, I made chow mien for him, with the blue cheese he likes."

Nathan's happiness left him as quick as it came. Clare could see that pain and sorrow on her brothers expression, but there was also something else, that she couldn't quite put her finger on.

She decided, and blurted it out, "He's been kidnapped."

Adam was undoubtedly puzzled, "What? Serious? We should go find him, come on." he hurried out the kitchen.

Nathan going after him, "Adam, there's no use, word is that he's in the Demon realms, and the Garde won't send any of their own."

Clare was shocked, and puzzled, "What? I didn't know that, I thought.."

Nathan interrupted, "You thought wrong Clare, Caidrian would've told you anything to get you here."

Adam added clearly worried, "Rumor has it that Calub's not your brother."

Clare laughed at him, but uncertainty filled inside her just as sudden, "What? No, Caidrian would have told me, you would've told me."

She looked at Nathan, who just shrugged, "Of course Calub's my brother, he's a Draiken, right."

Nathan stared at her, if she guessed by his expression, he was angry, her eyes searched for clues in his frown, waiting, "Yes, he's a Draiken, this isn't the time to talk about this, that's only speculation."

Adam scratched his head. He was wearing a black t-shirt and black jeans, no apron. The kitchen smelt flavorsome, first the steak, and then noodles and hot cheese, even chicken, it was making her stomach burn in hunger, her mouth watery, she conceded, "Fine, we can talk about it later, but I want to know the truth, no more bullshit."

Nathan dropped his head, the lines between his eyebrows still squashed together forcefully, "It shouldn't matter if he's biological or not, he's still missing."

She figured maybe it was a good time to just drop it, she would find out eventually, "I'm starved, I need to eat."

Clare gulped her food down, which consisted of steak and fries, in minutes. She sat in the corner on one of the couches, ignoring the other's who were clearly pre-occupied talking amongst themselves. Since they had left the kitchen, Nathan and her hadn't spoke much.

Kalbreal was still missing in action, but it didn't bother her, in fact she was more at ease eating when he wasn't there, she knew he'd probably stare at her. What he'd said in the bathroom made her cautious and worried her, but knowing parts of her were confused because not only had she lost her mother, her brother was missing.

She weren't really in the mood for romance, but with it said, she couldn't help the images of the stranger playing up in her mind, William, and his hands splayed on her breast. The way he brushed the sides, and the touch of his skin on her fingers, just the thought of it now made her want to just say his name aloud, find excuses to bring him up.

Finding out she was a Lightwatcher, and sitting with a bunch of new faces, not knowing who truly to trust, was enough to focus on. She thought of William, and the intensity of their encounters. It was as if she feared acknowledging or deciphering what she felt, her mind purposefully shutting out thoughts of him, with everything else going on in it. He had saved her, twice in one day, yet had no interest in meeting her, no want or attempt to tell her his name. But his words hung on her like a wind chime, made to move in the direction it was pushed, "See you soon princess", why,

"CLARE." Nathan screamed, making her jerk back into her seat, and squirmed, "FOCUS."

He kept his eyes on her until she rolled hers, and mumbled an apology, "The Orderian are arriving, they're going to want to speak with you."

She faced him, her plate empty on her lap. The purple light in the room making her eyes droop, her naturally dry voice seemed more distinct, when she said, "So what should I do?"

Nathan smiled, "Well sister." He handed her a glass of soda, "That's the reason why we're here, to discuss our plan of action, unfortunately I'm banned from speaking to the Orderian, don't ask me why."

"Fine, but first I wanna know why you and Caidrian are fighting?" He sat back, sinking in the chair, "We agree to disagree that's all."

"That's it? for a brother I really know nothing about you, besides that you surely know how to keep up with mystery."

He sat up straight, Alonso and Nadia clearly arguing about something, "Clare people change, you should remember that, that's all you need to know about Caidrian and I."

She was distracted by a young guy who approached them, bronzed skin, with distinctive light almost yellowish green eyes. His walk tailored to his narrow build. He acknowledged Nathan with a courteous bow of the head, and ignored the others. He was attractive, not as tall as her brother, but strikingly gorgeous, in a beautiful way. He looked like what one thought an Angel should look like, except for the bands around his wrist and huge ring on his index finger, "Hello, Clare, I'm Vincent Ipswich." His accent was thick medieval, maybe a bit British.

He extended his hand, which she took almost immediately, stumbling on her words, "hi, uh..I'm Clare." seating himself directly next to Nathan, he smirked.

She rolled her eyes, *'I'm Clare.' How much more of an idiot, can I sound, jeez,* She thought.

Alonso's eyes staggered in their direction, "What's Vincent doing here, I wasn't aware that we were meeting with the Nefilim?" Nathan's eyes widened, his back straightened up, clearly upset, "Watch yourself Alonso, he's my friend, I requested his presence, if you don't like it, I suggest you leave."

Her brother held Alonso's gaze, and so did Alonso. There was something perturbing about the situation. Nadia didn't seem to notice, she was too busy doing something on her cell-phone.

Vincent settled himself back into the chair, and carelessly started to play drumming beats with the pads of his fingers on the armrest of the sofa, "I don't care for childishness, call me what you will, it is I who shall out live you after all."

He gave Alonso a light smile, which didn't reach his eyes, before his attention focused on her and Nathan, "What's the problem, why couldn't you call Jullie?"

Nathan ignored his question, "Clare's approaching the Orderian tomorrow, I'm sure you aware of the news circling around."

Clare watched the two of them pass certain stares at one another. Nathan and Vincent looked a little too preoccupied in looking at each other, it was like a silent conversation taking place, she gestured, "Are you dating each other?"

Nathan smacked her head, she screeched, "Shit, why did you do that."

"Because you talking crap, and we exchanging info telepathically, its quicker."

Vincent laughed mildly before straightening his expression, "I'm versatile though."

He looked at her with alluring eyes. An unwanted blush crept in her cheeks. His tan complexion, and dangerously masculine features, the guy was hot, but he wasn't a guy she would go for.

"Seriously, Vincent," A familiar voice echoed, throughout the room.

Clare almost knocked the plate off her knees, but managed to grab it just in time and put it down on the table, before turning to the person in the room, "Where did you come from?"

Kalbreal didn't answer her, instead he shook his head, a scowl marred his face, "He's nine hundred years old, and a Caster."

Clare sighed, "Then you must be like what? Moving in the thousands?"

Nathan stopped both of them, "We're here to discuss the situation, both of you drop it, tomorrow at the court there's going to be a representative of the Advisors, it unclear who it's gonna be, but my guess whoever it is, might try and force authority, so that's where Vincent comes in."

Alonso walked toward them, "We still need permission from the Orderian and the Garde to go to the demon realms."

Nadia disagreed, "Not necessarily, If the Casters agree, their decision would over ride the other Orderian because it's partially their realm. Then It'll be a vote from the Lightwatchers.

Vincent smiled, "You've done your homework, but I'm not representing the Caster's tomorrow."

Kalbreal interjected, "Yes you are, Druscilla isn't attending, she's in Vancouver, and Jullie is unavailable."

Vincent muffled a string of curses, "I know I'm going to regret this."

Kalbreal tightened his lips, it was the first time Clare saw him look irritated, "I'll pay you, handsomely."

Everybody was quiet, all eyes on Vincent, "Okay, but Clare should approach them ALONE. Draiken women always have a way with words."

Clare wasn't certain she heard correctly, she couldn't believe he really expected her to talk to people she didn't know, alone. I mean they weren't even real people, they were a different species, plus her encounter with the few descendants she had met, it hadn't been the most comforting of situations. In fact she was certain that she made more enemies than friends.

Kalbreal agreed, "He's right, if they're going to be persuaded you should be the one."

Alonso challenged, "Say she does, what if they refuse, We are famous for our stubbornness."

Vincent got up, "I'll give my vote, and I would even try to persuade the Queen but your people, THAT's up to you."

The room fell silent after the conversation. Vincent left and Nathan smiled at Clare every now and then as they ate chocolate cake.

Nathan ran his fingers in his hair, which was already so messed up. Her eyes carried from one side to the other, every time he did it. He was irritated and on edge, and by the undisguised disgust on his face whenever he put eyes on Alonso, told her that any thought she had of Alonso and Nathan being friends were completely off course, because he clearly didn't like Alonso at all.

Nathan stood up and took her plate, "Give me five minutes and we'll leave, you must be tired."

He got up and went to the back, as he did this Kalbreal moved closer. She looked at his rich fire full eyes as they glowed in the lights, his jaw tightened, "Were you seriously born with eyes like that, it just seems... unnatural."

"To earthling, yes, but not in the Infinity."

"Infinity, you mean heavens."

"You may call it that." Just when she thought he would elaborate, he casually changed the subject, "I have this feeling about today, but I don't know whether it's good or not, but you should be careful." He said, "Do you plan on getting acquainted with this place, OR are you going to make me hang?"

She laughed at him, "Seriously, people don't use big words when they speak, and maybe I'll make you hang just a tiny bit longer, just to help you along with that over confident ego you got going on." He threw his head back and laughed, it was an unaltered laugh, the tension in the room seemed to dissipate almost instantly.

She stretched out her arms, when she rose from the couch, chuffed with the bit of glee she brought Angel-boy.

Peaking at Kalbreal, his neck extended as he stared at her, "But since you offered to take me sightseeing twice, how can I not." She walked away, smiling at his stunned reaction.

"Nathan, Nathan." Yelling, she neared the kitchen door, she was exhausted, the sleep kicking in,

The kitchen doors burst open, Nathan emerged through it, like the place was on fire, "What's happening?"

She smirked at him, he looked so disheveled, "Let's go I'm tired, I'm sure the Suns risen,"

"Clare, shit, sister, I thought somebody was strangling you, patience, it's not even two yet."

She turned to look at Kalbreal, his voice soft, and husky, "Come on lets go stand downstairs,"

She hesitated for a second, then Kalbreal said to Nathan, "Relax, I can't even touch her remember?" before she followed him downstairs.

Waiting in the middle of the steps, Kalbreal offered, "Lemme get you a drink while you wait for him."

He gave her a slight smirk, which she appreciated, considering their prior discussion. The guy was clearly hitting on her, and he was an Angel, she should've been happy and excited, but she wasn't, she could see herself becoming friends with Kalbreal, but anything more than that, No.

William had already left his mark, faceless or not, even if he was a beast, there was just something about him that called to her, and until she figured it out, she was off limits, "I guess it'll depend on the drink?"

Kalbreal laughed, "Are you flirting with me?"

She dismissed his ignorance, "I never know with you, whether its kindness or something else, but with me, you'd know if I'm flirting."

Nathan chuckled, behind her, "I have the exact same problem." Putting his arm over her shoulder as he spoke. Her gaze wavered to Kalbreal, searching his expression, but all she saw was his blazing eyes as he stared at her face in clear confusion and uncertainty pinned perfectly together.

Nathan gestured with his head to Kalbreal, "I'll take the bin out for Adam if I were you."

"Oh, yeah, I forgot, maybe I should take out the trash, I am an Angel after ALL." Kalbreal responded in a rehearsed tone.

Clare tried hard to stifle a giggle, Nathan just smiled wide mouthed, showing his teeth, which was perfectly straight, "Really, you going to go there NOW, that was four years ago, I was young."

Clare burst out laughing by her brother's exasperated look, "What's that about,"

He noticed her and said almost faintly, "A private joke, but let's just say it didn't end well."

Clare knew when somebody was lying or hiding something, and Nathan was definitely holding something back and so was Angel-boy.

"Nathan, door is that way," She said, pointing her finger towards left.

"Nah, there's a quicker way,"

"Ok."

Clare was too tired to argue, or ask any more questions, she needed a hot bath and some rest. Following him to the bar area, she watched as he moved a silver handle on the wooden counter and the bar shelves started to separate. The alcohol bottles didn't fall off the shelves, but rattled as they touched on each other.

It revealed a tunnel, a dark, pitch black one. She blinked and failed to readjust her eyes, she was that tired, "Wow, cool, what's this, a tunnel or secret passageway?"

Nathan amused her, "You're correct to both, it's a tunnel that leads to a secret passageway."

She followed Nathan into the tunnel. He said something, and a light burnt on the tunnel walls, visioning the way. Walking through, they turned left. The walls made of dried clay, ancient, not much decorated the walls, besides a few flowers she saw drawn on the clay, in what looked like crayon.

The tunnel smelt like desert sand, the temperature cool, it was clean and well maintained, "What does this writing mean?"

Nathan turned, and curled the corner of his mouth, as if she'd asked a question of utter importance, "Where one sin has entered, Legions will force their way through the same breach."

He paused before continuing, "It was written by a very extra-ordinary Lightwatcher, his name was John Rogers, early 1700's."

"Is there something to it?"

He faced her, hesitated, "Maybe another time, let's get moving." He turned and kept a steadied pace a little ahead of her. They didn't walk much further from the second left, before they came to a wooden door with bolts decorating its frame.

Nathan knocked a few times, the door unlatched itself and opened fully. Clare followed him closely, snapping his fingers, small freckles of light twinkled brightly in the room bringing light to the darkness.

"Where are we?" She asked as he rushed towards another door, on the other side of the room. She followed quickly behind him giving one last peak at the lights, "We're at the castle, right?"

"Yup, that was my room, in-case you ever need a quick escape," He walked a few rooms down and opened the double door, which opened into a larger room.

Nathan clapped his hands twice, and lanterns lit the expanse, with white and blue lights mirroring the walls in tiny circles, "Lightwatcher's generally need to sleep one cycle every month, depending on how strong you are, unless you've been injured critically, then your body might go into Shakara, a healing state where you could be out for months."

"How long's a cycle?"

"Twenty four hours."

"So you can stay up for weeks without sleeping at all, WOW.."

He nodded, "Yes, but there's more to it."

Clare lifted her chin up towards the ceiling, that was almost thirty feet high. The floor was white stoned with small crystals embedded in it forming spirals of red and navy blue color, "WHAT? No, that's crazy, Mom use to sleep every night, you're clearly messing with me."

"No, she wouldn't have been able to. A Lightwatcher's body tells us when to sleep, it's not something you can force, it's like peeing, you can't just do it can you?"

"So what happens if the Garde need to sleep in the middle of a battle?"

"Don't know, it's never happened, how's the room?"

"It's amazing, this whole place is incredible."

"Well good you like it. It's your new room, for now." The door closed behind Nathan when he left, almost instantly.

She spun herself around the room, visioning her mother smiling happily at her. She spun until her knees collapsed. Time passed, and the drug induced feeling faded, overwhelmed by the sudden downward spiral she burst out crying, "What am I going to do without you mom."

Twelve

L iam
The car window went up again, Liam was certainly doing his bit to annoy the driver, "Why in the realms couldn't we just teleport the whole way, or use the entry in Africa." She honked the hooter again, fury torched her eyes to a golden circle of crushed glass. Liam had gotten used to his sister's driving in the 1900'S.

He was too distracted in keeping them both from being tracked to really bother about the traffic that left them jammed in the centre of Southampton, London, or so she thought,

in actual fact...

He was pathetically mooning over Clare. His meeting with Kalbreal hadn't went as smoothly as he had hoped, it left him re-questioning his better judgment. It was a new habit he had grown accustomed to of late, but he couldn't get her out of his mind.

Having watched her for months, wanting to meet her, talk to her. Refraining himself from actually doing it, was the hardest part, but now after Kalbreal had confessed, his gravest concerns proved to be far worse. Liam knew now, he had no choice but to be close to her, it was the only way she would be protected. But if he did, was he to hold back, was she really worth it. All this trouble, that he now faced, solely to protect her. A visioned face of hungry green eyes drowsed as they searched for his, the permanent curve of her lips opening as he held her at the bayou. A scent of breath captured from her mouth when she gasped for him, honey mixed with luscious berries, assaulted his senses.

Her bodies response to him was a normal thing. Woman swooned over him, some dug out their eyes, just looking at his hands. However, it wasn't the case with his Princess, it wasn't one sided. They were linked in ways he didn't wish to comprehend just yet. The connection between them like a magnet made specifically to unite them as one. Once attached, he knew the magnet contained an unyielding glue, which will bind them for eternity.

But he could repel the magnet, at least for a little while longer, it was those damn breast that haunted him the most. She liked his touch, even in her innocence, her boldness in keeping his hand there, under the curve of her perky breast, it awakened something in him with every remembrance. A feeling that he himself thought would never rise.

His sister yelled him to attention, hitting her hands on his thigh, "Great, now you just ignore me, leave the window alone."

"You should have more patience at your age, but it just seems to worsen by the decade, no wonder Kole call's you a little vixen."

She didn't meet his eyes when he faced her, but her tone was serious, "Kalbreal told me what happened last night, Clare's body rejecting Franchesca's gifts. I knew it was her, the bearer and all, she's just so different, so deceptor-ish, you should have told me first." She turned into a small road, agitated.

She'd been more snippy recently, but he knew not to pry, his sister was the one woman who didn't like to share. He was going to have to dig it out of her slowly.

Liam's attention focused on the road ahead as they drove in a black BMW 3 series. Not wanting to draw in too much attention to themselves, "There was nothing to tell, I only confirmed my suspicions this morning, that's why we need to get to Asguard, once I'm inside, you'll have 2 days to get to her and please don't frighten her, she's vulnerable."

A solemn smile on her lips, "You seriously going to do this? The hero is suppose to rescue the maiden not send his sister, and ambush his brother into helping."

Liam sighed, "He probably knows, when have you known him not to dabble."

"Since he came back, something's changed, he's lost. He gets calls from the Da Vinci boy a lot, it makes it worse."

"Interesting, I'll look into it, he'll be fine. I'll talk to him as soon as things cool off, I promise."

They parked off onto a dead end, the road quiet, no one in view. She shifted gears, and drove into the wall, through the portal he made, and landed walking distance from the Stonehenge.

It was piles of rocks put together childishly, but an astonishing phenomenon to the deceptors. In actual fact it was one of the door ways to Asguard, not that it wasn't a mutable sight but Liam knew what lay beyond those doors, and he didn't like it, not one bit.

London was cold and dry, but he hadn't minded the weather since his body didn't respond to cold weather at all. It was midday and not a glitch of sun greeted the country top.

He wasn't one to admire anything earthly, he thought it a waste of time and admiration, especially for one who'd seen far beyond the boundaries of the known universe.

They jumped out of the car, and walked up the hill covered in grass. His black Italian silk pants showed as the wind blew his coat open. It also revealed the concealed weapons he carried, mostly two long swords, fitted neatly in a weapons belt, dangling on the sides of his legs, a precautionary, just in case things got complicated.

"We could've waited a few days." She muttered, "I really don't see what the rush is about."

Jullie was one who fussed and complained most of the time, except when things got really serious, but Liam trusted his sister and time again she proved her worth and her loyalties more times he cared to recount.

He confessed, keeping his pace, and long leg strides toward the stones, "She's becoming Lightwatcher again, but she has no name, the necklace is supposed to help with that, but now it's missing, these Angels are here solely for her, the Tempters won't be long behind."

Jullie stopped in her tracks, "That's impossible, a Lightwatcher with no name, Kalbreal doesn't even know that, does he? He believes that she'll stay deceptor."

"He doesn't need to. I figured it out a while back, it was confirmed once Kalbreal filled in the blanks. I need to figure out what the Asguardians know about the Angels and their reason for entering earth. I think it has something to do with the killings, they somehow connected as you said. Kalbreal's still hiding something, I need to know what, he isn't going to just tell me, this is the only option."

Jullie nodded, "How long does she have?"

"It's been weeks, she could have a couple more, it's hard to say exactly. I've never encountered this particular situation before."

They reached the Stonehenge, without a word, Jullie silenced by the news. She stopped to roll up her black jeans and straighten the collar of her loose black shirt. Her hair was tied up in a messy bun, and her boots now replaced by a nude Jimmy Choo stiletto, she had no make-up on but her skin was still flawless.

"This is it," Her Australian accent always reminded him of his mother, he brushed the thought off.

"I'll be fine, Julliette, they can't really hurt me, I'll see you in L.A."

"PLEASE, Be careful El, if you not back soon I'm coming to get you."

He rubbed at her chin, his head bent down to see his sister's small lips curve up. Her light small green worried eyes wishing he wouldn't do it, he knew that she hated the idea, "You worry too much, just like our mother," he kissed her nose, he never denied his siblings affection.

"Well somebody has to do it especially at the rate you're carrying on."

He wanted to tell her more, but he knew Jullie better than she knew herself, she pretended she could handle all that weight on her shoulders but it was eating her inside out, he feared what might become of her.

Once she knew, the whole truth, all of it, would she still be Jullie, he turned away from her, "I want a full course meal when I get back."

"Then you better hurry up brother."

She cut her hand with a small stone she picked up from the grass, and rubbed her blooded Palm flat on the Stonehenge. The stones absorbed the red liquid leaving no evidence that the blood had stained its grey blanket. She closed her eyes and in the old language said, "By the blood of my mother."

She walked to the side parallel to the one she stood.

Liam's eyes fixated on the distant view, as he prepared himself to enter the holy grounds.

It had been years since he last visited other realms, in fact, it was decades since he visited any realms until Khiron, now Asguard, it was still all too familiar with him.

Jullie opened her eyes, "It's not working, try your blood."

"Too risky, it'll work, give it time."

The Stonehenge shook, rattling like an earthquake. The stones started attaching to one another, enlarging in length, like gigantic LEGOS pairing together.

Liam stood with his legs slightly apart and his hands in his pocket, completely un-affected by this extraordinary occurrence. His black straight hair blew partially in his face, but he did not move or lift his hand to move the hindrance from his view.

What stood in front of them, was not rocks just laying around, but rocks that transformed into a lively beast- The guardian of the doorway.

Liam moved a step into view of the guardian. Jullie hid away behind a small hill top further below, by his instructions.

The guardian bowed his head at Liam, "Should I be concerned for the protection of those whom I guard."

Liam's eyes narrowed at the beastly stoned creature, as if the beast had insulted him, which he did, "Do you wish to stop me from entering."

"I cannot stop you, but those who do not know and cannot see, will harm you, is that what you choose?"

Liam stared up at the Stonehenge creature. It was piles of rock put together with no eyes only a mouth, if you would call a crack in the rock one, though it held the soul of the guardian. He looked behind him, checking to see the distance his sister had gone, and whether she was safe or not.

His hair settled back onto his neck, in its perfectly layered nape length, and he straightened his body as he stepped closer to the Stonehenge. The Stonehenge was an incredible six feet taller in height than he was, but Liam didn't deter and glared into its view, "Vasteal, what happens beyond my entering, you can not intervene, no matter what. You are to hide your knowledge of me, seal this doorway." His voice was hoarse and commanding, and to the guardian it was final.

The creature responded in action, its shape reformed and every rock of its body joined together forming a square arch, revealing the doorway. A white milky liquid appeared in the centre of the archway, taking the full shape of the square. Liam did not hesitate before he entered through the milky liquid, inhaling the familiar scent of musk and taking his leap into the Angelic realm, as the light around him sucked him in like a vacuum.

The air was purer and easier to breathe in Asguard, compared to the deceptors land. He jumped down, knowing there was a drop, and landed on the roof top of the golden empire. He stood there, to look out at that which was all too familiar to ignore. He stared across him, and then to the sky. It was no surprise that it was light blue, clouds never formed in the atmosphere of Asguard.

The land was a virgin to global warming and pollution, it was the purest place on the earths' plane. Asguard didn't rain, and it never ran out of water. Asguard was built solely for pleasure, and outstretched with rows of golden empires, all too similar to know the difference, like Khiron, and other realms. Which was why, he liked to stay with deceptors.

If you had been a new comer, it might've been inevitable for one to get lost. The trick was to look at the windows, some were crested in yellow and lime gems, others had a stone or two in a different shade. The one he searched for was further up land, with a white diamond on the far left, because he was the one who put it there.

He spotted Asguardians further North, as he moved to the end of the roof and checked around, making certain that he was out of sight. When he was satisfied that he wouldn't be seen, he jumped down, his coat lifting up behind him.

He landed flat on his feet from the fifty foot drop, dusted himself, straightened his charcoal coat. Placing his hands in his pocket, he strolled up the narrow path that was made from yellow gems, known as citrine.

He came across a few Asguardian children who smiled up at him. They were playing with alexandrite stones, confusing the colors with tricks of the light, whilst the other's guessed what color it would be next. He remembered playing the game when he was younger, but what seemed like yesterday had been worlds ago.

Asguard, unlike the other realms, was favored in its architecture, made specifically for the Angels' children. Rare gems laid to place their feet, whilst white spring waters glittered with radiance to bath in, even the silks which they wrapped on their body had been from the fourth of Infinity itself. But with all these comforts, Asguardians always wanted to return home, return to the Infinity, rise as an Angel and stand beside their own.

He lifted up a metal stick that was laid next to the ruby door, and rang it on the doors gem, making a soft melody noise.

The softest tune of humming birds played through the empire. He placed the iron stick back to the ground.

When the door opened, he hadn't straightened his back, the Asguardian in a black cotton robe showed himself, "Speak child, it better be important."

Liam straightened his back slowly, whispering royal blue eyes peeping through locks of black hair, which dangled in his face, he slid his fingers combing his hair back, eyes almost bored by the unappealing sight of the man, "You don't know who I am."

The man's snarled, his hazel eyes enveloping on Liam's gaze, "Why should I know you, Caster."

"Not accurate, but an," Liam's face lightened as he contemplated his words, "excellent effort."

The man was broader than Liam appeared to be, bulky muscle like Kalbreal, he looked in his thirties, but you never knew for sure with this breed. His hair was still ash blonde and no heavy circles surrounded his eye sockets.

Liam pushed the guy into the house and slammed the door shut behind him, his eyes engraved on the man, "You are going to do exactly as I tell you, do you understand."

Clare

A loud siren was what sprung her up, almost falling off the bed. Clare woke up to a familiar place, but not familiar enough. It wasn't London, it definitely wasn't the holiday apartment she and her mother had stayed a few nights ago. This was spacious, way too colorful compared to her mother's white obsession, and unreal, but nevertheless it was no stranger to her eyes.

The soft cushions underneath her body was confusing as she was unaware of how she gotten into the king size bed when she couldn't recall leaving the floor.

The room was dimmed with rays of sunlight shinning in through the slits of the red velvet curtains, concealing wide stretched windows. She estimated their height of more than fifteen meters. The room itself was bigger than her entire house in Cambridge.

Her gaze darted around the expanse, as she wriggled herself to the right side of the bed. Closing her eyes, she prayed, "Please, let this be a really bad dream, please, I swear I'll behave."

Part of her knew what she'd find once she opened her eyes, so she didn't need reality to sink in before she flung the blankets off. Padding her way across the room she opened the curtains.

The siren stopped, but her ears still rang with the noise. Standing in front of a glass mirrored door which led to a balcony, she stared at her reflection. Recognizing herself, the same messed up teenager, just more messed up than before, because now she was motherless as well, but wait not orphaned, because just before she lost her mother, she had found her father, what a happy story.

Hatred crept up into her veins at the ridicule of it. It all sounded like the perfect happily ever after, but the reality of it sucked.

Why was she being punished, or was she?

She felt torn, because parts of her felt betrayed, lied to. Even now, things were kept from her, but there were also the other parts, which never felt more alive, parts which craved to be like them, the Lightwatcher's.

Still wearing the jeans and t-shirt from yesterday, her hair tangled in a mass of knots, she looked like shit, she felt worse. But she still opened the door and stepped onto the high balcony.

Whilst the suns heat penetrated her skin, there was not much warmth to work with, but it did the job. Straight ahead, and directly opposite her, was a view of a tall grey stone mountain, solid rock but smooth surfaced, like it had been sandpapered. Scattering her eyes around Khiron was the only thing that seemed normal, the vision before her was anything but. The castles stood proud and tall and glistened in the sun. She saw some people walk with laptops and others run past.

The grass and trees still moved, but there wasn't many people downstairs. She expected it to bustle with people, but it seemed oddly deserted instead. Clare remembered that not many people lived there.

She inhaled the scent of musk mixed with something sweet, she couldn't make out what it was, but it didn't stop her eyes from burning with the need to cry. Her body yearned for a seed of relief from the horrifying image that held her mind prisoner when she thought of her mother.

The sights of Khiron was beautiful, but tainted in her mind, because she would always remember the loss that had brought her here, the pain she felt when she lost her only love, her mother, the woman who didn't love her back.

She willed herself, "Don't cry, you have to be strong."

The more she convinced herself, the harder it became to understand the reason to hold on, the reason to be calm. It was one day after her mother's death, and she felt frustrated, angry, sad, hurt, confused, it was mixed up, all there, she needed to burst, or an outlet.

From the corner of her eye she spotted a vase on the balcony, she picked the flowery pot up and threw it against the mirror door.

It felt good, exhilarating, so she barged into the room and started tippling everything she could find, screaming and cursing, "I hate you, I hate you, COWARD, you kept this from me, you lied to me, and then you left, you are a COWARD." She threw the white side lamps on the floor that reminded her so much of her mother, and basked in the small satisfaction she got as it hit the stone tub in the centre of the room. She attempted to tear the curtains off the windows, but when it refused to budge, she instead toppled the dresser.

Nathan barged in, "What in the realms are you doing, have you lost your goddamn mind."

"Get out, GET OUT," she snarled. Nathan completely ignored her and marched up to her in five long strides. He locked his thick fingers into her bony shoulders and held her tight, forcefully crushing her into his chest.

It was the last of her will gone. She surrendered into his arms, and burst out crying, she gave him all her heart ache, all her pain, and discretions in those tears.

She yelled, "What am I going to do." Her words sucked up by the tears, "How can I live on from this, I have no one, she's gone, she left me, she freaking left me."

"You have me sister, you'll always have me," he took her face between his hands, bent his head, searched her lost eyes, "I promise you little sister that this heart break of yours will only be temporary, there is a whole world out there waiting to bask in your light."

Haunted by the utter surety, and finality in his words, she shook her head, "How could you say that. Nathan she's your mother too."

Nathan raised his voice, "Clare." His eyes daring but firm in its gaze, "look at me, as long as my blood runs through your veins little sister, you will be STRONG, you will show no weakness. Our mother is gone, and the other's are far away, so right now you and I are all we got."

She looked at him, confusion masked her face, "Nathan what are you talking about?" He let her face go hastily, his gaze downcast, "Nathan what is it, talk to me,"

"Caidrian, he left, he bailed ok, let's just leave it at that."

Clare was lost for words she needed comfort but so did Nathan, so she reassured him, "We have each other Nathan."

She embraced him for what seemed like forever, both not wanting to let each other go. He pulled away first, took something out of his brown leather pants and handed it to her.

"My phone, how did you get it?"

He confessed, "Well, actually a friend of mine found it,"

She wiped her tears, tried her best to lighten the mood, "Your friend, Where's this friend, so can I thank him or her?"

He didn't look at Clare, "Preoccupied, but you're more than welcome."

Clare could see his brooding eyes showed a certain crest of loyalty to this particular friend, she could only guess it to be William, even though he stated that he didn't like the Caster. He had the same look on his face when he warned her away from William, it was a look of respect.

"Why were the sirens on?"

"The Orderian have arrived, it's to notify Lightwatchers that the seal is being opened, so they should be wary for any uninvited guest, hence the quietness."

"You mean demons and Tempters."

"Among other things, enough questions, go shower and change, I'll meet you out front."

She nodded, he was almost out the door, when he gave a backward glance, "Oh and wear the Armor on your bed, Nadia sent them for you."

"She seems nice enough, I don't know why you have issues with her. If you ask me, I would think she might even have a thing for you."

He gave her a crooked look, "Good thing I didn't. The ones who show you kindness so quickly are the people you should be most afraid of Clare, this is no fairytale, you trust the wrong person, you dead."

The words stuck in the air like a constant scent even after he exited the room saying no more.

She glared at the mess she made, "You trust the wrong person, you dead."

Those words were so true, but who did her mother trust. Shaking her head she laughed at the absurdity that her mother had kept this all from her. She never would've guessed that all this was real, even with the signs smack in her face, even living in the proof, she still had doubts.

Grabbing the brown Armor from her bed she walked out into the passage, down the lobby, and into Nathans bedroom where she showered and changed.

It was a good hour later when Nathan finally appeared at the entrance of the castle. He, like her, wore brown Armor, which consisted of leather pants and t-shirt that looked cotton but was much stronger, and lace up black boots that felt much lighter than they looked. She'd tied her hair in a high pony tail, so that it was out of her face.

"You all ready sister, come on, Kalbreal's waiting outside."

Clare followed him out the castle doors, and spotted Kalbreal instantly, wearing grey leathers and a white shirt loosely buttoned.

She liked the grey better than the brown. She was about to say something, but stopped when she saw the frown marred on his face. He didn't seem to be that thrilled to see her, but he was as confusing to read as Latin words in her mind, so she didn't let it bother her.

She spun around, "Is it just the three of us, I thought Nadia and Alonso are like your pals."

Kalbreal laughed, a streak of ginger hair dangled in his eye, the tip rested below his cheek bone complimenting his eyes. Hair so straight and silky always moving as he walked, "Your brother knows Nadia because they grew up together, I won't really call them PALS."

Nathan squinted in Kalbreal's direction as he commented, "She thinks she's the hottest thing since Megan fox."

A man approached them, just as they'd taken a small pathway between two large castles.

Clare had been quiet for the past ten minutes, admiring the view, trying to live in the now and not the past.

The stranger didn't walk all the way to them, but Nathan left her and Kalbreal to go talk with the man. She waited in silence, her lips pursed..

Nathan rubbed his hand on his face, as his steps closed in to her and Kalbreal, "I've been requested by Annabelle, I'll catch up later."

Clare's heart sank, was he seriously going to leave her with Kalbreal, as if he read her thought, Nathan sighed, "You'll be fine, Kalbreal will show you around."

She pouted, "Can't I just come with you."

Kalbreal moved into view just next to Nathan, "Come on."

She gave her brother one last snicker before he turned his back to leave. Her nerves rose at the thought of getting left alone with Kalbreal. He was undeniably alluring, there was no doubt, but he had a way of looking at her and tempting her, she knew it was an Angel thing, though she didn't have proof, but still, "Don't do any freaky stuff just.." she hesitated, dangling her hands carelessly in the air, "Let's keep the distance."

He grinned, and shook his head, "Fine, if that's what you wish."

They walked further down the pathway between two castles. Nathan left in the opposite direction, "So you admit that you've been messing with me."

"Maybe just a little, I can't help it, I don't socialize with deceptors very often, and you, mark-less, are so much like them, ambrosia is very seductive to deceptors, and I happen to be made of it."

Well that explained a lot, "Can't you tempt the other Lightwatchers?"

"Not worth it, they're partial Angels, too much effort. But I only did it to you once, I tried it in the bathroom but you rejected it."

"Not so lucky there, are you." She rolled her eyes, "You don't need ambrosia to get a woman Kalbreal."

"Since my wife, Azilina." The name was spoken with so much passion coming from Kalbreal's lips, "I've not been enticed by another, until recently."

Clare's breath caught but she said nothing, as her eyes stayed firmly on the ground, ashamed that she didn't share this Angels' sudden emotion. She lusted for a faceless Caster with breathtaking blue eyes, that spoke of water, ice and crushed diamonds, rather than an Angel whose body was made for obsession.

They walked to the end of the path and started up a small hill, with trees and smaller castles than the front end of Khiron, which would had still been considered massively large in the deceptors world.

Clare felt her heart somber on the quiet walk. Her thoughts on Kalbreal as he walked beside her just as lost in his own mind as she was in hers.

She thought about the part of him that had loved before, a part of him devoted to one eternally. The knowledge made her see that while she had never thought of getting married, he had lived it. She was barely grown, and he was beyond it, but still, if a guy could speak her name with so much passion as he had spoke of his wife,... She didn't let the thought finish before she turned her head to face him.

His eyes already glued on her chest, lips parted with an urge to say more, it took an effort but wisely he closed it, turning his vision straight ahead, "You are normally really talkative Clarebella, just like Julliette."

She smirked at him her eyes flattering sarcastically, "Now you are comparing me to some mystery girl, named after the famous Juliet? What's next?"

He didn't face her, but she could see the curve of his lips as he spoke, "Her name is Julliette not Juliet, she is family, we're here."

She stopped in her tracks, and stood in front of a very large castle, with gold beams near its entrance. The outside door was marked in blood with an unknown language, apart from it being the largest Castle on the road, it's exterior was like all the other castles, wrapped in gold and marble. Clare was confused as a knot twisted in her stomach, "Where are we?"

"Draikens residence."

Clare's nerves instantly went on red alert, "NO one told me I was going visiting." She raised her voice accusatory in her tone, "Let alone meeting my family."

The thought of meeting her mother's family, Her family, after all this time was beyond nerve wrecking, more so because she had no idea who she was, or what she was doing, let alone what to say, did they know about her amnesia. Her mind riddled with meaningless questions.

"What are we doing here, why? did Nathan tell you to bring me here?"

"RELAX, they your family, and they've been expecting you, your mother actually called them a while back."

Clare's eyebrows furrowed, darkening the green. She faced the door, lifted her hand to knock, but Kalbreal opened it, "Don't, it's rude to knock, ALL Draiken are welcome."

"What's the blood on the door?"

"It's not blood, its sytna, the mark of birth, your cousin had a son this morning." He walked into the castle. Clare followed obediently like a wounded puppy, not allowed to touch its master.

The Draiken castle was different in the inside. No open planned entrance like the Moonstone's, but instead a long narrow hallway. She passed a half a dozen of doors on either side of her already, but Kalbreal went further down. Her boots crunched on the emerald carpet, as she hurried down the lengthy walkway.

Kalbreal kept his pace a few feet ahead of her, his steps purposeful, as though he walked this path numerous times, which he probably did. He didn't stop until he opened the fifteenth door on the right, and disappeared into it.

She followed him, not having any other option, and stopped dead by what she was seeing- a large crowd of people, staring at them both, some completely awestruck.

All the people in the room continued to go about their business after a few minutes, when Kalbreal cleared his throat, and only then did she step closer to him to whispering, "Who are all these people."

"Your family," He laughed, "There's no need to be nervous Clarebella."

A man walked toward them from the crowd skilfully, as he manoeuvred his way through the people, some with using hand signals, or by a bare touch of their shoulders.

She tried to recognize these people. Some looked different, with ash blonde hair, and others Asian skinned, but there were some, including a little girl, hiding between a woman's legs, that she somehow felt connected to. The room was emptied of furniture, no chairs OR curtains, just an open room, with at least fifty people gathered in a circle.

Eyes pausing on the man who approached, her wide smile showing no sign of the turmoil which battled within her. He wore a charcoaled and mixture of grey, leathered pants, that was matte, with loops of leather, laddering right down to his ankle, where three hunter knives rested.

The powdery grey t-shirt with boots and empty weapon strapping's on the top, didn't camouflage the drops of blood that tattooed his neck. He could've easily been mistaken for a man in his mid to late thirties, but by what Clare knew about the Lightwatchers, it was most certain the late forties.

He took out his hand which Clare held without hesitation, "The names Zartieal Draiken." His Scottish accent was completely out of sorts with his physical description, "I'm Luela's father."

The man didn't let her hand go, but she admitted to herself that she didn't mind, not one bit. It was comforting, something that she longed for, "I'm Clare, Franchesca's daughter." "We know who you are child, you are ours, come now, meet your family."

Kalbreal smiled at her, when she looked at him for approval. She didn't understand what she searched his face for, but she got a nod as he followed next to her and Zartieal, making way to the crowd.

Zartieal hadn't let her hand go, instead he brought her closer to him and tucked it under his arm, squeezing her fingers gently, giving her comfort. The other Lightwatchers smiled at her as they made way for her to pass through to the other side, toward the fifty foot window.

The room was much bigger than she calculated at first entry, and smelt of roses and saffron. Hands on her back, different, unfamiliar, touching her, patting her shoulder, she felt at home, relaxed, welcomed.

Zartieal only dislodged her when they approached a girl seated on a chair, the one single piece of furniture in the room. The girl stared up at her, with a warm glow on her cheeks, and black downturned eyes. Her hair was black with loose curls, open and flowing down the sides of the chair just over her breast, not as long as Clare's, but it looked thicker and was damp, like she'd just showered, and slipped on the long white dress made of silk. Her tanned skin in complete contrast to Clare's paled one from her years in London.

Clare's eyes dropped to the girl's arms, as she saw something inside it- wrapped in a white woollen blanket, was a little baby.

She had this urge to run away, but a hand gripped her arm, holding her captive, it was an elderly looking female in her sixties, but the tightness of her fingers on Clare's arm was no sixty year old grip, "He hasn't received his name yet, still a wanderer."

Clare looked at the lady, noting how tall she was for a grandma, her shoulders straight, posture - perfect, and something oddly familiar about her, but Clare couldn't make out what it was, "I've seen you somewhere." It came out more of an accusation, than an observation.

"I'm your grandmother's sister, Aniela, this is my first great grandchild." She said, pointing to the baby nestled in its mother's arms.

The ladies grip loosening around her arm. Clare stepped behind the chair and looked down at the baby, whose eyes opened at Clare's stare, "I thought newborns don't open their eyes, he's beautiful."

"Our children are different." The baby's mother's voice was dry, but soft, it suited her, "We're born with our eyes open, souls like those of Angels, it's mostly why we are called Lightwatchers, because of the Igori. Names Luela by the way." She smiled at Clare and stood up. Handing Clare the baby so quickly, Clare didn't have a second to refuse or step back, not that she wanted to, she had experienced enough death, let her experience life too.

SHE WAS CROONING THE little male bundle, having had him for the past twenty minutes. Kalbreal bent down to her knees and sat flat on the ground. She could feel his eyes on her as she played with the baby's chin, murmuring "You're so handsome little one, you'll break many hearts, yes you will."

Kalbreal laughed, "I'm sure he will, it's close now."

"What is?"

"The naming, when he receives his name, he also receives his seraph energy, his Gazool, it what makes him half Angel."

She lifted her chin, her eyes still fixed on the baby who lay cradled in her arms, her nephew. "Is that why all the people are here."

"Yes."

She appreciated the opportunity, it was good to see a new life after that which she lost. She brushed the thought of her mother and stared deeper into the baby's eyes, "When do his parents name him?"

Kalbreal leaned in, his voice loud and clear so she could hear it in the crowd of noise, "His name is given by Adonai, when it's written on the Akashic it'll show visible on his skin, there is only one name."

Clare smiled and played with the baby, hearing the people as they talked and laughed amongst each other. Whilst she tickled the baby's cheeks she lifted the infant boy and laid butterfly kisses on his rosy cheeks, and inhaled the scent of newborn.

Kalbreal still focused on her as the minutes past, she smiled at the thought of how long he sat there watching her with a disbelieving look, she asked, "Do you wanna carry him?"

"When he gets his name yeah, of course, it's the only reason I'm here."

"Did you ever have one, a baby?"

He scowled, and tensed up, "No."

"Then you should, I want three someday. So do tell, what's the Akashic?"

He rubbed his chin with his index and thumb, "Something you shouldn't know about."

"Well, I can't argue there, you are the Angel, obviously."

Clare caught two girls around about her age, squealing, as they gossiped about Kalbreal, making it so obvious by standing at his back and gawking at him. They both wore brown Armor like hers, she was surprised that Kalbreal didn't even turn around to look at them.

She focused back on her bundle, and watched with a huge smile as the little ones tiny hand crept its way out of the blanket. Clare touched the little fingers carefully, having never touched a newborn baby before now, it was an all too new experience for her, especially when she stared into the baby's eyes as he smiled, the forehead of the baby's started to lighten up,

"KALBREAL, something's happening."

"What?"

Kalbreal got up and moved over to her, the child's entire face had a light under the flesh, making him glow like a pink crystal lamp,.

Clare's protective instincts rose, tenfold, as she held the baby tight, "Call his mother."

"It's too late for that, the baby's receiving his name, open your hands and remove the blanket."

The people gathered around her as the mother rushed through the crowd of people, with tears brimming in her eyes, it wasn't happy ones, but those that Clare had been all too familiar with in the recent past, those shed from loss and sorrow, anger and heartache. She averted her gaze from mother to baby, that squirmed in her arms. Her heart pounded as she decided to follow Kalbreal's instructions. Luela didn't seem in any state to handle it, and nobody stepped forward to assist, so it was now up to her.

Unwrapping him from the blanket, slowly, she kept him tucked to her chest. The baby now naked, she lifted him up, the blanket falling to the floor at the same time she stood up.

The baby's body alive with a glow penetrating through his flesh. Brightening with every minute passed, his heart pulsing, as crimson vines illuminated through his untainted flesh. The site breathtaking, pure, so Angelic, astounded her speechless. To think, she thought that nothing could amaze her after she had glimpsed the beauty of this realm,

But...

This energy, because that's what it looked like, felt like, beneath the skins' surface of the baby, was celestial, unearthed, inhuman. Keeping her emerald eyes on the boy, fascination clear on her face, she watched his vibrant water blue eyes change completely to green.

This she thought is a heavens miracle.

The infant's weight got lighter in her arms and started to rise from her hands, until he was in the air, floating on an invisible cloud. He didn't cry or moan, instead he kicked his tiny little legs, eyes wide open and sucked on his hand.

It was extraordinary, as the innocence of the baby flourished through the Gazool that now flowed through his body, Clare's mouth parted in amazement.

The other's stood further back, Kalbreal now next to her, amused by her astonishment, "You should stand back Clarebella."

She listened dubiously and took a few steps back as Kalbreal moved under the baby who drifted further into the air. Instinctively she turned her head, and watched as Luela cried bitterly in silence, held tightly against her father.

Clare could only wonder what was so horrifying when this spectacular occurrence was happening. What could make this young mother so mortal. She searched around, moving her head slowly from left to right for the father of the baby, but there was none, nobody who seemed enthralled enough to be anyway.

Kalbreal still stood closest to the baby, as the others and herself positioned at least four meters away. The emanating light grew brighter, until it was so bright that Clare, while struggling to keep her eyes open, could still see the light through her eyelids. When the brightness beyond her eyelids finally dimmed a good few minutes later, Clare opened them and saw Kalbreal as he held the baby. His free hand on top of the babies face, releasing sparks of fire. Directly over the child's naked body, his mouth whispering something, but a slight smile hadn't moved from his mouth. *Angel-boy really likes babies* she thought, *maybe William likes them too.*

Kalbreal faced them, and lifted the baby up above his head, "Arsheal."

The crowd gathered in, some bumped her, but she didn't move, as her eyes wandered back to Luela, who smiled, but with haunted sadness. Behind her, Clare caught sight of another figure, another female.

Clare tried to make her out properly by straining her eyes, taking in the girls light blue gaze, just like her mother's, that focused right at her. The female walked closer to Luela, who started moving toward the baby. Clare bumped and pushed, keeping the mysterious girl in her vision, she spun when she bumped into a big chest, taking seconds to get her bearing, but the girl was gone, just like that. She looked a few feet in every direction around Luela, nothing.

Facing Luela again, she watched as the mother stopped walking. Her mind made up, she moved forward to talk her cousin, to find out what was so wrong.

A female hand gripped her wrist, a soft voice whispered into her ear as the person reeled her in, "You aren't safe here, leave now, GO." American, she must know Nathan.

Clare spun around but the figure was gone, she hadn't known who it was, where it came from, but part of her believed it, and got her feet moving through the crowd, with determination.

She got his attention easily, when she yelled, "Kalbreal", he wasn't holding the baby anymore, instead he just stood there, looking at Arsheal when she called out to him.

She gestured with her chin to follow her, which he did. They passed through the crowd and slipped out the door, he didn't seem irritated, which was a good sign, "What is it?"

"We need to leave, it isn't safe, ACTUALLY a woman told me that, about yay high, big blue eyes."

She was puzzled by his response, or lack of, "What are you doing, why you closing your eyes?"

"I'm seeing what's the danger, probably Jullie who spoke to you but I don't sense her unless..." he trailed off,

"Unless what?"

"Nothing, Listen Luela isn't happy, her husband ascended an hour ago, but he's chosen to be a maker, she won't be able to stay with him."

Clare raised her voice, "Why not, she just had a baby? That's ridiculous; he'll obviously choose his baby." She shrugged, but looked up at Kalbreal's face, and knew that there wasn't anything at all obvious about the situation, "Why can't she stay with him if he's a maker? What does it mean to ascend?"

"Let's go I won't risk your safety, we'll talk somewhere else, come on."

She didn't know why or what it was which convinced her, but she listened to him, and followed closely as he took long strides down the passage, purposely trying to get out of there quickly, she, had to run partially just to keep up.

CLARE THREW HERSELF onto the soft lively grass, and faced the bayou waters, it was as soft as she imagined, and smelt of musk, the strongest kind.

A tree moved toward her, shading the sun from her face, a few minutes before Kalbreal left to fetch them something to drink while she stretched out her aching legs.

She placed her hands under her neck, lying on her back and stared up at the tree kind enough to shade her, watching the dance of its leaves as it provided her with entertainment as well, moving to a ballet in her mind.

She bent her neck forward, chin to chest, looking toward the water, as an image played up in her mind,

Phillip,

She wondered if he was ok, did he try calling her, she wouldn't know because she left her phone at the castle. She thought of her mother's death, it had been just a day ago, but felt like a week by the way the Lightwatchers carried on like none of it mattered. She couldn't fault them, life went on for them, they were born to die killers. Death was not the end because their souls lived forever, wow, she couldn't get her head around this crap.

She replayed the ceremony in her head, what could have went wrong, and that man, William, his faceless body, those unique eyes penetrating right to her very soul, as his hands wrapped around her, she remembered breathing in his very air. She rubbed her fingers together, remembering the feel of his cheek moving against her palm, as her fingers brushed his flesh.

"Princess," she whispered the endearment, the thought made her face heat up and a silly smile tickled her lips. It was the biggest brightness in her darkest hours and she would hang on to it, for as long as she could.

Kalbreal stood in front of her, blocking her view of the lake, holding two big cups of juice. "You shouldn't think so much," handing one to her, he said with a smile, "It ages you."

Clare grabbed a small stone and flung it lamely at him, which he missed, laughing, "Your brother said to meet us here, the meeting's in a few hours."

She sat up, taking both cups out his hands, and put his down on the grass, which was now flattened like a coaster, so Kalbreal can sit next to her.

She jumped by shock, when another tree joined them, and spilled some of the juice on her pants, luckily, it was leather. The tree dropped pears. Kalbreal picked up four, rinsed them in the lake and threw one at Clare, "You did not just wash the fruit in a lake full of dead people's ash." He bit into it, her jaw dropped, "Nothing mixes with the lake, you could drink from it."

"If you say so but if I get infected, it's all on you Angel-boy." The tree turned and dropped a pear on Clare's head, she scowled, as it returned to its original position.

It was ten minutes later when she lost the battle of silence, curiosity spurred her, "What happened with Luela and her husband?"

"If one is chosen to be a maker they can't have a family, they have to give themselves up completely."

"But why would he do that? Why would anyone do that."

Kalbreal bit into the pear and stared into the lake, he still stood by, "Sacrifice, not every Lightwatcher can be killers Clarebella. Luela is strong, a great warrior and fearless. Cedriel was given the gene, not the conscience. They married young hoping he'd ascend and at least be a teacher, but today when it happened, he had a mark that is rare, a mark that chooses his faith for him. In his case his path was forced on him, it's believed that sometimes a path is chosen for you, and if you follow, it shall lead you to unimaginable possibilities. My father once told me, that it's the path that makes the man, not the outcome."

"Your father is a wise man, can't you help him, you're an Angel?"

He didn't look at her, when she faced him, a frown creased between her eyebrows, she had to stare at the right side of his face. The outline of his features all matched perfectly, not one dent or hair out of place, so perfect, too perfect. His orange streaks just took it all and gave it a perfection you could never multiply. She wanted to hit herself for not being attracted to him, but she couldn't muster up enough guilt to actually do it.

Clare didn't know what it was about his eyes, when he turned his head to face her, he was standing five feet away, but that intense fire that erupted in his irises, said a lot of things, but one screamed out to her..., Kalbreal was hanging on to a deadly secret. A secret that she wasn't so sure she wanted to know. His jaw ticked, before his lips parted to say, "he's been blessed, it isn't a curse but a gift, an honor. Luela will accept it in time, she's strong."

Clare was furious by Kalbreal's lack of concern, he certainly knew how to get her revved up, she screamed, "Accept it? She has to raise a FREAKIN' baby alone, UNACCEPTABLE, you have to help her."

He moved in a blink of an eye, one moment he was five feet away next, he was right there, "There's no reason to shout Clarebella, I'm sitting right next to you." He paused, and muttered something, which she was pretty sure was curse words, way to go Angel-boy she thought, as she barred her teeth.

Clare got up and threw the juice on him, he could probably crush her like an ant but she didn't care about that in the heat of the moment, she just wanted to get as far away from him as possible. She didn't even understand or make sense as to why it bothered her so much, but it did, it grated her that life was so cruel, that her cousin would became a mother and a 'divorced' woman on the same day.

It was like Luela was given a gift of life but lost a part of her soul, nothing about it seemed right to Clare no matter how you put it.

Kalbreal stood up, and stepped in beside her, his eyes locked onto hers, she knew her face was red and her lips pursed, as she scowled at him, but her anger seemed to just brighten his mood. She looked at him, his face transformed into the sun itself as he smiled so radiantly, like if the sun had a face it would be his. She felt her furrowed brow drop at his amused lips, and found it harder to hold her annoyance at the infuriating creature.

"Fine." He lifted his hand, wiggling his fingers, a what-ever gesture, "If it upsets you that much I'll see what I can do, ok."

Their eyes stared into one another's for minutes, though it had felt not long enough when she lowered her gaze. She didn't want to give him the wrong impression, she had no romantic inclinations toward him. She saw him as a friend, an Angel who was pleasing to the eye.

Where was the harm in that, surely Kalbreal didn't really feel anything for her, he said so himself. He was married, she just reminded him of his wife, it wasn't the end of the world, but part of her, as sick as it sounded felt like she was betraying William. With one touch he'd claimed her, he was her compulsion, her secret slice of decadence, tainted and she hadn't even seen his face.

Kalbreal didn't need to know that she was obsessing over William. She had many unanswered questions, to which Angel-boy seemed to have most of the answers, and so did her brother.

The wicked gleam and sudden broad smile that etched his face had her narrowing her eyes, "What's the joke?"

"Do you still want to see my wings?"

She tilted her head, a grin playing on her mouth, "Will I die?"

"No, I can show it to you under the water, the lake's blessed with healing properties, it'll protect you as long as you stay emerged."

"Okay."

"Take out your clothes and get in the water and I'll show you."

She coughed out, "Angel-boy has seriously lost his mind."

"Angel-boy? You couldn't have chosen a better name, maybe hero or prince."

She snorted, recalling a similar thing he said to her in his room the day before, "Prince, huh, that'll be the day. ANGEL-BOY is much better."

Face flushed as thoughts of William assailed her again. Mind drifting to the faceless man that had touched her and comforted her, as one would their lover. *What's wrong with me,* she cursed her brain, cursed her skin, as it tingled with the urge to be touched by him. So lost in her mind, not hearing as Kalbreal spoke, his voice a background sound.

Cold water splashed on her face, bringing her back to reality, she screeched, "What the hell."

"You mind gazing AGAIN, you want to see my wings or not?"

She turned her back to him and started removing her t-shirt first,

"And I'm not getting naked, I'm wearing underwear, turn around."

He didn't respond to her, so she halted in her quest, and turned around to face him, but he wasn't there. She moved carefully toward the water.

Hair clinging to his face, curled around his cheekbones, his eyes blazing hot, looking more of a crimson red than orange, as he swam closer to the shore, his voice deep, "Hurry up," he called from the lake.

She discarded her clothes and at a last minute she had remembered her back, she didn't particularly trust him that much, so she slipped the t-shirt back on, she hadn't thought of why she hid the barely there mark on her back from anyone, but her instincts seemed to take over when it needed to.

Kalbreal didn't seem to mind much really, he deliberately refrained himself from the temptation at looking at her legs. She touched the water with her bare foot, expecting, well she didn't really know what she expected but the lakes water was warm under her feet and remained so.

The deeper she got, the warmer it felt. She swam closer to Kalbreal, who was now in the centre of the Saltril lake, she swam further in until he stood opposite her, "You okay?" at her nod, he said, "Count to seven and come down."

She nodded again, her hair wet floating in the water. Some of the water touched the inside of her mouth, it was clear, and sweet, she was tempted to swallow, but rethought it. After seven anticipated seconds were up, she took in a lungful of air, and swam down toward the lakes bed. Half down, she could see the sparks of fire, milky, blurry lava, she went further down, swimming deeper, holding her breath. Her eyes stayed open, not willing to lose a second of this, as excitement coursed through her, when she was less than ten feet away from him.

The heat from his body made the water hotter, her lungs getting heavy, she focused on the brightness, and she saw it, his wings. They were expanded about two meters wide and a little over three in length as it spread out. She blinked, water burning her eyes. She saw his face was normal, like he was breathing, his body flamed up in wrappings of fire, his eyes, it was so bright...

Her own couldn't handle looking much longer. She peeled them open just a tiny bit to see his wings one last time, but the water got too hot in the instant and she couldn't hold her breath any longer, she signalled him, that she was going back to the surface.

She swam up, and vacuumed in a large amount of oxygen, freeing her lungs, as she broke free from the water. Feeling exhilarated as fresh air soaked up into her lungs, her breathing barely regulated when the water scorched her skin.

She swam as fast as she could to the shore of the lake. Her hair barely covered her black panty as she ran out of the water.

She had just caught her breath, when she heard footsteps from behind her, she slipped on her jeans, "I could see it, but not for long, water was too hot."

"Pity, since you'll probably never get your name back."

His said it so bluntly like it was definite, but parts of Clare refused to believe it, she didn't say anything more about it.

"How did your wife die?" Her eyes widened by her loose tongue, turning to face him, and winced. Clare hoped she hadn't treaded too dangerously, and was about to apologize, when she found herself muted by the sight of him shirtless. His muscles, ripped, wet with droplets of water, she almost didn't catch his words,

"She didn't."

She lowered her voice, "but you said.."

"I didn't say she's dead, I said she's gone, you should listen more attentively next time, words can be very deceiving."

"But it sounded like you loved her, or love her."

"I do, but love is a broadened emotion."

"There you go again." She bowed at him sarcastically, "Sometimes you speak like a person, and other times you just shut a person out, your tone changes, do you even hear yourself sometimes, is that how all Angels are."

"I've been on earth for a while, but I am not a person, I am superior, an Angel, to answer all your questions would be to betray sacred laws. But I can tell you that there are limits to every emotion. My wife crossed those, and paid a price far more treacherous than simple death, and that's all I'm going to say about it."

Clare saw that look in his eyes, as he stood there, not moving, not blinking, unreadable, guarded by something too solid to break or crack. A tear fell from her eye, a single tear for a broken Angel, a tortured soul.

She wanted to press for more, but her heart couldn't give her courage to hurt the Angel, not now, and if she did, it would be as if she'd killed him a little inside.

She heard her name been screamed, "It's Nathan." She said quietly, "I think we should go."

Thirteen

L^{iam} The room was full of Asguardians, their frustrated moans and curses echoed in ancient tongue. Liam wanted desperately to silence them, instead he had made the situation worse. When he scoffed at Dukael, the elder in charge since Raphael and Armatos was in Khiron,

He had insulted them-

The Angels offspring, and called them wingless trash, after that it pretty much sealed his faith.

The discussion at present was who would take him to the Elvan domain. The mountain in Safiereal was made with a rare metal, which weakened all angelic descendants including the Tempters children. The idea was to torture him there, in hopes to seek vengeance, for burning there scrolls over a thousand years ago.

They slashed him continuously in the past hours with what looked like a scourge but was actually an Angelic laced whip called Dresta, made and named by Azazy-el, the master of weaponry himself. Unfortunate for them, it hadn't done the damage they had hoped. Eventually as the hours progressed, he was allowed a comfortable seat on a throne chair in the centre of the room. Though he was forbidden on the sacred ground, no one had stepped forward and asked him how he had entered.

Liam absorbed the attention, as he sat on the throne chair, left in view for all those in the room to see. He should have said something, but, his mind was not focused on the present, as much as they thought.

He was surely focused, but on something far beyond- a barely there woman with enticing lips that pouted when she teased you, or got so upset that she had to rein herself in. The woman with the most malicious yet seductive smirk that played on her mouth, when you dared challenged her, as it taunted its victim,

His Princess,

She was always ready to defend, and those wicked green eyes that were barely leashed, held a man captive, without knowing how deep he'd fallen until there was no way up. It brought him satisfaction, knowing he alone could see the smoky silver specks which recently dotted the rims of those hypnotizing eyes.

Her situation was the only one he cared about, he was still conflicted when it came to her. This uncensored attraction made him edgy and agitated. It messed with his control, and he needed to be in control, it was what made him, his father's child. It was the one thing that took precedence over everything else, it was the one emotion he honed himself to master, to utter perfection. Control was his greatest weapon, the one that had won him all his battles, and kept his secrets, just that, secrets. He fought within himself, an ongoing battle, a waging war, he wanted to be there with her, but there was so many risks, so many dispositions and too much at stake.

He needed more answers first, he needed to know, how many would have to die to keep her safe. How many Angels and Tempters he'd have to massacre by his blade, and how much danger he was about to put his young siblings in, he needed to come to a decision, was she worth it? All that blood, all those souls that would be spilt in her name, the name of one defenceless Lightwatcher, who now had the heavens and hell after her, because one single tear had landed on a two year old Lightwatcher, probably not,

He knew that her death would be the course in which the Asguardians and most of the Angels would take to protect their Prince, it was what they had done willingly for thousands of years. It was not the one the Tempters were taking, and it definitely wasn't the course he himself followed, not by a long ride, and he will sever the heads of any who dared strike against his princess.

He wandered his eyes, and extended his hearing, as he sought out Dukael, impatience and irritation riddled on the Asguardians expression. Liam could tell by listening to the extended thumping of Dukael's heart, that he was losing patience, and fast.

"There's rumors, he's partial Angel," One said.

Dukael whispered to the others who surrounded him, "We can't just defy the laws, there's a killer on the loose, if we break the laws we betray the Orderian oath we made to the Lightwatchers. The Advisors would order a massacre, they would send the Legions, and we would have no protection from them, they're merciless, our parents won't aid us in this, even if they wanted to." He paused, when no one interrupted him, he suggested, "We should wait for Raphael."

Liam yelled, his voice hoarse, but solid, as it echoed through the expansive room, "So now you're all scared of half breeds, I thought you Angels- pure bloods, what happened to being superior. The Tempters children you despise so much would never shy from a fight, much less from a pack of Legion half-bloods."

Dukael marched up to Liam, his purple eyes cut with frustration, as he ran his fingers in his red hair, which was now short and spiked. Liam would've probably blocked this from a mile away, if he wished, and proceeded accordingly, which would mean brutal death, but he knew exactly what he was doing, and here in Asguard there was no better way to get answers, because one thing was for sure, they hated ALL besides themselves.

He chimed, "Things could be much easier if you and the others just answer my questions Dukael." Liam pointed out dryly, as he sat straight up, resuming the position he stayed in for the past few hours.

Dukael kicked his face again, no blood spilt from his mouth. The marvellous thing with Asguard was that there was never bloodshed on the holy land, it didn't condone violence, so no matter how much it hurt, that, was as far as it went. Except if one shielded a Harpien blade, which only a full pledge Angel could command and unfortunately that list didn't include Asguardians who hadn't earned their way to the Infinity yet.

Though, he did know of a few who were not bound by the laws of the Harpien blade.

Twenty minutes later Liam felt a headache come on, the spell he put on himself fading. Soon he wouldn't be able to maintain this calm solitude, and if that happened, then so help them all.

"I don't know anything about Franchesca, or the killings and if I did." Dukael said proudly, as he boasted his bravery, "I still would never tell a filthy Caster," he spat at Liam's feet, instead of his face. The indecision saved Dukael his life by a hairs breath, because amongst the angelic breeds it was considered worse than swearing or name calling to spit in ones face, and if Dukael did, to Liam's brother, Kole, it was an excellent excuse to kill Dukael.

Liam was not among those who cared about that which seemed so minor to end a life, but he had killed for less, much less, so he'd play along. He stared at Dukael, contemplating his next move, but stopped, to imagine his brother's face, when he told him about this.

He kept his features emotionless as he was on the inside, the very thought made him cringe internally, because as much as he wanted his princess, he might never be able to love her the way she needed. But he wasn't letting her go either, she was *his,* whether he wanted her or not, and Kalbreal had better figure that out soon, because he was coming to claim the Lightwatcher that belonged to him, right after he sorted out what had taken him away from her in the first place, or who.

Liam blinked, "Kalbreal wouldn't be too happy about this."

Dukael spoke loudly, his eyes playful to a degree, "He's a minor Angel."

Liam thinned his lips, Dukael clearly entertained, but Liam was out of time, and his patience was wavering in and fast. His instincts didn't like his princess being so far from him while she was being hunted, even if he had appointed those to protect her, they weren't part of his eight, and Calub was playing captive.

"So you keep saying," Liam replied, "He's obviously fooled you all, either way I'll get the information I seek."

Another Asguardian stepped forward, Liam didn't know who he was, but by his stance and broad shoulders, he was definitely influential among the Angels' spawn, "You are really arrogant for a Caster and stupid coming into our realm, threatening our kind."

Liam stared into the ageless yellow eyes, painting a picture of someone succumbed with years of agony, unwanted, unloved, unraveling this male specimen piece by piece. The man stepped forward attired in a long gold silk robe like some of the other Asguardians had worn for this grandeur.

He didn't wait for Liam to respond, he just snapped, "Did you think we were just going to let you walk out because Kalbreal has taken an insane liking to you and your siblings, William Blackwyll. Do you think we do not know who you are, whose blood runs in those veins, look at you betraying an Angel at the first opening you get."

Liam thought for a second, as he rubbed his chin, still feigning a relaxed position in the chair.

Dukael now a few steps away from Liam, and the other man who now waited for Liam to speak, with a triumphant stare.

Liam shook his head, he was very disappointed in this breed of descendants, "Yes," he shrugged as a matter of fact, "Well," Liam corrected himself, with confidence that exuded all of them in the room, "Let me rephrase, no I don't think, I'm certain that you haven't a clue whose blood runs in my veins, because if you did, we'd not be having this conversation. And I did consider the repercussions of entering this place and when I added it all up, the decision was obvious, really, 'see the conceited bastards.'"

Dukael neared Liam, stepped in Liam's path to defend him from the wrath of the Asguardian who now clasped a sword in his hand ready to thrust it in Liam's direction.

"Tahros." Dukael called out at the top of his voice, "You need to stop, I am still in charge."

Tahros barked, "Get out of my way Dukael."

Liam could tell that he had over stepped his boundaries just a bit, but then again, it wasn't like he set any. His plan was to simply get answers, though he had to admit, he enjoyed the theatrical performance which was taking place.

Tahros thought he could take him in a fight, but Liam would wipe him out in barely the first tick of the clock, and he would do that soon.

A voice screamed from the back, "ENOUGH" it was unexpected, and feared amongst the Asguardians, because most of them sat down or quieted, even Liam had not expected it. He sat up, back straight, shoulders squared, eyes following the owner's voice.

Some, Irin possessed an uncanny gift, the mark of the knower, the Lightwatchers called it. The Angels called it Alurya. Liam had seen his fair share of them, but with the help of his brothers' sorcery and a pure crest stone versed by a Blackwyll, he created a force field shield that would protect him, and his siblings. He made sure his shield was strong and impenetrable as it blocked his hierarchy and identity with dominance only he possessed. He did it whilst he considered that voice and absorbed his surroundings.

The room was filled with gems and precious metals, most of

which was expected, among the Cherubs young. The base of the very chair he sat on was made from titanium and blue sapphires, whilst the sponge part was made from raven feathers wrapped in spiders silk.

He didn't need his suspicions confirmed when he could easily see that the Asguardians had been taking more stuff from the Infinity, maybe even stealing.

Liam was certain, that the law for removing treasures from the Infinity was very specific- only on the rarest of occasions, when an Asguardian rose, were they allowed to retrieve one thing from the Infinity to leave behind in Asguard, it was common knowledge amongst all Orderian.

He waited until he caught sight of the strange man, when he did, he couldn't believe his eyes, the words made out of his mouth, were as soft as a whisper,

"Aneil."

The man rose nearer to Liam, his black eyes narrowed on Liam. His once golden blonde hair that had once glowed at night, now white, and plaited down his back. He regarded Liam, taking his hand out to touch him,

"If you touch me," Liam threatened, "you will die."

Liam thought quickly, he needed to warn them, he closed his eyes, focused on Jullie, his mind whispered into hers, *"Warn Kalbreal, tell him Aneil is here, don't tell him my whereabouts, not yet."*

"Be safe," She whispered back to him, through the permanent channel in his mind opened for his siblings.

Aneil now stationed right in front of him scoffed "You know my name Lightwatcher, you have been schooled well, but not well enough."

Liam stared at him, wryly, he said, "Lightwatcher? Demoted from Caster to Lightwatcher, I should be offended."

Aneil hissed, "Don't undermine me child."

Liam stood up, clearly taller than Aneil, his spell had worn out, and so did his patience. Then he spoke, "There's a killer among you, seven Lightwatchers drained of their souls, in a matter of a week." His voice echoed in the hall, "Raphael's refusal to aid the Lightwatchers has now made you the prime suspect, I've seen those bodies, that is the work of an Irin, who says they won't turn on you? Asguard needs protection."

Pause

"Unfortunately for you, the Garde had already notified the Legions, as of two days ago. I don't need to remind you of the seriousness of this circumstance, Aneil is a Cherub, an Irin in rank. But this isn't his land, it's yours. The Legions would retaliate in death, they would show no mercy to a dying breed when none is shown to them."

The Asguardians were quiet, attentive, and patient. He continued, as his hands moved with subtle signals, captivating his audience, "I stand here not as Caster, Lightwatcher, or Asguardian, but as one residing on the earth."

His voice deepened, he wanted to be heard and he was heard, "The Lightwatchers WILL blame you for the killings of their own. I offer you protection on behalf of all Draiken AND Blackwyll. I only ask you to tell me who's the third Irin that arrived yesterday, speak his name and I'll bid you farewell."

Aneil was the only one who laughed at Liam. Dukael stepped back, and other Asguardians moved forward, their looks were thoughtful, as they considered his offer.

A lady stepped forward wearing a black silk dress, her crimson hair curled in golden pins. Black shadowed bronze eyes lined with coiled makeup, bloodstained lips oozed seduction, but her wild pheromones she gave off did nothing for Liam. It was surprising that some Asguardians still maintained the temptation gene from their parents, but mostly annoying when they tried to use it on other angelic descendants because it never worked, it only sent a silent invitation, one that Liam was not going to answer.

She purred, "I am Ulaidea, lady of Raphael, unlike the other's I do not coral with you, William Blackwyll." Her soft voice, made to allure a male to his knees, but only aggravated Liam. He liked his women warriors, those who could yield a blade.

"My years on this earth, has taught me many things," She asserted, "I am no fool when it comes to knowledge or wisdom, no mere Caster could have walked freely into Asguard, the guardians would have given their lives in our protection."

She faced the others in the room, raising her voice as her confidence tangled with her words, "Yet all the guardians are in their positions, unharmed, unafraid. We have questioned them countless times, yet all are ready to die for William Blackwyll, to be no more, for the one who my kind claim a beast, yet I see no hatred in those eyes, no fear, no torment, they are the eyes of a pure soul, but so was the Archangel Azazy-el, yet he turned out to be our biggest disappointment."

She paused, while Aneil remained quiet, his eyebrows gathered closely together, in deep contemplation. Liam felt a prickle in his nape, it appeared that Aneil was attempting to warn the third Angel, or Irin as the Angel in question was no minor Angel, but one of rank, but Aneil's attempt would remain just that, an attempt. Liam had put mental shields on the whole of Asguard, allowing no one to communicate telepathically beside himself. Yes, he was that powerful, it didn't even nick into what he was truly capable of. If these people knew who he was, they would be writhing in fear, not vengeance.

Ulaidea didn't face the other Asguardians but kept her attention solely on Liam. He was impressed by her observation, but not surprised, just disappointed, because his eyes gave nothing away. She sought a pure soul because it was what she wanted to see. Some made him out to be heroic when he could kill them without a blink or thought, he was merciless, but he had never killed without a reason no matter how small. He never blamed them, never bothered correcting them either, it was time wasted, though with every rare occurrence there were ones who saw him for what he truly was and those he kept close.

"Ista-el." She said finally, "I don't know if he or the other Irin are out to hurt the Lightwatchers or any other descendants but I do know that only Armatos was granted ward to the earth."

Aneil slapped Ulaidea, "Traitor, to your own flesh and blood," Her eyes fell to the floor in shame.

Liam moved with a speed faster than light, the sword from Aneil's hand now in his own as he guided it through Aneil's heart knowing full well that he had just killed the high rank Angel, and almost two hundred Asguardians had bared witness to it.

The Angels eyes widened with shock, as he took his last breath, before resuming into nothing. The Asguardians charged against Liam, dislodging them as fast as he was capable he grabbed Ulaidea by the arm. Sword in the other hand, the two of them ran for the door, which was, still meters away.

Dukael stood by the door,

Liam ran nearer, dragging Ulaidea by the arm.

Dukael pulled out a dagger from his belt, and grinned sheepishly at Liam, before he bowed his head, "You said piss them off El, not start a world war this wasn't in the plan."

Liam arched a brow, "Plans change."

Ulaidea looked from Liam to Dukael, her voice as shocked as her eyes, "You hold a Harpien blade and befriend an Asguardian, what are you."

He let her arm go, and turned on his toes, flinging the back of the blade across the face of one of the Asguardians, who was ten feet away, he yelled, "Dukael, take her to Safiereal."

He faced the crowd, who sought his death, as Dukael listened and ran for the door with Ulaidea trailing behind.

Liam's body started glistening streaks of electric blue, only letting enough kiss his skin, he didn't want to have more power.

"Blade, speak your name, live," He ordered in a steady and firm voice, as he commanded the Harpien blade.

Whilst he booted another Asguardian, another came up behind him as he attempted to past Liam. The intent of the Asguardian was clear, he was going after Ulaidea, she was still Raphael's lady. But Liam was faster, more trained in combat. He grabbed the neck of the Asguardian and flung him across the room, the Asguardian's bones crushed as he hit a hard wall on the left.

The Harpien blade he yielded started to change, as it whispered "Surta."

Two more Asguardians came toward him, as the blade glowed with the black angelic writing on its metal, before it transformed into its true self, a long razor sharp bladed samurai sword.

Liam glowed with the frost of his anger, his skin now slicked with beams of electricity and ice. The shield which protected his identity was actually a rare obsidian stone versed by a Blackwyll, the last breed of stone Verses on the earth. It also kept his abilities at bay, but his body was getting stronger, his power growing, soon there would be nothing to hide his fury, and the sparks that sizzled his skin, proved that soon meant now.

He didn't want the Asguardians hurt permanently. He was going to have to weaken himself, by electrocuting his mind, it was the only way as there were too many innocents in Asguard. Angels hardly ever conceived, with only two hundred and thirty seven offspring, amongst two hundred thousand Angels, in the last three thousand years. Killing them was just not done, even the Tempters refused to kill the Angels spawn unless for a valid reason, and that was what had brought forth the last war, the battle he had fought alongside Franchesca and Azazy-el, the war where thousands of Lightwatchers fell, the war that had earned Draiken his respect, the war of descendants.

Something sharp poked him in his lower spine, and four more followed, two on his neck, and one on his thigh,

Tranquilliser,

They were putting him down like a rabid animal, he had never expected that, but it saved him the trouble of frying his mind. The ground blurred and spun under him as he felt a boot connect with his stomach, and multiple hands fist his face, everything numbed as lots of them unleashed the anger they had worked up by the thought of him killing an Irin.

He pushed the rest of himself, to succumb to the darkness which would follow, he needed to do one last thing, reach Jullie, *'It's Ista-el, go, go now.'*

The whisper he knew would be enough as he closed his eyes and sucked in his last breath, surrendering to the darkness crowding behind his eyelids.

Fourteen

Clare strolled into the golden relished dome, her legs still lazed from the extra walking she done in the past four hours since she and Kalbreal met with Nathan at the bayou. She paced, up and down the long hallway of the Moonstone castle, whilst her brother lectured her vigilantly on how she should and shouldn't behave at the meeting today, what to say, how to say it, when to say it. Her head spun with information, but in the end of all that prepping she crashed, winging it was now her only option.

Now, she stood in silent admiration alongside a nonchalant Nathan, Alonso and Nadia. They were in a place to what could be described as a dome, surrounded by six large throne chairs made of white marble with black and yellow crystals embedded on the back rest and hinges of its body, rooted firmly to the ground. Kalbreal hadn't joined them, after he showed her his wings, he had shut off, she was only partially curious as to why, but felt more relieved than anything after Nathan told her as well, that Kalbreals scent was pure ambrosia, meaning he was a walking aphrodisiac and could only be warded off by strong descendants.

Her nerves mirrored by her tightened features as she scanned the area like prey on foreign ground. Nathan called it the dome, because from the outside, it resembled a semi circle marble slab in different shades of green, which swirled like a hypnotic illusion.

The inside was floored with underneath lighting and black walls glimmered from the correct angle. The six throne chairs, where they now stood smack centre of, was the only furniture in the expanse.

She yawned as Alonso started murmuring musical tunes and making dramatic humming noises. Attempting to withhold her laugh with a hand on her mouth, she looked up to see a huge grin masked on Nathans face. He leaned in, whispered in her ear-

"Weird right?"

She didn't reply, because at that moment she really listened to the tune Alonso hummed, and her laugh instantly disintegrated as something triggered inside her, chills spiked her spine, leaving a bitter taste in her mouth, and she knew that taste, fear.

Vibrations rocked the ground beneath her feet, just as her brother crushed her head to his sternum. She looked down to the white stoned floor, which mirrored a fluorescent crystal, in total contrast to the brown leather pants she was sporting and the black cashmere t-shirt Nathan got her as a good luck token.

The floor started its descent, the walls acted as the only support down the smooth ride. She recalled Caidrian telling her that their infrastructure was advanced, but a design as such made from marble, this she knew not even the Germans would be able to pull off.

"It's called an elevator," Nadia said aloud. Clare forgot she was even there; Nadia was exceptionally quiet since they arrived at the dome.

Clare not even half impressed, rolled her eyes, and pursed her lips, "I never would've guessed."

Nadia mumbled, "Anytime."

They stopped five meters below, four tunnels now in view, two ascended up on a slope and one went straight ahead before turning right three meters into the cave, but the fourth was dark, pitch black, no light or fires lit up its map.

She doubted and hoped they wouldn't go in that one, but unfortunately, luck had taken a zero percent interest in the life of

Clare Moonstone recently. She brushed off the nervous twinge in her belly before she followed the others in silence.

The smell of wet clay, assaulted her nostrils mixed with incense of honey suckle, she wasn't sure. The scents in the whole realm were all so overpowering and strong but the land itself was a lot to take in to worry much about the smell.

She cut into a corner as the dim floating lights on the roof, projecting what could be only explained as waves of light, gave her a clearer view. Frozen and bemused to see that it wasn't lights exactly but glow in the dark butterflies. Entranced by the beauty with the change in glows, she had to force herself to move on.

Focusing on the sounds of Nathan and Alonso's boots she asked, "Why do we have to wear brown leathers? Why can't I wear grey, is it suppose to symbolize something?"

"It's more like different strokes for individual folks," Nathan answered, slowing down to step in line with her, "It's the material that counts, grey leather is stronger and more flexible, great when hunting demons, because it's from the shells of the guiders eggs, it also protects you from being sensed by minor demons, and it's almost impenetrable."

He released a breath, as his boots crunched the earth beneath them, "Fortunately its grey, but the brown leather is good for shielding yourself from all descendants, the Garde wears them the most. The material isn't very strong, the color itself symbolizes peace, students who've ascended wear them often as well, it keeps their parents off their backs, it's made from the insides of the Khiron trees."

Nadia muttered, "The Garde are the peacekeepers after all," but loud enough for Clare to hear.

"That's horrible, don't the trees die, they seem so," Clare paused, "alive."

"Nah, we just remove branches, it grows back within a few

months, they don't really mind, they've been doing it since the angels first arrived, it's one of the reasons they exist."

Nathan gestured, with his finger to the end of the cave, as they grew closer toward the noise, "The chambers for the court, Luckily we're meeting only some of the Orderian."

Clare asked, "Do you think they gonna agree to help Calub?"

Alonso interrupted, with a nonchalant shrug, "If they don't we'd just do it anyway, we don't really have to obey them just yet, well Nathan does, but only the Garde condones the Orderian say in anything, besides it's not like we're addressing the Advisors."

"ALONSO" Nadia shouted, a meter away from Nathan, Alonso and herself, "Stop putting ideas in Clare's head, there are consequences when you defy the rules of the realms, even for the those who aren't ascended."

Alonso said "It's just a dumb treaty." He rolled his eyes, "I don't see why we have to pretend like we care, or need them, especially those Asguardians, I hate them, egotistical jackasses."

Nathan muffled in irritation, he sighed, "We have a peace treaty with some of the other realms." He explained to Clare, choosing to ignore Alonso's snarky comments, "That's how we keep most things strictly on a demon and Tempters basis."

Nadia added, slowing down, as they almost reached the open area, "There are certain rules that each of the realms agree to follow, in return, we offer them protection and agree to a fair trial if any crimes have been committed, amongst other things. That way no harm comes to the humans, you should thank the famous Blackwylls for that."

Alonso added, "There are still some who defy the Advisors, the highest order of our kind."

"True, but when there's a problem that affects other realms, we only call the realms concerned." Nathan continued, "We then discuss a common ground solution, if a major law is broken then we vote on a possible punishment, that is what the Garde do, think of them like policemen. In our case, we seek assistance from the other realms without the approval of the Advisors so this is a public matter."

Nathan stopped, and held Clare's arm gaining her full attention, the seriousness on his face made her flinch, "Asguardians consider themselves above law, so be careful, and don't heed what Alonso said, don't mistake his size for his honor."

Clare nodded and soon enough they arrived in a place which was enveloped with people, covering the eighteen row drop of metal chairs. She recognized some of them, from the moon ceremony.

As if they sensed her presence, most turned and stared openly at her, she had expected it. Nathan explained that it would happen because she was considered cursed, because she had no Angelic soul, but he didn't say that she would freak out, or that her palms would get sweaty.

Nathan warned her that morning, how news travelled like a lightning bolt, so she attempted poorly to shrug off the feeling, and narrowed her eyes in an even more poor attempt as she pretended that she was actually looking for someone specific.

The place was a sight for the well deserved eyes, a modern court, tenfold, with lots of chairs joined together as it curved into an oval shape, it was magnificent.

Ancient relic symbols and paintings sketched the walls with colors of blacks and reds and splashes of browns and white. White marble thrones that resembled the ones she'd seen first when they'd entered the dome lined up in a straight line centred the room. On the far right, people surrounded two crescent shape tables with cakes and biscuits and other delectable's, making her mouth water.

She looked around her, realizing but not shocked that Nadia, Alonso had scattered, including Nathan, *so much for small talk,* she hissed inwardly.

The small group of people further in front of her, whom she

remembered as the Elvan stared at her as if she was a forbidden fruit. She gave them a flippant what-the-hell-are-you-looking-at snub, she already disliked their princess Alexa, so it wasn't hard to despise them too. The Shapeshifter's stood on the opposite side examining a young Lightwatcher, like he was an alien specimen.

She noticed something interesting as she stood by her lonesome, how divided the room was. The descendants didn't mix very well with those who weren't their own, except surprisingly the Casters. They were the ones with the bands around their wrist, the only ones scattered amongst the whole crowd. Clare chuckled at the thought, shaking her head at the absurdity of this live picture. Who would've thought that the social ones were the most evil of the lot, but then again, who was she to judge.

She felt a tingle and a breezy whisper in her ear, "I see" the person said, with emphasis on the *s*, "that you are lost,"

She spun around, her long hair hitting his body. Her breathing hitched when she took him in, Kalbreal, all dressed up. Her eyes slowly descended taking in the charcoal suit lining his muscular body. His pants tailored to perfection hinted at the ridges of his thighs. His black shirt which was definitely a thick silken thread was left un-tucked, his jacket open. All together, with his markings on his ears he looked sinfully sexy, but those eyes,

Clare couldn't hold in her laugh, as the blush turned her face shades of ruby, she turned around properly to face him, "So someone's in a good mood, did your prayers get answered?" She said, taunting him with her eyes.

Kalbreal lifted his shirt slightly to show her a black edged blade, "See for yourself." She smiled as she looked at the blade which protruded out from its black sheath made with diamond edging, hmm, definitely an angel, "Nice, are you gonna give me the rundown of who's who, before I make a complete idiot of myself?"

He gestured with his hand, as a ghost of a smile shadowed his face, "We should sit higher up, I have a reputation with female Lightwatchers." He shrugged with a sheepish smile, "If we're going to commit sin we might as well do it privately."

Clare raised her eyebrow and smiled with a knowing look as Kalbreal ushered her to the top of the court. She had to admit, this playful side of him was definitely the side she wanted to be on.

When they sat down she saw a few people walking towards the marble chairs facing the audience, they wore green robes that were open in the front, "Who are those people?"

"Some of the members of the Orderian, look there, the first on the right." He leaned in closer to her, his voice a bare whisper, "The Elvan queen, Arexandra, the Shapeshifter master, Jaiden Pyn, the Caster Vincent Ipswich, his the son of Asmodeus you met him last night, and the sulking one sitting on the end that's Raphael, Prime of Asguard."

"They are seriously children of the Angels."

"Majority are descendants of their children, Angels don't conceive often."

She looked wide-eyed at him "Tell me something about the Angels, something I'd find interesting."

His jaw ticked, and his demeanor changed, she was almost certain that he wouldn't say anything, he'd close off, but Kalbreal surprised her, "We don't do marriage like the deceptors, we take consorts, most of the time by a blood binding to seal the bond, but in the Infinity there are those of highest rank, they are..." he paused, "different. If they find their true consort, their destined mate and complete the mating a true bond is formed, and the said beings' Gazool is multiplied. But if he comes into contact with his true consort, and neglects the pull, until the bond is formed he's Gazool or energy as some call it, cannot be easily controlled. The more powerful the being is, the worse the side effects. Which will be catastrophic if that said someone were to be roaming on this earth, which is why when they normally meet their true consorts they seduce them to hasten the bond."

Kalbreal stared at her, until she started feeling uncomfortable, was he trying to tell her something, he should just say it, why did he always have to be so evasive. The way he sat, the way he moved, she was beginning to see him as an Angel, a perfected being, almost flawless if it weren't for his mouth. She smiled at the thought, arrogance suited the bastard though she'd give him that.

"What?" she snapped unable to stop squirming under his patronizing gaze that saw more than she wanted to reveal.

"There's a rumor going around that Franchesca Draiken's youngest born is the son of Azazy-el, and Azazy-el being a prince means, that he is of highest rank, a cadre of hell, your mother could be his consort."

She sat there staring at him, pretending he hadn't just told her that her mother could possibly be the consort of the prince of hell himself, "I know Caidrian and her split up after I was born."

He faced front, eyes still drawn on her, "Franchesca was on a mission a year or so after you were born, she fled to Egypt landed in some trouble, and ended up in the mountain of Dudael." He stopped, waited for a response but she remained silent, knots forming in her stomach, "Azazy-el would've known that there was a connection, a few have been known to deny the true consort bond, but he isn't the type, your mother would've felt it too. A long time in a mountain, trapped with your true consort, the mortal mind can do crazy things, it's possible. I wasn't around that time, I asked William about it, knowing the twins wouldn't speak, but he didn't exactly answer my question, but a lot of the descendants believe that story."

At the mention of Williams name, she stiffened, but quickly brushed it off not wanting Kalbreal to notice her infatuation, because that's what it must be right, to her faceless Caster, "Are you trying to convince me or yourself?" she asked incredulous, "because

I'm not buying it."

His gaze was compensative, when he replied, in that deep masculine voice, "It could be partial truth, you must understand the truth is not what you convince people in believing, it's that which is forged."

There he went with the evasive again, she had no doubt that he already knew the truth, it was those fire colored gazes which had given him away. She also knew that most of what Kalbreal said had significance. When he spoke, it was always with that slight smile, arrogance of knowledge. A permanent expression that he mastered, his, not fake like some humans but real. She was certain that whatever questions she had, Angel-boy held the answers to most, but he wasn't going to tell her, at least not yet. She had to play his game, understand him, but she also needed to listen as a student listened to a teacher.

Clare looked at Kalbreal blankly, she not only changed the subject, but she altered its course, when she asked, "What's so special about Calub that a Tempter or someone else would want him and not kill him?"

Kalbreal sighed, not meeting her face, "Your brother isn't easy to kill, unless you are an Irin or higher, he has a certain type of protection, one similar to the mark of Cain, but whereas Cain's was bestowed on him, Calub was born with it and learnt to harness the gift at a young age. We shouldn't be discussing this now." His eyes pierced her with an ire of warning; she had yet to see on Angel-boy. They glowed a mica of black and orange volcanic eruption, "You can't tell anybody about this," she gasped at his feral growl, her eyes widened by the fear that crept in her, the tremor that rattled her hands.

She nodded abruptly, and dropped her gaze, and gulped. Kalbreal had so much Gazool flowing off him that she was overwhelmed; this was no minor Angel as Caidrian said. Clare was certain that Kalbreal was more powerful than he wanted people to believe, much more. This meant he must have had an important position in the Infinity. The question which had never occurred to her now lingered in her mind, like a rattling snake hissing in her ear-

What was he doing on the earth for the past eight years, there WAS a reason, and she was going to find out.

Clare squinted to get a better view as a lady, wearing a royal blue robe, walked toward a glass microphone, which stood in the centre of the court. Behind the lady sat the four people in the green robes.

Arexandra the Elvan queen was the first seated, with her platinum hair shining down her back, it wasn't hard to guess from so far up. Next to her was Jayden Pyn, and three other men, amongst them sat Vincent, with an unmasked confidence. Underneath his open robe, he wore a black leather pants and a powdered blue shirt. The sleeves of his robe folded up, revealing black strings and beads wrapped around his wrist, as if he sensed her, he turned his head and looked smack into her face, she quickly averted away, embarrassed she was caught gawking at him.

The lady who stood in the centre of the room was tall, with dark, short cropped hair and what looked like blue eyes and a heart shaped face and a bit wide hipped. She could've been in her forties, but judging by what Clare new of the Lightwatchers, the aging process slowed down after a certain age, so she could've been in her fifties, but still an airy of lethality marked her stance, when she addressed them.

"I am Annabelle, Sole Advisor here today." She paused, and the room went immediately quiet, "Members of The Order and Lightwatchers, a Lightwatcher has been lost to us, but another from the Moonstone and Draiken blood has returned, stand up Gabriella Moonstone."

Clare's heart thumped soundly, the beat heavy as she obeyed, without acknowledging Kalbreal. People whispered, eyes stared in horror, some undisguised disgust, "Gabriella Moonstone come child."

She walked down a middle pathway of iron steps, with each descend she took, her breathing escalated, her palms began to sweat

Step, step, THUD THUD

Cursing herself, urging her body to move forward, why was she so nervous,

Step, step, THUD THUD

A single drop of sweat beaded at her temple, she fought against her body,

Step, step, THUD THUD

She was so scared, she couldn't understand it, her mind told her to go, move faster, you have to save your brother, he needs you, but her body, her body wanted to flee, to run, and never look back, her body wanted to cower.

With sweaty palms, a fast pulse, she tuned out the people. Their disdainful eyes, never stopped its onslaught. She reached the very bottom where Annabelle stood, it took all her courage and willpower not to run, not to whimper.

She didn't turn to acknowledge Kalbreal, or Nathan, just stood there expectant, with her back faced to the crowd. Her heart never ceased its speed, her body itched as the leather rubbed against her thighs, she was sure that the cashmere shirt she wore was drenched with sweat under her armpits.

"State your case," Her gaze widened at Annabelle's abruptness, Clare stared at the woman, trying to get some read on whether this woman were among those who despised her or pitied her, but there was no injustice. Annabelle nodded slowly at her to go on.

Clare thought about what she was suppose to say, then gathered some courage and spoke, "I wish to be called Clare," She flinched, at the stupidity of how she sounded, "My birth name has been removed," It came out more a question than a statement, but it was enough to get the descendants whispering.

She refused to turn, knowing full well that they'll be staring at her in repugnance and loathing or sheer disappointment. The worst would be the pity, because to the Lightwatchers having no name, that marked you. Having your gift taken away was worse than being branded an axe murderer, or losing your memory at the tender age of ten.

Nathan had told her, "There is nothing worse than being stripped of your name, it's like ripping out part of your soul. I've watched it been done, seen the torture in the eyes of one who's been stripped. Most end up dead within a week, not many are strong enough to go through the change. The descendants may give you the cold shoulder, but their hate is fueled by their fear of a ten year old Lightwatcher who survived almost unscathed by that which has killed many. You have a strong soul Clare, don't let their masks deter you, when you have barely surfaced." She didn't understand why he told her that, but now she knew, it gave her a semblance of courage when Annabelle gestured, she turn to the crowd.

A bearded man stood up, he had a rough exterior that gave her the creeps, but it fueled her determination, because she saw him, he might've looked strong, but she caught the nervous tell in his left hand before he put it behind his back and sneered, "How can you be one of us if you don't even bear the mark, where's your name child?"

Frustrated, her mind drew a blank at her brother's lecture regarding laws, she snapped, "My father and mother are Lightwatchers, descendants of the archangels Mikael and Gabriel."

Her cheeks flushed, and a burn lodged in her throat as she swallowed her saliva, "I have amnesia, my names gone, but I'm sure you all know that."

Annabelle saw the tears in Clare's eyes, and retorted on Clare's behalf, "The girl has spoken her point, we shall call her Clare until her name has returned." Annabelle looked up to the audience, "We have more important matters to attend."

Raphael stood up from his chair, fair almost paled skinned, lithe, with long black hair barely touching his shoulders, and chiseled sharp features. If it weren't for those calculated yellow eyes that chilled her bones by the sheer hatred in them, she would've have thought him a striking beauty of a man. His voice scratched the air, "Why did you call upon us half-blood?"

Annabelle's head spun in his direction, her voice grave, "Do not downgrade her Raphael, you are still in Khiron, you would respect our young, name or not."

He ignored Annabelle, his eyes focused on Clare, who wore a scowl of her own, when he practically spat the words out, "I see your acquaintance with my uncle grows stronger every passing second."

His eyes shot to Kalbreal, "Isn't that so Kalbreal?"

Kalbreal reputed his remark, with a shrug, and shouted, "Since when do you question me."

Raphael turned his attention completely on Clare again, she resisted the urge to swear him, and shut him up, "I know why you are here, girl." He clapped his hand, as a cruel smile painted his face, "I refuse any help on my side towards your suicidal mission."

The voice from the back spoke, Clare turned to see it was Kalbreal, "Don't worry about him, I'll follow you, it's not like an Asguardian can yield a Harpien blade."

Raphael looked furious, "Your sudden affections for the little watcher devour your judgment Kalbreal."

Kalbreal argued, "You know the boy is good Raphael." His voice deepened and intensified, "Your father would be ashamed."

"Ashamed?" He asked, with mocking dispute, "For how long? you are a newer Angel on this planet, I have roamed dimensions as an Asguardian for Thousands of years, Azazy-el shaped the chaos of the world, any descendant of his will bring to the earths' destruction. I do like the boy, and will forever mourn his death but this is best left as it is, maybe if you haven't saved his sister..."

Kalbreal shouted, Clare could swear she felt a slight vibration in the air, when his voice drifted down, "Facts are not proven by rumors Raphael, Asguardians have always hated the Lightwatchers, seen them as a threat."

Kalbreal taunted him, "I won't be surprised if you are behind these killings, attempting to steal their souls, use their gifts, the same ones you have spent eons trying to earn, but they are born with. It must be hard that your superiority only extends to Asguard."

Clare looked at Raphael, the bitterness in his eyes and face so unhidden, she yelled, "What do you mean when you said saved his sister?"

Raphael hissed in satisfaction, "Little Clare doesn't know."

His quivering eyes met Clare's, his voice soft and husky, "Oh yes, Kalbreal defied death and saved your precious life after Kadreal put an order out for your death." He paused, facing the audience of people, who were so quiet, so still.

They were as shocked as she by this news. She didn't have to see the faces that made up the crowd, because she could feel it in the air, as it skilfully sucked the oxygen right out of her lungs.

"Clare's death was destiny," He spoke to the audience, "But Kalbreal just couldn't let that happen, could you uncle."

Clare looked at Kalbreal, unfettered tears poured down her face as she mouthed his name, without a sound.

Raphael wasn't done confessing the Angel's sins for all those to hear. She wanted to stop him, to tell him it was wrong, it was so horrible, her heart-ached, but she couldn't move, she barely remembered to draw air into her lungs, frozen in one spot.

"When an Angel saves a life they leave cracks, the fallen are able to get through them, if you want to blame someone for the deaths of your people, blame Kalbreal." He paused, "He just had to intervene all those years ago; he knows that whoever it is killing you, wants the girl."

Raphael raised his hands, his index fingers pointed toward the ceiling, "How many sins did you commit Uncle to save one ten year old girl? And how much more death will befall the realms and your own family, before you see truth? The girl must die it is the only way, she might be female, Kalbreal, but the outcome is the same, she must die, you know it and I know it. The Irin will come for her, there are even a few Tempters who see that, you know HE would come for her, I'm surprised she is still alive."

Kalbreal stood at the back, his voice a catatonic boom in the hall, as the ground shook, he growled, "ENOUGH," His voice echoed through the court, vibrating in Clare's ears. People got scared, some even held on to their swords and guns, getting ready for a physical onslaught.

Raphael pushed on, not at all deterred by Kalbreal's fury, which was weird, and made Clare wary, as to why Raphael pushed the issue of her dying.

She felt scared as involuntary hopelessness curdled inside her. If what Raphael was saying is true, then the angels would come for her, she didn't know why, with no memory, no one who would give her answers. Who would protect her, she presumed her brother would want to, but how would her brother save her from Angels and Tempters, when he was only half of one. She was as good as dead, because it was impossible, and she didn't need to be one of them to figure that out.

William flashed in her mind, and just the thought of the faceless Caster grounded her, especially when Raphael focused his intention on her, "Why do you think Kalbreal is here, all these years? Have you wondered why Clare? He was exiled; he had no right to save you."

Raphael's words poured out like acid burning her ears with the deception laced in his voice, planting doubt in the descendants head, goading Kalbreal, aiming for a fight, but why.

What was it that this Asguardian was trying to prove, he spoke on but she blocked him out of her mind, as she slyly slanted her gaze to where Kalbreal stood, and the breath she held, left her in complete relief.

Kalbreal was shockingly calm, which meant he foresaw exactly what Raphael was aiming to do, she caught the last part of what Raphael was saying, "...Gabriel favored Kalbreal, still a full Angel plus all the perks that earth has to offer, taking up residents with Tempters' children, you are not even mentioned in scriptures uncle, must be really low on the mark."

Kalbreal laughed, it was infectious as it echoed right to the bottom, where she stood five steps away from Raphael, "Jealous?"

She looked at Raphael and then at Kalbreal, she had enough of this, Kalbreal was an Angel, he didn't deserve Raphael' bitterness, and she certainly wasn't going to put up with it a second more, if there was one thing Clare would be remembered for, it was her big mouth.

She narrowed her eyes, vehemence in every word she yelled directly at Raphael, "Angels are supposed to be kind and merciful, your parents are Adonai's soldiers, yet you belittle an Angel, to prove what? Who has the bigger balls?" She turned to the crowd, dismissing Raphael, "Kalbreal might be exiled but whereas other Angels would've killed an innocent girl, he saved me, for whatever reason. Now I may not remember any of this, but I've been to church like the deceptors and I'll tell you that the bible speaks of Angels being good and pure, but where is the goodness now? Where was my mercy when the very Angels I was taught to trust tried to kill me? Where is Kalbreals, because he chose a conscience and saved my life? I pity all of you if you think for one minute that Kalbreal is anything less than great. If Adonai wanted him powerless, why is he still a full Angel? Why is he able to hold a Harpien blade, the same blade only an Angel can hold, right? Someone told me, that the truth is not what you convince people in believing, it is that which is forged."

A man from the crowd stood up, she didn't notice him, straight away, because she had her eyes trained on Nathan who was two rows from where she stood.

When she turned her head, she was almost surprised by the black suit and blue shiny tie he wore, it was so human, his hair multiple shades of blonde. His eyes a saturation of purple and pink, entranced her. He was as tall as Alonso if not taller, chiseled cheekbones and a sharp bridged nose.

His voice heard loudly by everyone, was husky as he commanded attention, "You have suffered much grief, yet your belief in Adonai is not swayed by the actions of Kadreal, Clare, and knowing that your actions could cost young Calubeal his life, you defend an Angel in front of all five hundred and eighty six descendants. I have not seen that honor for centuries." He gave a slight smile, and bowed his head at Clare, which earned a few gasps in the crowd, "We are merciful to those deserving, it is in my ability to bestow a gift if the receiver is worthy, accept my gift Clare, remember that which you have lost."

Kalbreal glided through the air, his body a flame of fire, landing in front of her as he roared, "NARZA." Which Clare knew meant no, but it was too late, a shock of lightening struck her brain, she barely heard Kalbreals voice, when he yelled, "Armatos what have you done."

Clare fell to the ground, hitting it hard, her body possessed into a temporary trance, something she had never felt. An igniting blast shot through her spinal cord, her brain shocked itself with small electric currents, causing the cells in her body to pin prick, and convulse, into a semi epileptic state, and a final relief washed over her.

She felt it when it happened, she felt.. awakened subconsciously for the first time, as her mind took her to another place.

A LITTLE KID, a girl, with light brown short hair, smiling at a lady and a man, who sat on a bench in the middle of a snowing seasoned park, she didn't recognize these people, and focused on the girl as she said, "Ok mama and papa, I love you."

Her mind moved quickly to an older girl about seven or eight, whom she recognized as herself, except the girls' hair was black and her eyes... Clare couldn't make out her eyes, but they weren't green, was it her? She looked similar to Clare, but the girl was engaged in martial arts, with a young version of Caidrian and a little boy, who looked similar to herself that she knew now, with brown hair and green eyes.

Flashes and glimpses of her brother Nathan when he was younger soared through her mind like a slide of clips, first a teenager sparring with the girl she presumed must've been her. His scratchy voice, "Sister, sister, be strong, the stance determines the skill." He glided his feet and swept her legs off the ground.

The images faded like dust, and another appeared of her mother so happy, chasing her around a big wooden floored house, and then, she spotted Raphael teaching her knife throwing and angelic words, "Armah, water, remember that one Ella and you get chocolate."

Another glimpse with Raphael, his kind eyes looking to the ceiling as a young Clare called to him, and ran into a lounge area, squealing, "Uncle, uncle," he grabbed her around her waist, like a little doll when she jumped on top of the brown leather sofas and tickled her. She wailed, screeching in delight, "Uncle, I swear it was Nathan."

Something about him was different, yet there was a familiarity to him, a softness behind that hard exterior, not the cold Asguardian that cursed at her with the stench of venom on his lips.

She flashed to encounters with Caidrian, the scenes didn't play out, but she was remembering, a shrill of hope sparkled inside her, as she recalled him taking her to an abandoned building, things went wrong that night, and they were attacked.

Caidrian fought two demons, shooting them with guns. She was scared at first that night, she froze up, until she thought they were going to die, then a dim light shone around her body. She flashed and caught an image of her ten year old self, as she gracefully glided a sword through the air, slicing a meaner demons head off.

She seemed fearless, her moves faster than she could catch on a blind eye, her reflexes were amazing.

The memory quickly desiccated into another vision, one more real than the next, (her mother sitting with Calub, helping him with his trick cards, she saw her little brother, his innocence to the world reflecting through her mind, his magician tricks in the lobby of the faculty always well served).

She then saw the training room, with different sections, she recalled her mother telling her, "People can't know." and a door opening into darkness

Then everything slowed and played out, "Let's go, come on guys, UNCLE," She was ten, her hair was black and her eyes covered by an extremely long fringe, as she screamed from the bottom of the stairs,

Raphael walked passed her and touched her nose, "I'm out, Ella girl, enjoy."

Franchesca walked downstairs slipping on a pair of black pumps, "Where's your brothers?" Ten year old Clare rolled her eyes, "Calub's in his moods, Nate's pretending to be sick so he can see his girlfriend, and uncle's out."

Caidrian was driving, and Franchesca sat in the front seat, Clare sitting at the back with her head peeped out between the two front seats watching Caidrian drive, she remembered that she really wanted to drive, but Caidrian refused, so she watched him instead, so when Nathan finally took her secretly she wouldn't disappoint.

The traffic was light that evening, the cold stifle. Caidrian brushed her hair back, and blessed her with his rare smiles. On a sharp left, a bright light blinded ten year old Clare's eyes for a second, it took her a good couple of seconds to recover, but she knew instantly that it was no car or any earthly thing, no it was an Irin a powerful Angel, who stood in the centre of the road.

Young Clare was excited, "Mom, that's an Angel."

Franchesca yelled, "Put your seat belt on honey, sit back." Her mothers' voice was scared, nervous, she had never heard her mother frightened before, but she did it, and just as she locked it, the car was flipped.

Young Clare felt her head hit the windscreen, and the Angel was right there, reaching for her with his hand. When she felt a heat, and saw an orange flame behind the Angel, it was another Angel, she saw wide spread wings licked with flecks of fire, before young Clare was out, unconscious. Waking up to a familiar voice,- Kalbreal, he said, "They want to kill her I can't hold them off forever."

She remembered him touching her head, all her thoughts sucked out, vanishing, gone. The pain of something been ripped out of her, the hollowness, the feeling of loss, she saw him, removing all the past of her life, so they could make a new future, "I suppressed her abilities and hid her gifts, they shouldn't be able to track her, I also removed her name, to be sure. She can pass as a deceptor. I don't know for how long but it's longer than she will get if you don't run."

She heard someone else there, another man, but she felt herself waking up from whatever spell she was under.

CROWDS OF PEOPLE SURROUNDED her, mumbling, some

talking louder than most. She rubbed her head, and got up, seeing her brother beside her in a crouched position. She flung herself into his arms, and he gripped her tight, his hair tickled her cheek. She didn't let him go, but bent her neck back to give him a smile, which faded when she saw his brow line, furrowed "How long was I out?"

"Half hour give or take, but it felt like fifty lifetimes, I'm sure I have some grey somewhere."

"I think I just got my memory back, not everything, I can't remember my full training, and stuff about being a Lightwatcher, but I remember you and dad, and Cal and his tricks, enough to know that I'm a Lightwatcher, and you my brother," he smiled with his eyes but it was forced.

Clare had a strange feeling that her brother hoped that wouldn't have been the case, she caught the flash of worry, before he discarded it, "Wanna get up?"

She nodded, and looked in the front, where she now stood hugging Nathan and locked eyes with Kalbreal. He didn't hide his emotions, there was no doubt of the unhappiness sketched on his face, his eyes seemed hotter, blazingly so, but why? Did he think she would hate him? He saved her life, by risking his own, a true selfless act, if anything she liked him a bit more, but now wasn't the time to dwell on the past, she needed to focus on the future. So she ignored the questions and emotions that now swirled internally as she walked up to the centre of the stage, with a new form of confidence and surety and approached the stand, with a quick nod to Annabelle.

"Lightwatchers, and Orderian," the room quieted after a few minutes, some took seats, whilst others stood, "I Clare Moonstone, stand before you, as a Lightwatcher BUT most important as a sister, I know it's not my place to talk." She looked at an older man, a member of the Garde, "I am a minor in your eyes, but I seek guidance in my elders and assistance. I don't ask you permission, my mind is made up, I am no servant to the Garde or the Orderian, and since the

Advisors are not forth, well you get what I am saying."

A woman spoke from the crowd, "You are a child, you can't go on a quest it's forbidden, you haven't even ascended."

Clare ignored her, "We are suppose to love and care for our families, that's what makes us part human. A Tempter has my younger brother, a minor, I don't know why."

She paused and looked at the Elvan queen who sat in the front row, "And even if you help me, I offer no guarantee on your return."

She sighed, and lifted her head toward the Shapeshifter's huddled in the corner, "This is a suicidal mission, and maybe death is the fate I am choosing, but yesterday I was a human girl with no siblings and no father."

Her throat threatened to clog, but she fought her emotions as she revealed, "I watched firsthand the wrath of a Tempter, as he ripped my mother's heart out of her chest, and held it in his hand, like his greatest prize. I saw that hunger in his eyes, but here I stand ready to fight, be it death I walk to." She inhaled a lungful of air, and faced them head strong, "I ask you, LIGHTWATCHERS, SHAPESHIFTER, ELVAN AND CASTERS, will you join me? Or would you stand against me?"

People started whispering, including the Orderian amongst themselves.

The Elvan queen who had been quiet the whole time stood up, "I shall send my own,"

The Shapeshifter, Jayden yelled thereafter, "I second that,"

Nathan stood forward, with Nadia, Alonso and at the end stood Kalbreal.

Clare smiled at the lot who stood in front of her, "Thank you."

THE ROOM WAS ROWDY, as the people caught up with news and conversations, completely disregarding all the drama that had taken place twenty minutes ago.

Clare had just spoken with one of her own, Draiken, when she spotted Vincent, "There's one who can be of grave use to you Clare, he's in the mountains of Aquadore, him as an ally might just save your life."

She smiled at Vincent, he leaned in closer to her ear, a hint of a smile brushed his lips as he whispered, "Nikolai Blackwyll, I suggest you go alone."

"Thanks Vincent," he winked at her and walked away.

Clare's gaze shifted, it landed on Kalbreal across the room. He stood alone, lost in his mind no doubt, and she just couldn't look away from the gingered hair Angel, who was now part of her past and possible future.

She didn't know how to feel about his link to her past, or that he had purposely defended her, by going against his own. She couldn't hate him, because if she was honest to herself, she would've been dead if it weren't for his betrayal.

She got to live a normal life, as Nathan had put it, because having amnesia made it easier to accept that she was being hunted to death, by Angels. Having amnesia made it bearable to live with the outcome of having her soul forcefully ripped out of her, leaving her bare. The same thing she had hated and chastised herself about, the same sickness that she tried so hard to reverse, was the same thing that had kept her breathing for another eight years, given by one selfless fire Angel named Kalbreal.

She still didn't know why the Angels wanted her dead, but knowing what she knew about Kalbreal, knowing the sacrifice endorsed from saving her and the determination he set on keeping her alive, she was certain that she could never part from her Angel, because that's exactly what he was, her Angel.

She dropped her gaze, when he turned to face her, as if he could feel her eyes trained on him. It should have freaked her out, that he knew exactly when she watched him, but it didn't, and she was in no mood to analyze what that meant.

Capturing those visions in her mind again was harder than she thought, with all the chattering and laughing going on around the room, so she focused on facts instead. She knew that girl was her, but she was different, young and fearless, with raven black hair, and the eyes, she couldn't remember the eyes, it was always blocked, maybe it was a trick of the light but she was almost certain it glowed, ha, she'll remember eventually. Nathan explained that her memory could take days to unravel, depending on how fast her brain was able to process the information.

Clare knew that there was more, much more behind those locked memories, and maybe the reason for her mother's death laid there waiting to be reborn. She had to try and piece together the events which transpired when she was younger. Her instincts told her that she needed to do it soon, because something was coming and it was coming straight for her.

She looked at Kalbreal, whose back now faced her, and knew her feelings for Angel-boy had altered. True, he had been a constant in the last few days, since her life turned into turmoil. Seeing him now as not just her one time savior, but the reason for her continual existence.

Clare smiled at the memory of what he'd meant when he said he'd saved her twice. Now when she saw him, she found it hard not to see a broken Angel with blazing wings, and even harder not to look at him as one who had shifted a place in her heart.

She sighed, because even with all Kalbreal's flaws now just a minority, he did not have midnight blue eyes that glimmered in the darkness, or the touch that possessed her from the very first time. So though there was a small part of her that felt for Kalbreal, he was not the one she yearned for. Not the one she craved like an addiction, writhing for her next hit, not knowing what she was addicted too. That one, his name was William, and he was coming for her. She felt it in her soul, as strongly as the shudder that rippled through her at the mere thought of her faceless obsession.

Clare caught Raphael's seething gaze on her, like a hunter waiting on its prey. She frowned at the bloodlust in his eyes, a complete one eighty to how kind and generous he once was. She remembered her mother calling him "Labiel," she mouthed the name, soundless, what did it mean?

There was more to it, more to this, something was off with that picture, she just couldn't wrap her head around it, but she would, tonight. She had never been more glad for her photographic memory, which she purposely hid at school, not wanting people to think she was a geek with good looks. Nope, she had saved it for University, where it was cool to know it all. Unfortunately, with Angels trying to kill her, she wasn't going to get the chance to test the theory of that one.

She walked closer to mouth of the cave, as she thought of Calub, wondering how he was, if he was safe. She knew deep in her heart that she was doing the right thing. Saving him was what she had to do, regardless of Angels and whoever the hell else trying to shorten her life span.

Clare was just about to walk out of the room when she caught Raphael moving toward her. Her hackles rose instantly, but quickly dissipated when a man stopped him in his tracks.

Phew, that was close, she inwardly groaned.

The Asguardian was not to be trusted and given the chance, he would slice her head off without a second thought. At that moment she mentally made an enemy list, and gleefully placed Raphael at the top.

What became another problem in her list of puzzles was, who

was killing the descendants and why did it sound like the Asguardians were covering it up, and blaming her. It seemed she was centred to everything. In the human world she wouldn't mind, it was semantics with popularity, but in this world, well that just seemed to make more enemies. And with Tempters and Angels already gunning for her, her future was just getting dimmer by the second.

She wasn't aware that she stopped and leaned against the wall of the court's entrance, being lost in thought. A man from her right called out her name, snapping her out of her buzzing mind. She turned her head surprised to see it was the Shapeshifter Alpha, Jaiden,

"Yes, Orderian" she said in a respectable manner, not wanting to lose his alliance. Though he looked like a man who couldn't care less about formalities, she wasn't going to compromise her brothers' safety any further by a slip of the tongue.

She eyed Jaiden with an appreciative glance, capturing his ruffled spiky bed slept blue hair, and hazel eyes that slanted upwards, hidden behind thick long lush eyebrows. He stared right back at her, as his bridged nose flared. Talk about hotness coaxed in olive skin, Jaiden Pyn even walked like a tiger on a prowl. She wandered if he purred, while suppressing the urge to fan herself as the sudden flush of heat crept on her.

Since she woke up from her sleep induced trance, she had been getting a lot of hot flushes, similar to when she was ovulating. It must have been a side effect of getting her memory back, but she wasn't going to ask her brother about that, no way.

When he stopped in front of her, he gave her a knowing smile. Clare instantly dropped her gaze as a sudden blush pinked her cheeks, glimpsing his suddenly extremely interesting black combat boots.

He cleared his throat, and she reluctantly lifted her head, to stare into his eyes that now looked black, and primal, his voice thick and gruff when he said, "The Shapeshifter I have for you is in Los-Angeles, I called him, he'll expect you to meet him midday, in two days, be there. His name's Thomas Browley, brown hair, about your height, tattoo on his body of a butterfly you won't miss him, I don't think he'll make it sooner, he'd take you to the entrance of the demon realms, your brother has his number."

He paused as if contemplating what to say next, "Never lower your head Clare, especially if you plan to confront Kole, he'll eat you alive. If you can barely look at me, you wouldn't last ten minutes with Kole, especially if he's having one of his moods."

Clare laughed, completely puzzled, "Kole?".

He looked at her confused, "Nikolai Blackwyll?"

She bit her lip, trying hard not to say something snarky, "Thanks for the info, I'll talk to Nathan."

"Malibu beach, Thomas."

She nodded as Jaiden walked off, taking a sec just to admire his delectable back view, she turned to see Nathan, Kalbreal, Alonso and Nadia at the entrance of the cave, gawking at her.

Startled, because she'd been caught standing by the entrance admiring Jaiden's asset, she raised her eyebrows to say *well-what-the-hell-are-you-staring-at*. She hadn't seen them pass her to leave the court, not that she was really paying attention. Nathan was the one to drop his head and shake it, while Alonso and Nadia gave her knowing looks. Kalbreal on the other hand, looked almost worried, not angry, or jealous, but worried..,interesting.

It was comforting to know that she hadn't been launched, but she was really hoping to slip out unseen, because this Nikolai character peeked her curiosity, "You guys don't have to guard me, I feel fine." She shrugged as if it was no big deal, "I know my way around, go have fun."

Her brother held his hand out so she could take it, "Psst, we aint gonna be having fun here little sister, when there's a party to attend."

She smirked at Nathan and took his hand, "hmmm party, music and booze kinda party?"

They all laughed, except Kalbreal, who had the same distraught look plastered on his face,

Nadia added, gathering Clare's attention, "There's a whole lot more than deceptors booze. The Garde all left for their stations, including your father."

"Yeah, I didn't see him at the meeting," She gave Nathan an expectant look, who had his head dropped to the floor, as they made the way back toward the elevator, "Aren't we suppose to go with him to Washington?"

Kalbreal chipped in, "We will," his gaze speculative. She guessed the Angel wasn't sure whether Clare was angry at him or not. She'll have to fix that, after meeting Nikolai Blackwyll.

Nadia remarked, "If we live through the next week."

Outside of the dome, Clare was just about to make up some excuse when Nadia tugged on her arm, "Clare and I'll see you boys at the Jakenson palace."

After a brief hesitation from Nathan and a teeth grinding from Kalbreal, the boys eventually left and Nadia pulled Clare further away from the dome, "I heard you talking to Vincent Ipswich, I know Nikolai Blackwyll, he's a drunk, and a womanizing liar. He has no remorse for anything, just going to him alone is a suicide mission especially in his recent state, he's deteriorated, what if he kills you Clare?"

Clare went completely defensive, for reasons she couldn't possibly understand, when she practically growled, "Well it's a chance I'm willing to take. Vincent's alright, I don't think he'd have told me about Nikolai, if he didn't trust the guy, and I need all the help I can get, Casters can be helpful." She shrugged as if the decision was simple, totally not true, but Clare didn't like explaining herself to someone else.

Nadia sighed, "He prefers the term Warlock, if you going, at least take this."

She handed Clare a silver gun, it was a 9mm, serpent symbols engraved on the handle. She recognized it as the seals for death, "Lemme guess, demon gun?"

"Ah, I see you picking up that memory fast."

Nadia and Clare walked around the building into the open sky. The sun had just set, and the darkness started creeping into the shadows.

Clare felt chills crawl up the flesh of her spine, she didn't know whether it was her nerves, or the fact that the mountain of Aquadore looked like a nomads mountain,

"Clare focus, the guys will meet us at eight, that'll give you two hours to get there, change and get back. I'll meet you at the entrance cave, exactly at 7.45, with a change of clothes, don't be late."

She nodded, "Weird that you helping me, but thanks."

Nadia looked serious, "Go, now, before I change my mind."

Fifteen

Liam

The night sky was starless, his body bumped onto something sharp causing him to wince. Hands tied in the front as they pushed him up a long staircase, regardless of his offer to walk on his own. Liam was seriously being tested. In other circumstances, he would've ripped their throats out without so much as a glance, but keeping up a weak front was the only thing stopping them from tranquillising him, yet again. Things hadn't went entirely the way he presumed it would, now a prisoner of Asguard in the Elvan territory, Safiereal. Alexandra nowhere to be heard of or seen.

Liam had relied on been captured in the hope of getting more information by now, but instead, he was pushed quietly across a staircase which led to the open grass-way toward the Elvan mountain, "Raphael, stop this now. I mean no harm to your kind, the only law I broke, wasn't even a law in itself."

"I'm not in the mood William for your petulance, I would have killed you the moment I found you, if I could. Kalbreal is a betrayal to his own kind, weakened by a nameless mortal half blood, he forgets his loyalties. What I do to you, would be a fine reminder to him."

"This is about Clare isn't it. You know who she is."

"Oh I do." Raphael assured him, "In actuality I know enough, that she won't live much longer, not after what Armatos did."

The Asguardian who held Liam pushed him, but he didn't fall, he front flipped, landing on his feet, not even looking at the other Asguardians, but focused on Raphael.

He inquired, not surprised by Raphael's nonchalant reaction to his strength, "Armatos, what did he do?"

"He gave the girl her memories back, it'll take time to all be returned, but Kalbreal had linked it to her legacies. Unfortunately, she doesn't have her name, all that power without the Gazool to maintain it."

Raphael shook his head, "Disastrous."

"What." Liam felt the air around him dense, as he fought to control his rage, and the coldness that threatened to seep through his pores, "It's too soon, I'm not... I'm not ready."

Raphael stopped, and faced Liam at the end of the stairs, "Not ready? You can't save her, you're a Caster, a beastly monster, she would need an Archangel at least, to save her. One of the highest stature to return her name, and even then, the prince himself would come for her."

Liam completely ignored this, he was thousands of miles away, attempting to reach his sister, but he couldn't, something was off, she wasn't responding.

Liam's face was cold, his big blue eyes smaller and darker. He lifted his chin, though still taller than all the others who surrounded him, "This changes things, changes everything."

Raphael grabbed a sword, "Changes what Caster?"

Liam looked at the heavy metal binding his hands, "Release me."

The chains opened at request, Raphael lifted his sword, but Liam stood there not moving, "I don't want to hurt you Raphael, but if you stand in my way I will not hesitate."

Liam's body changed before Raphael and the other two members of Asguard. First it was his skin, glowing, then his eyes that resembled cut diamonds, and finally the blinding royal blue light that flamed around him, like a fire which seeped out from his pores, bringing the touch of the fire of ice.

His hair still black, matching the coat he still wore buttoned up. Features still visible, he decided that he would not show his full self, not yet anyway. He bent his knees, without a word or an acknowledgement of Raphael he jumped high up into the sky and landed in the centre of the Elvan territory, at least fifty kilometres away.

He was careful to land in an empty spot. People stopped to look at him, but it was a show he'd given the Elvan one too many times for anybody significant to bother much. But the kids never got over the thrill and that helped to calm him somewhat.

He wasn't far from the castle door, which was made of black glittering stone. *The land of the fallen stars,* he thought, as he moved toward the castle.

Liam had always favored Safiereal, even with its darkness attached to the black buildings and slight stench of demons ichor. It hadn't stopped him from receiving semblance from the aged buildings. Maybe it was the fact that he and his siblings had resided here eons ago, or helped build the very buildings. Maybe it was the Gazool he had hidden in the very ground, he didn't care.

On arriving at the castle wall, Liam hit his hand on the black stone wall, it melted down like liquid gold. As soon as he stepped in, the wall began rebuilding itself, leaving no sign of entry.

The ceilings and the inside of the castle was made of cement and titanium. On the edges of high narrow archways stood fire stands, also made from titanium. He focused on the voices, his walk brisk but silent as he advanced toward the one he sought.

He didn't stop or slow his pace but walked through the half opened door, "AREXANDRA." He yelled, accusatory in his voice, his body back to its original self, "Demons, they intend to enter your land, I take it you know this."

The white hair queen didn't so much as turn to face Liam, "Very clever William, did you hear them."

"They call my name, WHY?" He inquired accusingly, "You gave me passage, unharmed, un-hunted, my plan was working. Why did you betray me Elvan."

She faced him, her shining teeth glistening in the reflections of fiery lights emanating from a small fire place behind him, "I didn't do such, I promised you that you'll be unharmed by my people, hunted not by my own, William, and I delivered."

"Don't dissemble me Arexandra, I've lost my patience, SPEAK all that you know NOW!"

"You can't come into my Land and threaten me!", she retorted.

"Do you need reminding of what you truly look like, without my generosity?"

Her eyes glanced widely at him, she snarled, "You wouldn't, we have been kind to you and your siblings for years."

"Years, are not enough! As long as I possess the power to undo that falsified beauty of yours, you will be in my debt."

The queen's face rippled and etched with hopelessness as she sat on a throne made of tinted red glass.

The bottom of her cream dress gathered at her feet, she sighed, "I don't have a choice, you not the only one we've made deals with. Being ugly is a small price to pay for staying alive and getting fed, so if you are going to threaten me, then so be it."

Liam remarked, turning his back to Arexandra. "Ah, He knows what I did."

The door shut, with a loud angry bang as Alexa stormed in. Her hair was back to blonde, her beady black eyes wild with fury. "Maybe if you did what you were created to do mother, then you wouldn't have to make so many deals, especially not ones with the devil."

She was wearing Garde clothes or, as Calub always called it, 'disturbing brown leather garments.' Swords, daggers and her famous two guns strapped up around her thighs and waist, in her very own private style of chain and leather weapon satchel.

Alexa's eyes reached Liam, as she blatantly dismissed her mother, "He hasn't arrived yet, we've got time. Once we reach the main gates, we have to run east."

"No, we fight." He turned his back to both mother and daughter, "I never run from Tempters, especially when they're after me."

The queen stood up, "Alexandra you would betray your own kind so easily?" her eyes dark, as she growled angrily, "If you choose to side with him, you betray us all. You would have no place as an Elvan, you could never return." When Alexa ignored her, Arexandra exploded, "You forget how the Lightwatchers treat the Fuized, you wouldn't be any different, they would never fully accept you."

Alexa walked up to her mother and stood directly in front of the snarling queen, expressionless and confident, "I already have no place, I'm not like you either, but I'm doing what I was made to do. I'm a star with the blood of an Angel, I was made to kill demons, and drink their blood, maybe if you just did the same mother.."

Her mother gripped her arm, which was just wicked in Liam's opinion. BUT Liam decided not to intervene, he knew about having a mother once. He missed his, she was mostly kind and nurturing in her own way, nothing like Arexandra. The Elvan queen was clearly crazed and self-centred.

Alexa shook her mother's hands off her arm, and stalked away. She paused, her back faced to Liam, and bound herself by ancient words, "I follow your path William Blackwyll," Her allegiance to him now carved.

Liam jerked his chin, as a silent bye to Arexandra, and stated, "Weapons"

Her mother's voice echoed as she screamed, bellowing, "ALEXANDRA, ALEXANDRA." Alexa didn't look back as she walked out the door knowing there was no turning back.

Liam was silently impressed; it was about time she stood up for herself, "The Asguardians want my blood too."

They reached the outside of the castle door, darkness now filled the air around them, but Liam knew that look in Alexa's eyes, she said, "I was at the meeting in Khiron."

Liam heard as much, Jullie kept a close eye on Clare during the whole meeting. His sister was always the prevention type, nobody hated fixing anything as much as she did, "Clare got her memory back, I heard."

"Not just that, I was spying from afar before Clare arrived, Raphael knows who's Franchesca's son."

Liam hadn't expected that, "Dukael, I sent him here, he'll be able to track the boy before Raphael, that kid must stay safe, he's our only leverage to get Azazy-el's alliance."

Liam concentrated again on reaching his sister, the voice swallowed itself inside his mind, "*I'm busy, the Tahore isn't going to track itself, I'm close. Oh and Clare's on her way to meet Kole.*"

"*There's a few hurdles, I'm gonna be late, lemme know when you see her. It's time, do it quickly, but be careful, Kalbreal isn't to suspect a thing.*"

He didn't hear her reply, instead immediately altered his attention to Alexa who barely held it together, he knew he was going to regret this, but... "You can stay with us Alexa, until you sort something out."

She looked at him and nodded, he could feel the relief the gesture brought her. He knew she wouldn't last with the Fuized in Khiron, she loved the war and adrenaline too much for that. Liam was no fool, he knew the Lightwatchers would ignore her talents, and keep her as a Garde. It was the highest they ever allowed Fuized to go. Alexa was a born killer, keeping her in detective work was a waste, and Liam hated wasting, especially when its uses were vast.

The two of them moved forward, through the crowds of Elvan,

whilst street lamps lit the way.

"Kalbreal and Clare are getting closer by the minute, I suspect he feels for her."

Liam faced the moon, it was full, glowing brightly, he knew it would change in the hours that followed, "And the point is?"

"I know you have feelings for her William, or you wouldn't be doing all of this, just to know something you already suspect is certain." She smiled her teeth white and straight, annoyingly so, "She's different from your usual taste, but she'd make a fine consort by your side."

"Consort", he walked closely to her, whilst his expression gave nothing away, he snorted, "I don't do romance."

"You'll change your mind eventually, we all say such, look at my sister, died in the heart of battle for that she loved, or Azazy-el poised into helping us for the protection of a son, who doesn't even know he has a Tempters blood in his veins. Or myself, willing to give up a prestigious title to fend for the sister of the man I love, who would never love me back."

Liam stood there expressionless, "Dukael's at the stone market with Ulaidea."

Alexa smiled, "That's going to be interesting, Raphael's whore."

Liam corrected her, "Ex-lover, she'll be staying with us as-well, so behave."

Alexa snorted, "Julliette isn't going to be pleased."

"I'll send her traveling for a while."

Dukael was spotted a few feet away, with Ulaidea behind him, wearing a black robe covering her braided hair and crown. Walking over to him and Alexa, Dukael's warmly smile, plastered on his face in obvious delight to see Liam unharmed.

Crowds of Elvan busied around as fruits, gems stones and fine jewellery were displayed on silver trestles and titanium bowls, for swopping or buying.

Dukael not interested in anything besides Liam, as he chastised, "You made me hurt you, purposely, all for nothing."

Ulaidea dropped her hood, also oblivious to the market on goings, "I want to join in on the fight."

Liam crossed his eyes to Alexa and back to Ulaidea, "No, I have other plans for you two, I need you to track Ruheal, Raphael knows his identity, he'd kill him."

Dukael was flabbergasted, "Raphael has gone too far, the boy's innocent."

Ulaidea interrupted, "Ruheal's in Ireland, I could get there fastest, Raphael plans on handing him to Allistor to kill."

Alexa yelled, "Allistor is involved, why?"

Ulaidea with kind eyes now strained on Alexa's snarly face, sighed, "They want to lure out Azazy-el and kill him, I'm not sure why, sorry."

Liam rubbed his neck, before putting his hands behind his back, this was not good news, it confirmed that there was a higher mind behind this. Someone who knew how to kill Azazy-el, that meant at least an Archangel, and if the archangels were involved then he knew for certain it wouldn't be long before they found Clare, they'd want her head. "They'll have to go after Kalbreal first, Raphael must be stopped."

Dukael didn't look happy or convinced by the idea , "Won't his father be upset, angering an ARCHANGEL, it isn't a favored option on my part."

Liam's voice was icy, when he said, "I'll face them all, if I have to!", *to keep her breathing*. Liam could see the sky changing, the moon becoming red, the atmosphere darkening, time was near. Soon there would be demons everywhere, scouring the realm for him, out for his blood, hungry for his flesh, "I need you all to be vigilant in your quest, Alexa and I'll clear a way for you, do as I say, stay safe."

Ulaidea touched his face, but Liam flinched, moving his cheek out of her reach. When she made to touch him again, she was shocked, stuttering, "But I thought you.. I.." he walked further down, not looking back.

He hated when woman thought it was okay to make assumptions and throw themselves at him, he took what he wanted from whom he wanted and he was never in need of females.

Alexa said, in last thought, "He'll let you know," She smiled at Ulaidea, before she ran up to Liam. "

Alexa, you know how Asguardian woman are."

"It was funny," She shrugged, "It's what Calub would have said."

Liam sighed, "True, ready to kill demons?"

She took out her guns, shook her hair out, and smiled as others watched with amazement as it got thicker and sharpened on the edges, dangling as far as her knees, like razor blades, before she said, "I'm keeping count this time, you tricked me last month."

"I didn't, it was twenty three."

They both sped up, and started climbing a block of what looked like flats. Alexa in the lead, he climbed a few blocks behind her, he could hear the demons screaming, the ground trembling.

He took the next climb, turned to see an Elvan child screaming at the bottom, he kicked out his legs and free fell, front flipping, landing on his feet, stationed to the ground.

He yelled, "Adaula."

The child obeyed and ran, seconds before the demon's tail whipped at him, but he had already moved. Standing behind the demon as the swords fell from the building where Liam had only moments ago climbed with Alexa. He jumped up, grabbed them both, and crisscrossed the claymore swords around the demon's neck, slicing the blades cleanly across. The demon shrivelled.

Liam was already plunging another, the Elvan screaming, which annoyed him immensely to see none of them jumping to fight. He plunged his hands into two demons hearts and ripped it out. Easily killable, Gumanta demons, souls who possessed the dead bodies of deceptors. The Elvan were useless.

The gunshots started, and the counting followed as he jumped up taking two small Dragonfiely demons by their wings, he spun with them and flung them hard against the walls, without even a muscle strain. He saw a shadow in a green robe, and arrows coming from it, bemused he wasted no time as he grabbed at one of the arrows that flew past him and spun it across toward another Dragonfiely demon, which was feeding off an Elvan corpse.

The shadow jumped down landing next to Liam, "Vincent, did you know?" he yelled.

The crossbow never rested and the arrows never ceased, the Caster's hands moving too fast for the human eye, but his voice as calm as if he'd just woken up, when he said "I didn't, I was on a date."

Liam ran off, toward Alexa, her hair holding three demons captive as she shot at them and stabbed at another with the other hand, still counting, "thirty five.... thirty six..."

Liam joined her and threw his sword into one of the demons. He hadn't turned to any inner strength, knowing full well that this was just a small warm up, test-the-waters theory, and if there were two things Liam was unbeatable in, it was war and death. Without even breaking a sweat, he took the demons' lives aware of the outside eyes who watched him. He made their death look as easy as counting, because to him that's what it was.., easy.

Clare

After Nadia left, Clare didn't want to draw the attention of the other Lightwatchers, so she kept a safe distance from any passers and kept closer to the darker parts. She didn't feel as scared as she expected to. The knowledge that even when the sun was gone, the invisible seals kissed the air with fractals of light, was like a safety net on its own.

The mountain of Aquadore looked as scary as it could've been, with a few caves, but not enough to cut her tail and run.

Clare found the entrance quickly, when she approached closer to the mountain. Taking her first steps with caution into the mountain, cautious of getting caught in any spider's webs as it was pitch black, but nothing, all she heard was water dripping.

Looking around, she realized that she hadn't thought the whole plan through. Where was she going to start searching, was she going to scream and just wait for him to come to her, she had no real course of action. After a while of careful thinking, she saw the time, on her phone, "Half hour gone just thinking, where are you Nikolai."

Walking up the stairs, she made her way higher up through the cave. When she was sure she was deep enough, she put her torch light on, muttering, "Apps you just gotta love them." The stairs spiraled in well crafted black stone, made of the same stone as the mountains exterior.

Clare assumed it was naturally this way, but then again nothing in the realm was ever as it seemed. She spotted some drawings on the walls, stopped and directed her flash light towards them. They were letters which looked like they were written not so long ago, "With each kiss my heart leaps, everlasting Adrian." Wow, she thought, as she walked further up the stone stairway. Seeing more messages on the walls, lots of them, the higher she went, "Steil, may your soul burn brighter than the ancients."

"They all dead,"A voice from higher echoed. Startling her, she gasps by the sultry voice and deep British accent cutting the air. Frightened and completely unaware that he was going to say anything she lost her balance, and fell down a few steps, hitting her knee on a sharp point of the cave walls, "Oh, shit, that hurt."

"You should be more careful."

She got up and dusted her pants, her knee hurt, but she told herself not to show him the satisfaction, "Kind of hard to do, when voices just pop out of nowhere." She shouted back, flippantly.

Clare walked up the stairs moving closer to the guy. A bottle just missed her head as it swung passed her, breaking on the wall of the cave, "What the hell dude, are you tryna kill me."

She finally reached the top, where the guy was, her senses strained by the potent stench of brandy and knew it had to be, "Nikolai Blackwyll?"

"You know my name, so I take it, there's a reason for your madness."

Clare tried to look at him but it was too dark, she couldn't see a thing only hear his voice. Not sure what he sounded like, maybe twenties, or thirties, she wasn't sure, it was the manner in which he spoke that gave Clare the impression that he was older than she thought, much older. She started walking closer to Nikolai, she saw the shadow of him, back crouched up against the wall, knees risen up to his chest. A bottle dangled loosely from his fingers in the centre of his legs. Her torch light went off, she didn't bother putting it back on,

"Vincent Ipswich sent me, I need a man with your talents,"

Nikolai laughed making Clare feel like a fool, "Your flattery will get you nowhere with me, young watcher, I am over a thousand years old, heard it all."

Clare checked her phone, she had one hour to get back before the others noticed she was gone, her leg throbbed, and she had just about enough patience with him, "OK dude, listen, I was trying to be nice, if I was flattering anyone, trust me, it wouldn't be in a creepy cave with some drunken, old guy, whom I have no interest in getting to know, no offense."

Nikolai got up fast, as if the wind carried him in the air like a faltered feather, and grabbed Clare by her neck pushing her against the cave walls. She let him without flinching, knowing how to protect herself in these situations but choosing not to, she needed him to trust her. He flicked his finger and the lights in the cave was lit, he looked deep into her eyes,

"I. Am. Not. Old."

There he stood, piercing her with his darkened green eyes and brown short hair that fell onto his face slightly. He was fair but not paled skin, he looked young, like a matured twenty year old. Clare couldn't tell, his skin up close had no open pores just flawless. Nikolai stared deeper into her eyes, loosening his grip around her neck and lightly touching her face before turning around.

"You have Draiken blood in you, intriguing, so you remember who you are."

Clare felt nervous, he was tall and thinner than she envisioned, not at all what she imagined him to be. He had slightly broadened shoulders and black and silver bands on his wrists, similar to Vincent. There was something about him, she couldn't put her finger on it, but knew.., "I'm a Moonstone, Clare, my mother WAS a Draiken, she's dead, and my brother will follow soon, I need your help." She neared him, "Wait, wait, you look like, familiar, have we met before?"

He wore black jeans that were dirty and a grey t-shirt, with a black chain on his neck, "No, maybe it was a crazy fan that has you confused, I have plenty."

Clare didn't believe him, she rolled her eyes, he was drunk she presumed. Nadia was right. She stared at her phone. Nikolai sat back down on the cave floor, "Why do you keep looking at your phone Love, do you have somewhere else to be?" he paused, not smiling at her and sipped another drink of his brandy, "I knew Celeste Draiken, actually, a real charmer until she tried to burn me on a stake, the twenties, memorable times."

Clare nodded, "So, are you going to help me?"

"It depends Love, what exactly do you need me to help you with, you don't have a clue about anything do you."

She confided "Finding my brother Calub, he's been kidnapped

by a Tempter, and I do have a clue, I'm not the one wasting away a two hundred pound bottle of brandy alone in some cave."

Nikolai choked with laughter "Well if that's what you think, then No, I'm sorry, can't be of assistance."

From a sideward glance he looked at her, "but Vincent said.."

He got up, "Vincent does not control me Love, his words are meaningless, and for the record I don't sense any Moonstones in your genes. You might want to check that up will you." Pointing to her knee.

She wanted to leave but her knee was throbbing, a sharp pain shot through her right leg concentrating on her bruised area, "My knee is fucked, shit, ah, it's all your fault." She paused, biting all the words she craved to spit at him, "Could you at least help me downstairs?"

Nikolai looked at her, obvious that he was thinking about it, "Well that's what I just said. Fine, but next time don't be a party crasher, I happened to be having a great time." He hurried her, "Come on Love I haven't got all day, you might not believe this but I do actually have somewhere to be."

He lifted her up with a quick sweep, and held her gently looking at her while he walked them down the spiraled staircase, "For a drunken Warlock, you are really sure stepped."

He gave her a slight smirk, as if amused by her conclusion, "Who said I was drunk Love. You see a guy in a cave, drinking, and a little dirty, and you presume him to be a drunken Warlock."

Clare looked at him as he walked, clearly unable to defend her perception, "I'm sorry, ok, I'm just disappointed that you won't help me, I don't get it."

His hand slipped a little while carrying her, the one around her waist moving now and again, touching fractals of her skin. He got to lower ground, a breeze blew slightly. Behind the smell of brandy was the smell of a really alluring scent. It was a perfume she didn't recognize, something addictive. She didn't know what it was, but it caused her bones to tingle and heart to skip beats. His eyes were small, but not too small, when he smiled his mouth moved up more to one side as his eyes sparkled. But there was that familiarity, a sense, that she knew that face, maybe a passerby but she couldn't shake the feeling. Maybe he was the guy, the one who saved her, but no, the touch was different. Nikolai had a darkness to him, and haunting features.

He was gorgeous and sexy, no doubt, but so were a lot of the Lightwatchers, "Why won't you help me, I can pay you if you want."

"Your rescue mission sounds a little farfetched, a Tempter won't just keep a Lightwatcher, especially not now."

There was something in his eyes and his tone that made Clare feel that she could trust him. She couldn't understand it, especially because of the obvious fact that she had just met him, minutes ago.

"Raging hormones, you really should conceal your emotions, you don't want to attract the wrong attention.", he spoke and arched his eyebrows being sarcastic.

She sneered, "Excuse me." They were almost by the entrance of the cave when she wiggled, "Please, just put me down, I can walk from here,"

Nikolai listened, "I feel your emotions, when I touch your skin, you would expect a Lightwatcher at your age to know the basics, there is no need to be embarrassed."

She said, "Thanks for the suggestion, I can make it from here, clearly."

Clare paced herself in the front, limping, "There's no need to follow me, I'm fine" She limped out of the cave.

"Don't be silly Love, I'm on my way to the Jakensons' palace, I take it you'd be joining me shortly, OR maybe a bit longer by the look of things?"

"Joining you, I highly doubt that."

Nadia came running towards them, a bag in her hand. Clare presumed it was clothes for the party, "Clare, get dressed quickly, Nathan's looking for you."

Nadia gave Nikolai a stabbing look of disgust, "Missy I will turn you into a walking cactus."

Clare quickly intervened, "Nadia, stop, you are being rude,"

"Me?, I am rude, Nik here is the rude one, messing with my head,"

"What? How is he doing that?" Clare looked at him, back at her, "Wait, Nik? you two, know each other?"

He smiled and crossed his arms, "This is going to be interesting! Go ahead tell her."

Clare sighed at Nadia, waiting for her to explain, "So, is anyone going to tell me what's happening, is there something between you two, or..?"

Nadia stood there not saying anything, which grew on Clare's nerves, not only was her leg in pain, but now she was probably going to have to play peacekeeper by the way the two exchanged looks.

Nikolai blurted out, "Oh for the sake of time, she had sex with Caidrian and paid me to help him forget, sorted, now change, let's go."

Clare dropped the bag on the floor, "WHAT?" Her jaw fell down, she hadn't expected this, "YOU SLEPT WITH MY DAD?",

Clare grabbed her hair and tied it up then started taking her clothes off quickly without thinking that Nikolai was still there.

He turned his back to her, she saw it and smiled at his action, other guys would have looked. His eyes staring seriously into the sky, like his years on the earth had sucked all his life source away, tainted by agelessness.

Clare shouted at Nadia, she was furious, "I could just KILL you Nadia, but right now I'm just going to pretend that I didn't hear any of this." She gave Nadia one last grave look, "I'm done, let's go."

Nadia thinned her lips, and flared her nose, "Will he be joining us tomorrow?" she said pointing at Nikolai,

Clare replied "No, he is just a drunk like you said."

He cleared his throat without facing them.

She looked at Nikolai when he yelled loud enough for Clare to hear him "Let me fix your leg."

There was silence between the three of them, the stillness of the night and the sparks of light glimmering between their vision. The stars sparkling, unaffected by the intense circumstances which lay before Clare, like the diamonds they were. Clare inhaled deeply, taking in the air, the pain was bearable. Clare knew it would heal, but hidden in her, was the need to have someone care for her. It made her nervous when a person showed any interest in her, but now it was worse, probably her hormones, she thought carefully before she answered, "Fine, if you want to."

Nikolai turned to her and walk the distance until he stood in front of her, he stared thoughtfully, "I suppose I am lost for words."

Nadia answered, "Maybe you were going to tell Clare that she's looking gorgeous."

"No." He shook his head, "That's not it, actually blue, is not your color Love, and you should remove the bra, straps are vulgar."

She surprisingly started laughing, "Thanks for the honesty, are you gonna fix my knee?"

She bent down slowly on the floor, falling straight on her butt, Nikolai had his hand already holding her waist to ease her gently down, "Wow, you have speed,"

He caught her eyes on him as he lifted her dress to reveal her knee with his one hand, whilst his other hand, loosely nestled on her back.

Clare's bones felt like crumbling, he was gently touching the skin of her leg, slowly gliding the dress higher up, moving it up to her thigh, her heart thumping uncontrollably.

He looked normal, not nervous, like he had mastered it. He closed his eyes and smiled, "Hormones, Love."

Clare jerked her leg out of his hand, he took it back, grabbing her leg with a firmer grip, pulling it closer to him, with a edge of roughness, that made her moan silently with pain.

Keeping his eyes closed, he said loudly, "Be still."

His hand started flaming up , like the fire burned through his skin, and slowly burning out, leaving his hand red and hot to the touch. She could see the veins in them as he placed the said hands on her knee, his touch gentle, but not delicate, it had a hardness to it, and heat, lots of heat.

Clare could feel the hotness penetrating through the skin of her knee, accompanied by a soothing sensation. As his hand cooled, the pain in her knee subsided. She pulled her knee away again and said in a soft tone not even she recognized "Thank you, for that."

Nadia who was quiet, coughed out, "You two clearly need a room, this is just creepy."

Clare defensively blurted "He was fixing my leg."

Clare checked her cellphone, as she got up "It's eight thirty!"

She turned to talk to Nikolai, but he was already gone, "Which way did he go,"

"He's a dick, he does that just to show off, you won't get use to it."

Clare gave Nadia a sarcastic look, "Like you sleeping with my dad?"

Nadia pulled Clare's arm, "look, get over it, we go on suicidal missions, we are hunted by demons and Tempters all that time. If you aren't focused we going to die, so pull your finger out your ass, people have sex, deal with it."

She stormed off, Clare marching after her, "But you made him forget."

"Well it was complicated, we do stupid things sometimes, when we aren't thinking."

"Bitch, I don't like you."

Nadia shot her a frightening look "Clare, when you get over it let me know," she walked faster, and was out of sight.

Clare walked alone again passing the Masonner's house, turned the corner road to the crafts shop and walked further up the hill. She saw a boat, just aimlessly floating on the water, with a man whom she recognized instantly, "Alonso!"

He beamed at her, "Ay, Clare, looking hot. Come on your brothers waiting."

She walked up to the boat, Alonso was wearing a blue jeans, and a light purple shirt, loosely buttoned at the bottom only, showing off his ripped chest. He jumped out and hugged her tightly, "The party is blowing, I mean literally, and Kalbreal is drunk, so I would keep my distance."

She sighed "Ok, Angels drinking, that's a first, how did you get stuck on boat duty?"

He laughed "Oh yes, Kalbreal drinks the hot stuff. Honey, this is my boat, your brother said you'll be here shortly, thought I'll just save him the wait."

Alonso looking a little drunk himself, she looked at him carefully "Okay, shall we go?"

He warned her jokingly "Just mind my house it's all messy, I'm hoping the Casters will help fix that in the morning, oh and congrats on getting your memory back how does it feel?"

She inquired, "Your house? Are you a Jakenson?"

He replied, starting the speed boats engine, "Yes, Alonso Jakenson."

She confessed, standing next to him, as the boat docked off, "I don't really have all of it back." She yelled louder, "I could remember some stuff, but unfortunately I'm still quite lost in the Lightwatcher's book of 101." She asked as an after thought, "Isn't your name

Alonsoleus?",

"Yes," He paused, turning the boats wheel, his hair blowing all over the place, "but didn't your brother explain to you why we shouldn't say our full names?"

"No, he didn't, why is it a curse?" She went close to his side as the boat slashed at the water, "Nothing will surprise me at this point."

He sighed, naughtily at her, "Much better, say your full name and see for yourself."

She felt a bit nervous, but did as he asked, "Gabriella Moonstone." She waited patiently, but nothing happened, "Is something freaky supposed to happen, because it's not."

She said her name again, mindful that the boat slowed down, "Gabriella Draiken." But nothing happened,

Alonso gave her a awkward look, "Ok, watch this," he put the boat off and they stopped in the centre of the water, "Alonsoleus Jakenson," his eyes lit up just like her mothers had, the day she died, only much dimmer.

Clare took a step back, "Woah, that's impressive," his eyes came back to normal. "So what sort of weapon is that?"

He laughed at her, "It's your true self, you just activate the Angel side of you. What you can do with it, is up to you, we all have different gifts and strengths. Some of us have legacies, the ones with them have brighter lights like your mother."

She nodded, "Just like a wingless Angel with an off and on switch."

"You can say that."

Sixteen

The Jakensons palace was across the bayou, it was one of the few places in Khiron that was actually built with brick. The palace was newly built and the exterior of one that you would see out of the realms. It was white with a red rippled roof, and red window panes. On the entrance of the doors and windows, were bright small lights that could be spotted clearly from where Clare was.

The palace was a far distance from the bayou waters. As she got nearer to the palace, Clare could hear the hard rock music playing, and catch glimpses of people dancing outside the palace. The engine blades cut through the water, bumping her up a few times here and there. Her hair blew back, pulling her as it was very long. She'd meant to cut it this year, but kept putting it off, now it was bum length and full of big heavy curls. Alonso stared at her for a moment, she caught him, asking hastily, "Drunk?"

"Nah, I'm just wondering, whether you scared, or nervous, about tomorrow?"

She felt a bit flushed, "I never thought about it that way" she was standing next to him, their shoulders bumped, every few minutes, "I just imagine my brother, all alone in some scary place, if dying is what it takes to save him, it's a sacrifice I'm willing to make."

"Clare I know some of us are going to die, I just hope you aren't one of them." The words he said, with a smile across his face made her stomach tickle, it didn't sound convincing, she brushed it off.

Alonso turned away from Clare "We here".

She lifted her dress and jumped carefully out of the boat. She was almost on the grass when she noticed Nathan approaching her with excessive speed, he was screaming something but she couldn't quite make out what the fuss was about. She stood there waiting for him, she turned on her right and saw Nadia, who was also walking toward her.

She heard Nathan screaming louder, "Clare RUN, RUN Clare."

Her heart began pounding, she started running, but a hard thing hit her head, sending her falling hard on the sand. It took her a minute to register that somebody was pulling her legs, she started screaming, she told herself, '*Focus Clare*'.

Clare opened her hands, which were already stretched out in the front of her. She clutched her fingers tight, making a fist, like she was about to do a push up, and twisted her body using her hips. The person still dragged her on the sand, but her back now faced the ground. Looking behind her, she spotted Nathan, he was fighting three other guys. She looked in the front to see who was pulling her, her heart almost collapsed, it was Alonso, what was going on? She bent her legs towards her chest, with tremendous speed. He held onto her legs, and she pushed them front, injuring his chest and sending him tumbling.

She got up and ran, Alonso running after her.

She spotted Nadia, Clare screamed, "Nadia help, help," She ran faster than Alonso, she was an athlete after all. Clare bolted for the lawn, relying on Nadia for assistance, all she got was a solid punch in the face from Nadia.

She fell down, "Nathan, NATHAN,"

Nadia booted Clare savagely in her stomach, "I am going to enjoy killing you Clare."

Clare turned to face her, "Why, are you doing this?"

Nadia smiled and kicked Clare again, "You and your mother are the reason we are being killed, didn't you hear what Raphael said." She kicked her harder this time, Clare howled in pain, "biiiitch"

Clare grabbed Nadia's foot, when she would have hit her again and pulled it. Twisting it, until Nadia screamed in pain.

Clare got up and kicked Nadia in her face, leaving her on the ground. She searched outside for Nathan but he was nowhere to be seen. Her body was throbbing in bruises, her stomach in pain and face bleeding. A pair of hands grabbed her from behind, it was a huge older guy, "Get off me, leave me," She started screaming, swearing, cursing frantically as the man hurled her away from the house.

The music was loud, her voice disappearing in the heavy metal song, she tried consistently to free herself, it was no use.

The man dropped her down at the bottom of the bank near Alonso's boat, "What do you want from me?"

The man didn't answer her, he just took a sword out of his belt, and smiled wickedly at Clare. She knew he was going to kill her, she blocked her eyes waiting to die.

Nothing happened, she opened them seeing Nathan, "Come on, let's get out of here, Kalbreal's been drugged with demon blood, we have to get to him, there's more of them."

He threw her a gun, as she said, "Nadia, and Alonso.."

"Clare I know, come on."

He lifted her up and she started running behind him, they got to the door of the house and inside waited more people with swords and guns.

Clare looked at Nathan horridly, what were they going to do, she knew they are going to have to give up. She put the gun down on the floor but was surprised when Nathan screamed at her, "This isn't a movie, pick it up..." before he could finish his sentence he was fighting a group of guys, five to one.

She felt a graze of a sword on her wrist, she turned, and was kicked down by a man twice her size. He had a sword in his hand lifting it up to kill her, she started screaming. She tried to get to her gun, no use. The blade touched the skin of her chest and next thing the man fell down next to her. Behind him stood,

-Nikolai.

"Sorry I'm late Love, had to take care of the two o' clock," he offered her a hand, and handed her a sword, "Try not to drop this one, will ya."

He smiled, and then vanished, jumping in the air with a sword in one hand and a gun in the other, shooting people down, his targets precise. His blade moves were something else. Clare had never even seen this on television, she stood there flabbergasted.

Nathan was slicing the guys and fighting them hands on, kicking them, but there were more, there were a lot more.

Clare got up, and a lady jumped from somewhere right in front of her. Clare took the blade and shoved it through the ladies chest, she pulled it out, her eyes widened, but she had memories, she killed before. She bolted fiercely pushing her way through towards the stairs, going straight up to look for Kalbreal.

The upstairs was empty, quiet , the music stopped, leaving the noises of guns and screams instead. She heard furniture break, glass fall. She sped up and looked in the first room , nothing, the second room, nope, but she opened the door with a silent caution.

She took a steady breath and opened the third, she saw somebody laying unconscious on the floor, their head against the bed. She walked closer, it was Kalbreal, she pulled his hair, talking in small whispers,

"Kalbreal, wake up, Kalbreal wake up,"

She heard a noise coming from the passage, she spoke to him again kicking lightly on his legs, "Angel-boy, get up." Nothing was happening to him, the voices got nearer and so did the sound of quick steps.

Clare got scared, and started kicking him harder, still he didn't respond, "Dammit!"

She kicked him aggressively, and in a blur he was up, nearly knocking her over in the process. Her eyes filled with fear, she wasn't sure whether it was because of him or them, "We have to go."

He looked incredulously at her, "Go where? What's happening?"

She uttered incredulous, "You're an Angel, find out dip shit."

He closed his eyes, and she saw a light flash behind his eye lids, he opened them seconds later. Pushing her aside and grabbing her sword at the same time, he rolled over and struck the sword in a person, just as they got there.

Clare's nerves were shot, "That was just scary, really, really creepy and scary."

"Where the others?" They got out in the passage. There were more people, who started coming up, they were Shapeshifter's, blue hair, and white leathers on.

"Oh shit, Kalbreal, what do we do?"

Her heart felt like it might stop, as her breath clouded, "KALBREAL."

"I fight, and you stay here."

A Shapeshifter grabbed Kalbreal, and they jumped down into the crowd, leaving Clare alone with four other Shapeshifter's, one of them grabbed her, and another injected her with something, "What the hell did you give me?"

Nikolai appeared from thin air, in between the other Shapeshifter's and the one holding Clare, he sliced their bodies in seconds. They barely screamed before they morphed into tigers, all three of them.

He quickly threw a knife at the guy who held Clare, hitting him aimlessly in his shoulder. The Shapeshifter moved back.

Clare ran to Nikolai and held the back of his t-shirt. He looked at her, she looked at him, really looked at him. The reflections of light, showing the wetness of his skin, and the sense of surety in his eyes that she was safe. He spun fiercely, looking at her face to face. He grabbed her waist, and pulled her close to his body leaving no space between them. Besides their lips, he smirked ravishingly, "Hold on Love."

She saw something in a flash, it was dark, and she felt a sudden light headed feeling. Within seconds they were somewhere else, at first she didn't know where she was, but then it occurred to her, she was in her room at the realm.

Nikolai was breathing disorderly, "Nikolai, Nikolai , your heart, it is beating too fast, you need to sit down." She touched his chest, trying to find out what's wrong.

He started pushing her away from him, taking in and out breaths. "Go.. go, back."

He sat on the floor in her dark room, she could hear him gasping harshly for breath, "Quiet, someone is here, shoo," he whispered.

She stopped talking and took his sword out of his hand gently, it was almost completely in her hand, when he grabbed the tip of the sword, and said,

"Narba"

The sword went flying through the wall, and Nikolai sat back. A glass mirror with a light appeared where the sword was, and through it came people approaching from the inside of the mirror.

Clare scared started jittering, sitting next to him. Nikolai held her hand, "They're allies." And he was out, unconscious. She slapped him a few times, "Not again, aaah fuck."

A lady from the mirror emerged, leg coming out first. It was a high army boot, heelless. The woman came fully out.

Clare stunned, the woman looked like the girl from a PS game. She had on a light grey leathered full body suit, carried a bow and arrow in her hand, ready to attack. Her shoulders up, breasts out, well toned. Brown heavy hair which curled slightly at the bottom, not as long as Clare's, hers back length.

Clare shouted as loud as she could, "Who are you,?" the girl walked quickly to her. Clare could see her features clearly from the lights that shone through the room from the mirror. Her eyes a light green, similar to Clare's, but she had bigger eyes, rounder.

"Help, where are the others?" She asked touching Clare, and turned back to the mirror. Two adults emerged, a tall man and lady, who looked like the woman.

The older one had blue eyes, like Clare's mother, and straight black hair, she spoke quickly, to the younger woman. The older lady was quiet tall, very thin for an older woman. There was something about her that reminded Clare of her mother. "Go help the others, I'll see to Clare." she walked briskly to Clare, "Clarebella, oh baby your arm."

Clare looked at the lady confused, before observing her right arm.

She clapped her hands for the light in her room to come on, taking a proper glimpse of herself. Her dress was ripped in places, showing midsections of her torso, and pieces of her legs. Her hands stained with dried blood. The dress strap ripped out, showing a black bra. And the sight of her arm, her veins stood out, purple marks marred her skin, her hand and wrist stained in color, like it was turning black. She jumped up, "What is happening to me?"

The ladies eyes widened, "Clare it's just a drug, don't panic."

"How can you say that, Nikolai, he's,..he's," she turned to look at him, he was gone.

"He was right here," Clare said, pointing to the floor, her mind wrecked, like she was going insane.

"CLARE, he's alright," The lady tried to calm her down.

Clare's rushed out, "Nathan, Kalbreal, they were attacked, and- and Alonso he was tryna kill me," she spoke quickly, the words poured out of her mouth like gasoline.

Clare felt a hot hand slap her across her face, it was the lady,

"Snap out of it, you've been drugged by a Soren plant, I need you to calm down, if the liquid reaches your heart, you'll be in a comma for two days."

Clare shook her head, the lady smiled at a man's voice which came from the back of them. Clare focused on him, a tall muscular man, short brown hair, fit and young looking forty year old, "The others are on their way,"

He stared at Clare, like he wanted to just grab her and hug her, but she just couldn't make out his face. Was it someone she knew, no it couldn't be, she'd gotten some of her memory back, she would have remembered, or maybe not. "Clare" was all he said and nodded before he walked to her room door.

The lady held Clare up, putting Clare's hands around her shoulders, "Clare, you need to go through the portal."

Clare jerked, and started raising her voice, "No, no, I..I don't even know you." She staggered at her words, slurring, "M...mm..my friends, my.. my brother, Nathan, and Kalbreal , they need my hhh..elp,"

The lady grabbed her arm, "Clare they fine, we need to leave, now,"

"No, I'm not leaving them."

Clare pushed the lady, and an invisible force field shot through her hand like a gust of wind, being released from her inner self. The lady went flying through the air, but landed on her feet. Clare's body felt numb and she encountered a sharp pain on the side of her stomach, "AAAH, aaah."

The bedroom door flew open, she saw what looked like a demon, but it wasn't, it was a guider. Similar to the bird she seen on her arrival at the realms, except this one seemed evil, like different, its wings darker and beak harsher.

The lady who was a few feet away from the guider, grabbed something from her belt, and shoved it into the birds' mouth. The guider squirmed, and Clare saw it attempting to fly in the room, but somebody was holding a chain around its neck.

The bird continued to flap its wings, but the person behind it grabbed harder. The guider's stomach underneath it, started protruding, it seemed like it was burning from the inside out, until it splattered everywhere.

Clare just managed to block her face with her hands. She peaked after it exploded and saw the lady had taken cover under a blue force field. The lady had her knees facing the floor, she continued staring at Clare.

Clare started feeling dizzy and her vision began to blur, but What she was seeing, the man who stood in front of her, was he real?, or was it a delusion, she tried focusing her eyes.

The blonde hair, the big eyes, standing in front of her, the same height, the familiar light powdery blue eyes. The difference about him was the grey leathered outfit, maybe she was losing her mind, she was drugged, it couldn't have been him, it just couldn't be

Phillip.

She tried to get her voice heard, but the words were lost, her vocals muted, all she could hear was the familiarity of his tone as he spoke.

"Clare," she could hear him speaking, "Clare, Clare," her name. He swept her off her feet, lifting her up, even his thick arms were familiar, carrying her, cushioning her head by his neck, his known scent.

She heared other voices in the background, one could have sounded like Nathan, saying something,

"We were compromised, is she alright, at least we all alive."

She heard Nikolai, "Let me take her, she needs to be healed,"

She felt her body moving, she was being carried by another, her head feeling lighter.

She could hear the people speaking even though her eyes were shut, she heard the young girls voice, who came from the portal, "Kole, you can't heal her, you drained, she'll be fine,"

"Tash, she's your sister."

"I will heal her." She heard Kalbreal say.

The girl replied, "See, Kalbreal will heal her."

She heard another person, it was the old man from the mirror, he was saying,"Let's move it, they coming,"

Clare could feel herself drifting through something, a liquid, something similar to the gates of the realm. She felt a numbing pain pass through her shoulder, she felt like she was dying. The pain was unbearable. She let herself go, her mind and body easing into a distant sleep.

Seventeen

A glass chandelier hanging directly above her was the first thing she saw when she opened her sleep filled eyes. And a hand holding her was the first feeling she felt. Foreign spaces, keeping calm, she searched the room. Her gaze searching for a clue to tell her where she was. From the white cotton bedding, feeling thick and warm, to the vanilla scent of the room, she closed her eyes, and opened them again. This time wide-eyed, the hand on her made her nervous, she started turning slowly, trying to get the persons hand off her chest.

Eventually managing to get free, slowly she put her feet on the white and green Egyptian carpet.

She stood up, feeling a sudden wave of dizziness, taking some time to get her balance. She started to think, recalling- what was the last thing she remembered.

"Nathan," she said aloud, waking the person who was laying next, "Clare."

The voice sent a shock wave through her veins, her eyes opened with radiance, she turned to the person, almost lost in tune. There stood a thin, tall fair guy, with perfectly styled blonde hair that was not too short or too long and light powdery blue eyes, with thin lips that pouted when he spoke as if he flirted with you, everytime.

"PHILLIP?"

There he was, her best friend, her first crush, standing opposite her, but all she could do was stand there in horror. "Clare relax it's me, Phillip, well aren't you going to say something, anything."

"What are you doing here Phillip, what am I doing here?"

"Clare you've been sleeping for three days, you were drugged."

"What, why didn't you wake me, I..." she looked around the room, and back to him,

"I have to go," she went for the door and opened it.

Phillip shut it closed instantly after, he turned her around to face him, "You aren't going anywhere especially not like that." She glared at him, but his eyes painted to her chest, she looked down.

"Oh shit," She squealed, when she saw what she was wearing, a hot shorts and a white vest, with no bra.

Her hands in front of her breast, she counted down from ten. "I have seen it all you know."

In normal circumstances she would have laughed by his remark, but now all she did was stand there. Contemplating whether he was good, or bad. Should she trust him, could she. Chastising herself for thinking so low of him, she dropped her hands. Of course she should, he is practically family she convinced herself.

"You are absolutely correct, I should change, is Nathan here by any chance."

"He's downstairs, I'll call him." He opened the door, "and please, don't get any smart ideas, we both know how that turns out," he said pointing to the window, and shaking his head.

She rolled her eyes, "I won't, I promise, you should go call Nathan, I'll wait."

He paused for a second, his head shaking before he left.

The door closed and Clare skidded to the windows, opening the black cotton curtains and the window, she checked the drop, too high to jump.

She went to the cupboard, eyeing the clothes hanging in it, grabbing a black pants and t-shirt she quickly changed into her bra, which hanged over the dresser, and the clothes.

Locking the room door, she grabbed the sheets off the bed and tied them together. She pulled the curtain off the railing and joined it to the bed sheet making a rope, which she'd learnt watching years of action movies.

Searching the room for something to tie the sheet onto, so she could escape through the window, she knotted it around the leg of a wooden dresser. Keeping calm she slowly put her first foot down and then the other, dropping her body weight onto the sheet. It was scary, but she reminded herself she was a Lightwatcher. She braved up and lowered herself closer to the ground,

"So much easier on TV."

Clare looked down, and wrapped her legs around the sheet, bumping into the wall. She wanted to scream but managed to hold it, the pain was bearable she told herself. Her hair opened now blocking her view. She shook the mass out to get it away from her face. When she finally managed, she felt the sheet slip, and looked up, the knot was opening.

She checked how far she was from the ground, still too far to jump and land with all her bones intact. "How big is this damn house." Aggravation setting in at her dilemma.

The knots started separating further, she lowered herself just below the first knot trying to hurry down before it opened. She carried herself down faster but the knot opened.

Clare fell with the white sheets, she didn't scream, but tried to grab onto the sheets which followed her. She braced herself for the fall, and closed her eyes. She landed, but not as she thought, she was caught midair,

"Hello Love."

Out of breath from the fall, she huffed, "Nikolai."

He tilted his head eyes focused on hers, she could smell his scent, alcohol and perfume riddled behind blazing fire, sending unwanted tingles through her body.

"That was quite a show."

His right hand that held her body up, touching the bare skin of her back. His fingers making light feathery circles on her flesh. Her body tensed, "Why are you always saving me?" Accusatory etched in her words.

"Why do you always need saving Love?"

She got down from him, he exclaimed, "I make you nervous."

She bent her head down, trying to camouflage her expression, the truth was he did make her nervous. But so did a lot of people. She was not used to being touched by so many guys, especially handsomely dangerous ones but that wasn't it, there was something wrong with her emotions.

"I don't have time for this, I need to find my brother."

He snarled, "I suppose you haven't been downstairs?"

She lifted her head, "Excuse me?"

"What's the rush, your brothers fine, maybe a little full of shit but fine."

She yelled at him ridiculed, "I mean CALUB,"

His smirk didn't leave his face, "Yes, last I checked, you only have one brother Love, unless of course you are not Clarebella."

"Nathans also my brother, maybe those thousand years of yours are finally catching up with you."

"Nathan is your cousin, considering that I saved your life, on numerous occasions, some gratitude would be good."

He walked a few steps away from her, then turned back, "And don't be so jealous Love, because I really think I'm good for another twenty thousand years or so."

She wanted to slap him, he just knew how to rile her up, "Along with your modesty, maybe forty," she retorted, marching up to him and stamped his foot, her face frowning with anger.

"Was that suppose to hurt? Some deceptors way of making your point?"

She exhaled blowing her cheeks up in a huff, the string of curses tipping her tongue.

"I see my services are not needed anymore." They both turned, Interrupted by a voice.

She smiled, unaware how long he was there for, "Kalbreal!"

He gazed at her bleakly, she thought, *so unreadable.*

Kole and her eyes met again, his expression changed like a sudden breeze, impatience now masked in his eyes. Was her emotions transparent, well maybe a little.

"I see," Nikolai's voice hardened, unfamiliar to Clare, but then again she barely known him, "You are in the Angel's hands now."

He was gone before she could say anything, phew gone, in a flash, she really needed to get use to that.

Kalbreal smiling observantly, now that Nikolai was gone, like he eased up. "It's really disappointing that you want to leave without saying goodbye."

His eyes gave something back to her, a secrecy, one that hadn't been there before.

She shook her head, "I didn't think you'd want me too."

Touching her fingers slightly, he then held her hand fully. His skin perfect, his touch so smooth, she'd never felt a more subtler one, and more easing hand, it was alluring.

Up into the air towards her bedroom window, he lifted her, disappearing in seconds and reappearing in the room. Touching her face lightly, his hands smelt so addictive. She didn't know what it was but it was sweet. She couldn't believe it was happening, she couldn't believe he was touching her. "I am really glad that you are okay Clarebella,"

She turned her face slowly away from his hand, and he vanished.

She stood there, frozen to the ground. It was the first time Kalbreal had touched her, and when he did, it was in that way, an intimate one. Something changed in his eyes, she saw a different person. Not a warrior or avenging Angel, she saw a guy, who was trying to shield his emotions from the world, only leaving specks of it undisclosed. Clare wasn't going to entertain that thought.

Nikolai's broody face flashed in her eyes, there was something familiar about him, an unidentified line, that drew her in, he knew how to pull her. But that wasn't what had her troubled, it wasn't what confused her-

It was William, the only one who could do that. She didn't know who he was, or what he looked like, but in the time she was asleep, he was all she dreamed of. His touch, his eyes, his voice, it was just him who crowded her mind. Was she going crazy or fooling herself? She felt like she was metal and he was the magnet, and no matter how different they were, they would be destined for each other.

When she'd woken up, she ached with a longing inside her chest for him, for a stranger. It was getting harder to brush the feeling away, harder to pretend that this craving was so much more. Focusing on what Nikolai had said, that was what she did, her brother was here, she needed to find Calub. Then she would find him, find her William.

She looked around the room, the white painted walls, two small green circular side lamps which stood on separated brown wooden tables that matched the headboard. She walked to the dresser, seeing herself in the mirror. Her hair was straighter and shorter, a lot shorted. Somebody had cut it, she liked it, just falling aimlessly over her breast and stopping a good few inches above her navel, not curling as much. She saw a new person, she didn't recognize herself, her hair was darker, something about her eyes and features were sharper, reflecting her inner emotions. Her dark rings were lighter, she attributed it to the sleep she had.

Loud voices drifted from downstairs, laughs. She walked to the door, opened it. One of them sounded like Nathan laughing. She followed it through the house, down a large spiral staircase, the place she was in had at least five floors, she was on the second.

Reaching the bottom of the house, she saw the glass sliding door which led to the back of the monstrosity. The grass had a wide stretch of planks made of cement. There were five guys outside shooting archery arrows wearing white body suits, and practicing in the outside field.

"Morning, you look lost."A guy behind her greeted, causing her to spin around.He himself wore a white leather outfit just like the others.

"Where exactly am I?"

"L.A HOL," He replied.

She smiled blandly at him, "hole?" "The HOL, House of legions, crazy, hey? I still can't believe this place, it's huge, I got here yesterday, I'm Ale."

He walked away, joining the others in training. She carried on passing a place which she presumed was a hall, and moved further down into a large lounge area with beige couches. She continued towards a door, still following the voices.

She opened it, barging into an office room, with a round wooden table, and chairs. Around it were people scattered talking and laughing, everybody in the room just looked at her, blankly. A girl whom she recognized, stood up, walked up to her and extended her hand.

"Hi, nice to meet you too, I'm Natarsha, call me Tash"

Clare overwhelmed by the room full of people, "Oh."

She looked at the girl, not knowing what else to say, luckily Nathan intervened, hugging her, "Hey sleeping beauty has finally woke up."

She hugged him back, speaking softly, "You're ok, did you see Calub?"

A young man stood up from behind a chair, he was tall, like way tall, with dark brown straight hair that was gelled in a messy style that enhanced his dark green eyes. He wore a white uniform like the others she saw, he smiled showing off his perfectly straight teeth, "Who me?"

Clare tilted her head, her eyes widened with excitement, "Calub?"

She bumped Tash, "OW, where's your manners."

She ignored her, and walked around the table towards him, "Is it really you? You're all grown up."

She squeezed him tightly, holding him around the waist, getting a good look at him, "Ouch, are you trying to kill me."

She stopped, and standing on her tippy toes started kissing his cheeks, "Sorry, are you ok, gosh I missed you so much, I thought you were dead, or worse, being tortured by a Tempter, thank god you're fine."

He nodded gleefully, She wanted to cry, he looked so big, it had been years since she'd last seen him. He was a little boy, now he was taller than her, "Bow to that, I missed you too sis, but you know I was never kidnapped, right?"

Lost and curious Kalbreals eyes were, staring at the floor, planets away. She looked around the room, there were three other people, all wearing white, except for Tash, Kalbreal and Nathan.

She registered what Calub just said, her eyes darted on Nathan, who held a smile, "What's going on, why were we, almost killed yesterday?"

Nathan sat down on a chair, "Yesterday? You mean two nights ago, it's Wednesday."

A tall lady walked in the room, "Clare, come with me." her voice commanding.

Clare shot the lady a defiant glare, but something about this lady told Clare that there was no negotiating. She followed the woman towards the lounge area, "I see you know that your brother is all well."

Clare sighed, "Yes, but I don't understand what's going on, did you hear from my father?"

They sat down opposite each other in the lounge. A man came in with a plate of food, it was macaroni and cheese. He left it in front of her and sat down next to the lady, who spoke, "You should eat."

Clare looked at the man, "What exactly is this place, House of legions?"

The man said, "My name is Wesley Ravensword," his voice was very deep, he had no specific accent to his tone, "This is Sofia Draiken.

Clare sat up and took the plate of food, she started eating. She was so starved, and to be honest the moment she heard Draiken, she felt relieved, "How are you related to my mother?"

The lady and man passed discerning glares at each other, the woman smiled, "Franchesca's my sister."

"Clare I need you to listen to what we tell you, before you ask any questions, can you do that." Wesley asked, his tone gentle. Nerves raked her body' her guard going up. A hand touched her shoulder. She looked to her right, it was Calub, his reassuring eyes causing her reluctant nod, "Fine."

"The Legion, is a society of extra-ordinary Lightwatchers, in 1047, a woman named, Areana Legionnaire founded the first group of legions- A group of Lightwatchers whose abilities exceeded far beyond the others. When they ascended their abilities were multiplied, and they received a gift, called legacies." Sofia continued,, "As legions we are trained in ancient angelic skills, in Elvan and Naturah magic, as well as human martial arts. Over the years our numbers have grown, now we are positioned everywhere in the world. We are the warriors of the light, but known as the assassins."

Calub spoke, "The Garde kill minor demons, but their jobs are mainly to handle disputes amongst the realms and peace treaties, allowing descendants to live among the deceptors. We do the killing, the dirty work, some of the Garde are secretly Legions themselves, working both sides, our informants, like Nathan was, but."

Clare ate another morsel of food, "Another history lesson, so what does this have to do with me,"

Sofia smiled, "When Nathan was young, Lightwatchers started dying by the dozens, so we took help from the Asguardians. They sent their own to stay in some of our faculties, and even the HOL's, but the deaths continued. A war amongst the Lightwatchers and the other realms brewed, blaming each other."

Wesley interrupted, Clare could see the story got to Sofia, "As a Legion, our work can be dangerous, one night, Sofia was at home, unexpected, an Asguardian named Varemeal snuck into the HOL."

Sofia put her hand on Wesley, he stared at her. She faced Clare, "He attacked me, I fought back, but I was drugged with ichor. Too weak to fight further, my eight year old boy, Julius, attacked Varemeal, and killed him."

Sofia lowered her eyes, and Calub squeezed at Clare's shoulder, "But not before Varemeal drove a sword through my sons heart. After his death I feared the worst, I got scared and panicked and did what any parent would do in my circumstance."

She paused again, and looked at Wesley, he nodded at Sofia to carry on, "I sent my eldest daughter Natarsha to stay in the Los Angeles faculty, and I took my three year old daughter, Clarebella, and eighteen month old son, Calubeal, and gave them to my sister to raise as her own."

Clare put the plate down, her eyebrows gathered, her stomach twisting as the taste of food no longer appealing, was she hearing things, no, it couldn't be.

Sofia's voice rose in anguish, "I didn't know that I was putting you in more danger, I swear it, until eight years ago, when you killed your first demon. There was something special about you Clare, kids don't ascend so young. I still don't know what it is, but the Angel of war came for you, claiming Metatron had ordered your death. That's when Kalbreal showed up the first time to save you instead and remove your abilities and memories. He told Franchesca to hide you, which she did but my sister had secrets of her own, deadly ones."

Wesley got up, as if the look on Clare's face said something, "I have always loved you Clare, I sent Phillip and his family as protection for you, all those years, I swear I don't know how they found you, I think your sister and them could know something."

Sofia added, "They are all so secretive but they will protect you with their lives."

Clare frowned, raising her voice, "FIRSTLY, YOU. ARE. NOT MY MOTHER. Secondly you are lying, if you really were my mother, you would know that one of my abilities is telling when someone is lying."

Sofia stared at Clare, tears pouring out of her blue eyes, sorrowfully, "Clarebella please."

The woman walked up to her, Clare put the plate of food down, "Don't you dare touch me," she held up her hands to her chest, "You are not my mother, my mother is dead,..dead!"

Calub whispered, "It's true Clare, I'm sorry, but it's true."

She turned to Calub, he believed it, he really believed it, why, "You can't seriously believe her, when did you find out?"

"I've known," he swallowed hard, "for eight years, straight after the accident."

She felt like she was losing her mind, "Calub, they are lying."

Her voice rose, she made an effort to convince him, but his eyes told her there was no hope. She faced Sofia, pointing her finger at her, tears brimming in Clare's eyes, "I'm going to find out the truth, all of it."

This was too much. Just when she thought her life couldn't get any worse. Just when she thought she had seen the light. When she felt a breath easier than it had been, she felt worse. It was burning her out, she felt clustered, like she couldn't breathe. She needed air, space, distance, she needed release.

Clare pushed Sofia away.

"STAY AWAY FROM ME." She spat, "YOU ARE A LIAR, YOU ARE ALL LIARS."

Sofia fell on the table, and remained there, shocked as Clare quickened to the door.

Clare ran out of the room, crying. She went straight for the front door, opened it, and ran for the gate. It was miles away, but she didn't stop. She quickened her pace, when somebody was standing there out of nowhere. A guy with black jeans and a white loose shirt which was buttoned almost to the top, and rolled up sleeves with black bands on his wrist, dark glasses, that gave off a darkened inside to his style. She slowed down, wiping her tears, sniffing in her snot.

"I thought I'll stick around, I gathered, you might need my services after all Love."

She was glad to see him, he gave her a devilish smile, as she drew herself closer to him.

"Teary eyes and bare feet, you don't intend on staying do you?" His face gave her what she searched for, and right now she needed someone who would make her forget that her world was in turmoil. That everything she had known was all a lie and that she was now a stranger to herself.

"Well you figured right, how do I get outta here?"

He didn't have to say a thing to Clare, she could see it in his smile, feel it in his words, that he was there for her, no matter the consequence. He took out his hand from his pocket and looked feverishly at her.

Clare could feel his heated gaze staring, his black shades hiding his eyes but not the intensity. She took his hand, without a second thought, "Are we going to teleport or something." She sniffed, "how do you do that anyway?"

"Not with difficulty."

He dazed at her as if searching for the right words to say, "I should warn you, Love, your man will not be pleased if he finds you with me."

"Last I checked I didn't have one."

Nikolai didn't respond, he held her hand tighter and walked towards the gate. He touched it, and the gate swung open. They carried on walking. Clare was surprised and nervous at the same time, she had never walked alone with a guy besides Phillip. She thought a bit about him, but anger just filled her heart, thinking about him, the lies he told all those years.

They walked down a pathway, through some trees, like a mini forest. The trees weren't tall but big trunks and full of green leaves, the place smelt like a grave yard. They carried on down, and stopped when they reached the beginning of a road. Nikolai took the lead and approached a black sports car. She tried to keep her mind out of thoughts.

He let her hand go which felt sweaty, so did her body. He had a really hot body temperature, and the heat in Los Angeles wasn't helping either. Years in a cold city didn't help adjusting to weather like this. The car clicked open.

"Aston Martin Vanquish," Nikolai spoke of his car as though he could never be more proud.

"Nice ride," she said, "I guess the Warlock business pays well."

He smiled, and paused but didn't answer.

Clare walked to open the passenger door, but he was already there, "Thanks."

Nikolai took out his glasses when he got into the driver's seat, touching his rear view mirror, "Your hair, it'll take getting use to Love."

"Is that your idea of a compliment?"

"If I were to compliment you, you would know it."

She shook her head, "Guys, just seize to amaze me."

"Are you referring to me or your love puppies?"

They drove down the road, a sign read, 90211, Beverly Hills she gagged at the thought, "love puppies? Are we going to have a problem."

He spoke vial to her, "Your two undying lover boys, Phillip and Kalbreal, it became quite obvious when neither left your side in two days, creepy if you ask me."

She challenged him, "How could you be certain unless you were there too."

He laughed at her remark, "Don't fool yourself Love." He sighed from the corner of his eye, switching lanes, "I have had my fair share of romance and love triangles to last me ten lifetimes. Thousands of lovers all ending with the same tragedies, betrayal, hatred or death."

Curiosity crossed her face, "So what?, you just giving up?"

"I won't put it in that context, one cannot simply give up on something inevitably out of your control." He smiled, keeping his eyes on the road, "but in response to your question, I have acquired myself a distraction," he said pointing to his bottle of brandy under his seat.

She was lost with words, she didn't know whether to be happy or disappointed, she was hoping Nikolai had not brought his bottle on the trip. She turned her head to the tinted window dismissing the Caster. Sightseeing was better than where the conversation was going.

Clare didn't pay attention when he spoke, she was wrapped up in thoughts of her own new life. Her last few days of hell, she didn't know what she was doing. Her mother, now not her mother, her brother, now her cousin. Her name, first not her name now technically a shortened version of her name, her head ached. They turned, she saw a sign which read, "Sawtelle Boulevard"

"I take it, you haven't been to Los Angeles before?" His phone rang before she replied.

He put it on speaker, "If you called to scrutinize me, I'm not in the mood."

A voice on the phone replied, "Where's the girl, I saw you leave with her."

It was Kalbreal, Clare shouted, "I have a name you know."

"What are you doing with Nikolai? He's a thousand years older than you, and not in the state to be alone with you."

Nikolai smirked, amused by Kalbreal's transgressions, "Don't be jealous Kal relax, she's in great hands, where's the trust."

"I'm unable to track her, you put a blockage spell on her," Kalbreal anger coming through on the phone, "I'm calling Jullie, maybe she can talk some sense into your madness."

Nikolai interrupted pointing out, "She's not a dog, and if you do get a hold of my dear sister, lemme know." He cut the call and drove a while before parking off in front of a restaurant. Clare didn't pay attention to the name. She did pay attention to a group of girls gossiping and flattering their eye lids at Nikolai when he jumped out of the car, but he didn't seem to notice, or just completely ignored them.

They both walked into the restaurant. It had a beach feel to it, bamboo tables and chairs, open bar, and a few outside tables and chairs where people scattered around eating hot dogs and ice cream.

Clare's foot got poked, she had forgotten to be more careful as she was barefoot, "Shit, I'm bleeding."

Nikolai turned around and lifted her up, carrying her to the back of the restaurant, "For a legion, you're more dangerous to yourself than anyone else." She pursed her lips as usual, when she got angry.

He just laughed, putting her down on a long red sofa and took her foot lifting it as he stood up. Positioning it in the air for him to examine, like a rag doll, "Your feet are huge, what size are these, ten,

I'm shocked you even felt that?"

She pulled it back, "It's an eight, and thank you very much for the concern, but I'm fine. Can I just go for a walk now, some fresh air."

Clare didn't wait for a response, she got up and walked towards the front of the restaurant. Nikolai didn't stop her. She limped onto the road, her feet hot from the heated tar. Blood dripped out under her foot on the road and pavement. This was not ideal, but she didn't care.

Clare crossed the road, and made her way towards the beach sand. Her stomach growled from hunger, making it known that she hadn't eaten enough. But, she was more angry than anything else.

Her mother who was not her mother was dead, her best friend turned out to be a LIAR, and Kalbreal's open affection was giving her mixed signals. She didn't even recognize her own brother and didn't know who she could trust. What hurt the most, was that though she had so much to deal with, she couldn't stop thinking about him. The faceless man, his scent, his hands pressed against her chest, sucking all that power from her body like a vacuum.

"William."

And to top it off, she was stuck with Nikolai, who was purposely being mean to her. His words saying one thing but his actions speaking another, and his constant alcohol smell wasn't lightening the situation.

Clare walked on the sand, more like stomping it like a kid, toward the ocean. There were American's everywhere- men surfing, teenagers wearing bikinis and lots of fully breasted older woman, some even wore thongs.

Clare rolled up her pants to the top of her carves, and sat by the shore of the ocean.

"Your outburst and lack for appreciation is rather surprising, if I must point out," Nikolai said before he sat next to he, she ignored his remark.

He tilted his head trying to catch her attention, but she just stared into the ocean, with tears nestling in her eyes. He looked at her not saying anything. Finally turning to face him, his face was soft, "Stop staring at me, there are woman practically naked walking around, look at them."

He handed her a burger, "I don't want to stare at other woman."

She took it and opened the burger quickly. Clare was starving, even if she was angry, she was hungry. While she ate, he slowly put his hand under her foot that was injured. She felt the heat surging threw her foot. He lowered his face, his voice soft, "Have I cured the pain."

Her eyes locked in on his, while her teeth bit into the burger. She chewed slowly, and swallowed, it tasted like sticky cardboard, she shook her head, "I'm afraid, my pain might not have a cure."

The two of them sat there not saying a word to each other. Time passed, the waters hit her feet wetting it. The sun blazed heavily on her head, making her hair hot. Sweat dripped under the t-shirt she wore, but she didn't care. A week ago she would have cared a lot, about silly stuff, that seemed so important, but now it just made her feel shallow. Because now, nothing really mattered, there was no purpose. Why didn't her mother (Franchesca) just let her die.

Clare cried silently, the tears rolling down in silent depression. Not wanting him to see her so fragile, so vulnerable, she got up and started running, but this time he ran after her. She paused further down, putting her hands on her knees, out of breath, crying. Nikolai touched her back, she didn't think he'd follow her. Standing up straight facing her back to him, the water touching their feet. Away from the crowd of people. He spun her around, his hands cupping her shoulders, and bared witness to her tears,

"What taunts your selfless heart, my love?" He asked like they lived in another century, in another world.

He touched her skin, silently wiping the tears falling on her cheek. The heat from his hands was so unreal, mystified with his touch, like a dark calming overcoming her.

"I don't know who I am," She snuffled her confession, "I feel like I'm burning in this hell that has no end." She said wiping her tears, "I mean I have no one who I can trust, there are lies no matter where I turn. I watched my mother die, protecting a daughter who was never hers. I see a brother I do not recognize, with parents I don't remember, and you talk about me being loved. But why is it that I have never felt more alone."

Grabbing her by the waist, he turned around to see if they were being watched. Then fixated on her, with a weary look, eventually he smiled, "Hold on!"

She closed her eyes, feeling a sudden lightness, but evil lurking into her veins. She opened it again, to the feel of a strong breeze, blowing at her back.

They stood on the top of a high building- the Eiffel Tower! Clare opened her eyes wider, lost in her own vision, while the strong winds blew her hair back causing her to almost lose her balance. Nikolai grabbed her by the hand, steadying her.

Clare amazed by the view, she couldn't believe her eyes, was it real, "Where are we?" she asked loudly.

"Paris, I feel it's only suiting, since you are hell bound and all."

She laughed, the tears melting away with the cool breeze. Shaking her head and lost for words, Nikolai beckoned her to sit beside him. The sun setting, its last rays of red, teasing the oceans sky with its burning beauty, she said, "I have no words to describe it."

"I can think of a few," He responded.

She faced him, his eyes fixed on the sunset taking in the view of the ocean. Seeing his unchained features clearly, the tips of light reflecting the darkness in his eyes, making them seem grey rather than the dark green she knew them to be.

The lump on his throat, echoing distinctive features. She could almost hear his heart racing, pulsing. He caught her eyes on his, but she didn't flinch. She sat there hoping that this could last forever, bitter and sweetness soaking up her body, the knots in her stomach racing in circles.

Nikolai said to her, raising his voice, "My eyes have seen all these wonders across the world, but it's never the same. Every dawn brings with it uniqueness like no other."

She turned her face mesmerized by the view, birds flying so freely in the air as the darkness took over the sky. Clare inhaled and closed her eyes, taking in the unaltered air.

Nikolai dazing at her face, speaking softly into her ear, "I have seen it you know,"

She tilted her head, her hair falling in her face, leaving one eye visible to him, "Seen what?"

"Hell."

"Was it anything like mine?"

Piercing her viciously with his irises, as if rekindling an emotion of destruction "It is by far, much worse."

Curious she asked, "So, how did you escape?"

He laughed, expectantly "I met an Angel actually, she spoke, and I laughed. When she cried, my heart fell, and for that moment, I was free. We danced, and all that love I had whisked away so selflessly, came back to me in that instant. But then she fell, and like a sleeping beauty awakened, she opened her eyes, and I realized at that moment, that Angels don't love demons."

The words echoed through her, the possibility of it being her was none. She had not danced with him, or known him enough to have sparked such emotion through him.

"I have seen demons and I have seen Angels, Nikolai, and you stand by far the fairest of them all."

His jaws tightened, Clare could see the history and loss that layered behind his eyes, and all that sorrow, that came with it. As she moved closer, he turned his face shadowing his emotions.

"Don't! You should stay away from me."

"Nikolai, don't push me away."

The night, bringing its darkness in shades of grey, she sat there looking at him, her heart raced. Clare could not believe what her eyes foretold. His eyes changing into lights of red and orange flames, before her very own, burning behind his lashes. Blood red sparks visioning itself, diminishing his once pure inhuman greened eyes, into something dark and heavenly at the same time. Her breath rose, her mind contemplated grasping realities. She kept her gaze strong, clenched to his face.

A symbol of a star appeared from under his skin, on his left temple. Faming sparks of lava shone through it. He looked at her, she could see the light reflecting parts of his cheekbones, enhancing his flawless skin in a twilight of fire, "Nikolai, your.."

He pierced her vision with a lava glare, flaring his nostrils, like the heat burned untimely through his Armored flesh, "I'm a monster, a beast, not so sweet and charming now, am I Love."

Nikolai stood up daring not face her. She got up on the tower, her hands shaded with dirt from the roof, walking after him, her bravery showing not one of a human.

Losing her balance she slipped off the top of the Eiffel Tower. Falling down, Clare didn't scream, she welcomed it. The peace and adrenaline of letting go. She was mid-air when appeared in front of her, grabbing her waist, his grip not faltering, like a parachute clutched to her body, lifting her slowly and vanishing into darkness.

They didn't go back, instead they appeared on the Wickery bridge. It was afternoon, sun still blazing, not yet setting, quiet.

He let her go, as if he meant to push her, "What were you thinking, are you trying to get yourself killed, you are reckless with your mortality."

Clare didn't reply, she couldn't help staring at him. His eyes blazing like a tamed fire. She touched his face, catching herself and biting her bottom lip, trying hard to control herself. But it was useless, she hadn't felt this lustful emotion before, she tried to resist the temptation, but it was too hard to contain. Her body wouldn't let her, she found herself going towards him. Her lips on his, kissing him urgently.

Nikolai responding to her kiss, holding her cheek in his hand, and grabbing her tightly with his open one. She continued kissing him, not taking time to excrete the carbon from her lungs, the urgency of heat pouring between them, like it was the only time they would ever get. They kissed like the world was going to collapse separating them for eternity.

He stopped pulling away, his face returning to normal.

"Clare, no, this is wrong, what's the matter with you, your emotions are chaotic, it's your body changing, you need to control yourself."

Ignoring him, she kissed him again, their mouths perfectly fitting into each others, matching each movement in sync. He grabbed her around her waist, touching the skin under her top. Her breathing louder, more impulsed, she put her hands under his shirt, feeling his back muscles flexing beneath her very touch. The hotness of his body penetrating through her hands, making her feel clammy.

He pulled away again, "Fuck, Clare, control yourself, we need distance." Walking speedily away from her. Gaining distance, with his hands on his head, she could hear his hastened breath and cursing words. Clare stood there, stunned, unable to gasp for air or believe she could feel this inhibited lust so quickly. Lust, she didn't know why, kissing him, touching him, it felt wrong and right at the same time. What was happening to her, she didn't feel this way about him, she knew she couldn't. He was cute but she just met him, this was wrong, she missed William, she needed William, *oh gosh what had I done.*

She tried to make sense of what she just did. Her life was falling apart, she lost everything, with nothing more to lose. It didn't mean anything, it was lust, and it helped take her mind off stuff. He was beautiful in his own dark and twisted way she thought, and she had never kissed a guy like this before. Nikolai turned and walked back to her, she was still too exasperated to say or do anything.

He shouted angrily, "You could have an angel at your side, but you choose the demon instead, you are choosing wrong, if Kalbreal found out about this it will crush him."

She hadn't thought about it that way. But she couldn't say kissing Nikolai didn't feel good. There was something about him, something familiar. She still couldn't shake the feeling, even kissing him. She walked closer to him, taking his hand in hers, he flinched, pulling away.

"I'm bad when it comes to decisions,Nikolai, I know." She cried out, "You not the first guy I kissed without warning, but Kalbreal wants more from me, I can never give him what he wants, when I already gave my heart to another." William, she thought, she had given her heart to William. "I'm messed up, So to answer your unasked question, I have a right to make mistakes and be reckless and decide to kiss a Caster because he is hot, and feel nothing but lust, but it wasn't right, and for that I'm sorry."

She turned to face the sun, trying to conceal her tears, "I lost everything, Nikolai, don't you get it, nothing is ever going to be the same, I'm always going to be broken, my brother said it will get better, but it just gets worse, there's no end to this." She faced him, "besides death and bloodshed."

He walked closer to her, uttering words she could only hear, "I do get it Love, believe me, but I can't be your distraction."

"I wouldn't either."

"You got it all wrong love, No matter how many lifetimes I live, and demons I kill, I would never be worthy of an Angel, even if it's just for lust." His words bitter but he believed them. She could feel it in his words.

Clare touched his face, smiling sadly, "I'm no Angel."

He clenched his jaw, "No Clarebella, you are by far more gracious, and you belong to another, you said so yourself, and let's hope he doesn't castrate me when he finds out about this, because he will find out."

He grabbed her arm, teleporting them inside his car, they sat there, silence speaking between them.

Clare, stunned by his words, she didn't know why, but she felt so fragile, and angry at the same time. She didn't know if it was because of him, or the obvious, that she had a lot to take in.

She met the woman who given birth to her, only to be told that she had given her up. She had looked into her real fathers eyes and saw nothing but love in them. Nothing like Caidrian, but this was different. She conjured up the way her father would look at her when he'd finally met her, and Wesley's was more, more than she had imagined. He loved her, she knew it and felt it. How was she going to face them, it was all too much. She jumped out of the car.

Deceptors gathering on the pavements, attracting attention to herself, kinda hard not to when you were leaning on a Aston Martin.

Her eyes darted to him, searching for something. He was a drunk, a Tempters son, she hated that she betrayed William, and was grateful for Nikolai pushing her away, making her see reason. She just hoped that William would understand.

But one thing was clear, she needed something to do, to keep her busy. She was so far away from home and didn't even know where home would be now, but one thing was certain, she wasn't leaving Calub behind. Pushing her hair out of her face, Clare jumped back into the car without a word. He started the car, driving the alien roads as the traffic began building up. The minutes in the car, felt like hours to Clare. Words unspoken to each other, were more said with the tension between them. He turned into a road called Beverly Hills 90210.

Eighteen

Nikolai slowed down turning into a driveway with a black gate. The automated gate revealed another paved driveway with a mermaid fountain on the right. Clare didn't say anything else. He pulled up to a yellow mansion, with high top tinted windows as big as the Whitehouse and face brick walls.

Bending over her, he opened the cubby, "I forgot to give you something,", he took a journal out and handed it to her.

"I don't want it." She said, pushing it back.

"It was Franchesca's, she never could get herself to write in it growing up." He paused, as if contemplating the right words to use, "I think it's best if you hang on to it," Jaw taut, he sighed, in defeat, "I know you feel that I've hurt you, and but trust me Love, I am a big chunk of evil."

Not wanting his pity, or to admit that he was wrong, and she was riddled with guilt and regret, she took the book and without a backward glance jumped out of the car, still barefooted. She was walking toward the house, when a Calub ran toward her. Now changed in to a blue shorts and a black golfer, carrying a pair of shoes in his hands. He looked so tall, and grown up, not the little boy she remembered, who had teased her- grizzly.

Clare could see the innocence faded from his face, nearing her. There was something else that made her heart somber. She'd seen the same thing in Nathan. It was the pain of loss, the guilt of killing, the weight of it all.

She pasted on a smile, which wasn't difficult to do, "Hey."

He threw the shoes on the ground, for her to slip on, "I thought you weren't coming back, you just vanished, good thing Kole phoned."

He looked behind her, "You are in deep shit man, Kalbreal and my dad went flip after he called you."

Nikolai- Kole smiled and ruffled Calubs hair, he was inches taller than Calub, but much tinier built. Her brother looked buffed, he had muscles showing on his arms, which gave the impression he was older than her.

"Good thing I'm immortal." Kole declared, comically.

He didn't look at Clare, before walking toward the house, chatting to Calub, who clearly, had a bond with him.

The mansions walls were washed in bright red as you entered. Two meters down the centre was a big staircase leading to the upper part of the mansion. On the left was an open-plan lounge and dining area, with a see through glass piano, and black leathered couches, complimenting the black and glass dining table.

The place was fitted in ceiling lights which tempered to a dull glow in the room.

On the right was a passageway, which Clare followed, leading her towards a room with a satellite plasma television and beige couches. Further down, was an entertainment area with a pool table and bar area, which fed off to four glass sliding doors.

She opened the door. On the terrace was black tweed couches with green cushions and a matching outside table, leading to an Olympic size pool.

"Lost in thought!"

She turned, facing Phillip, "Hi, I..I didn't know you were here, I was just checking the place out."

He arched his eye brows at her disapprovingly "I leave you for less than a week and you are already breaking my heart."

She was surprised, and confused, not knowing what to say, he had never spoken to her like this, "I didn't know it was mine to break,"

"Everybody is waiting in the kitchen," he walked off. Clare followed a few steps behind him, through the passage. He turned grabbing her by the arm and pushed her against the wall. He moved so close to her, that she could smell his unfamiliarity, something different about him.

His voice etched with sharpness, "I forbid you from seeing him."

"What? don't tell me what to do." She flinched trying to get away from his grasp, but he was too strong. Snarling at his scared and angry face, she spat, "You didn't want me before, and I don't want you now, so deal with it, you are being a dick."

She pushed him hard against the opposite wall, and stormed towards the kitchen where the others waited.

The kitchen was separated from the lounge and dining area, it was four times the average size and in the centre, were two separated black marbled tables. One of them had a sink and stove, with silver pans hanging from the top, and at the other sat, Tash, Calub, Kole, Nathan and a girl who looked Elvan. She was holding onto Nathan and smiled showing surprisingly normal teeth. Her platinum hair saying otherwise, which sat on her shoulders and didn't do much for her paled skin.

Clare could have compared her to Snow White. They all turned at the sound of her entering except Kole. He sat, staring blankly at a glass of brandy in his hand,

"Where are we?" she said finally, walking towards them.

Tash replied, "Kole's house, ours not far from here."

Clare repeated, "Ours?" sarcasm splattered out,

Tash got up slowly, walking towards Clare, she had a hardness to her as did them all. She was older than Clare, but something familiar about the way she made her lips.

She dressed different from the night before, her hair now curly, wearing black denim pants and a light pink t-shirt, "I'm your sister, in case you forgot, WE live at the HOL, house of legions, you are one of us now."

Clare rolled her eyes, she was already regretting why she was back, "Good to know, so why are you all here? Why am I here?"

"Were you hoping to be alone with Phillip," The girl holding Nathan spoke matter of factly, she had a constant flirtatious smile on her lips.

She giggled at Nathan, who shook his head and kissed her absently on the head.

Clare felt her body tense, with all their eyes on her, including Kole. He pierced her with his snake like green gaze, which she recalled was grey at the Eiffel tower, before they became firing lava.

Tash looked at her, "It's a quiet obvious that Phillip is in love with you, he sends my friends messages all the time, about you, quite cheesy if you asked me."

Phillip remarked, "Unfortunately," abruptly bumping Clare, "for Phillip, it appears Clare's heart dwells for another."

Kole saw him, and in a flash was standing in front of Clare, with his drink in his hand, giving Phillip a grave stare.

Clare was nervous, her brother Calub was grinning, enjoying this.

Tash gave Clare an impatient look.

Kole still devilled eyeing Phillip, the tension heating up between the two, like the heat of an open fire, "Quite unfortunate for you."

"Well," Tash said, "aren't you going to tell us."

Clare stood stunned not knowing what to say.

"Yes Clare please, enlighten us," Phillip's voice was loud enough for all to hear his sarcasm, "Who is the man who got you so wrapped up."

Kole stared patiently at her. While she was still trying to gather her words. Nathan didn't look as impressed as the others, in actual fact he was more annoyed than anything, but kept quiet and waited patiently like the others.

They all had death in their eyes, all hidden with secrets, but Kole had dark ones. He was suddenly pushed across the kitchen floor by a eye catching bright light.

Nathan jumped to his feet, Calub already there helping Kole up. His glass now shattered in tiny bits across the black tiled floor, with the liquid splashed onto the cabinets and walls. Clare could smell the brandy, a small piece of the glass cut her hand. She looked at the blood as her wound healed, she then lifted her head. Kalbreal stood in front of Kole, his face and body a blaze in orange and red flames with high watts of light shining through it. Clare compared it to the sun at its highest peak, because she knew that he was not in his true form. An angels true form would be with his wings, the house itself would disintegrate with that much heat.

Clare was a bit surprised that she didn't disintegrate by looking at him as she had been led to believe she would at the bayou.

Tash standing next to Clare remarked playfully, "Well we all know who you have wrapped around your finger after all little sister."

Clare couldn't hold the blush in her cheeks from showing, maybe it was out of relief, "You are going to have to take some getting use too Tash."

Her attention swung full on Nathan, he was shouting at them, "She is still a kid Kalbreal, come on, it's normal to lash out and leave."

Kalbreal pushed him, "He crossed the line, stay out of this Nathan."

Kole got up, "Kal, calm down she's fine, what in the realms is wrong with you."

He shouted louder at Kole, "You have no right, what if something happened to her, what if she hurt the deceptors or worse killed them."

Clare was astound and upset, *hurt deceptors* she thought, she would never, she could barely remember much but she would never hurt innocent people. She walked slowly towards Kalbreal, his body on fire, the heat a lot to bare, but he was more beautiful than she had ever seen. He had all that lightness which you'd dream of the Angels having. His eyes did not meet hers but she knew it was beautiful, in its glowing sun. The thought made her desire to move closer to him.

Calub moved next to her, grabbing her arm, "Easy there tiger, you not able to resist the temptation, you are still nameless, don't go too close you will die." Calub let go of her arm and folded his arms, "He's been like this the whole day, you know. I mean the blazing part, he can't control it, apparently some Angels glow when they angry."

She shouted at him, "You are enjoying this." Smacking his head, "Get upstairs now, go watch a movie or something, or phone our father. Let him know I'm fine."

Calub looked at her in disagreement but obeyed, storming out. She turned just to make sure he did. While Clare might have not been with him all these years, she was still his older sister and felt the need to reprimand his inappropriate behavior.

Kole kicked Kalbreal back, but he didn't flinch, it just made his body glow more.

"STOP IT, KALBREAL, you are fighting because of me, I would have left with or without Nikolai." She screamed at him, remembering to keep her distance.

She wanted to kick herself for defending him. Maybe it was the guilt for leading him on, for kissing him, or calling him a drunk Caster, but it was done. If Kalbreal wanted to fight it should have been with her, not Kole.

Kalbreal turned without fully facing her, "You should get out of here, Clarebella." He warned, "I will talk with you later."

Kalbreal And Kole both disappeared before Clare could say

anything more. Nathan, Tash and Nathans girl ran outside through the kitchen door. She followed them to an open garden which was mostly grass but had a few pot plants. She wondered how big this yard was, including a few scattered Christmas and hedged trees.

Finding Calub already standing there as she turned the corner of the house, she didn't say anything.

She kept replaying Kalbreal's words, they were final and made her quiver. Clare barely knew him, but being the cause of the Angel's fiery temper, scared her. He was an Angel after all, and could snap her neck at the blink of an eye if he chose to. Fear crept up through her as she moved toward Nathan and Tash, seeking safety in their vicinity.

Kole and Kalbreal still fighting, Kole mostly just blocking shots from Kalbreal. His movements had speed, but at times seemed to allow the occasional kick or punch. Which must've been painful considering their size difference. Kole was much smaller and slightly shorter than Kalbreal, not to mention Kalbreal being an Angel and Kole a Caster. She ran toward them but stopped to hid behind a tree out of view.

"Putting a blocking spell on her." She heard Kalbreal, shouting.

He kicked Kole, who flew a meter at least above ground landing a few feet away from Kalbreal, "I have left you since you got back, to waste your immortality yet again," he kicked Kole again. Kole didn't move he just took it, the pain in his face said it was bearable, but it hurt, "But not at the expense of Clare, you should know better Nikolai, you left me for a year, a year Nikolai, and you come back like this, I don't know how they put up with it."

Clare felt her heart shuffle, the way Kalbreal had spoken Kole's name, with so much passion, "Jullie is on her way, we have things to discuss, Liam won't be happy by this." Kalbreal's back was turned on Clare. Kole was still on the floor, his gazed fixed to the ground.

Parts of Clare felt guilty, it was her fault, she should have left alone. But a small part of her was glad she went with Kole. He made her feel better, like he'd known her and knew exactly what to say, and what not to. Kalbreal's body started cooling down, to a light glow, he was still angry but calming down. "What happened last year is done, mourning time is over. Clare is under my protection, don't defy me again!" He knelt down, Kole still on the floor now looking at Kalbreal, "We don't have time for this, I have known you too long." Pause, "It's time you accepted the faith of those whom you love."

"You talk as though you are older than me. But I forget that you have claim to her. She was distraught when I saw her, I was acting out of kindness that is all."

She peeped behind a tree not wanting them to see her, for the first time she saw Kalbreal with all his guards that he hid so well, falter, as he sat next to Kole, silently.

She didn't know what claim he meant, but Clare didn't want to interrupt this unexplained occurrence, the son of a Tempter besides a pure blood.

Clare never considered them so close, a Caster and an Angel, together, sitting under the same sky. Different blood, but still brothers in a way, and there she was, guilt filling inside her. What had she done, kissing Kole? She couldn't understand his resilience before, but now it stood as clear as the setting sun behind the two men. She'd called him a mere distraction and kissed him, never thinking about Kalbreal and the implications of her actions. She now understood it, realizing what he had to lose.

Clare spotted Nathan and the others further down surrounding a tree. She stepped out from the one she hid behind to face the both of them, Caster and Angel staring at her. Seeing Kole, his eyes unfolding everything she needed to know, as he turned his tormented face away.

She looked at Kalbreal, not knowing how to see him anymore, because at that moment, in front of her, sat a guy, in love with a girl, with hope that she loved him too. But Clare knew, she, who he loved, loved another. Was it infatuation?, she wouldn't know, not until she faced the unknown stranger- William, whom her freshly wounded heart secretly desired.

All Clare knew at that moment was that she had definitely caught the eye of the handsome Angel and Kole's reasons for choosing to deny her. She didn't fault him. She knew in her heart, walking towards them, sitting silently next to Kalbreal, that she herself couldn't bare to lose her Angel.

The others joined them, on the floor, Calub sitting between her legs, his arms resting on her knees. The white haired girl sat next to Clare, breaking the ice, "I'm Safira Starcrest, Nathans lover."

Clare put her arm around her, "I'm Clare, the sister, are you Elvan."

Nathan shouted in Safira's face, "I told you." back to his cheerful self, he laid flat in between Safira's legs, "Sister-sister, she's a Lightwatcher, I told her not to dye her hair, Elvan wannabe."

Tash yelled, "It's better than the blue." They all laughed, except Clare who just smiled, not knowing the joke, shared amongst them.

Phillip walked toward them, she didn't know where he had disappeared too, "I'm sorry Clare, I was a dick."

She bent her head back and lifted her hands, gesturing that he should hug her, which he did. Everybody started jumping on top of them besides Kalbreal and Kole. Kole got up and smiled, walking slowly to the door, leaving the others hugging and laughing.

Calub was screaming, "Get off, you guys are suffocating me," still stuck under the lot.

Kalbreal sitting on the side of Clare, amused, pulled Calub out by his feet. Clare was stuck under, her back flat on the ground. Nathan got up first, flinging himself to the ground. The others finally throwing themselves on the floor. Laying under the sky, soaking in the remains of the sun.

Nathan said, "Oh yeah, Clare got her memory back."

Calub smiled, "So does that mean you are going to kick my butt?"

Clare laughed, "No, I can't remember everything, when I try to think of my training or anything pertaining to the Descendants, it feels like it's still being blocked somehow."

"Your memories back." Kalbreal answered, "but as long as your body fights its true nature, your mind will reject your full memory from revealing itself, especially that part. But it's also linked to your Legacies, removing it meant also removing your memory of it."

Calub said, "So hypothetically speaking if her Legacies were to return, she would regain her full memory unaltered right?"

Kalbreal nodded, "I took it away myself, it would be impossible for it to return so quickly, she might have her gifts and minor strength for now, but that's it."

Nathan smiled lightly, changing the subject, "Tell Clare about the Watchers."

Kalbreal faced her and she faced him, but not before she caught a glimpse of Kole screening them through the upstairs window, drinking from a bottle, which Clare knew wasn't juice.

She smiled at Kalbreal, "Start with once upon a time."

He laughed as she faced the darkening sky, but proceeded as she asked, "Once upon a time, when hell seized to exist, lived angels and humans in harmony, all under the protection of the watchful eyes of Adonai, THE GREATEST CREATOR. One day Adonai said, "I shall appoint two hundred of my Seraphs to stay on earth, you will be called IGORI." And just like that, two hundred of them came to existence on earth. Their jobs were simple, spy on the humans but do not help them and do not befriend them. For years the IGORI obeyed, until one in particular, Azazy-el saw a beautiful maiden. Her skin was as white as the purist soul, and unable to help himself, fell in love and married the maiden. He stayed on earth for many years, defying Adonai's orders, and bore six beautiful children. But all was short lived and soon, others followed him. Revealing secrets of the Infinity to mankind, making them wise and curious. Teaching the humans trade, weaponary and science thereby empowering them. Adonai, angered by their betrayal, banished them from the Infinity and cast them into a place so evil and treacherous. But for the first betrayal, he ordered his loyal Raphael to trap Azazy-el in the mountain of Dudael. Now, however Azazy-el roams free."

She looked at him, "Is any of it true?"

Nathan laughed, "Yes unfortunately, which is why we are all here."

Tash added, sitting up, "If the Igori didn't fall there wouldn't have been a need to create us."

Clare got up off the floor, "Anybody has a phone?"

Tash lifted her hand, pointing, "They all inside, why?" "Time!"

Kalbreal answered, "Six, are you tired?" "No, I'm hungry, is there anything to eat here?"

Kole stood by the door, it was another entry to the house. Clare gazing tiredly at him, decided to talk with him. She moved closer toward him. Ignoring her attempts, he walked back into the house. But she went after him, following him through the passage and pulled at his arm. But he didn't turn around, he continued to walk to the back part of the house, still ignoring her efforts to talk to him, to reason with him.

He stood outside, face to the pool, with the sliding doors open. Clare paused by the door, her nerves started to seep through. It was darkening where he stood, still holding a bottle of alcohol. She moved closer, his back still facing her, drinking from his bottle. She gently took the bottle from his hand and turned him around.

He turned away, not wanting to look at her. She put the bottle down on the floor, and turned him around again. He resisted harshly, "I'm hoping you will leave Clare."

"I'm sorry, for what I said, you aren't just a drunk and you definitely don't deserve the status of a distraction, for lust."

Kole spoke with a silent shudder, "You really shouldn't fool yourself Love, if you think I care what you think."

She held his face with her eyes, tugging on his arm to face her, "I didn't know that Kalbreal and you were so close, if I would have known."

He shouted, "What?" his small eyes, stuck on her like needles, "You would what? Huh? You wouldn't have kissed me, Twice?"

She took a step back, "No, I wouldn't have."

Kalbreal jumped down from the roof, the floor underneath him trembled slightly. His eyes bewildered, confused, unbelieving, "You KISSED him?"

She neared herself to Kalbreal as Kole vanished with his bottle. He must've known Kalbreal was listening, "I didn't mean to, I swear, I was messed up, it meant nothing."

He kept his eyes on her, soundless. Clare could see the tension in his shoulders. She now realized that his feelings for her was not new or shallow, but something which had developed over a period of time. "It was stupid," she didn't falter in her apology, her green eyes locking on his.

"Clare don't, you don't have to apologize to me. I could read your mind if I choose, but would give you a chance to answer truthfully."

She touched his arms, he was wearing a light shirt which was rolled up and opened three buttons down, revealing the markings on his chest, her hands itched to touch it, but she kept them on his arms.

Kalbreal pushed, "What is it?"

His skin was smooth but rock solid. She could feel his strength, her mind dazed, losing her grips on reality. She felt the heat from his arms, he was addictive. She felt herself feeling things she shouldn't. She wanted to stop touching him but couldn't let go. She was losing her mind, what was happening.

She felt a sudden shock in her brain and blue eyes showed itself in a flash. It was like she'd been awakened from a slumber. A heat, that which was provocative, cooled by something more enticing to her own. It was him, she knew it, he must've been watching her. Clare closed her eyes, hoping to glimpse at it again, those blue eyes, 'William'.

Kalbreal pushed her away from him, bawled by whatever it is he had witnessed, "Unrequited love, how unfortunate, luckily I can take the choice away." She slapped him, and his body started to glow lightly.

Kalbreal had pushed the line, he had messed with her feelings again, messed with her mind. Let him kill her if he wanted, she didn't care, especially if he thought he could just do with her as he pleased.

Clare turned away, hurting by his actions. Considering she actually had feelings for him, genuinely, maybe not romance but she felt for him as a close friend. She hated him for wanting to force something that wasn't there, take her choices away, to suit himself. Crying, she walked into the house.

Clare's breathing speeded up as he stood there in front of her face to face. Appearing before her like a prince blown there by a breeze. His hair falling into his eyes, he was dangerous, a true Angel. All the muscle and charm any woman could dream of, but not her. No matter how breathtaking he was, she was not going to jump into his arms.

He lifted his hand to brush her skin, but she took a step back, resisting the urge. "Clare, my intention is not to cause you pain, but you make it hard not to. You are naïve to think for a second, that William would fall for a helpless girl. He cannot love you Lightwatcher. You who cannot even deal with rejection, or death. I can give you what he can't, I can love you. You are just a job to him, nothing more. He will break your heart and shatter it to pieces, without even blinking."

He paused, looking at her, "Clarebella, you've barely even met him. He refused to have any contact with you, yet his vision holds strong power over you, it's very disheartening."

Clare wiped her tears and ran pass him, knocking him hard, but getting hurt in the process. She ran up the stairs taking two at a time, opening the first room she could find and threw herself on the bed, crying silently in the dark room, "William I need you."

Nineteen

C lare
     He stood by the door way, she looked at him, teary eyed, but remained cuddled up on the bed. He moved closer to her.

     The door closing behind him silently, the lights in the room dimly lit. Like a majestically woven trance, he stared deeply into her eyes. His expression hungry with desire, his eyes glowing with the traits of a hunting panther. He stalked her. A heavy rhythm heart, Clare got up quickly, not removing her eyes from this man. Her body entranced, her mind unable to absorb anything else besides his need, his desire, his craving. He grabbed her wrist, keeping his eyes on her. Blue, they're so blue, breathtaking, astound by his magnificence her pulse raced.

     His lips slightly parted, his confidence unwilled, intimidating her. He lifted her hand to his nose and inhaled deeply, staring in her eyes. Clare's stomach knotted, her body ached for his touch. His body drew closer to hers. She closed her eyes allowing him to take over.

     He gripped her jaw with his free hand and inhaled again. This time her mouth parted as she felt his eyes burning into the depths of her soul. Their lips barely touching, she moaned as sparks electrocuted her with ecstasy and passion. He bit onto her bottom lip, pulling it in the most seductive temptation she had ever experienced.

     His lips touched on hers, her mouth opened in anticipation, she dared and opened her eyes, staring at this man through her eyelashes, gasping for air.

His kissed her, in that brief second as the air flushed out of her mouth, rushed and hard. Deeper, giving her his tongue, he gripped her jaw tighter. Her legs trembled with need, urgency. The kiss increasing. A possessiveness like no other, marking her, biting at her lips, sucking on her tongue. Losing themselves in the moment, his saliva sweet to taste, mixed with hers, rough, and greedy was this man.

Hands on his shoulders, nails digging in. His muscular body flushed against her as she pushed forward, closer to him, cutting even the smallest distance between them.

His shoulders tensed as her moves became urgent, pulling him down. He followed, throwing her flat on her back. Her chest heavy with escaping breaths. The room like a furnace, or maybe it was just her.

He halted, looking at her attentively as his brow furrowed, what was he thinking? Clare, vulnerable, she wanted more. But he just stood there, his breathing eased. His eyes a seduction to her body holding her hypnotized by his confidence, seriousness, his maturity and surety, at what he was doing. He lifted her middle finger. Slowly bending down, he bit on it as her body convulsed with the passion the act solicited, sucking it into his mouth, she arched her back. A silent invitation. His eyes never leaving hers, but his hesitation evident. She bit at her bottom lip plumped from his erotic deliverance.

He gripped at her neck, she arched it, head back, giving him access to the long length of her neck. He devoured it, sucking parts of her flesh, hard. Her body shuddering under his touch, her skin building up a cover of wetness. There was no doubt of this mans intention, he was marking his territory. This was a claiming, a promise.

She grabbed at his arms, beckoning him to come closer to her, touch her. Her back arched, in need, but he didn't budge. Her chest up and back bridged to match his movement, panting for further bodily contact. But he kept his distance, devouring only her neck. Leaving her body aching, paining with want, with an unfulfilled need.

Her legs shook as she moaned, uttering "please, please." He stood up and stared at her as her heart skipped a beat. His jaw taut, his nose straight, a masculine piece of art. The hardness inside him, a badness, that made her body reed.

One hand firmly gripped her neck, the other pulling her hair, keeping her head afloat. Craving more she reached up, hands under his shirt. Fingers digging into his muscular waist, a silent moan escaped her as this sexy, tall, and well toned man bit into the crevice of her neck, before sucking the skin gently. His callused hand released her hair, flattened on her thigh, making slow massaging motions. Her breath shortened, giving herself to him, moaning hush sounds of pleasure.

He didn't stop kissing her jaw, neck, and collarbone, he knew what he was doing, a master of seduction, her seduction. His hand moved up her thigh, passing over her pants, up her stomach, he squeezed her breast, "Ah" she cried, her body burning from pain and pleasure. She tugged at his belt, his grip unyielding as it captured her wrist, she had to stop.

He yelled "Stop."

He pushed her flat on the bed, her brain in waves, eyes dizzy, her body tight with anticipation, she squeezed her legs tight together to hold her arousal,

His eyes furious, dark, Was it need? Or something else, "Control yourself Clare, I'm not here to service your needs princess, not tonight, not like this."

She jumped out of the bed, something struck her, it no longer felt like a dream, it was real, these feelings, the room, her instincts rose, she glided her hands through her hair, hoping to find a knot to pull at.

Her breathing heavy, need still there, she urged herself to keep it together, stuttering she asked, "who are you?"

She was across from him, on the opposite side of the bed. His unflinching gaze held her frozen, his back so straight, shoulders so broad, she felt like an ant in front of a giant, "How did you get in here, why are you kissing me." The last few words came out as a breath barely audible to her own ears.

Turning away from her, he switched the main lights on, back still faced in her view, layered black straight neck length hair moving with his reflexes. Just this stranger's hair spoke of untold perfection, masculine as the jagged edges played touch on his jaw.

Turning to face her, she stopped breathing. His features so sharp, his strong jaw line shaped his face, chin prominent and golden glowing skin. Deeply stained pink fleshy lips, tightened, but they weren't plump. She knew all to well that it was males lips, the one that spoke of experience.

His eyes, his eyes, tanzanite blue, staring straight at her. She had never seen a man more beautiful, she had thought no one more finer than Kalbreal but this stranger to her eyes, he was in a league of new heights, big deep blue set eyes, with the sparkles of finely cut diamonds, his cheeks hollowed, giving him sharp distinctive features, his face dirty, his stubble a day old at least, she was a goner..

His anger which vibrated off him was the only thing keeping her from the brink of her sanity, managing to barely keep her composure. Watching closely, his fingers on his right hand, as he glided his thumb on their tips. She could feel his eyes on her, as she watched his hand. Looking up at him, his face showing no emotion, no sign of anything. He'd managed to hide his anger, he was not the man who had just mauled her, claimed, as one would to a lover. This was no man, he was no Angel either, there was no league he'd fit.

His perfect gentleman posture, so cold, she shivered but why did he kis- "The stronger the mind the harder it is to control."

She knew that deep voice, oh yes, how could she forget,

He hadn't answered her question, but made a statement. The black suit pants he wore was dirty now that she paid attention, the cut fitted him perfectly. She could still feel the tingle in her fingers.

The same fingers that itched to touch the curve of his waist line. He had no scars, she could tell by the long slash mark of his creamed shirt revealing the apex of his torso's hairline. Eyes tracing the happy trail, forgetting that he was looking at her, she stopped right at the top button. How was he so mouthwatering, she moaned,

"Control yourself"

Eyes narrowed she snarled, startled by his loud words that ordered her to only obey.

His arm just below where his shirt sleeve folded up, had a navy blue tattoo of a pentagram with weird symbols surrounding it, and another on his neck. His voice, accent less, but his attire so formal, like a business man, maybe he was, but Clare couldn't be sure.

"Our connection is sexual, you need to control it, breathe." His voice sounded distant now, almost like an echo.

"You're in a semi dream." His stare not wavering from hers, his face expressionless.

"Dream?" It was a sound of disbelief, "You mean I'm dreaming, so all this didn't happen." She let out a lungful of air, holding a hand to her mouth,

"fuck." She huffed, "gee whizz, Whoa, okay."

She bent down to touch her knees and stood up again, "No wonder you so damn gorgeous." She exhaled, showing her relief as she looked at him, standing there.

His mouth twitched with the barest hint of a smile, amusement, she amused him.

"No." the smile wiped off his face, "I actually exist."

This guy seemed like a real hard ass, Clare thought, as she shook her head in exasperation, did he forget who he was talking to! "I know you exist dummy, or should I say William. How are you here? I... how am able to talk to you, where are you. I need you, there's things happening and I need you."

"I know, but now's not the time, Princess." His voice deeper, eyes seethed with that blank confident expression.

She ignored him, "When William, why do I feel like this, I don't

know you well enough, and we just did all that, as though I know you."
She pointed toward the bed, as her face turned Crimson.

"You will, when the time is right, I will be by your side. But now
I don't have much time princess." He was so relaxed, calm, when she
was flipping out, "You are quite the curious one, aren't you, just like your
mother."

"Which one?"

"Franchesca, since she raised you I presume it is only fitting, she
wears the title."

"You look so much younger, not a day older than 25, still older than
me. I...I can't believe it, you here." She brushed the thought off, "How do
you know her, My mother."

"I am the one who trained her."

He looked like someone who was charming and petrifying
dangerous at the same time, a male who woman would kill for, "Your
gravest threat, is lurking in your midst, princess."

She knew it was him, her William, well not HER William. She
doubted he would want the title, he was clearly to powerful to be hers, "I
want that title, don't ever think otherwise princess, you are mine Clare."
Clare's eyes widened, at his confession, it was so resolute. Final.

He paused, eyes glittering, dark, "The soul thief, as I would call
him, hides their true nature, I believe he has the protection of a powerful
Tempter. I'm a little pre-occupied at the moment so you are going to
have to save yourself for now."

She could hear his tone was all business, "Everyone seems to think its
Azazel" she said.

"No, Azazy-el isn't strong enough yet and he is an ally, this one is
stronger than Kalbreal. The others around you are unable to sense him,
he grows stronger by the take, don't be fooled by his charms, he waits
patiently for your Legacies to be drawn back to you, it has to be willed to
him unless he is of a higher rank than an Angel."

"Do you know who he is?" She asked and he dropped his eyes off her *for a second, it was the longest second of her life.*

He looked at the blue pentagram, Clare followed his eyes still a few feet away from him, but she could see it fading, "Your mother had something with her, the night before she died , a necklace, it looks like this," he said pointing to the mirror, she could see an amulet. A yellow diamond, with a shimmering substance inside it, she moved closer. He moved closer to her, his shoulder touched the back of her hair, he was so tall.

"You need to find the necklace, before anyone else does." His voice was subtle, but strong in its power, "Try to act normal, but be wary, my princess."

"What's all this about? what does it do?" She asked.

"Find it, and you will find out."

He started walking away, "One more thing," eyes changing before her very own, jaw tight, perfectly bridged nose slightly flared, but alluring nonetheless. The dirt on his face not merely enough to hide his captivating blue gaze, "If he is not of your blood, you will not touch him, understood."

His cold vision seethed with hers, a challenge to deny him. She'd never seen possessiveness before now, but she thrilled it. She wanted this from him, as crazy as it sounded, she wanted him to want her, this stranger to her eyes, but she didn't agree. He was just that, a stranger to her eyes, she needed him with her, "No, I don't understand, you being ridiculous, come to me, and tell me that, maybe I'll listen. I'll try and find the necklace but that's it."

His expression brazen with anger, his whole mood darkening, "No one says no to me, don't deny me this." She stared him in the face, wanting to kiss him, bite his lips, instead she bit the corner of her bottom one, "I just did."

It was a declaration, but one of pure subtlety, "We will discuss this matter in person, princess, and believe me when I say that you would wish you said yes."

She widened her small green eyes, "Fine," pause "but answer me one question."

"Considering your defiance, I say not."

He moved toward the door she gripped his arm, he tensed, her head tilted to face him, "Why are you helping me, risking your life?"

"I too have picked a side, and who said I was risking my life? I'm saving it." He walked through the door, and slammed it shut. He was pissed, for a guy from her dreams.

Liam

Vincent peeped through the red tinted glass, "How long before he wakes."

Liam opened his eyes, "I was never sleeping, I tried to contact Jullie, I know she's there, but I'm unable to reach her."

Alexa wiped the last smear of ichor off her blade, with a old tattered cloth, "It's the air, the demons skin is poisonous to most, even Tempters themselves cannot withstand the effects."

He knew that was not his reason. It was something more, a presence of some unknown being lurking around.

Liam sat on the bench, next to the candle light. They had taken shelter, having succeeded in killing the first round of demons. Alexa had brought them to a secret hideout near the Elvan mountain, it was a small wooden cottage, with red stained glass for windows and hand carved rosewood chairs, there wasn't much to go on, besides that it was small, hidden and dirty.

Alexa straightened her back, "how long before round two?"

Liam faced her. She'd cleaned herself up, but her clothes like his and Vincent's were torn, and stunk of ichor. Even with the years of experience they had killing demons, the smell still guttered at Liam, nauseating him, he could taste the bitterness in his mouth.

A thought crossed his mind, as he watched Alexa, how did the Elvan drink ichor. Picturing how Alexa indulged herself with the green substance, he brushed it off.

Vincent sat next to him, "Seen Clare, did it not go well for you?"

Liam considered the question with careful thought, but no smile crossed his face, "Satisfactory, I need you to do something for me."

Alexa stood up, "I can feel the air thickening, we don't have much longer."

Liam stood up, joining her, "We must clear a passage for Vincent."

Vincent raised to his feet, "You want me to leave?" he was as confused as he was shocked, but not surprised when Liam insisted, "You need to inform Wesley, and have him order an immediate lockdown on Safiereal, nobody goes in, and nobody comes out."

Alexa was quiet. Liam slanted his eyes to her, fear riddled its way up into her mouth, but she brushed it off, toughening herself up. She put the sword back into its sheath.

Liam had done well over the millenniums not to get too emotionally attached to outsiders, but when he looked at Alexa, he thought of Clare, and how easily Kalbreal enticed her, using his allure to attract her.

He needed to get back to her, protect her, but his only chance of saving her was finding Raphael. He knew that if the Asguardian knew about Azazy-el's son, he definitely had knowledge of Clare, and it wouldn't be long until he went after her. At least he knew Raheal was safe, which meant extra protection for Clare.

"Aren't you afraid of the risk you are taking, it's extreme, considering, you know.." Alexa Whispered.

Vincent looked at her, "Considering what?"

Alexa's expression changed, she opened her hair, and lifted out her blade, "I hope she's worth it."

Liam stood behind her, ignoring her. Clare was not up for discussion to anyone. Signalling Vincent to get ready to move on his go, Alexa crept out of the cottage.

Liam followed on close to her side. He picked up a scent, iron and musk, riddled with brutality, "Raphael is close, I can smell him."

The sky was blood red, the air heavy to breathe, but it didn't bring him down, nor Alexa. She moved slowly, out of the bushes, where the cottage was hidden. She knelt down besides a small bush of wild orchids, hearing voices. Liam copied her crouch, Vincent hunching instead.

Alexa bent her head, signalling Liam to come in front of her. It was no sooner that he confirmed his senses. It was Raphael with two other Asguardians, but there was somebody else, a fourth footstep. He listened in, lengthening his hearing.

Raphael's voice was harsh and hard, "Dukael has escaped. Ulaidea, my lover, I want her alive. She's with Dukael."

"I do not take orders from you." The unknown one seethed, grinding teeth, "We have an agreement, we share a mutual interest. Do not forget I am a Cadre Tempter."

Liam knew that voice, that arrogance. He thought, it was so long ago, then he heard it, the wind. He felt the breeze, the wings, and he knew, anger filled up. He closed his eyes trying to calm it, but he couldn't. The nightmare was too fresh, too violent to let it slide. He moved out of the bushes, standing straight. His posture never left him, even in times like these, when the poisonous fumes weighed on his body.

"Allistor."

The fair haired Tempter narrowed his vision, eyes glistening black, sucked in a deep breath, "I cannot sense you, who are you?"

Raphael unsheathed his sword, his mouth parched. Liam knew the poison had affected the Asguardians more than himself.

Liam taunted Allistor with his smile, "I am that which you should fear."

Raphael's eyes sparked up a sudden rage as he threw the sword at Liam. But Liam was too fast, with only a look, the sword went up in blue disintegrating flames.

Allistor grinned wickedly, "Who is this foolish boy who taunts me with childish tricks."

He stared at Liam, but referred to the Asguardians to answer.

Vincent came out from the bush, "William Blackwyll, father."

Alexa still ducked behind the trees. Liam shook his head, in a deep inhale, he glared at Raphael who held another sword.

Allistor raged in disbelief, "Father? I'm not your father child. I father no one, besides that of my first consort, Daleyan, are you Daleyan's boy."

"No," Liam answered, amusement intended, "He is the son of Taliya Ipswich, the only son."

Allistor's beautiful white wings, which had flapped constantly, had come to a stop. He folded it in, his eyes softened.

Liam felt a sort of remorse for Vincent, he watched the hopefulness in the Casters eyes, the longing for a father.

Allistor remembered, "I have not forgotten Taliya, your mother. My heart fell the day she died, how tragic, wasn't it."

Vincent jumped forward into mid-air, his movements brisk, guns in hand, but Allistor just booted him.

Liam did nothing to intervene, but watched. One like him had all the patience, it was rarely he let it falter.

Allistor pounced back, "I should have killed you, but I showed you mercy and this is what I get."

"You killed my mother, she was no threat to you."

"Yes, but to Lucifereal she was. She knew of his children and was suppose to deliver them to us, but she failed. She knew her faith, she didn't even beg, not even for you, how pathetic. I thought you dead by now."

Vincent got up off the floor, not dusting himself off. It was Liam who remained cool and collective. Raphael's lack of patience shedding through his eyes. The other two Asguardians finding the air hypnotic, had taken seats on a large rock.

"Fair enough Allistor." Liam acknowledged, "I would show you mercy as you have your son, but in our next meeting I will show you the same faith you had shown Taliya and Daleyan."

"Ah, young William lacks no confidence in his capability of handing me my death." He took a step back, his blonde hair blowing in the wind.

Liam often wondered what became of the Tempters' souls when they fell. He remembered Allistor, with his blue watery eyes and bright smile, though Allistor had no knowledge of him now. He watched Allistor flap his wings, freely.

Allistor was never made an Archangel like most of the Cadre who ruled hell. Unlike the others, his wings remained always, a continuous reminder of his ranks in the Infinity. It made him a ruthless Tempter. The blue visionary eyes which Liam had recalled, were replaced by blackness, the color of his soul. A sign which most Tempters refrained from- killing innocents.

When it came to Azazy-el, he had compelled himself from harshness and murdering innocents. Though he broke rules, it was ones he felt strongly about. A well thought out decision. A smile crossed Liam's thought as he concentrated on the people in view.

Alexa rolled out of the bushes her eyes fuming with rage, "It's a trap, there are demons surrounding us."

Liam didn't quiver, "Allistor, call off your demons." His tone was a direct one of command. His own blue eyes brightened with the chaos it would release if his order was not addressed. Liam was not one you said no to, not when he was like this.

"They are not mine, I have no jurisdiction here, but you knew that already."

Allistor's wings flapping higher, the whiteness of his feathers washed away by the reddened sky. He began to lift off, "If you really must know, my hunt's for Azazy-el, I heard he knows the identity of the Prince of souls."

Liam remained cool, it seemed that Allistor had just answered his question for him, "Prince of souls huh? What do you want with him?"

"It's not me who wants him, young William. There are greater threats than a member of hells Cadre, ones only Lucifereal would not fear."

"What could be more threatening than hells Cadre?" It was more of bland statement, really.

"Those who seek the rein of all, of course!" Allistor looked up at the blood red sky, redness all around them. The suffocating air working its poisonous glooms on all. Even the Tempter seemed fragile. But Liam stood his ground, there were still demons to fight.

Raphael contorted into heading for shelter. Liam kept his eyes of Allistor, but his mind reaching Vincent, *'Prepare to run, Allistor will try and kill you. Take the back entrance, jump into the lake. I slipped a stone in your pocket, hold it tight it'll take you to where you need to go. Tell Jullie all that you heard here today, she would know what to do.'*

Alexa pulled out two short swords, squatting on her knee, back straight. Liam could hear them, the demon cries. He knew once Allistor left, he would inform Lucifereal of what happened today, but if he left first, Vincent would die.

Allistor was wicked beyond that of saving, *"run"* the words spoken were short and final, and only heard by Vincent. Allistor charged at Vincent when he hit the ground hard with his boots, running back toward the cottage.

Liam jumped up, his body ablaze in its majestic glory. His skin as glittering as the rarest form of diamonds, a burst of blue and white energy flowed into his fingers, making his body blaze brighter by the second. With it grew something long, strong, held in his hand, it grew. The blazing blue and ice trickles of fumes proceeded through the unearthed weapon, forming a wide cut, long length, sword. His eyes brightened, the ice now frosted with smoke around him.

Allistor stopped as he witnessed the transformation, his wings flapping in the air. Liam focused only a fraction on Vincent, he could hear the water, he was safe.

Allistor screamed, the sound of an anchoring siren. With it, he saw the demons from the sky charge ferociously at him. Liam dropped himself down to the floor, landing flat on his boots.

Alexa was taking on a dragonfiely. Liam's fumes blazing in its blues and his eyes still adorned with its desirable beauty.

Allistor as he suspected left, flew off, but Liam knew this wasn't over, not until Allistor's blood had touched his blade.

He focused in on the battle in front of him, fighting the demons as they charged him. With swift and quick glides of his sword, not making much effort, they grizzled down to dust as they met their fate with his blade. This round had taken him minutes.

Alexa still fighting at his side, loyal not to him but to Calub. But, he knew this battle he fought was not for Clare, but for another. Another long forgotten- Roselletta.

With the shields up, it'll be days and many battles later before he left this place, and as his blade greedily consumed the death of its enemy, William relished in one thought.

He would hunt Clarebella Ravensword down and claim her. And anybody who tried to take her away, will know no worse death than the one he'd deliver.

A note from the Author

THE STORY CONTINUES in The Angel descendants and The Prince of Souls, which will be coming out April 2018 So stay tuned and get ready because this is only the beginning.

I hope you enjoyed the book and used the dictionary.

Please let me know what you think.

Send me an email: shanrk@zoho.com

Shanaazk47@gmail.com

OR POST ON GOODREADS: http://www.goodreads.com/author/show/15220814.Shan_R_K

Don't miss out!

Visit the website below and you can sign up to receive emails whenever Shan R.K publishes a new book. There's no charge and no obligation.

https://books2read.com/r/B-A-DHHG-AFDT

BOOKS 2 READ

Connecting independent readers to independent writers.

Did you love *House Of Legions*? Then you should read *Shock Me Twice* by Shan R.K and Kady - Co!

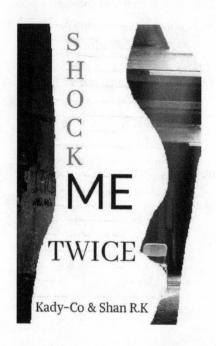

Eight (8) year old Kady Co releases her first co- written Novel, Shock MeTwice.

Small town secrets have a way of coming out.

In Liston Hills, those secrets can land you in a whole lot of trouble.

Especially if your name is Percy Daniels

Our town is divided into two sides, the rich side and the South side.

Years ago the Billionaires and the South'ers joined up, when Mason Bray left his preppy little life and attended **Liston High Public School.**

That was a one time occurence, but now the Snow brothers show up.

My name is Lannie, and I am hiding a big secret, and the Snow brothers know what it is, but that isn't the reason for our story.

Someone kidnapped Percy and the Snow brothers want me to help them find out who.

Seems like the whole town is blaming the bikers.

That was my first shock, I can do with a second.

So please feel free to **Shock Me Twice**.

A Young Adult fictional book written by 8 year old Kady-Co and Shan R.K

Also by Shan R.K

Catch Me, If You Can
Shock Me Twice

Liston Hills
School Me Season 1
School Me Season 2
School Me Season 3

Love Hate and Billions
Kylie Bray

Secrets Of The Famiglia
Capo Dei Capi

The Angel Descendants
House Of Legions

The Satan Sniper's Motorcycle Club
Beggar
River's Keeper
Zero
Beauty's Breath

Standalone
Faces Of You

Watch for more at https://shanrk.com.

About the Author

I am a born and bred South African Author.

My passion for writing was not something that suddenly happened. I was born to write words as one is born to die.

My stories are dark and twisted. The Characters are people who we all can relate to.

They are either personas of a certain belief of mine or they are characters portraying the different types of people in our world today.

I love writing fiction and bringing a world alive with words. I believe that a voice is not just one spoken but one seen too.

Since I have started writing I am able to show you that which I wish to scream.

I enjoy reading at any time of day.

My favourite book I have read to date would be Angels blood by **Nilini Singh**. My ATF Author is a definite **Jamie Begley** and my BR series is split between Infernal Devices by **Cassandra Clare** and The Black daggerhood brothers by **J.R Ward**.

The longest book I have written to date would go to House of

Legions- A paranormal romance about a Lightwatcher and Angel.

The best book I have written would be Beggar - A MC suspense/ romance series.

The best idea I have ever had would be to start my blog Liston Hills School me. It is a live online novel I started working on a year ago.

If I could describe myself I would say I am shy but also friendly.

Read more at https://shanrk.com.

About the Publisher

Author, blogger and Graphical designer.

CPSIA information can be obtained
at www.ICGtesting.com
Printed in the USA
BVHW031442311019
562602BV00001B/160/P